Lost in Lombardy

Inspired By a True Story

LORNA NELIGAN

Lost in Lombardy

Inspired by a true story

Published by West Cork Publishing, New Haven, CT

Paperback ISBN: 979-8-9896668-0-5
Hardcover ISBN: 979-8-9896668-1-2

Subjects: | BISAC: FICTION / Women. | FICTION / Coming of Age.| FICTION / Travel / Europe / Italy.

Book design by Bailey McGinn
Author photograph by Mia McDonald

To Frank, Ava, and Maeve – my believers

A journey of a thousand miles begins
with a single step. —Lao Tzu

$ 3,245.00

April 1, 1990

One-way ticket on Alitalia to Milan ♥♥♥	- 557.54
Three huge samsonites - spring, summer and winter	- 251.02
Dresses, jeans, shirts, sweaters buy a trench coat?	- 648.98
Accessories - shoes sunglasses, raffia hat	- 354.56
Putumayo garden squirrel for Matteo's parents - MUST WRAP!!!	- 134.78
Last minute lowlights/haircut w/Serena ★ MUST CONTACT HER AUNT MARIA WHEN VISITING SICILY	- 75.00
EUROPEAN ADAPTOR FOR HAIR DRYER	- 24.89
Groceries - bagels, chicken, veggies, pasta, butter	- 18.48
Bon Voyage dinner and drinks with Hannah, etc.	- 48.00
Final phone and electricity bill goodbye 212!	- 54.00
Ridiculous early termination NYC lease fee Boo Dinkins!	- 600.00
JFK preboarding prosecco, tube of lipgloss, lifesavers, gum	- 10.00

MAY 3, 1990 - no bills, no debts $431.75

CHAPTER ONE

WHEN MY FLIGHT REACHED cruising altitude over the hook of Cape Cod, it was goodbye, America, ciao, Italy. Since I'd left the check-in desk, an indescribable joy had glued a smile onto my face, and the lunacy of love was to blame. I was on my way to reunite with Matteo, my soon-to-be-fiancé, and begin our forever dolce vita. Besides romantic gondola rides in Venice, our endless to-dos included eating tortellini in the food heaven of Bologna and sipping bubbly prosecco on an Amalfi terrace. My off-the-charts excitement could have powered any cute Tuscan village or Florentine art studio with years of free electricity.

Still grinning, I unraveled my earphones while the captain rattled off arrival details over clicks of unbuckling seatbelts. Fifty degrees. Morning clouds. Sunshine in the afternoon. And the strong tailwind would deliver us to the gate half an hour early. And me into Matteo's arms.

I glanced over to my loafer-less seatmate who was skimming the glossy pages of the Alitalia magazine. A Botticelli-like portrait of a serene woman with a rose-pink pout glowed on its cover. Intrigued, I plucked my copy from the seat pocket, and her knowing gaze said it all—she was in love, too.

I sighed, flipping through the elegant pages of stunning photos, imagining my new life in Como. Of course, friends thought I was ridiculous to leave my fantastic job and jump on a plane for Matteo, but they had never experienced an intoxicating connection like ours. The original plan was that *after* he settled in Italy, we'd use vacation time and long weekends to see each other as much as possible. But at the airport, sneaky Matteo surprised you-know-who with a pre-engagement ring, and everything changed. He said it wasn't the let's-get-married one, but to me, it was close enough, a token to prove our amazing love would continue overseas.

With a rebel yell, I quit my nine-to-five a week later and bought a one-way ticket to Milan. My decision made sense since we talked about our future nonstop—like when we had kids, what would we name them? He liked Mario, and I loved Aurora. Both sounded so pretty when he rolled his Rs like a true Italian.

How we met was classic New York. After a hectic day of analyzing linen lab dips with a wishy-washy designer, I left the office late. The only thing on my mind was a heavy-handed drink at O'Shea's happy hour. Oblivious to Cupid's plan, I squeezed into a crowded elevator, weighing the pros and cons of having tooth-picked Swedish meatballs and overcooked weenies as my dinner.

However, when the doors closed, a fragrance matching the freshness of an open jar of honey with a tinge of rosemary and leather overtook my senses, and I forgot the free hors d'oeuvres. Like a bee searching for sweet nectar, I had to find the source. Beside me, the sweaty bike messenger with a silver whistle around his neck was a doubtful origin. I buzzed to the yawning woman in a pink prairie dress and matching pastel sneakers, staring at the gray floor. Nope. On to the next person—a raven-haired man with a jagged jawline softened by a poetic nose that a sculptor could never replicate. His full lips parted into a smile when our eyes met, and the unexpected gap between his front teeth added a charming flaw to his perfection.

That's how it started—a simple good night turned into an introduction, and Matteo joined me on my walk to O'Shea's. My colleague and best friend Hannah had escaped work early and was already a Long Island Iced Tea ahead of me when I arrived at our table with this gorgeous guy at my side. Her face said it all, and when Matteo joined us, her elbow jabs bruised my ribs whenever he looked away. Matteo's Negroni order confused the server until he offered him the recipe of equal parts gin, vermouth, and Campari. Before Matteo took a sip of his amber cocktail with an air of James Bond elegance, our drinks clinked, and I was in love.

From then on, Matteo made me feel strangely dangerous and yet safe as we grew closer. Prone to moodiness, he said his smiles were infrequent because happiness wasn't alluring in men, and I loved the challenge he presented. He was also beyond stunning. Women glanced at us and then at me. How did *she* get *him*, I imagined them thinking?

It's not that I'm unattractive. A friend at college said I fitted the Victorian profile with my oval face, wide-set eyes, and small, pouty mouth. Hannah said I needed to accentuate my positives with more make-up, but I never did. Anyway, Matteo said I was already perfect.

Things had moved fast after that memorable whiff of his outdoorsy Luca Rosso cologne a year ago. Named Rosso Certo, it was a sizzle for *every* Italian man. Matteo moved in a month later with a suitcase and an electric typewriter after his consulting gig finished at an international company's racing car division. While I took the subway uptown to collaborate on fabric boards with ready-to-wear designers, he struggled to enter the sports marketing field. Matteo was the ideal candidate—he climbed mountains, rode motorcycles, and played soccer on a United Nations team in Central Park. Yet his resume tread water in the application pool, and my dinky studio slowly became an anxiety-ridden cave with pages of the *New York Times* classified section, rejection letters, and shiny annual reports stained with coffee cup rings.

I'm not going to lie; it was difficult. My parents questioned if his education was enough or if his visa was valid. Then, friends wondered aloud if anything hidden in his past prevented Matteo from succeeding. Flynn, my older sister, even suggested he had a criminal background. I couldn't believe it.

But he and I never lost hope. The East Village, with its wild and unpredictable grit, sustained us. We would share a cannoli on Mulberry Street or split an order of French fries at Lucky Strike on two-dollar draft beer nights. During that time, AIDS seemed to be touching so many of my friends and colleagues, and dear Matteo helped me through the endless trail of unwelcome news, especially when Damian, my close friend and the best neighbor in the world, got it.

Twirling Matteo's ring, my smile faded as I remembered Damian's contagious laugh and hilarious comments. I missed him so much. He would have never pooh-poohed my decision to move to Italy. He would have cheered, *Jayne, you do you.*

I stared at the pillowy clouds, blinking back tears. Thank God Damian had lived next door to me in that rent-controlled building. I wouldn't be on the plane if it weren't for him. Fresh out of college, my first job had been selling American medical tour packages to the People's Republic of China. After a tough day of negotiating for hot water in a Beijing hotel room, runway model Damian passed me in our apartment's hallway carrying a load of laundry. I guess my slumped shoulders and space cadet stare must have said it all because ten minutes later, he knocked on my door and invited me over for gin and tonics.

At his place, I let loose, and after debating whether Princess Diana or Madonna was the most beautiful woman in the world, I declared that fashion was my dream career. The comment must have affected Seventh Avenue's master networker because the next day, Trendary Fabrics phoned me for an interview as a fabric assistant. I got the position, and my salary, as well as my confidence, increased significantly. I invited Damian for a mega thank you celebration at the Royalton, and he told me before dessert that he had AIDS. I couldn't breathe; an iron anchor sunk my soul to the bottom of the ocean. Too proud for tears, he waved it off with a cough and called it a "fait accompli." He used his college French whenever possible—even when delivering devastating news.

Luckily, weeks later, I met Matteo, and he helped me make a homemade chicken soup that Damian loved, but of course, it wasn't enough to save him. An overnight hospital stay extended into weeks, and when he was discharged, Damian left for his parent's house in Long Island, never to return to his beloved city. The beautiful Sag Harbor funeral service, packed with emotional admirers, was one for the record books and even written up in *Women's Wear Daily* by the iconic fashion writer Maria La Motta. Usually feared for her swashbuckling pen and ego-devouring comments, Maria ended the moving piece with a Dr. Seuss quotation for his friends: "Don't cry that it's over; smile because it happened."

I think of it often.

A week later, an older woman and a bell-collared tabby cat moved into his empty place. As Matteo's fruitless interviews continued, I avoided her for no rational reason. Our darkness lifted when a friend called Matteo about an opportunity that ticked every box for his career—except the location, which had him banging his fist against the wall.

Italy.

First, Matteo yelled no way, never, forget it. Then it simmered to a maybe. He zigzagged across my creaky floors for two long days, trying to find an excuse to stay. Matteo battled against Sinatra's if-you-can-make-it-there syndrome of New York success, so returning to his home country constituted a paralyzing failure. Nevertheless, the overall practicality added to being flat broke ruled in wisdom's favor, and he finally ended his turmoil with a yes.

My gaze turned to the front of the cabin. The dinner cart rolled up the aisle, and I glanced at my watch—six more hours.

"Lasagna or chicken," the tall flight attendant with a husky accent asked as he handed me a napkin and utensils.

"Lasagna, per favore," I said, unlocking my table. "And a vino, per favore."

He grinned at my language attempt and presented a mini bottle of red wine.

"No, grazie. Bianco, per favore," I said, smirking at his puzzled expression. Red wine-stained teeth were not going to ruin a perfect reunion.

After loading the luggage cart with my three overpacked suitcases, I burst through the arrival hall doors, ready to detonate with happiness. A handsome guy cradling a bouquet of red roses hurried past me, and his female recipient squealed for joy as I funneled through a crowd of anxious faces, searching for my Matteo. He was nowhere to be seen, and a sudden fear that I had told him the wrong time caused me to slow down. I thought of the previous day, clenching the handlebar. Matteo hadn't called me before leaving, and when I'd contacted his office, his assistant had said he was visiting a client in Milan. He must have been too busy for a bon voyage.

Near the arrival hall's bustling café, I spotted Matteo's tall frame in a navy pea coat leaning against the wall. When I waved, his gaze met mine, and I ran joyfully into his arms. My eager lips met his, but our barebones kiss was as passionate as opening junk mail. He quickly released me, and I blamed his shy restraint on a terminal full of strangers. Or maybe it was my breath from the pre-touchdown coffee. Before I could comment, he swiveled around to grab the handle of my luggage cart. "Andiamo," he said in Italian, meaning let's go.

With a big smile, I regretted my pettiness and thrust my fist into the sky. "Andiamo to us," I laughed.

So, with my three bulging suitcases crammed into the tiny backseat, I squeezed into Matteo's Fiat, rejuvenated by pounding adrenaline. We cruised up north to our love nest on the shores of Lake Como and near the Swiss border. For a half hour, his head bobbed to my caffeine-fueled babble of "I can't believe I'm here" until I ended in a walrus-sized yawn. That's when Matteo slipped in his we needed to talk about *something*. Something must be important, like when I'd find employment or if we wanted to switch our anniversary trip to Positano instead of Rome.

"Honey. Don't worry. I've done my research. And I grabbed all the business cards from my Rolodex. Network, network, they say. And Silk City Como has a ton of mills."

"It's not about working …" He shifted into a lower gear as he slowed for a gas station. "I need to stop here. Let's talk about it later."

I glanced at his tense jaw. My stomach dropped. Was he fired?

"How's *your* job?"

His face brightened. "Better than I imagined. I love it. My boss said my orientation was the best he ever had. He said my New York experience made me an asset to the company."

I clapped and gave him a peck on the cheek. "That's beyond fantastic. See? I told you so. You are unbelievable, you know. Was that why you didn't call me before I left? Too much celebrating? My mom thought it was weird, but I told her it was work. She made me feel like something was wrong." As soon as I said the vague word "something," my confidence dampened. I looked over at his right hand lying on his lap. Why wasn't it roaming up my thigh and other places like it did during our drive up the Taconic to see Flynn? We almost went off the road with his antics. "There isn't. Right?"

He glanced in the rearview mirror and frowned at my suitcases. "You brought so much stuff."

"Matteo, you asked me to come live with you. Start this big adventure together. I need clothes to do that, silly." He shrugged, and when I leaned closer, it hit me. His usual Rosso cologne was missing, and I sat back, wondering where his signature scent had gone. "Remember the ring you gave me? At the airport? This?" I said, showing the ring on my finger.

"I do." The car swerved to the pumps, and he parked without another word. I waited for him to grab and kiss me, lamenting he was having a dreadful day and was sorry. I'd be so relieved and cry tears of joy as I scolded him for scaring the hell out of me. But we sat in silence while I stared at a dead fly lying legs up in his dashboard's dust, and he gripped the steering wheel like a driver's ed student. A tourist bus idled near us, and I turned to watch a group of men smoking and joking as the driver paid the attendant. Had Matteo forgotten about our earlier life? The visits to Queens to see my parents? Barbeques at Flynn and Ambrose's place? Sex on Sunday afternoons? I took a deep breath and crumpled in pain. Did I just come to Italy to get dumped?

His door opened suddenly, and he jumped out with a quick, "I'll be back." My chest caved, and I gasped. When I'd left him at JFK, he'd said he couldn't wait to show me his country. He was excited about our new adventure. Second thoughts happen to other couples. Not us.

Neither of us spoke when he returned to the car. He peeled out of the gas station and drove the last miles like a Formula One racer. The breathtaking lake appeared like a sexy seductress, taunting my uncertainty while the encircling mountains laughed. The joke was that my arrival answered his pleas for undying love sprinkled over vignettes of cheesy pasta, glamourous boat rides, and warm embraces under Como's mulberry trees. No one with a pulse could resist his heartthrob accent, especially me, who considered gelato a food group. I resisted the urge to ask for an explanation, remembering his lackluster kiss. So, we sat as lifeless as the luggage behind us, afraid to talk.

It wasn't a good sign.

Matteo's second-floor apartment was a stone's throw from the lake, and he left me in the apartment to unpack. Hours later, he returned, stating he made a reservation at his favorite restaurant next to Villa D'Este, an exclusive villa where all the top designers stayed when they did their Como mill tours. I had armed myself in a low-cut little black dress, and his eyes caressed the curves of my body like they always did, making me feel better. He took my hand when I stepped onto the vaporina, a sleek boat created solely for Lake Como, and I flirted as if my life depended on it. I was not going down without a fight.

After we sat down in the restaurant, I entertained him with fun details about the over-the-top bon voyage party our friends had given me, but he seemed disinterested and kept turning around to check out the other diners. That's when I started to feel inadequate. The waiter must have sensed my pain because he refilled my wine much more than my water. I was coherent when we left the restaurant but fell asleep on Matteo's living room couch from jet lag and too much vino. A hand-drawn smiley-faced note was on the refrigerator when I woke up the following morning. Matteo scribbled he'd be away, using work as his excuse.

So, while he hid somewhere, I whirled into an emotional smoothie, rehashing what had gone wrong and what to do. Walks along the lake-shore left me crying my eyes out on a scenic bench, hoping for an answer. Locals gawked in concern. Even the gliding ducks seemed to feel sorry for me. A week before, welcome-to-Italy sex had occupied my thoughts, not an exit plan.

However, Matteo had to make the first move. I wouldn't contact his office for details, even though his obnoxious telephone begged me to dial. Alone in his rustic apartment, I corncobbed my French manicure while my unpacked suitcases stared from the doorway like anxious children who wanted to play outside. On the coffee table, my overused wine glass pirouetted above a tulle skirt of mascara-blotched tissues. Even more depressing was my pocket-sized notepad pulsating a pathetic bank balance of my stupidity. Payback for shopping like I'd won the lottery.

Of course, I went Sherlock Holmes and searched his apartment for evidence of another woman. But no raunchy thongs or lacy bras hid in dresser drawers; no condoms lurked deep in coat pockets or trash cans. One unexpected item, however, offered hope—a train schedule for the Lombardy region—and I opened it.

Milan was the capital of Italy's Lombardy region and less than an hour's train ride south from Como. And besides Matteo, the only other person I knew in the whole country lived in the Quadrilatero della Moda – Milan's golden ground zero of haute couture. His name was Gino Morelli. Being one of Europe's most prominent fabric vendors, his office was on the most must-visit street for fashionistas, Via della Spiga. A well-connected character with a never-ending list of new luxurious mills to show and hot designers to promote, Mr. Charisma always appeared grinning in paparazzi photos, either hugging celebrities or dining with supermodels. Whenever he visited our office, Gino was pampered as a super VIP. And, thanks to his in-depth knowledge of textiles, impeccable ability to spot the rumbling of a trend, and pick-up-the-phone contacts at all the top mills, we were privy to all cutting-edge atelier designs. He was, in a way, our secret weapon at Trendary.

It was getting late, but I grabbed my backpack and ironically found his phone number in my "The Most Romantic Places to Visit in Italy" folder. After throwing the gag-worthy file into the garbage, I dialed before my courage wavered. My body stiffened when I heard, "Pronto?"

"Hi," I said as I began to pace around the room. "I mean, pronto? Hello? Gino? It's Jayne Boland from Trendary Fabrics. I don't know if you remember me. We met five months ago at our New York office. I work with Jim on the big accounts, and I—"

"Si. Jayne. Jayne and the Italian fiancé. Matteo, right? I remember. You brought biscotti for someone's birthday. Chocolate chip, you told me. I loved those."

Funny that my contribution to our office manager's celebration should have been memorable to him. I hoped he hadn't gotten a burnt one on the bottom. "Yes. That's me. I can give you the recipe if you'd like. It's easy. And, for the record, Matteo and I are *not* engaged," I said with a high-pitched laugh, touching the corner of a suitcase.

"Oh. Not yet. That will be soon, I hope. Matteo is waiting for a special place like Portofino. Or the Boboli Gardens. So, tell me, where are you lovebirds in my beautiful country? Milan?"

"Unfortunately, not Milan. I'm in Como. At Matteo's apartment. But, Gino, I'm calling to see you and discuss if there are any job openings in Milan for me." As a first-generation American of Irish-born parents, I had the fringe benefit of dual nationality and could work in Europe without a visa.

"Oh. Okay. You're now in Como? I was just there on business. But sure. We can meet. You let me know when you are coming here, and I'll show you my city."

"That sounds wonderful." My heart raced. "But … I was wondering … are you free tomorrow?"

His voice rose in surprise. "Tomorrow?"

It would be Saturday, and I cringed at my desperation. "Yes. I'm so sorry; I know this is all last minute, and you're probably asking why this person is calling me so late at night. It's just that … I'll be available all day," I said. "And solo. Could we grab a coffee? I mean, espresso. My treat."

"Hm. I *do* have an appointment in the morning for a special order. I could see you before they come. How about ten at my office?"

My eyes darted to the timetable, and an eight o'clock train arrived before ten. "Sure. Ten sounds perfect. I'll be there. Thank you, Gino. I've got your address, so I look forward to seeing you at ten. Grazie. Ciao. Bye."

I hung up, thrilled that he said yes. But I needed to pull myself together and focus. Where was my resume? I couldn't forget my dictionary. What would I wear?

Behind the front door, a rattle of keys sounded, and I glared at the entrance as Matteo stepped sheepishly through the doorway. "Well, look who's returned," I said, crossing my arms. Gino's conversation boosted my battered confidence. "What's your name again?"

Matteo glanced at the coffee table and then at my suitcases. He was probably disappointed I was still there. "I'm sorry. They needed me in Torino."

He was an awful liar. "Please don't start the Torino bullshit. You left me alone for five days. I got the message loud and clear that we're over," I said, blinking back tears, "but can you explain what happened from the ring at JFK to now? You didn't even give us a chance."

Without a word, Matteo walked over and hugged me. My body convulsed as I bawled buckets into his chest. He smoothed my hair, soothing me that *everything will be okay*. Except his okay was not my OK, and I collapsed onto his couch, accepting that he and I were officially ex-lovers. And ex-hand holders. And ex-best friends. When I finally looked up, he started. "I'm so sorry, Jayne. I didn't know this would happen. I love you, but …"

"But *what*?"

"It's hard to explain. I loved living with you in New York. I really did. Meeting you was the best thing in my life. I had an incredible time with our midnight walks to see the big Christmas tree, all your fun friends, the Jets football game when they finally won. Only it was so hard for me trying to find a job. I never told you, but I was depressed and never thought I'd get work.... It was the worst. I could see my failure in everyone's eyes, including yours."

"Matteo, I never considered you a failure. I was always your biggest cheerleader. New York is a tough city. I know. It will eat you alive." I tried to maintain my composure, taking a deep breath. "So, you're saying I remind you of that awful time?"

"No. I'm not. It's more complicated than that. And I'm not blaming you in any way. But now, I need time alone—to fix my ego. A fresh start. I can't do it when you're here."

I stared at the coffee table, trying to decipher his words for any iota of hope. But he basically said my presence suffocated him. That hurt. With a big sniff, I wiped my tears, and our eyes met when I reached for a tissue. "Why didn't you tell me all this before I got on the plane?"

"I wanted to tell you face-to-face."

His selfish admission stoked my frustration, and my eyes darted to my little notebook of expenses. I was broke. "Well, don't you have good manners. Give me a break. Why didn't *you* fly to New York and end this like a *real* man?" I snapped. "Face-to-face in Manhattan."

His mouth opened to respond, but the phone rang, and he hurried to escape my hostility. "Pronto." His face broke into a big grin. "No, no. We're not in bed."

I stood up and walked towards him, ready to punch someone. "I knew it. Tell Miss Como Hot Chick I'll be out of here ASAP. He's all yours, sweetie," I shouted.

He put his hand over the receiver. "What? Stop. You're being immature." He then raised his finger for peace and continued. "Right. Right. Hannah ... Hannah ... wait. Jayne is right here."

"Hannah," I said, gulping back tears. She had called daily for updates, although she was unaware of the breakup because I'd prayed it was just a slight hiccup. Our tight bond started with after-work cocktails and partying at throbbing neon nightclubs, followed by sloppy breakfasts. After Matteo and I declared our girlfriend-boyfriend status, she followed our relationship like a romance novel.

"Hi." My news would be crushing. I turned away from Matteo, sucking air through my teeth. "Hannah, I … I've lied to you about Matteo and me, and it's not exactly what I said. I'm sorry. The whole hot sex thing and our great meals on the lake were bogus. There was no personal chef or whipped cream massage, either. I made the whole thing up because he dumped me as soon as I got off the plane. I didn't want to accept it, but he just triple-confirmed it's over. Finito, as they say over here."

"What? Stop. Are you kidding? This can't happen. You two are perfect together."

"That's what I thought, too. I guess we were all wrong," I said, swinging around as Matteo slinked out of the apartment, clutching a bag of clothes. I found my wine glass and told Hannah the tragic story between woeful wails. "I'm wrecked, Hannah. He just left again and is avoiding me like the plague. He hasn't spent one night here—only a pathetic kiss in the terminal. It was like I was his grandmother or an old aunt. I can't believe it. I left everything for him. The whole thing was a charade, and I don't know what to do, but one thing is for certain. This sucker has gotta get out of here."

"What an idiot. Does he know what you gave up? That rent-controlled apartment? Plus, you loved Trendary and had just gotten a promotion."

I stumbled onto the couch. "Don't remind me. Any garmento would have killed for my position at Trendary."

That was another reason to be furious at Matteo and his revelations. I had high hopes for my fabric sales career. Design teams from big-shot manufacturers like Ralph Lauren and Calvin Klein met in our Trendary Fabric showroom to discover the newest textile hot spot or earth shattering trends. By shadowing my boss, Jim, I had learned to play a big part in dissecting each season's poetic definition and had loved watching game-changing styles come alive through each designer's mood board. Nothing was more exhilarating than that stiff white foam board pinned with obscure antique swatches or tattered Ivy League rowing team jersey's cotton thrust into my hands under the command, "Source these fabrics." With bloodhound madness, I'd sniff through mill books and visit showrooms, searching for the perfect swatch to construct a dream garment.

My first solo project was a torn pocket from a vintage British battle uniform, and I hunted for the same olive-drab wool in gabardine in a flea market basket of military swatches. After a dozen mill samples and thousands of lab dips, my hard work appeared on the catwalk that season on a strutting supermodel oblivious to the gallons of sweat invested in her one-of-a-kind palazzo pants. But it didn't matter. She had her assignment, and I had mine. And I loved it.

"Well, at least you didn't do anything stupid like marry that monster. Come back and start where you left off. I know it's tough, but you forget about pasta boy."

"I'd want to forget. But I love him," I sobbed. Hannah's words sounded so final. "How do you wipe your brain of the memories of a year spent with the man of your dreams? Maybe it's cold feet. Matteo *did* say he loved me."

Hannah's voice perked up. "Wait. What? Did he? Today?"

"No. When he gave me that stupid ring before he left, I don't know why he didn't end it over the phone like normal people do. I asked him why he waited to tell me *after* I arrived. Do you know what the swine said? He said he wanted to tell me face-to-face."

"Jesus. What a jerk. I hope you gave him a face-to-face slap. Oh, Jayne, I wish I were there to hug you."

"And now I've got only four hundred bucks to my name, so I can't even buy a plane ticket to Dublin," I moaned. "I should ask him for the money, but he's got so much debt from moving over here. We only had one meal together, no sex, and I've been crying nonstop. No wonder there's a huge lake here – it's full of tears since it's the saddest place on earth. The only positive is that I now know Como because all I do is wander the streets. Locals probably call me the rejected American. *Rejecta Americana*, or whatever the hell they say."

"Wow. That's tough."

"Exactly. I wonder if I hallucinated the whole relationship. Did I?" I rose and turned the bottle of pinot grigio over above my glass, but it was empty.

"You didn't. It was real. I saw the whole thing from day one. It was a beautiful love story."

"Yes, it was." My lips trembled. "Flynn was always suspicious of Matteo, and I thought she was overly protective. But my dear sister was right. I hate to say this, but he used me."

"No, he loved you. Fiercely."

"You think so? That makes me feel better. It was good while it lasted, I guess. Let me go. It's late, and I need to digest this horror with sleep. My mom always says things look better in the morning. And please don't tell anyone at work. Especially that talkaholic Jim."

Jim had done a weird snicker in the hallway on my last day. When I'd stopped to ask what was so funny, he'd confessed that an unofficial office pool had started, predicting I'd be back within a month. Taken aback, I'd faked a laugh, assuring him I had dated enough guys to know this was the real thing. Still, he'd patted me on the shoulder, saying he would hold my spot till Memorial Day, just in case.

Hannah snorted. "Don't worry. I won't mention it to Jim."

"Oh, I forgot to tell you. I called Gino, and I'm going to see him tomorrow. He knows everyone, so maybe he could help me. It may be the biggest waste of time, but at least it's a day away from this claustrophobic box of gloom. Keep your fingers crossed for me."

"I will. That's great, though. Yes, leave that place as soon as possible.

Gino is beyond wonderful, and he'll figure out what to do. Maybe there is a job for you in Como after all?"

I gulped. "Como? Nah, no thanks. Not after this. Milan is my first choice."

We said our goodbyes, and after hanging up, I threw icy water on my puffy face and brushed my teeth. I looked out the bathroom window and spotted a woman walking her white chihuahua under a streetlamp. The scene reminded me of my family, and homesickness hit me.

My Irish immigrant parents gave Flynn and me a great life. Our house on 88th Street in Howard Beach was always a hub of activity, and our neighborhood hummed under the purr of JFK and LaGuardia inbound and outbound air traffic—a constant reminder of what I may be missing. Naming jetliners on their approach became a backyard game we played while licking our dripping popsicles. Sometimes, I'd wave like a kidnap victim, hoping passengers would notice me, as Flynn yelled, "They can't see you!" I swore one day I'd be on an Air France jet to Paris or sipping coffee on a Turkish Airlines flight to Istanbul. Travel was a no-brainer for my future, and Matteo offered me a chance to experience the unknown sooner than expected.

Now, I wondered if my wanderlust was frivolous. Disillusioned, I crawled between the bed sheets, ignoring the earthy smells of Matteo that still haunted each fiber. Unsettled, I stumbled out of bed and down the hallway to open the bulkiest piece of luggage I brought. I had appointed it as my winter suitcase. How presumptuous, I thought.

After placing it on the floor, I zipped it open. My hand zoomed past a perfectly packed down jacket and hand-knit Irish sweaters. Finding the familiar soft fur, I pulled out the small monkey I'd had since I was a baby. Its name was Toasty, and it was my security blanket for sleepovers, camping, and even college.

The glass amber orbs of Toasty's eyes still shone its beloved starry stare of love, and I placed it on my chest. Thank God Toasty made the final cut.

$431.75

- 2nd Class Train ticket to Gino/Milan -4.00
- Gettoni's for payphone - too heavy for wallet - dirty -20.00
- Cappuccino and cornetto - 2.00
- Tronky candy bar - choc/hazelnut Nutella?? - .86
- Pizza slice for lunch - not as good as Domenico's in Little Italy - but free garlic knots - 3.00

$401.89

$ = 1,000 lira
$ = 5 francs
$ = 1.6 Deutsche marks
$ = 125 Spanish pesos
$ = 1.80 British pounds
$ = 6 Danish kroners

CHAPTER TWO

TOASTY HAD JUST MET THE WHITE CHIHUAHUA, and both eyed a juicy hamburger when, suddenly, a noise jolted me awake. My hand shot out from the duvet's meringue folds to grab the receiver from the nightstand. "Hello?" I croaked.

My mother's voice blared one hundred decibels louder than a fire alarm at a rock concert. "Jayne, listen. An American Airlines ticket to JFK is waiting for you at the airport, and you can be on today's flight home. The woman there couldn't have been any nicer."

"Wait, what? Mom." The digital clock read six-twenty-eight. The alarm would blast in two minutes, so I fumbled to turn it off before becoming officially deaf. Hannah must have called her after we hung up last night, and my mother had probably already contacted Interpol and the White House for a rescue plan. Ugh. The feds were on their way. "No, don't call anyone. I'm fine. I can't—"

"Listen. Hannah called to tell me what happened. She's a great friend, Jayne, and we're both worried about you. And your father is furious," she said matter-of-factly. "He's ready to go over there and get you himself. Enough is enough. Come home. Why didn't you tell us this had happened?"

I put her on the speakerphone and slid out of bed, cursing loose lips Hannah. I stopped to repress a primal scream and grabbed Toasty from Matteo's unused pillow for moral support. "Mom, first, please don't shout. The phones work the same as they do over there. Second, I didn't tell you exactly for this reason. You don't have to worry. And please, no Dad. Third, thank you *so* much for the offer, but I'll figure it out. I'm going to stay and make it work." The words tumbled out of my mouth like Las Vegas dice, landing on my table of chance. They might have rolled around in my subconscious while I slept, yet I liked their conviction.

She tutted. "Jayne, these decisions need months of planning. You can't do what you did before and expect a good outcome. You're alone; you've spent everything to get there. Where are you going to live? Not with him, I hope. He should be ashamed of what he did. Especially since you supported him for so long."

There it is, I thought. Jayne and her knee-jerk decisions. Trusts people more than they deserve. Frustrated, I took the portable phone and rejoined the conversation when my mother segued into how preppy Lawrence Harpsbell, this finance guy I'd dated twice before Matteo, was doing. How did she know he'd bought a duplex in Tribeca?

"Mom, that doesn't matter now. I got myself into this mess and will get myself out of it. The last thing I want is for you and Dad to bail me out," I said, remembering my teen years spent warding off bill collectors calling our house after dinner when my dad became unemployed. It was an awful time, and to stop panic attacks, I used to babysit and work every weekend at a shoe store to help with the bills. Dad got back on track months later but calls after nine p.m. still triggered a sludge-like dread.

"We want to help ..."

A headache twinged at my temples. My liver must be waking up. "I know that, and I love you. The plane ticket offer is so sweet. I can make it on my own and don't need a man or anyone else to help me out of this disaster. But I do need a mega cup of coffee," I said, turning to the kitchen. "So, let me go."

"Didn't your boss say you could have your old job back? And what about your friends?"

I wished I hadn't mentioned Jim's offer on the car ride to the airport and was careful to respond, searching the cupboards for a mug. "He did … Remember I told you my friends made that huge Italy-shaped chocolate cake for my going-away party, and it had 'Good Luck Jayne and Matteo' plastered in white icing across the whole thing? If I go back now, I'll look like the biggest loser … I mean, one week in Italy, and it's over? Can you blame them for thinking that? I can't. I'd be the butt of their jokes forever."

"They don't care. They love you."

I unsealed a can of coffee. "Everyone warned me about Italian men—don't trust them, they're womanizers, they'll cause you pain. For the past year, all I did was defend Matteo and his subspecies as the nicest guys who would never hurt anyone, and *now* look what happened. I'm the poster child of ding dong dumb," I moaned, opening the silverware drawer for a spoon. "The stupidest person on Earth."

"You might have been a bit naive. Don't be so hard on yourself. You were in love."

"Well, look where that got me." I had to be tough and face the facts. At least Matteo wasn't married. Only that would have been worse. Getting misty-eyed, I aborted my pick-me-up since I had only forty-five minutes before catching the train. "Mom, look, I can't give up yet. I'm going to meet one of our vendors in Milan today. Just tell everyone Matteo and I are figuring things out. That's it. And these phone calls are super expensive, so you'd better go."

My mother grumbled about how I never listened. "What about Flynn? Are you going to tell her?"

"Not yet. I will." Flynn's life was too cliché with her lawyer husband, Ambrose. We used to call each other ten times a day about stupid stuff, and I was her maid of honor; however, we floated apart after she married. Our daily what's-going-on dwindled to monthly, and I blamed it on her new life and then motherhood. Their move from a tiny place in Queens to a center hall colonial in Millbrook seemed to seal the deal, and it was like she relocated to Alaska. Also, two and four-year-old Kate and Quinn were a handful. "She never liked Matteo, so she'll be thrilled."

"That's not true. She was always watching out for you. You should tell her …"

"I will, but not today. Hearing Flynn tell me how I wasted money isn't a priority. But, Mom, everything will be okay. Again, thanks for the ticket offer. You and Dad have enough on your plate. Como is incredible, and I'm in one of the most beautiful countries in the world, so it's not *that* bad. It will be … an experience."

"Experience? You barely speak the language."

"I've got a brain, Mom. And I know enough to get by. I'll call you later. I love you. Ciao."

I hung up the phone, thankful for her sweet concern. After the fastest shower in history, I sat near the window to put on make-up. Birds chirped as dawn broke over a Romanesque church in the nearby piazza, and I smiled, applying my eyeliner. Birds had tragic lives amongst prowling cats or squirrels eating their eggs, yet they still sang, I thought. I'd go to Milan and connect with Gino. I wasn't staying another minute in the backwoods of Italy having another boo-hoo fest since Matteo had given me a root canal welcome—adventure would happen. Plan B had started. I put on my tinted gloss and smacked my lips. Watch out, world. Jayne Boland was on a mission.

I caught the train and cruised down its thin corridor, searching for a passenger-free compartment. On my third glance through ochre curtains, one appeared empty, and I jiggled open the stiff door, relieved to be alone. After plunking into the window seat, I pushed back my cuticles, musing if my mother's offer was the best solution while staring at Como's green mountainous hills.

"Aspetta!" A beehive of teenagers swarmed into the corridor, and I braced myself as a harried chaperone ripped back the yellow curtain, checking her reservation number. The unruly high schoolers gawked as if I were a three-headed giraffe until she led them away under a collective groan.

Thankfully, two well-nourished gray-haired ladies bustled in and took opposite seats, acknowledging their intrusion in prim nods and filling the compartment with lavender perfume. I mumbled ciao and pressed against the cool glass as their shopping bags crinkled into the luggage rack. The heater warmed my feet, and I blinked to stay awake as my body relaxed into the velour seat. I hoped my fleeing instinct was correct.

Doors slammed shut, and whistles blew before the train jerked forward on the tracks. Pretty villas glistened bye for now under a morning's dew as the train labored south. The disappearing Mount Boletto triggered another trickle of salty tears, and I sniffed in peace until the conductor clicked his hole puncher for my ticket. After raccoon rummaging through my bag of wet tissues, the two women swapped worried glances when I handed him the damp stub. "Mi dispiace." *I'm sorry.*

Minutes later, the heavier lady with a jingling gold charm bracelet pulled out a waxed paper item, distracting me from replaying another series of "Why me." When a chunk of apple strudel appeared from its folds, its overflowing raisin spiciness awoke my breakfast-less stomach.

Glancing at the compartment door, I swallowed an imaginary cinnamon roll of air, hoping a pastry-laden coffee trolley would make the usual rounds.

"Buona," she said to her friend, licking her sugared lips. The peppery smell teased my senses, and she caught my wide-eyed interest. Blushing, I diverted my attention to the outside to the stunning Po Valley, transfixed by large flocks of birds rising above green fields and time-forsaken villages awakening as my two steamy circles formed onto the glass. The little towns I was supposed to visit alongside Matteo, I thought, swiping away grey clouds.

A soft weight slipped onto my lap, and both ladies beamed when I lifted my gift with a surprised gape. "Grazie," I said, unwrapping the delicate package. The buttery pastry melted in my mouth, and I flashed a thumbs-up between swallows. Satisfied, they returned to their conversation as I flicked stray dots of confectionery sugar from my black coat, enjoying my treat. The day was already improving.

Half an hour later, the train arrived at Milan's Centrale Station, and I snatched a tourist map before leaving the station. The frenetic atmosphere of honking horns and squealing brakes against the backdrop of neoclassical architecture kindled my spirit, although the gunmetal clouds seemed unfriendly. The noisy market around the train station had vendor stalls with colorful rows of shiny vegetables and pyramids of perfect fruits, and sellers yelled out prices to entice customers. People smelled cantaloupes or pointed at artichokes, clutching straw bags loaded with produce. Others haggled and joked as they opened purses or wallets, enjoying the bargaining process. It felt worlds away from the Saturday morning yawners in oversized New York Giant's sweatshirts grabbing mediocre coffee at a Bowery bodega.

On the boutique filled street Via Montenapoleone, gorgeous men in well-tailored jackets and casually wrapped scarves passed by on Vespas or bell-ringing bikes. Red-lipped women in perfectly belted trench coats clutched chain handbags worth a month's salary while a cotton mesh bag of fruit dangled from their other bejeweled hand. Sunglasses hid any gaze, and the overall elegance cemented my decision to remain in this fashionable aquarium of people.

When I hit Corso Venezia, I slowed to gather my thoughts. Catching my reflection in a shop window, I unbuttoned the top button of my black coat, hoping my A-line black skirt and Ferrari-red pussy cat blouse wasn't too much. I pinched my sallow cheeks for a bit of color and smiled to wipe away self-doubt. Today would decide if I had a future in Italy.

Gino greeted me like an old friend, kissing my flushed face before a friendly hug. Dressed impeccably in a tailored navy blazer, white button-down shirt, and jeans, he had that irresistible and effortless chicness of Italian men. I even detected a wisp of his Luca Rosso cologne when he turned away. Classic.

"Thanks for meeting me on such short notice, Gino. I should explain why I called out of the blue," I said as he guided me to a dove-colored armchair. I stopped mid-step to gawk at the endless shelves of dusty swatch books and tidy rainbow rows of vibrant yarn dye samples that resembled the professional chaos of Trendary's showroom. Bolts of pearly lace and embroidered cotton leaned against the doorway, and my arms opened wide with a grin, almost toppling over a half-dressed mannequin. "I'm honored to be here. This is where the magic happens."

"You like my den of creativity?" he asked, tilting his head.

"Like it? I love it. This office is so you. It's a designer's dream. Imagine if you had the Ralph Lauren team here. They'd rip this place apart." I turned to Gino. "And that William Morris line you did last season was legendary. When Vivienne Westwood used it for that full-length cape and then shot a layout in the Scottish Highlands for Elle? Wow. Your prints always make history."

"Yes, and it was an editorial piece in Italian *Vogue*, by the way. She can drape fabric like no other. Sometimes, I get lucky when the fabric stars line up. Here, please, sit." Gino took a piece of black woven twill and stretched it out. "I just got this swatch from an upcoming collection. See? This cotton fabric can stretch, but it's more than leotards and those dance leggings. The possibilities are endless in the hands of the right designer. Can you imagine what this would do to the garment industry? Haute couture pants that have elastic stretch? No more tight waists and stiff silhouettes. Don't invest in leather because belts will be as popular as Charles Manson at a playground." He held the cloth out to me. "Feel the hand of it."

The textile's luster slipped through my fingers like silk. "Wow. This feels fabulous. What's the thread count? Eight hundred? Feels like superfine broadcloth." I stretched it between my hands. "That's a lot of give with the elastic. I can see what you're saying. Mega potential."

"They can do it in a satin weave, too. That's why mum's the word. You must be one step ahead of the snakes to survive in this business. It's from your Como. From a little family-run mill." He threw the cloth onto a glass table and took the chair nearest me. Up close, he scanned my face with a worried look. "Jayne, Hannah told me what happened. You don't have to give any details. I know it's painful, and I'm sorry. Italian men can be dangerous."

"I'm sorry Hannah called and gave you my soap opera worth of problems." I smoothed my skirt, realizing Hannah had just ruined the privilege as my confidante. I didn't need sympathy from Gino—just advice. I slapped my hands against my thighs and forced a smile. "Yes, my warp and his weft weren't as strong as I thought," I said, referring to the basic concept of woven fabric. The warp threads ran lengthwise, and the weft threads were horizontal. The higher the count, the tighter the weave.

"I'm sorry. He sounds like a real jerk."

"I prefer a stronger word for him. And I'd say our relationship is now at burlap level." My voice rose. "I'm still at his place which is beyond difficult. But I'll get through it. I'm not the first person to get dumped. Only he's not the reason I called. I need to think about surviving in Milan without him. I've got my Irish passport, so I don't need a visa. I'm legit."

He sat back. "Hannah mentioned that, too. I wish I had work for you in the office. However, I've got Tatiana as my assistant and Giacomo in sales."

I waved my palms in front of me. "No, no. I understand. I don't expect you to hire me. And thank you for making time to say hello. I just wanted to know *if* you think there is anything in Italy for me. Or anywhere in Europe? At a little mill or supplier that might need a young American?"

"Hmm ..."

While he thought, I rose and went to his mahogany worktable that was full of designer sketches, random polaroids, and notes. I picked up a mood board pinned with a soft peachy suede and a snippet of Chinese silk with a green dragon motif. Fingering the threads, I daydreamed about the chance of having a job in Europe.

"That's from Como," he said. "Can't beat those silkworms."

"I know. I sat under a lot of those mulberry trees." Como was known as Silk City. Grand houses existed because of the exquisite textiles and high-quality materials from the Lombardy region. Luxury brands like Chanel, Gucci, and Versace created masterpieces from mills that churned out once-in-a-lifetime woven fabrics and knits. Employment with any heavy hitter in the region would boost my career—having international experience on my resume would open doors. The hope of becoming a fabric buyer for a big fashion house wouldn't be so far-fetched. I turned to Gino. "I'm a quick learner. You know I've got great experience, and Jim taught me the ropes since day one."

"I know. Jim is a legend." He came over and pointed to the board. "You'll see that on the runways for Spring '91. Versace."

"Gorgeous. Are there vendors I could contact? Or mood boards I could source? Any mill that needs a dynamic New Yorker?"

"So, you're fluent in Italian?"

My confidence sank. Matteo had taught me only basic travel phrases and courteous responses. It was my fault, and I should have practiced more with him. "No. Not yet. I'd be better if I took classes ..." I said, wringing my hands. "I've been using my dictionary."

I could tell it was the wrong answer. Yet Gino didn't give up. "How about French? Paris may be a possibility."

I gulped back the *je t'aime* I'd said too many times to Matteo. My once-romantic ability to say I love you in ten languages was now childish. "No. Sorry. Remember, we Americans aren't too good in the foreign language department. At least I'm not. Of course, Matteo's English improved, and I was hoping the vice versa in Como, but it looks like *that's* not happening."

Gino's enthusiasm waned, and he sat down, clasping hands behind his head and thinking aloud. "Let's see. Your number one problem is language. Unfortunately, Italian mills have locals with dialects that even *I* have difficulty understanding. Their reps usually speak five languages. How about Spanish?"

"Nope. Adios and te amo are as far as I can go. Plus, burritos and all that stuff. How about international sales? Could I meet the English-speaking designers who come to Milan? Answer the phone? Be a rep that way?"

Gino leaned forward in his chair. "Jayne, it's different over here. We flip back and forth with languages. If someone needs sample yardage in Berlin or Paris, they call, and we send it over. Your place, Trendary, is our lifeline to the big US manufacturers and retail market. You've got a massive audience we could never connect to, so we need your office to be our go-between. Jim is fantastic, and our sales have been growing each year." He paused for a moment and looked out the window. "New York has much more potential for you, but I understand you want to stay since you're already here. The only possibility is a gig in the big fabric shows. You know, like Premiere Vision."

Premiere Vision, called PV by fashion insiders, is a huge fashion event held twice a year in Paris for three days. Over a thousand woven, knit, leather, denim, and other textile vendors take the opportunity to inspire industry professionals with their exciting fabric under one roof. At Trendary Fabrics, an invitation to PV with the sales team was the holy grail, and I never got the golden ticket to go. "That would be great. But it's *only* seven days a year, and I'd need a more permanent placement if I'm going to survive."

"Ah, yes." He put his elbows on his desk and tapped his fingers against his cheek. "Okay. So, you don't know any European language but need employment. There *is* this place called the Colony Church that everyone says is a great resource for people. This huge corkboard in their front hall is full of help wanted and for sale notices. Who knows? You might discover a posting there."

Nuns in long black habits scurrying along stone hallways came to mind, and I wrinkled my nose. "Working in a church? I don't know ..."

"No. No. It has nothing to do with religion—it's only called a church because it used to be one. Now, it's a type of community center. Lots of people go there—and not only Milanese. And they've got tons of listings ... even apartments. It's, how do you say, worth a shot. Can you teach English?"

"I never had to. It can't be that hard," I said with a hopeful chuckle. "Thank God I'm fluent in one language."

"You can get work like that," he said, snapping his fingers. "Everyone wants to speak like J.R. Ewing. That whole get-my-gun cowboy way."

J.R. Ewing was a mean-spirited hustler on the hit show Dallas about an oil-rich family in Texas. His one-liner insults were legendary. "*You're a half-breed, Sue Ellen*," I drawled.

"Exactly." He stood up, glancing at his watch. "Look, I'd love to take you there, but my client will arrive in five minutes. I usually recover on Saturday mornings, but the bridal season is coming up, so it's all about sequined brocades and lace. Belgian or French. Beads or crystal. They drive me nuts," he said, whipping out a card and jotting information. "Here's the address of the church. It's about a ten-minute walk. An old brick-red building. Easy to find." He handed me the details with a wink. "I feel good about this. Let me know if you have any success."

"Will do." I stuffed the card into my pocket, trailing him to the doorway. I turned and gave him a little hug. "Thanks, Gino. You've been super helpful."

"You're welcome. And next time, I'll take you to Bar Basso, and we'll have a special martini as your official welcome. Don't let what happened with this Matteo fool ruin Italy for you, okay? Give it a chance. It's a great country. You'll see."

"I hope so," I said. "Fingers crossed."

A steady rain fell, and I popped open my mini umbrella, zigzagging between pedestrians and puddles on the cobblestones towards the dark red church. It wasn't a pretty building, yet it seemed popular with dripping bicycles and muddy Vespas gathered outside its pillared doorway. I splashed up the stairs and pulled the chilly brass handle into a vestibule full of backpackers, locals, and people of every age. Above the crowd, a massive board with hundreds of colorful flyers held each gaze like a cult leader.

I approached humbly, clutching my notepad for phone numbers as I joined the concentrated stares. The words "Immediate Hire" blazed across half of the printed announcements and ripped tabs from flyers landed into my bag. Signs with *roommate wanted*, but just the female-only ones interested me. No male issues, thank you.

Salaries and prices were confusing in the advertiser's currency, like the German mark or French franc. I focused on the Italian flags since dealing with foreign currency exchanges was not my strength. Tracking daily fluctuations was a full-time chore unless you were a mathematical genius. Ten French francs were equal to about two thousand Italian lire, and the dollar was valued slightly over one thousand lire. It was mental gymnastics, and my multiplication somersaulted in the room of distracting voices.

A woman around my age arrived beside me to gaze at a thumbtacked index card. I shifted to the right to give her room, noting that her bright blonde pigtails, Nordic knit cap, and mountain boots reminded me of Vikings and skiing. We smiled at each other and broke the ice when reaching for the same roommate-needed advertisement.

"Veni," she said lightly, ushering me to go. "Per favore." *Go. Please.*

"Grazie," I said, reaching to pull off the tab.

She gave me a side glance when she ripped off her tab. "Di dove sei?" she asked. *Where are you from?*

"New York City."

Her mouth fell open at my unexpected answer. Impressed, she switched to English. "*Working Girl* is my favorite movie. I loved New York and the craziness of Wall Street. I want to visit one day and eat a bagel on the Staten Island ferry, just like Melanie Griffith. My body is for sin," she laughed.

"I loved it too." A jab of homesickness and the phantom taste of a bagel's warm dough with a schmear of vegetable cream cheese hit me. Why do you only appreciate those little things when you no longer have them? "The Lower East Side has the best bagels. Remember the name Katz's Bagels—best in the five boroughs. Get the lox, too," I gushed. "Where are you from?"

"West Germany. I came here to be a bus tour guide. I've got a post in Florence next month and came to see Milan," she said. "I'm Nadia."

"I'm Jayne," I said, now curious about positions as an English-speaking tour guide. However, most massive diesel buses I'd seen were full of West Germans or Japanese travelers. Another language impasse, alas. "Milan feels a bit like New York, I think. Same energy."

"Cool." She squinted to read a poster on the top of the board. "Where do you live in the city?"

The dreaded question. "Um … I don't *actually* live here." I wiped the clinging raindrops off my coat to avoid her gaze. "I'm staying in Como up north."

"The lake?" She paused, calculating the distance. "Isn't that an hour away? Are you moving then?"

"Well … um … That's a good question. I don't know. I left Manhattan for my boyfriend, who lives in Como, but we broke up. I'm at his place now, which is super awkward," I said, snatching the nearest tab and pretending to read as my lips quivered. *Stop, Jayne.*

She understood at once and grunted. "I'm very sorry. It happens a lot here. Italian men aren't dependable. Everyone knows that," she said before realizing its impact. She flipped her pigtails and fixed her hat. "Sorry. You're American, so you don't. Are you staying at the hostel tonight?"

"No, but it's an interesting idea," I said, wishing I had thrown clothes and a toothbrush into my bag. Basically, I had no business being at his place—I was literally trespassing. He had responsibilities and needed access to clothes and his bed. His random stopovers to pick up a suit and accessories had been incredibly emotional, and I hated the bitter bitch I had become in his presence. Ten-dollar-a-night hostels with shared showers, strange guys strumming guitars, and creaky bunk beds hadn't been on my radar, but I had no choice. A week in a two-star hotel would leave me penniless. It was the only option. "I'll go to the tourist office and ask for a list."

She touched my arm and leaned forward. "Look at the ragazza alla pari jobs," she whispered, pointing to the other end of the board. "They'd be perfect for you."

"The raggaza alla what-a jobs?"

She motioned me to follow, and we threaded through the crowd, arriving under a section marked by construction paper balloons with strings of yarn hanging from them. She pointed at the decorations. "Childcare is here. This is the ragazza alla pari section. Babysitter. Nanny? Mother's helper? I think that's the way you say it in English."

"Yes. It is. Wow, there are tons of ads," I said, breathing in the opportunity. "I babysat before and like kids …"

Her eyes danced. "Yes. Yes. You live with a family and take care of their children. For you, the best thing is that you leave Como and have your room and board. Then you can decide what to do next." She winked with a grin. "Many women do that over here."

"Do you think I could learn Italian?"

She shrugged. "Why not? It's practice. Maybe you go to school at night."

My mood lifted at this sudden safety net. I'd never thought of babysitting as employment in Italy; nevertheless, I loved kids, so how hard could it be? And I'd have temporary housing while figuring out my next move.

I inched over to the special section and studied each listing. Mother-tongue fluency was popular with embassy addresses, while others sought a live-in au pair for forty-five hours a week. The pay was approximately four hundred bucks a month, which meant enough savings in six months for an apartment's first and last month's rent plus realtor commission. How expensive was language school?

"This looks great. Thanks, Nadia." Why not be a nanny? I began to pull tabs off for the English-speaking ones, adding the bunch into my bag. More people crowded into the foyer, and I stepped away, feeling content with my possibilities.

Nadia and I said bye for now at the doorway, and my frigid toes squashed against the cold concrete for mercy, but I ignored the pain. Being a nanny was a plausible short-term plan.

I cashed twenty lire at a newsstand for gettonis, the metal discs used as tokens in Italian payphones. The clunky coins weighed down my skirt pocket, and I spotted a free booth a block later, ready to start my cold calling.

"Here goes nothing," I said, inhaling the fumes of the departing smoker as I deposited the coins into the slot. The first phone calls in my barbaric Italian ended with two hang-ups, but my luck changed after a self-imposed pep talk for the next call. It was successful, and I lucked out when two mothers took pity on my Italian and switched to English. Agreeing to meet each woman that afternoon, I left the phone booth rejuvenated with the possibility of potential employment.

The first appointment was in the Brera district, near the Duomo, and I soaked up its appeal. Picturesque cobblestone alleys had Juliette balconies above charming starched tableclothed restaurants crowded with locals. In between, local butcher, grocer, and shoe repair storefronts added flavor to the chic neighborhood. I crossed the tram tracks at an intersection and rechecked the address before fixing my hair and lip gloss on the brass nameplate. It was showtime.

After being buzzed entry into the building, a lively woman with a pixie cut answered the door and led me into the mid-century furnished apartment. I tiptoed across a Lego-jumbled floor as she kicked a soccer ball down a hallway and spotted a framed signed jersey from the AC Milan soccer team hanging on the wall. Matteo's favorite team, I thought, rolling my eyes.

After I politely declined her offer of coffee or tea, she blinked a few times and began. "You like Italy?" she asked, sinking back into the overstuffed couch. "Your first time?"

"Yes. My first time. I love Italy—such a beautiful country. Love, love, love Italy," I exaggerated. "I can't believe how beautiful Milan is. The parks, the Duomo. This neighborhood is great, too … Como has charming little areas just like it."

Her brow furrowed. "Como? Did you come from *Como*?"

I froze. "Um. Yes. Is that a problem?"

"No," she said. "But Como is far from here."

I understood her hesitancy. Nervous, I spilled over my paint can of reasons. "Yes, it is. You see, this guy I came to Italy is up there, and he is now my ex-boy*friend*," I assured her. "I'm staying at his place temporarily … till I find, you know … suitable employment."

"Okay, I understand," she said with a sympathetic nod. My story was familiar, and from the curtain of mistrust that swept across her face, not one of her favorites. "So, you want to work as an au pair in my house to escape him."

Her rendition sounded awful. "Not exactly. I think Milan is perfect for me." I took a deep breath. "I love kids and played forward on my high school soccer team," I said, pointing to the ball. "Do you have boys or girls?"

Her face relaxed. "I have three wild boys who love to play football or, as you say, soccer. They're okay in school but need to speak better English. My husband is French, and he speaks only a little, and I'm better but not good."

My hand went to my chest. "I speak perfect English," I said with authority.

She smiled. "Yes. You do. There is an international school in Milan, and to speak English good is the requirement on the application."

I refrained from correcting her. "Okay. I can help them." I was ready to sign up, and all I needed was a bed and a bathroom.

"We travel to Ponza. The boys play on the beach all day, and we rent a house for July and August."

My spirits lifted. Matteo had told me about Ponza—a beautiful island like Capri without tourists. "Sounds wonderful." I grinned. Beaches, ocean, homemade truffle carbonara—I'm there. "I hear it's out of this world."

"Yes, it is. When can you leave if you have this … this situation with your friend in Como?"

"Whenever you'd like," I replied. *The sooner, the better.*

"Can you come in mid-June? The boys can get to know you. And you know us."

My shoulders sank. That was six weeks away. "Mid-June? Are you sure you don't need me now? Help with homework?"

"Now? No, we don't need you now. The boys are in school all day, and we need someone when we leave for the beach. They'll have time to learn English then."

I tucked my hair behind my ears. "Okay. But I was hoping for a position sooner."

With this new development, she put her finger on her chin before speaking. "I'll ask at the school. I'm sorry."

"Okay. Thank you. That would be great." After exchanging friendly smiles, I scribbled Matteo's phone number on my little notepad. "This is the number you can reach me," I said, handing her the paper. "If you hear someone needs a ragazza alla pari now."

She wished me well, and I plodded down the stairs, worrying if every au pair position was only for the summer—which would *not* be in my favor. Three gritty phone discs slid between my sweaty fingers as I calculated my odds, wondering if I'd need more if the next appointment were also a bust.

Disillusioned, I trudged onward, debating if a detour to a travel office would be wise to take my mom up on her offer. I almost tripped when two kids skipped past me on the sidewalk, and their mother yelled for them to stop. They were the same age as Flynn's kids, Kate and Quinn. And just as rambunctious.

The animated children, full of innocence, were unaware of how life sometimes could be cruel. They waited for their mother, and I passed with a smile while growling inside about Matteo's rejection. Saying the Earth was flat would have made more sense, except he wanted out, plain and simple. We dreamed of our future and walked through neighborhoods in Forest Hills to find our perfect house. What happened?

Once, he proclaimed that I was inconsiderate because he didn't like to be known as "my Italian boyfriend, Matteo." He argued that people instantly thought the worst because of preconceived stereotypes. I told him people loved Italy, and he was being paranoid. And then he accused me of only liking him because he was from there. He said I would never introduce him as "my New Jersey boyfriend."

"Ridiculous," I said under my breath. "Really?"

But there was no doubt our relationship had jumped all the relationship hurdles in our first month. My dad wasn't exactly handing out cigars when Matteo moved in with me, and I had second thoughts after my casual offer became a done deal. Yet I never regretted the decision, especially after the loss of Damian. Until now. What if he hadn't moved in with me, I wondered?

I had ten minutes before my next stop in the historical center on Via Manche with a voltaic-named woman, Electra, and meandered past the majestic Milan Cathedral in the Piazza del Duomo. Tourists milled outside diesel-puffing coach buses or snapped photos of its thousands of Gothic carved statues and spires piercing the now bluebird sky. I hurried under the Galleria Vittorio Emmanuele II's arch onto its beautiful mosaic floor, marveling at the glass-vaulted arcades and luxury storefronts. Clattering dishes from swanky cafés and spellbound tourists added excitement, and the pricey exclusive boutiques with elegant, dressed mannequins posed for perfection quelled my apprehension.

I found the dancing bull mosaic that I read in my Let's Go Italy book.

Placing my heel between its hind legs, I spun around three times for good fortune, ignoring the blank stares of shoppers. Laughing, I wished Hannah were with me as I absorbed the cosmopolitan buzz of vibrant colors, soft chiffons, and gorgeous drapes of beauty. In awe, I pursed my lips, speculating about the dire possibility of finding a mill stint in Italy. Sourcing was my passion, and Milan was the origin of high quality fashion craftmanship, different from the artistic cities of Florence and Rome. Destiny brought me there. It would be fantastic if I learned Italian and Gino could help me make it happen.

Dreaming of my next steps, I exited onto portico-covered streets toward the next appointment. An unshaven man in a Fair Isle sweater vest motioned to the excrement-splattered pavement where a sign read *500 lire a bag*, which was about twenty cents. Next to him, a young couple surrounded a little boy holding out his palm. A pigeon landed on it and poked at the seeds on his pudgy hand, and the parents grew excited when another attempted to land on him. I shuddered as the father fumbled to take a photo with his Instamatic camera.

"Signorina?" the vendor called.

"No. Grazie," I responded, watching pigeon wings bat against the child's face. Disgusted, I turned away as one bird fluttered high into the domed archway. A large raindrop landed on my hair, and my fingers touched a blob of jelly. When I looked up, a blinking pigeon peered down from an ornate pillar's gargoyle, cooing.

"Dammit," I said, staring at the grey mess. I turned to the man, shaking off the feces from my fingers. "Il birdo crappo on my head."

The family giggled, and the cheerful man gestured with raised arms. "Buona fortuna per sempre," he said with a toothless grin. *You'll always have good luck.*

Humiliated, I gave him a thumbs-down. Thanks, bull. If this was real Italian good luck, I was really screwed. The Duomo's bells tolled the hour, and I broke into a jog, pulling pigeon refuse out of my strands. A touristy restaurant had its door wide open, and I beelined to the restroom for a quick fix. Inside, a kind woman tried to help me with my dirtied hair with a wet paper towel, which didn't help my tornado survivor reflection. Exasperated, I said grazie and almost bowled over the hostess when she karate-chopped my stomach with a menu as I sprinted out the exit.

"Scusi," I cried as I ran to my following interview.

$ 401.89

Espresso - need 2 sugars - due zucchero - .50

Ticket back to Como - can't believe its over - goodbye Matteo! -4.00

International Herald Tribune - no NY Times - only at special stores -1.50

$ 395.89

MATTEO

Love Sucks!

4:02→4:45

CHAPTER THREE

"DON'T WORRY, JAYNE. Matteo said Italians are *always* late."

My self-encouragement didn't soothe my anxiety as I stood outside the building, trying to catch my breath. A silver Mercedes and a navy Range Rover idled nearby, and I wondered if my potential employer was a diplomat or owned either. The street seemed posher, and I wished I had worn earrings as I adjusted my bag and licked my dry lips, studying number eleven Via Manche. Flanked by two ceramic containers overflowing with white flowers, the massive, eighteen-foot green door with a shiny brass kick plate gleamed with power. Needless to say, another fruitless appointment would be the end of my Italian job hunting.

I poked the entry bell, and a middle-aged man in paint-spattered overalls appeared with a Scooby-Doo-looking dog drooling at his side. He ushered me into the echoing red-and-blue tiled entry and introduced himself as Pedro and his dog, Dante. Judging by the jingle of clinking keys, I guessed Pedro must have been the guardian who played door attendant, the chief fixer-upper, and the property manager. He wanted to know who I was, and I tried to explain in broken Italian until he finally cut me off with a pained expression. "Signora Electra di Caneva e al terzo piano," he said, holding up three fingers. *Electra di Caneva is on the third floor.*

"Grazie." *Thanks.*

He escorted me to the gilded, ornate birdcage elevator while his dog sniffed my coat. I patted Dante when we stopped, and Pedro screeched open the metal door. He moved aside and gestured for me to enter. "Per favore." *Please.*

"Grazie," I said, pushing the two inside wooden doors to enter the cabin. The floor bounced under my weight, and the acrid smell of polish matched the shiny brass railings outlining the interior. I jabbed the number three circle, and the lift jolted into action. Luckily, a small mirror was above the controls, and after tousling my hair to hide my bird poop drop zone, I dusted specks of dried dung off my shoulders.

"Aspetta! Signorina!" *Wait. Miss.* The cry echoed below as Pedro ran to the elevator with a shadow while Dante barked excitedly. I pressed the red stop button ten times, but the elevator refused to obey.

"Scusa," I apologized, hitting the button again. Besides Pedro and Dante, a well-dressed newcomer was peering up at my ascent. His arctic laser stare drilled into my soul with an unforgettable intensity, and my knees buckled. The man was my fashion hero, Luca Rosso. The most famous designer in Italy. A legend. I loved his elegant clothes. His wonderful colognes. His undeniable mystery.

"Mi dispiace," I cried again while the small cabin sped up the mechanical cavern. "Great," I added, listening to Dante's barks fade away with my courage. "Five hours in Milan, and not only was I rejected, and a bird shat on me, but now the king of fashion hates me. Maybe someone is telling me to forget this dream."

The elevator passed the red-carpeted steps that twisted upward as it ascended the shaft slowly. I would have appreciated the touch of old-world romance if I weren't so overwhelmed. When the lift stopped, an infant's wail grew louder as my body wedged through the tight door flaps, still in disbelief about dissing the designer of my dreams. I quickly checked my breath outside the door and rapped its brass knocker with a cheek-ripping smile, ready to sell myself.

An auburn-haired woman whipped open the door, holding a sobbing baby in a powder-blue sailor suit. Her candy-apple lipstick and bottle-glass green eyes popped like Christmas tree ornaments against her pale skin. Her appearance caught me off-guard because, minus the screaming infant, her unfiltered beauty was unexpected. I already felt out of my league in her presence. "You're late," she stated, stepping away from the door. "And I don't like late."

I was afraid to move. "Yes, I'm sorry. What happened was out of my control."

"Excuses. Come in. And take your shoes off. God knows where you were."

When I entered, I bent over to slip off my shoes and placed them next to her Gucci loafers with the horse-bit buckle. After prying her baby's cherubic grip from her oversized pearl choker, she handed me the hysterical child with an exaggerated moan. I tried to complete the squirming hand-off but nearly dropped him when he lunged toward her. She sized me up with a toss of her hair while I held him tightly. "See if you can stop this release of emotion. He doesn't like people who can't read time," she said with a slight accent before leaving in a huff.

The upset baby bounced in my arms, and we both watched her leave to the back of the apartment. With snot blobs bubbling from his nose, I tried not to slip on slick herringbone parquet floors as I paced around the room. Her home was different from the earlier woman's. Beautifully decorated with imposing antiques, the pale green pillows and soft yellow chairs warmed the cold, gaping oil portraits that seemed to judge me from each wall.

"Hush, little boy. Mommy will be back soon." The child quieted, staring at his disappearing mother with shock that I shared. When she was out of sight, he howled louder than before, writhing to escape my arms. "I think he needs you," I called, holding his cauldron of mucus away from my blouse.

The blasé woman ignored my plea. "He's fine," she finally shouted from a room. I stopped in my tracks, confused at her abandonment. Was there another child in the bathtub? A medical emergency? I sniffed the air for any smoke while the baby rubbed his nose, creating a web of stringy mucus glue between his tiny fingers. I held him like a wet cat as I hovered near a fragile antique bench, fretting if it could collapse under my body weight.

"Mommy must have had an emergency, and she left us *all* alone," I cooed, searching for a tissue box on a built-in bookcase lined with Chinese bowls and porcelain dishes. With no tissues in sight, I reached for the closest object—an ivory horse with a flashy black tail. The delicate figure swooped before his blubbering face as I oohed and aahed, attempting to hypnotize his cries away until she returned.

"Watch the pretty horse fly," I sang. His eyes blinked in wonderment, and suddenly, the infant's hand shot out with snake-like precision and latched on to the figure. I tugged it from his tight hold and gasped once the horse was free. The tail was missing.

"Shit," I whispered, glancing behind me. I gently tried to pry the porcelain piece from his tiny fist, peeling away each finger one by one. He puckered his face and bellowed at my audacity until I finally won. Panicking, I wondered if hiding the broken piece in my bag was the best solution. Doubtful, I finally placed the statue and missing tail on the shelf where it had been.

Glancing for another distraction, I spotted a stuffed dinosaur underneath a leather chair and grabbed it to stop his almost hyperventilating hysteria. "Look who wants to visit," I said, marching the dinosaur up his little leg with funny roars. It didn't help, and he head-butted his disapproval onto my chest, leaving a river of nose debris. Losing patience, I went to the top of the hallway and listened for any signs of life, worried. "Hello?" I cried out. "Do you need help?"

Nothing.

I took a step with caution. "Is everything okay?"

A door clicked open, and the woman sashayed down the hallway in wide beige pants and a long black sweater—a different outfit than before. Her heavy-handed fragrance ambushed my senses as she paraded around the furniture as if walking between pool cabanas. She pivoted like a socialite, and I expected an opera-length cigarette holder with a throaty request for a light.

"I'm desperate for a nanny who drives because I'm planning a big trip through Italy and may cross over borders to other countries. I haven't decided which ones because everyone is too busy to call me back. Oh, look, he likes you," she said, flicking a hand at her son. "Usually, at this point, he'd be having a tantrum on the floor, which is very normal since my little man can't express his emotions with words. Isn't that right, il mio dolce bambino?" She blew him a kiss. "He doesn't like people in general—that's all me. See how he focuses on my face so intensely? They say he's brilliant for only nine months. The doctors think he may be a genius. Takes from my side, of course." She extended her hand. "I'm Electra di Caneva, by the way."

"Hi. I'm Jayne Boland," I said, taking her soft grip. She focused on the shiny swoosh of her son's snot drying on my shirt and then visually inspected me as if I were a curious specimen. Thankfully, she wasn't my height and unable to see the splotch of bird turd in my hair. "I'm the person who—"

She raised her hand in protest. "Hush. I know who you are." She veered to a dark satin couch and crossed her long legs as she sat. "Come and sit. Let's chat," she said in a sultry talk show voice.

"Okay." Nervous, I gauged the two embroidered chairs flanking the couch and took neither, cradling the now calm baby. "I can drive. Long distances are not a problem for me." She looked at me, expressionless. "Um ... what's his name?" I asked, jiggling him as I played the part of a potential nanny. "He's so sweet *and* smart."

"Alessandro Carlo Alfonso Benedetto di Caneva," she said with pride, reaching up to fix the hem on his dangling pant leg. "He's a big boy, isn't he? Soon-to-be tall and gorgeous like all the men in my family."

My arms ached from his weight, and I shifted him onto my hip. "He's got great genes, especially in the muscle department," I laughed, choosing the sturdy leather chair against the wall. I gave Alessandro the nearby stuffed dinosaur, and he shoved it into his mouth, causing Electra to jump up and snatch it away.

"That dirty toy was on the floor where germs breed. My son could get a bacterial infection, leading to organ failure. Or worse, poisoning from lethal toxins from pesticides and chemicals and God knows what else."

"I ... I didn't know," I said as she yanked the baby from my arms. "I'm sorry."

"Sorry, won't help when he's in the hospital. Or when they operate on his little body." She stepped back, pointing at me with a shaky finger. "What is that spot?"

My hand flew to the bird poop, and I tried to shrug it off, patting the mess. "This? It's a funny story. A pigeon dropped a gift on the way here. It means good luck, right?"

She scoffed. "If you believe a bird relieving itself on your hair predicts your destiny, then I guess so. You must wash your hands *immediately* because you are not transmitting any strange avian disease to my son. Have you heard of the bubonic plague? Go! The door is on the right, and I will change him out of his contaminated clothes."

I rushed into the bathroom in a tizzy. To say that the appointment wasn't going well would be the understatement of the decade, I thought, glancing at the bidet. Hoping to find a hairbrush, I knew another failure would be the deal breaker for my life in Italy. After putting my hair in a bun and dusting white flakes from my shoulders, I grabbed a pink old-fashioned perfume bottle for a pick-me-up but as soon as it sprayed, I realized it was a nasty air freshener. "Dammit," I coughed, fanning the fumes away.

"Are you okay?" she said with icy politeness on the other side of the door.

"Yes," I replied, grabbing a towel to flap in the air. "I'll be out soon."

The door suddenly opened, and an object flew into the bathroom. "Wear that."

A white plastic shower cap lay on the navy-and-gold tiled floor. "You must be joking," I said. I picked it up with a moan and tucked stray hairs under the ridiculous bonnet, grimacing at my miserable reflection. "I needed this before to protect my clothes."

When I returned, the room was unnaturally quiet, and the baby scrunched his face at my new helmet while his mother smiled with satisfaction. The blond and periwinkle-eyed Alessandro clashed against her dark hair, and she appeared older than most young mothers in the direct sunlight, but maybe the dreaded lack of sleep caused her creases. Alessandro tugged her choker to suck its pearls, and I refrained from expounding the dangers of swallowing dirty, sweaty beads. Instead, I stared at her paintings as she gathered her thoughts before pulling him away from the necklace with a scowl.

"Stop with Mama," she said softly, balancing him on her lap as she reached behind to unclasp the choker. When she lifted the jewelry, a small pink scar appeared at the base of her throat, and she noticed my stare. "Ugly, isn't it? I've had it since I was a child."

"No ... it's not." I didn't know what else to say and scanned the room for diversion, noticing the half-hidden horse on the shelf. "Oh, before I forget, he broke the tail off that statue," I confessed, pointing to the tailless horse. "When he was upset."

Her face fell. "My little boy did *that*?"

"I tried to calm him with it, only when he grabbed the tail—"

"Okay. So, you're blaming an innocent child for doing what doctors consider an age-appropriate, natural reflex. Of course, *you* bear no responsibility for ruining a valuable piece of Nymphenburg porcelain. Jayne, let me ask you this. Do you know how to care for a baby?" she demanded. "Have you ever changed a diaper? Do you have a degree in early education or childcare?"

"Yes, I mean, no," I said, my cheeks growing hot. "I'm sorry about the horse. Yes, about diapers. About education, no. But my sister, Flynn, has two children, and I have watched them since they were newborns." I neglected to add that I hadn't babysat in two years since Flynn had moved to Millbrook.

The woman tilted her head for more information, so I proceeded. "My B.A.—my degree—is a Bachelor of Arts in East Asian Studies, and I graduated from Colby College."

"East Asian Studies is not very practical for childcare." Her eyelids dropped to half-mast. "I've never heard of your school before. Where is it in Ireland? Near Trinity in Dublin?"

"Ireland? No. It's in Maine."

She snapped to attention. "Maine? In America? Where they have those … those moose things? You told me you're Irish on the phone."

"I am. But also, American. My parents immigrated to America. When I called this morning, I said I had an Irish *passport* to work in Europe. And yes, there are moose in Maine." From her glazed expression, I was losing her. "My school isn't famous like Harvard or Yale, but it's still great. My other major is history," I added, for whatever it was worth.

She sniffed approval. "History? Like Art History?"

"Well." My confidence flat-lined. In my only art history course, I got a solid C. I had needed the three humanity credits and thought it was an easy class, but the final centered on a piece of obscure artwork other students swore wouldn't be on the exam—a medieval sculpture of a monk. She could quiz me on the dusty, ghoulish faces on her walls, which would be a disaster. "No, not art. History is like history. Like World History," I said quickly. "All this … this olden day history."

My dismal answer bordered on gibberish, yet she shrugged with mild interest. "Well, my family has centuries of history—we were one of Austria's founding families, now Northern Italy. Alessandro loves the subject," she said optimistically. "Homer's *Odyssey* is one of his favorite bedtime stories."

"It is?" I regained my composure. "Yes, of course. Babies love epic stories." Her eyebrows rose. "I always talk to babies about the past. You know, educate them when I can."

She smirked. "And where did you do this educating?"

I gulped. "For friends and neighbors," I said, praying she wouldn't demand references. Besides Flynn's gang, the last kid I'd watched must be out of high school.

"Which family did you work for before? The Rockefellers are in New York, aren't they?"

Her expectations needed to be lowered like a yacht's sail. "Yes, they are. However, I changed fields after college," I said. "I worked in Manhattan until a week ago before I came to Italy. In fashion." I pulled out my resume and smoothed out the creases. "It's all here."

She put on her cat-eye readers and seemed intrigued as her finger traced every line. An occasional nod made me feel better. "Your last business was Seventh Avenue in New York's fashion district. Not like Avenue Montaigne in Paris, of course, although still known to have one or two noteworthy designers," she said, examining my outfit with renewed interest. "My mother had a blouse just like that. So … it is, how do you say, simple? This house, Trendary Fabrics, I've never heard of them. Do they show at Paris Fashion Week?"

I ignored her subtle jab. "No. We deal with big designers who do the show in Paris. But we are not a house per se. Trendary sells fabrics to top American designers, and sometimes to international houses who came to New York." I leaned forward. "I saw Luca Rosso downstairs. He's my fashion god. His last collection was incredible. Does he live in this building?"

She clicked her tongue. "You mean the tailor? No, he only has his office here."

The tailor? Who was this woman? "Oh."

She folded my resume. "You have quite an interesting life."

I nodded, still digesting the tailor comment. Alessandro was asleep on her lap, exhausted from his blubbering. He looked so sweet.

"How old are you, Jayne?"

"I'm twenty-four," I said, taking my resume from her.

"Mio dio," she grunted. "You are old. I don't understand *why* you left your fashion thing in New York to come to Italy and be a ragazza alla pari. You had a wonderful career and *now* want to care for babies in Italy? It makes no sense. Why did you leave America? Did anything happen?" She leaned closer. "Are you in trouble?"

Trouble was a loaded word. I took a deep breath to explain my rehearsed "I love Italy" speech, except this woman wasn't stupid. She had every right to cross-examine how I'd landed on her doorstep. "I …" My insides twisted, disliking Matteo more than ever. Me trying to sell myself to this condescending Italian woman was beyond degrading. Yes, lady, I had a fantastic life in Manhattan with no complaints. And cool clothes to prove it. I gave it up for a fickle guy who landed me groveling at your feet, you with your brilliant gooey-nosed baby, for mercy. Call it off-the-rails pride. Or stupidity. Whatever it was, I was still trying to understand it myself.

I swallowed to recalibrate my response. "You're right. It makes no sense, and I should explain myself better. My boyfriend Matteo left New York a month ago and asked me to follow him. I got here a week ago, and I don't know what happened after he left, but he ended the relationship as soon as I landed. Since I am beyond shattered, I'm trying to figure out what to do since everything I own is in Como," I lamented, turning away from her poker-faced stare. "I don't blame you for being suspicious."

"I believe you." Her face softened. "There must be reasons for this … failure. Number one, is his mother alive?"

I hesitated. "Yes."

"Any brothers? Sisters?"

"None. Just him," I said, sitting back.

Her hand flew up in the air. "Okay. Case closed. Like Alessandro and me, his mother feels no one is good enough for him. *Especially* a foreigner."

I took a deep breath. "I don't think Matteo considered me a foreigner, and I've never even met his mother."

Her eyebrows leaped. "And why not?"

"Because," I replied, realizing she had me, "I just didn't."

"Okay, so you traveled across the world for her son, and his mother isn't there to greet you? This is a problem," she tsked, picking off a hair from Alessandro's suit. "Can you cook? And I don't mean the simple American thing you do with a shake in the bag or that talking glove."

I was afraid to answer. But curious about how she knew American food products like Hamburger Helper. "Um … I cook the basics."

"Mio dio. I am afraid of what the basics are. American food is full of fat. Starches like fried rice. Those morning round things you put tree sap on?"

"You mean pancakes? The tree sap is called maple syrup," I replied. However, she was right. Matteo's ability to throw together incredible risotto dishes or homemade lasagna with high-quality ingredients was gourmet-level. Our friends had wanted him to open a catering company—Matteo's Meals. The fact that I fit into her American stereotype was annoying. Sunday morning pancakes, meatloaf with mashed potatoes, and the occasional macaroni and cheese were my culinary contributions.

I continued. "It's a little different now. It's the *nineties,* and it's not about cooking to please your man. And for your information, I did make nice dinners, and Matteo never complained. Yes, he taught me a thing or two because he loved cooking. Al dente, herbs, and that stuff."

"Thank you for that correction. Syrup." She made a funny noise. "The man had to eat—that's why he cooked. You needed to show your passion for him every day in the kitchen. In Italy, we love to create a beautiful meal and seduce a man with food." She wagged her finger. "This could be the reason why he doesn't love you."

Ouch. "You're making it sound like it was my fault. And food isn't the reason. There are other women, I think. I'm trying to find a job and get my life back on track," I sniffed.

She jumped up and hurried down the hallway, taking the baby this time. Maybe she thought exposing my sadness in front of the tiny tot could induce emotional scarring, and she needed to put him under a bright light for detoxification. Alone in the room, I glanced down the hall, listening to her talk to her son in Italian. She was right. Chef Matteo stirred a lot of passion with his swaying hips and the sweet kisses he'd offer when I'd investigated a garlicky aroma. His love was in every bite of food. His charming smile of satisfaction while I swooned over his tasty surprises. How had I not seen that?

I turned to the front door and quietly rose. An exit from this bulls-eyed sabotage just required a grateful thank you very much; your boy is adorable; I hope you find someone and arrivederci. The vestibule was directly behind me, and I watched the hallway while my feet slipped into my kitten heels. Second thought: Forget the see ya; she won't care. I'll save her the awkwardness or offer another brutal freebie on why Matteo didn't love me.

I tiptoed and grabbed my coat. Take the next train back to Como or go to a travel office and buy that plane ticket. Put it on Mom's credit card and worry later. It was morning in Queens. She was right. I should beg Jim for my career back. Could I get a flight home tomorrow? Today?

I snuck to the door and twisted the handle, but her humming grew louder, and I skidded back into a chair, twiddling my thumbs with a smile as she reappeared with a fresh-faced Alessandro. She held out a box of tissues and stopped short, noticing my shoes. "Oh, you're leaving? Here," she sighed, "take as many as you need. Believe me, I'm not saying it is all your fault. This man is awful. Not your Principe Azzurro."

"My principe what?" Azzuro was sky blue, so I was confused.

"You know, the Cinderella Man. Prince Charming. Someone who loves you for you. We call him the Blue Prince here. Not your white horse one with the slipper thing, but the same idea. The man of your dreams."

Since my ego was lower than hell's basement, her fairy tale reference cracked my Hoover Dam of sadness. Realizing Matteo would never be my Blue Prince was another brick thrown at my heart.

"Now, now," she said, tutting as I sobbed. "You will find him one day."

I blew my nose. "I'm sorry for all … all this emotion," I said, shoving the damp wad into my bag as I stood. "Thanks for being so nice and letting me come here. Your little boy is beyond adorable, and your English is great, by the way." I dug into my coat pocket and handed her a bunch of gettoni. "This is for the broken tail. It's all I have."

She took the coins and slowly guided me to the doorway. "Thank you. That's kind to say I speak English well. I went to university in Vienna and then moved to America for a month, where I had a great teacher but didn't enjoy my life there. It was too … what's that word? Complicated?"

"I think it's complicated in every country. Thanks again," I said, accepting a wad of fresh tissues.

"Jayne, don't feel defeated. You are not waiting for someone to rescue you, which shows me you are a strong woman. Believe in yourself, and best of luck."

"Thanks. Bye, Alessandro," I waved as the door opened.

Suddenly, Alessandro opened his arms and leaned toward me. Electra, stunned by his action, took a step closer. "He … I … Wait. When can you start?" she said, letting him fall into my chest.

"Really?" His warm chicken nugget body pressed sweetness into my chest, and I squeezed him slightly. "I don't know. I was going to go back to New York."

She fixed the baby's curls, admiring him until her lips flickered into a smile. "Alessandro likes you, and his happiness is paramount. And I like the fact that you are a good listener. It will make you a great driver. Yes, you can return to your old life in New York, to the way it was. Except you are here now, and you can start tomorrow if you'd like."

Her offer was the sun peeking over my dire horizon. I wanted to hug her. "Tomorrow?"

Pleased with my reaction, she took Alessandro back and nodded. "Yes, the day after today. Get your belongings from that dreadful man in Como and come back." She turned away and pointed to a staircase I had missed against the apartment's white walls. It led up to a balcony loft, and I stepped back to see a lilac bedspread ruffle through its wooden rails. "I've got enough space for you to stay here. There's a single bed, and you can use the smaller bathroom. I'll pay you at the end of the month," she said with a sense of closure. "Four hundred and fifty thousand lire. About four hundred American dollars. Food is included, of course. Any of your expenses are your own, but otherwise, I'll give you my credit card for all our purchases. Is that okay?"

"Yes. Wow. Okay… That sounds perfect. I'll go to the train station now," I said, thinking aloud. "Pack tonight and be back here tomorrow."

"Great. And you've never crashed a car? Or had a ticket for speeding?"

"Never."

"Excellent. I plan for us to leave Milan in two weeks and then return in September. My life needs to be more balanced with my son, and I must handle a personal situation." She bee-lined to the elegant writing desk and scribbled on a pad as I waited by the open door. "Here's my number," she said, ripping off the note. "Let me know what time you will arrive."

"Thank you so much," I said, taking the paper.

"And here, take your gettonis," she said, handing them back to me. "Call your parents and tell them you're in safe hands."

I nodded. "I will."

"And Jayne?"

My stomach lurched, fearing she had changed her mind. "Yes?"

She pointed to my head. "I'll take my shower cap before you leave."

$ 395.89

Bottle of Pinot Grigio - 5.65

Shampoo (need conditioner for oily hair-not dry) - 4.50

Focaccia (near station-good!) - 2.00

Train ticket to Milan - 4.00

*NEW LIFE * HOPE *

$ 379.74

GOOD BYE LOSER

CHAPTER FOUR

AFTER SHOWERING in Matteo's apartment, I towel-dried my hair, staring at the three suitcases. One Samsonite would have to stay behind. Matteo couldn't refuse my request since my parents had stored his antique couch and ski equipment in our garage free of charge. His priceless treasures would have to be collateral to ensure my suitcase's safety, and I lugged the biggest one to the hall closet and shoved it into the darkness. Closing the door, I snorted at the irony—the highly recommended ski pants I'd bought would never see the light of day—another waste of money.

On the entry table, the answering machine's red light was blinking. Since I had left Matteo's phone number on assorted answering machines, I should play the messages. There could be an offer better than Electra's, but I highly doubted it.

The tape in the machine rewound as I poured a much-needed glass of wine. While I sipped, my mom's Irish lilt made another plea to take the plane ticket. Flynn's garbled message followed, and I learned that one of the kids had chickenpox, and she was so sorry to hear the shocking news of the breakup. The next one was a woman panting and moaning the words "Matteo," and I erased it, seething. It had to be one of his conquests, and I shut off the machine, realizing he had entertained himself for the past month with hot sex. So much for my nightly monastic existence of TV reruns and bowls of unbuttered popcorn.

I called my mom, Flynn, and Hannah to update them on my new position and gave Electra's telephone number for emergencies. Hannah still hoped for a reconciliation, but my mom begged me to not only be careful, but to come home. After the conversations, my mind juggled glass balls of confusion and disappointment, ripping every happy picture of Matteo and me over the garbage can with disbelief. There was no turning back.

After nine, my body needed real food besides thick, oily bread. Matteo wasn't back from the office, and I hoped to dine alone. Electra's eye-opening conclusion that my cooking was why our relationship had failed hurt, and I decided to tackle that problem.

"I'll prove her theory wrong," I said, pulling out pots and pans. Minutes later, as the linguine boiled, I threw red onion and juicy tomatoes on a hot skillet, flavoring as if Julia Child guided each shake of herbs. Garlic chopping had the same intensity as open-heart surgery, and more olive oil flowed into the skillet as my spirits lifted. I raised the flame and fried the garlic, filling the room with a luscious aroma and the familiar, comforting smell of delicious food.

A commotion sounded at the door, and I steadied myself for Matteo's entry, placing a frisée salad on the table. He would waltz into the room and pretend nothing happened, thinking I'd made a special romantic dinner to attempt reconciliation. But I'd never forgive him for what he had done. I gulped more wine. It was his last supper. But at least it would be good.

A knock rapped on the door, and a British accent shouted, "Matteo. Open up. It's me. Susan."

I put down the wine glass. Was this the woman on the answering machine? "He's not here," I yelled in her direction.

Her tone changed. "Is that you, Dory?"

Dory? I bolted to the door like a crazed Rottweiler. "No. There is no Dory here."

"Oh. Are you the American?" the woman asked from the other side.

I flew open the door, and a brunette chewing gum stood with a massive bouquet of roses in a glass vase. Flowers for me? My soul cartwheeled, and I opened the door wider. Roses were his apology for his awful behavior? "Oh, sorry. I was cooking. Aw, those are so beautiful. Please, come in."

She stepped in, sniffing the air as she glanced down the hallway. Her high-waisted jeans had a patch of cherries sewn on the leg, and she cocked her head to the bedroom with a smile. "Is he here? Having a little lie-down?"

"No, no. Matteo is still at work. Here, let me take those from you. Thanks so much," I gushed, putting out my hands. "They're gorgeous. And I didn't know you guys made late deliveries here."

She stepped back with a laugh. "What? Delivery? Wait. Do you think? Oh, no, they're not for you, sweets. They're for Matteo. We all thought *you* were gone."

"We?" I sputtered.

She didn't answer and hurried past me to his bedroom with her gift. "Matteo, you're not hiding from me, you scoundrel, are you?" Flabbergasted, I followed, and she placed the arrangement on his dresser with care. "I guess you're right. Poor guy works so hard. He loves the smell of fresh roses, you know," she said, arranging the flowers. She inhaled the blooms' scent and turned with a twitch of her nose. "Don't you?"

Her appreciation didn't impress me, and I folded my arms. "Excuse me, but who are you?"

She pointed to herself in disbelief. "Me? Who am *I*? I'm his English tutor."

"Matteo doesn't need a tutor. He speaks perfect English."

She hooted in disbelief at my comment. "Are you joking? Matteo wants to speak correctly. His grammar is terrible, and he said his accent is too … New Yorky."

I snorted. "He said that? I don't believe you. All he wants to be is a New Yorker."

"Ahh, but that was before." She scanned me up and down. "Jayne, right? Matteo said you were uptight. I can see that now. Still, I have to say you are much prettier than the way he described you. You've got great hair. What shampoo do you use?"

"Shampoo? Are you serious?" A sudden, acrid smell stopped my response to the insult. "Damn," I hissed, running back to the kitchen into a layer of smoke. The pan was ablaze in orange flames, and I frantically searched for the potholder while turning off both burners. Susan joined the chaos by fanning the fire with a magazine from the coffee table, making the room smokier. "Stop doing that. You're making it worse."

"I'll put water on it," she said, dipping a giant soup ladle into the linguine pot. Flashbacks of a Girl Scout fire-prevention course popped into my memory, but before I could yell stop, she poured the fluid onto the greasy pan, lighting up the room like a bonfire as pyrotechnical flames licked the ceiling.

I freaked, searching for a lid to cover the flames. The closest was next to Susan. "Get that," I yelled, pointing to the glass top of the linguine pot. "Quick. Throw it on to cut off the air supply. Hurry!" She hovered it over the flame, then dropped it onto the blaze. The inferno ended within seconds.

"Holy crap," I said, clutching my chest.

"Look." Susan directed my attention to the ceiling to a big circle of black soot. "He's not going to like that." She began to cough like a lifetime smoker. "It's so smoky," she wheezed.

I flung open all the windows, and minutes later, the fresh breeze brought the air quality to a breathable level. Susan had already taken refuge in his bedroom, and her annoying voice chatted behind closed doors. She was probably relaying the fire mishap to Matteo.

I knocked softly and opened the door. "The air is better. You can come out," I said, peeking in the doorway. The intruder turned, and a tsunami of anger surged. Susan was wearing the sexy little black dress I had unsuccessfully worn to seduce Matteo. I had left it draped over a chair as a subtle reminder to him of what he was missing. The worst part was that her curves looked better in it than mine.

"Is this your dress?" she asked sweetly. "Is Azzedine Alaia expensive?"

My eyes darted to her throat. One minute of a tight grip … "Out," I said, pointing to the door. "OUT!"

She stared wide-eyed. "Out? Me? I just saved your ass."

"Since when did you and I become friends?" I picked up the vase of roses while she unhooked the dress, throwing insult after insult my way. Half-dressed, she grabbed her jeans and scrambled into the kitchen as I followed her with the unfazed flowers. She defiantly snapped up the gift-wrapped squirrel I bought for Matteo's parents in one swoop and turned to me. "What are you doing with that?" I sneered.

She snapped her gum. "What are *you* doing with those?"

I stepped forward. "I'm returning your student's roses to you. Take his lovely gift and get out of here." She didn't budge. "Your threat means nothing, by the way. I don't care what you do with that stupid squirrel. Go ahead, smash it."

She blinked with feigned innocence and let it drop. "Whoops."

I pushed the heap of broken ceramic pieces with my foot. "Thank you. You just did me the biggest favor. And if you don't leave right now, this twenty-pound ball will be airborne," I warned. "Ten … nine … eight …"

She almost fell over, jamming a leg into her jeans. "You know, if you played your cards right, we *could* have become friends," Susan said, zipping her pants before rushing toward me to take the heavy vase. She gave a wry smile, and I gnashed my teeth before she fumbled at the door and disappeared with a big slam.

I turned around to the mess. Gross gray clumps gelled in the skillet, and the linguine floated like planks from a shipwreck. With a moan, I swept up the shattered squirrel mess and dropped the pieces into the trashcan. My wine glass needed an immediate top-up, and I ripped off a piece of focaccia and stuffed it into my mouth. "He said he talks too *New Yorky*?" I scoffed at the stove.

I chewed, bewildered. Susan, Dory. Who else? Oh yes, the groaner on the phone. Ugh. I looked above me. How many hundreds for that damage? Shaking my head, a rose petal on the floor caught my eye, and I picked up the fragile ruby pad. I touched the softness against my mouth, tortured at being alone in a country where the man I adored wanted me to leave.

I had to get out of this funk. Life would be better in Milan. Electra seemed nice, and her baby sweet. And I'd be traveling, at least. Maybe Portofino, Capri, Sicily. I dropped the petal into the pot of linguine and toasted an imaginary Matteo with my goblet of wine. "To us—two strangers who met in a Manhattan elevator one moonless night. A press of plastic that changed our lives," I said. I thought of Luca Rosso but continued. "But destiny is full of bad buttons waiting to be pressed. Here's to the right floor. Upwards forever without you darling. Ciao and it's time for one of us to get off."

Matteo's noisy departure awoke me the following day, and I crept out to meet his rumpled clothes thrown over the living room chair. A new spicy soap scent cut through the smoky aftermath, and my stomach knotted again.

"Matteo? Where are you?" I said, picking up a shirt before scouring the apartment. He must have slipped in before dawn to dodge my wrath or questions. "Damn."

I hurried to the nearest window and spotted him strolling to his car. Annoyingly handsome in his navy pinstripe suit and sunglasses, he fumbled with the last overlap of tying his tie. He'd seen the chaos from the fire, and I hoped he wouldn't send a bill for the torched ceiling and burned skillet. A smile broke over his scowl, and I craned my neck, expecting Susan or another goddess to be naked on his hood, though I almost laughed at the long-stem red rose stuck in his windshield wiper.

"Sly one, Susan. You brighten every room you leave."

As if he heard me, Matteo scanned the block, and I ducked behind the counter when his head snapped in my direction. The car door shut, and I peeked out when the engine rumbled to life. The wipers swiped the stray petals away, but it was sickening to see his macho grin.

"Good riddance," I snarled. "There is a reason roses have thorns."

I called Electra and told her my arrival time. In my last-minute rush, I grabbed Matteo's ring and held it to the light. The pretty little ring had once held dreams in its three petals of gold, platinum, and a diamond in the center. "Your promise of love failed, my metallic traitor," I said, sticking it into my bag. Before leaving, I scribbled a note about my big suitcase staying at the apartment since I could physically carry only two pieces of luggage with my backpack. My message was brief since Matteo didn't need to know the details, and the Rose Queen would fill in the blanks. I glanced at the charcoal spot on the ceiling with an eye roll. "I tried, Julia. I tried."

$ 379.74

Taxi to Via Marche - 6.00

Cappuccino and cornetto - 2.00

Air mail stamps, envelopes - 6.48

Soap, toothpaste, razor (forgot at Matteo's) - 8.20

$ 357.06

★ organic store Via Felice Casati
put on Electra's account

CHAPTER FIVE

"CIAO. ALESSANDRO'S SLEEPING," Electra whispered as her attention dropped to my two suitcases. She frowned with disapproval. "How terrible. You brought your whole life from New York and look what he's done to you."

I tried to be cheery and forced a goofy grin as I entered the apartment. "I know. It wasn't what I signed up for, either. I'm sorry I've got so much stuff," I said, dragging the luggage through the doorway. A vase full of fresh daffodils was on the coffee table, making me feel more welcome. I turned to Electra. "Believe it or not, I had to leave number three at his place."

She tutted her annoyance. "Don't tell me any more of this awful story. It would be best if you forgot about him. And that suitcase."

"I'm trying." Enough of my shattered love life, I thought. The repetition of misery was tiring. I needed to get over the shock of a failed romance and took a cleansing breath, glancing around. Bright sunshine enhanced colors in the paintings and furnishings; the old drab curtains from yesterday now radiated a lemon fleur-de-lis pattern, matching the wildflower bouquet full of daisies on her desk. After I slipped off my shoes, Electra ushered me under a barrage of hushes, guiding me up the carpeted stairs to the loft. The charming little beige carpeted area with a twin bed and chest of drawers was sweet and simple—a perfect sanctuary to heal my wounds.

She took a bundle of white towels off the dresser. "These are your towels, and the sheets are washed once a week," she said, plopping them on the bed. "On Monday."

"Okay … I love this place. It's so nice." A lilac coverlet lay over the bed with a folded navy blanket nearby. A low pine bookcase held children's German, English, and Italian books in one corner; cardboard packing boxes with marker-scrawled labels were in the other.

Electra seemed satisfied with my approval. "It is cozy up here to read with Alessandro. Animal books are his favorite." Browsing the titles, I didn't see *The Odyssey* in the bookcase; however, I noticed three boxes of tissues on the night table, which I appreciated.

After Electra left me to settle in, I unpacked while she wrote a letter at her dainty writing desk with a decorative gold border. Sporadically, the baby monitor pulsated electric violet next to her, and she paused whenever the static grew louder.

My pants and shirts slid into the mothball-filled drawers, and I relaxed. Through the skylight, an airplane's contrail streaked across the ceiling skylight like an arrow released into the mile-high sky. Off to JFK without me, I thought. I would have been on it if it weren't for Electra.

Below, Electra cleared her throat loudly, and I went to the loft's railing. "I like the skylight," I commented, hiding the tissue I'd been using to dab a tear and pointing to the bright opening. "It lets in a lot of sun."

"Yes. Lots of vitamin D. It's a benefit of being on the top floor," she said and nodded, holding a piece of paper in one hand. Her index finger curled in the other. "Can I talk to you?"

My body tensed. "Sure."

"I know Americans love to talk. But the telephone is very costly in Italy," she said when we were face to face. "It's considered an extravagant luxury for us. The government squeezes every last cent from its citizens with its heavy charges."

"Don't worry. I'm not going to call anyone," I said, feeling defensive. "And if I did, I'd go outside and use gettonis at the public phone booth."

"That's fine. If there is an emergency, please use my phone. On the other hand, if you need to call friends and talk about pizza or movie stars, use pay phones." She yawned and pushed in her chair. "Follow me," she ordered, heading to the kitchen, which was surprisingly small. The vintage wallpaper of assorted birds gave the room life, and a bowl of red onions sat on the black counter with a small refrigerator purring underneath. The Moka espresso maker on the old four-burner stove was well-used, and the milk-white cabinets had simple chrome handles surrounded by smudges. She opened a door onto an outside balcony where a grimy garbage can and charred Hibachi grill full of cigarette butts awaited.

I turned, surprised. "Do you smoke?"

She sneered at the Hibachi. "Oh, those? I never come out here anymore, and I should throw that out. It's quite disgusting to think I smoked all those Gauloises. At least a pack a day until I quit."

The image of her smoking alone on her balcony struck me as sad. Her mystery deepened. "It's good you stopped. Better late than never."

She grunted. "Well, for me, that unhealthy habit was beneficial in a way. Even *great*. When I stopped smoking and my stomach revolted, the doctor gave me medicine for an *ulcer*. The pills didn't help, and I got a second opinion. The doctor was as shocked as I was. I can still see his face when he told me. My ulcer was my beautiful Alessandro. You know, I'm almost fifty. He's my little miracle."

"He is. And you look fantastic."

She smiled, patting her cheeks. "Thank you. I started to use olive oil to moisturize my skin years ago. An old Italian secret. Greeks love it as well." She clapped her hands. "Now, back to business. You know what this box is?" she asked, pointing to a black square above me. Inside, a disc revolved slowly, and the word KILOWATT was on the metal side.

"Isn't it an electricity meter?" I said, watching the flat silver wheel rotate.

"Yes. As you can see, it is slowly moving. Except when *you*," with an exaggerated emphasis on you, "take a shower, the wheel goes like this," the woman said, swirling a finger in the air like a turbo blade. "Hot water eats up kilowatts and my income. The government is very sneaky and will rob me in any way they can."

"I don't know the government policy …"

"That's not the point. Electricity is expensive. Ten lire a circle," Electra interrupted, pointing to the sluggish wheel's rotations. "See. Only the lamp and monitor are on inside, and it's going so fast."

I frowned at her exaggeration. "So, you're saying I can't take a shower?" I joked, ready to pack my bags.

She touched my hair, and I flinched at the intrusion. I hoped she wasn't going to bring up the bird incident again. Or bring out the shower cap? "It's exceptionally long, your hair. Of course, you must wash it. You can turn off the shower when you clean it, okay? You must be very quick when you rinse," she said, demonstrating her suggestion. "As you can see, I'm not poor; however, I don't like to waste money on frivolous things."

I opened my mouth to respond, but the baby monitor crackled to life with Alessandro's loud cries. Startled, we stared at each other. "Should I get him?" I asked, unsure of my role.

She nodded, and I scrambled down the hall on the hunt for Alessandro. The first room had a washer and dryer with a daybed. Against the wall, Gucci and Giorgio Armani shopping bags crammed the seat of an old, wooden highchair. "I guess you like tailors," I said, blowing air between my lips. "Whatever."

I hurried to the adjacent room that had to be Electra's. A crystal chandelier hung over her bed, and silver-framed photographs and perfume bottles crowded her nightstand. Against the wall, an open armoire held an orderly row of earth-toned silky shirts, and a neat stack of soft sweaters was on a chair next to it. The large frilly bed had an open Italian Vogue magazine and an Etro-looking scarf next to it.

Behind the last door, Alessandro stood in his crib, gripping the top rail with Santa-red cheeks. I scooped up his warm body so fast that he didn't register me as a stranger. The diaper was ready to bust its plastic tabs, and after wrestling him onto the changing table, I completed the undertaking quickly. After powdering his backside and wiping his nose with a monogrammed washcloth, I presented Alessandro to Electra in the living room like a prized animal at a 4-H fair. "Here he is."

"Alessandro, mio bellissimo bambino," she gushed, holding her arms wide open. I plonked him onto her lap, and she cooed as he played with the buttons on her shirt. Uncertain of my next duty, I meandered to the window while waiting for instructions.

She kissed his cheek and caught my eye. "Alessandro needs his afternoon baba," she demanded as if I should have known, not taking her attention away from him.

I dashed to the kitchen but stopped, unsure what to put in his bottle. I retraced my steps and tapped my finger against my lips. "Umm … what does he take in his bottle?"

"What do you think?" she asked between his bursts of giggles from blowing raspberries on his stomach.

I said what came first into my mind. "Milk?"

Her amused face dropped in horror. She brought Alessandro back onto her lap, shielding his ears. "Milk? You want to kill my child?" she hissed. Alessandro, detecting trouble, buried himself in his mother's chest.

I gulped. "No … I—"

"Well, I'm glad you at least asked. I never thought I'd have to teach you about childcare, yet here we are." She marched toward the kitchen, seating Alessandro in his highchair before pulling out a canister and showing it to me. "I breastfed Alessandro for five months, and this formula is as fine as breastmilk and is organic and non-GMO. Plus, it has DHA and ARA for brain development." Her eyes narrowed. "You know what those are, right?"

My mind went blank. I thought about Matteo's marathon-training supplements taken before his big runs through Manhattan. She glared for my answer. "Vitamins?" I guessed.

"Vitamins? No. They're fatty acids with omega three and six," she wailed. "They are essential for a baby's brain development. Very, very important."

"Thank you. Got it," I said, faking a smile. When I babysat during high school, it was a no-frills service for little kids—pizza or pasta with a spoonful of tomato sauce and a handful of cheese topping. Then, a TV show, ice cream, read a story, put the kids in bed, and call it a night. When Flynn's kids were infants, she had everything laid out with specific instructions. And she never quizzed me.

"Alessandro likes a warm bottle," Electra instructed, running the bottle under the faucet. She dripped a tiny drop onto her wrist. "Perfect. I want you to feel this. The temperature should always be soft and warm. Like a cow's tongue."

I touched the tepid drop of milk. "Okay. I got it. Cow's tongue," I said, acting like I had received the nuclear codes.

In his highchair, Alessandro took the bottle, and his clear eyes ping-ponged between his mother and me, sucking the contents. "Is your bottle yummy?" I said in a baby voice.

"No, no, *no*. Mio dio. He's not a small dog. Don't ever talk to Alessandro with that voice. It's not acceptable for his verbal development," she scolded, putting the formula into the cupboard. She looked back and swatted me away from him. "He doesn't like anyone to engage in a conversation or stare at him like a zoo animal. His concentration must be on one thing at a time to enjoy the full sensory experience."

"Okay." I was unsure what to do, so I grabbed a tea towel and refolded it, afraid to look anywhere.

"We'll leave for a stroll when he's finished. Hopefully, he can walk soon. He's trying day by day."

There was an awkward silence, and I opened my mouth, hoping to spew an intelligent question. "How is … is his development?"

She stepped back in horror as if I struck her across the face. "His development? Who are you? Jean Piaget?" she said, wild-eyed.

"Who?" The word was out of my mouth before I could stop it.

Her mouth dropped, and the crooked lines of her bottom teeth glistened. "Jean Piaget is the most *famous* children's psychologist in the world. My son is perfect in every way, and there is nothing wrong with him."

"I'm sorry. I never meant to say there was." I studied the flooring as she busied herself while muttering. She left me to watch Alessandro, and, not wanting to spoil his feeding experience, I opened a cabinet containing expensive rows of organic ingredients. Sealed bags of organic beans and cereals lay on the counter in a wicker bowl. On a shelf, nursery rhyme-themed fruit jars and others had the label *natural* plastered on them.

I picked up a jar labeled "cavallo" with a picture of a horse. Its contents resembled gray whipped cream; the others were pollo, coniglio, and agnello—chicken, rabbit, and lamb. I picked another with an ostrich called Struzzo and snorted. "Ostrich? And she's worried about me?" I said aloud.

"You ready?" she said, flying into the kitchen and almost causing the jar to drop out of my hands. "The radio said rain in the forecast." She shut the cabinets and gave me a frosty glance. "I'm sorry. Were you hungry?"

"No." I stepped away. "I'm fine."

She picked up Alessandro out of his highchair. "Okay, then. Andiamo." She snickered a tight smile. "It means 'let's go.' You speak Italian, right?"

"No, but I know what 'andiamo' means, and I was hoping to learn more Italian. Maybe take night classes ..." I mumbled, following her out to the closet in the foyer. She pulled out an oversized stroller, reminding me of the WWII amphibious vehicles used at Normandy Beach. The typical carriage royal babies in bonnets peer out from with a sprinkle of corgis and ponies nearby. I stepped closer, hoping inside there wasn't a ruffly aproned uniform.

"I don't know if I mentioned it, but in your loft upstairs are children's books in Italian. Read them at night to help you learn. I'll help, of course." She wiped the dust off the handles and seemed to snatch spiderwebs from the inside. "We'll take this out today."

I peered into an aged, corn-yellow lined interior with a little pillow with strange stains. The nose-twitching chemical smell matched its antiquity. "Was this your carriage?"

"Yes, it was my pram. I've got pictures of me in it in Monte Carlo with my parents," she said, taking a suspicious Alessandro and laying him into the crinkly hollow of a toxic plastic cage. His face reddened with fear, examining the sides while trying to understand his new location. She tucked a cashmere blue ribbon-laced blanket around his body. "He always has this blanket when we go outside. The color of water soothes babies. Did you know that?"

I tried not to laugh. "I ... I can't say I did. Thanks for the tip."

After struggling to position the boat-like stroller into the elevator, I descended to the lobby with its handle wedged into my stomach, cutting off the circulation to half of my body. Electra marched in front of us when we got outside, and I played the childcare role, pushing the sidewalk-wide carriage and avoiding mowing down innocent people. I smiled at their humorous smirks, hoping we didn't have to go far.

We arrived at a vinegary-smelling antique bookstore on a nearby street. Colorful Old-World maps and prints of historical battles or etchings of ancient Greek monuments lined the walls. A glass case packed with leather-bound books stood in the middle of the room, and Electra stopped before it, crouching to examine the books on the lower shelf. Two salespeople spotted our entourage and flocked to Electra with a welcoming buzz of oohs and aahs as they stuck their heads into Alessandro's pram.

"Basta," Electra said, conductor-like. *Enough.* A hush fell over the group, and Electra stepped away to study the prints, taking more time at one than others. The women eyed each other with concern, and I stood by, observing Electra's peculiar behavior while Alessandro slept, oblivious to it all.

Suddenly, she swiveled to the group and lashed a volley of hardline questions. The group raced around like a disturbed anthill, trying to answer her inquiries by pulling books from shelves. A brave woman took the lead and tried to gain control, while another leafed through a notebook, licking her thumb with each page turn.

"No. Mio dio." Electra's voice rose, and another woman in a green tartan skirt flew out from the back area, hurrying across the oriental carpet with flapping hands. Her sudden appearance agitated Electra more, and a shouting match ensued while the ledger holder escaped to the back area. Electra slapped her thighs in anger and stormed out of the store, saying a couple more mio dios combined with words I didn't understand.

Alone, the group studied me as I clutched the handle of the baby carriage. I smiled and took a step backward, pulling the cumbersome pram to the exit. When I turned to open the heavy door, my arms could not hold it, and I struggled to leave. The bulging chrome bolts on the carriage wheels screeched when I pushed forward, scraping a thick line along the glass. Realizing my dilemma, the woman in the green skirt reluctantly came over, admonishing me with forceful tones.

"Mi dispiace," I apologized, struggling with another attempt. She lifted the rear of the carriage and helped me forward, cursing. "No parlo Italiano. Grazie mille." *I don't speak Italian. Thank you so much.*

Her face softened, and she held the door as I inched forward. "I say your boss is a bitch," she said with a heavy accent. She lifted her chin in the direction Electra left. "Because she's a Contessa doesn't mean she's better than everybody else."

A Contessa? Is that the same as a countess? I didn't know how to respond before the door closed in my face.

Across the street, Electra, in her brown plaid blazer and folded arms, waited. I hurried toward her as Alessandro's body bobbed back and forth, awakened from the chaos.

"They said my book was ready," she steamed, eyeing the store. "I need it. I'm a busy woman; they know my time is important. But they tried to say I had the wrong date. I will never go in there again," she said. "They'll miss their best customer."

I glanced back, blood hurdling in my veins. Thoughts of the French Revolution entered my mind, and I expected an enraged crowd of peasants with pitchforks and raised fists to come flying around the corner. Electra's attention shifted to me, and she pointed at the store. "You were in there a long time. What did they say to you?"

My intuition said to play ignorant. "Me? Nothing. The carriage was stuck, so the lady in the green skirt helped me leave," I said, glancing behind me. After two hours with this woman, I was already losing it. The big question, *Are you a countess,* was on the tip of my tongue, but I risked having her throw me out into the street. Was Contessa an Italian slang word—did it mean super-bitch?

A drop pelted the carriage, and her hand caught the next one. "We must go home. Raindrops make Alessandro depressed."

It was an hour before dinnertime, and things had settled down. Electra left the house to complete an errand while I played with Alessandro and his stuffed lions, bears, and other animals that littered the nursery. The room was a decorator's masterpiece with ocean colors mixed with sailboats and teddy bears, and a signed photo of him in his mom's arms sat on his antique dresser.

I picked up the framed picture on his white chest for a better look. Electra's high cheekbones highlighted soft, mossy twinkles of happiness, complementing Alessandro's Nordic coloring. His traits must be from his father, whomever he was. Electra never mentioned him, and I sensed it was taboo since there were no photos of a man with her or Alessandro in the apartment. I put the picture down and pulled out the top drawer, full of old photographs. I reached for a black-and-white image of a couple in front of the Roman Coliseum. The woman had Electra's strong jaw and the man her deep-set eyes. Two young girls in white frilly dresses stood on either side, and I squinted for a better look. The sad-looking younger girl with curly hair was clearly Electra. The other must be her sister.

Other photos were mostly black-and-white scenes of country houses or weddings of strangers. One was her family under a beach umbrella, happily eating sandwiches. My favorite was Electra and her mystery sister on a pony with her father tightly holding the reins. She must have been ten years old. From what I could see, hers had been a privileged childhood.

I carried the rambunctious Alessandro, bored with his toys, into the kitchen for the daily teething biscuit that Electra left for him; she said it helped his incoming molars. As he happily gummed the brown cookie, my mind drifted to what Electra had told me about storing my suitcases in the building's basement. Alessandro wriggled to sit on the floor, so I sat him down with his truck on a construction road rug before running upstairs to retrieve a bag from my loft. A little field trip to the basement seemed a clever way to break up the monotony of our day, and hopefully, I'd spot Luca Rosso again.

I got a suitcase and double-checked it was empty. Besides a white sock and a paper clip, Matteo's letters with red kisses and other love symbols were its only contents. I opened his last letter again, hunting for clues to his fading love that I may have missed. "*I can't wait to see you. I love you so much. There is so much to see in Italy. We will take trips everywhere together.*" The canyon in my stomach widened. He'd be arriving at his apartment soon, and my farewell note would greet him. What would his reaction be?

Above me, a deluge of rain pelted the skylight, reminding me of soggy walks through Central Park, bagels from Barney Greengrass, the occasional Guinness at McSorley's, or burger at J.G. Melons. Places we went as a New York couple. With a moan, I tossed the letters into the trash, taking the suitcase to the stairs.

"Alessandro," I choked. At the bottom of the stairs, Alessandro's little hand lay on the second step, and his cookie-covered face grinned up at me. Ignorant of the danger, he wiggled his hips, gurgling with happiness at his newfound exercise. He missed me in the two minutes I was gone. Behind him, the hard floor shined below like a slick villain, ready to catch its next victim.

"Stay there. Don't move," I said, slowly lowering the suitcase as Alessandro's fat fingers gripped the beige tufts of the stairs' runner. I gasped when he popped up and wobbled like a breezy sail. Afraid to have him climb the steps, I crouched like a cat and crept quickly down the stairs. "No, no, no, Alessandro, the best little guy in the world," I said softly, maintaining eye contact with his guiltless blues. "Don't move. Cookies. Baba. Yum yum up here for you."

To my relief, he placed his palms back on the steps. His body twisted to look at the truck behind him. I felt faint, but my arms swooped him up, and he wriggled for freedom while I kissed his face repeatedly.

"I'm sorry. I should never have left you alone. So stupid of me," I confessed into the soft-scented hair. "I'll be the best au pair you've ever had. I swear, I swear, I swear. You're my number one priority. Numero uno. Not Matteo."

$357.06

Book on childcare (ENGLISH) — 8.00

Jar of Nutella - 100 calories a tablespoon — 2.12

Cappuccinos, eight cornettos, assorted candy — 37.50

Two hundred gettonis - need stronger wallet — 40.00

$269.44

CALL HANNAH!

3 teaspoons = 1 tablespoon

GETTONE TELEFONICO

Shops closed Monday morning
Sunday/closed for lunch

CHAPTER SIX

AFTER THE FRIGHT WITH ALESSANDRO, I focused on nothing but my duties for the following weeks. Electra gave me her son's schedule, and soon, I followed his routine with drill sergeant precision from the crack of dawn to lights out. Fresh diaper. Bottle at seven. New diaper. Fruit compote and yogurt at eight. Playtime to ten, Montessori toys are preferred. Park. Organic lunch at twelve. Park again. Feed ducks. Nap. Music time. Mozart Monday. Beethoven Tuesday. Chopin Wednesday. Bach Thursday. Vivaldi Friday. Saturday was my choice. But only Wagner or Tchaikovsky if sunny. Brahms for sleep, constipation, and indigestion. Haydn and Verdi Sunday. Dinner. Bath. Read story. Bed. Repeat.

Sometimes, interactions got a bit dicey between Electra and me. Periodically, she veered out of control when we bumped into her acquaintances. Instant amnesia developed because I suddenly became an Irish nanny. The first time I tried to correct her, an icy glare stopped me. I don't know if it was because she didn't want any association with the red, white, and blue, or an Irish nanny sounded swankier. When I asked her why, she said it was for my safety, quoting scathing articles from Italian journalists about American politics and rampant crime. I tried to argue pro-American stances, but that was a waste of time. Since she liked to quiz me about current events and relished my inability to answer her with facts, reading her discarded international newspapers at night in bed with Toasty became routine.

Also, my meals improved with the help of a kids' cookbook, which also helped my Italian. I learned the difference between battuto and soffritto and to never sauté onions and garlic together. Jars of baby food collected dust as I delved into recipes with my handy dictionary ready to help while Alessandro played at my feet. I wondered why I never tried to cook with Matteo. Learning his risotto secrets or how he seasoned it to perfection could have been fun.

For most meals, I was the sole chef for one-tooth Alessandro and became a blender whiz with steamed organic vegetables, pastina, and a sliver of the night's meat or fish. Electra and I often split a plate of pasta, or we'd make a roast chicken or fish with polenta, the creamy cornmeal side dish. A gourmet restaurant was nearby, so occasionally, she'd send me to get take-out, which was always a welcome change. My only downfall was non-negotiable jolts of caffeine and sugar, fueled by my mid-afternoon Nutella sandwich. While Alessandro napped, I wrote letters or sent postcards to friends during each sugar high surge.

Days bled together and being busy with activities was the best panacea to heal my soul. I kept sane with Corso Venezia shopping excursions to buy Alessandro clothes, toys, or organic groceries, plus touring glamorous neighborhoods and pockets of hidden elegance while he slept in the carriage. I was comfortable in the city, and the gray-haired barista at the local café treated me like a regular with a ciao Jayne each time I entered. Every day, he selected a crescent brioche, the addictive cornetto, from his special stash behind the counter—a hand-to-heart gesture that made the unfamiliar city feel more like home.

Yet an ogre lurked in the apartment: tedious ironing. I'm not talking about the occasional collar on a shirt or wrinkle in a skirt. This back-breaking grunt work was jail time. When Electra had innocently asked if I could iron, I said yes, bring it on. Unaware of her trap, I thought of my prom dress from high school, and the time I'd even ironed a shirt for Matteo before an interview.

"You can? I thought Americans didn't iron," Electra said with suspicion.

"No, we Americans are proud of our ironing," I said with a smile, pushing an imaginary steamy metal object on an ironing board.

"You are? Fine. Then, I don't need to hire someone to do it. I'll show you the clothes." She led me down the hallway to the daybed. It was against the window, but a mountain of laundry blocked its view. "There you are," she said, pointing to the freshly laundered clothes. "Everything is washed and ready."

"All of that?" I gulped. She must have concealed the lump after the clothes and sheets came out of the dryer. Since Alessandro's wardrobe was endless, it was easy not to miss them. The pile had to be three feet high. "Needs to be ironed?"

"Yes. My little man is running out of shirts and overalls." She dragged an ironing board from behind the door and then opened lacquered doors under the alcove bookcase, pulling out the iron. "And we need fresh sheets."

She left me to start my task. Embroidered scalloped-edged crib sheets and Alessandro's fancy clothes were the first items I picked out to assess my skills. Labels from French and Italian high-end fashion baby boutiques were ubiquitous—but soft shirts with Peter Pan collars with jumping bunnies or chugging trains mixed with eye-popping racy lace lingerie and silky camisoles. I dreaded the latter and tried not to overthink her shoestring thongs and mesh corsets or compare them to my everyday simple cotton essentials.

"I'm off." She peeked in with Alessandro in her arms. "Oh, be careful of my satin and lace. Just steam those pieces. Like you'd do to your own. We'll be back after lunch," she said as the door closed.

I smirked at her comment, agreeing that I should have invested more in vivacious undergarments. After the door shut, my stomach rumbled with hunger, and I sighed like a deflating balloon. "Sure, bring me back my lunch. A panini? Prosciutto and mozzarella? With a basil leaf," I murmured, wiping steam droplets from my face. I glanced at the pile that seemed to have multiplied and groaned. "Stop. You're like frigging rabbits."

There was a knock at the door. Electra must have forgotten his sippy cup. "Just wait," I said, unplugging the iron. "Okay. The last place I saw it," I panted, opening the door.

But it wasn't Electra and Alessandro—only a tall, elegant man in a long trench coat with a sales pitch grin. "Buongiorno," he said. *Good day.*

I looked down at the hall for Electra, and she was gone. "Buongiorno."

He took a step forward, and his eyes darted past me. "Electra e qui?" *Is Electra here?*

"Non. Se n'è andata." *No, she left.*

His eyebrows rose, and I was proud that I didn't need my usual bird dance of gesticulations to clarify my meaning. Not pleased with my answer, he breathed deeply and zeroed in on a stack of Alessandro's diapers on the table. "Il bambino?" *The baby?*

My mouth went dry, suspicious of this inquisitive intruder. The man had the same coloring as Alessandro, and I paused before answering. Was this his father? "No," I said slowly, shifting my weight.

His expression turned smug, and garbled sentences flowed so fast that I gave up any translation after the first one. He turned away and left me speechless in the doorway as he hurried down the red-carpeted stairs.

I closed the door, bewildered. Who was this nosy guy? As I returned to iron, I stretched out my aching back and flexed my stiff arms from the repetitive motions, wondering about the man's identity. No one ever stopped by to visit. An hour later, as I folded the last garment, I heard the front door open. "Cou-cou," Electra announced. "We're home."

"Hi. After you left," I said, hurrying out, "this man came looking for you."

She took Alessandro out of the pram and held him. "A man? Was it Pedro? He wasn't downstairs."

"No, no. It wasn't Pedro." I brought my melodrama down to a simmer. "He was tall and blond. He asked about Alessandro."

Her arms tightened around her child, and she jutted her chin in anger. "He did? Tell me everything. He has no right to come into this building."

Her severe reaction was unexpected. "He knocked on the door, and when I opened it, he asked for you. I said you weren't here, then he asked if the baby was, and I said no, then he spoke so fast I couldn't understand him. I heard the word 'aperto.' But it might have been the word for open or also department. It was too quick. I'm sorry."

Her lips formed a thin line. "So that's all? Nothing more? He didn't leave anything? Just quick like that."

I nodded. "Yes." I thought she'd have more questions, and she never asked the man's name or for a more concise description. And what would he leave, I wondered?

"Jayne." She took the diapers off the table and stuck them into my stomach. "Don't ever open the door when I'm not here," she huffed. "There are many Milanese you can't trust, and some like to start trouble." She mumbled, rubbing her temples. "This stress is killing me, and I will take an afternoon nap with Alessandro, so don't disturb us. We need peace."

"Okay," I said, watching her leave. It wasn't my fault the man came—I just answered the door. I spotted Alessandro's baby bag under the carriage and pulled it out. Little did I know that opening a door would equal treason, I thought, taking out the usual junk and adding more diapers. I wish I understood more about her stress and could somehow help her.

In the stroller pocket, a paper bag had *Jayne* written on it. Opening the curled edges, I pulled out a piece of focaccia wrapped in oil-stained ivory paper. The tomato and cheese topping triggered my taste buds, and I felt better. "If this is for that disease called ironing, I accept your apology," I said before taking a big bite.

After dinner, I fell asleep while reading an Italian fairy tale about a whale, but soon awoke to Electra's booming voice. It was after midnight, and the one-sided conversation grew louder as I placed my dictionary and the book on the floor. Half-asleep, I buried under the lavender covers to escape the noise of the argument, hoping Alessandro wouldn't wake up.

"I told you. I need to speak to him," Electra repeated into the portable phone, her voice growing angrier as she left the kitchen and moved into the living room.

Was she calling the guy who had come to the door? I clucked my tongue under the warm covers. "He's asleep and doesn't want to talk to you, Einstein. Call him tomorrow. Go to bed," I said, curling my body tighter. "You'll wake up Alessandro."

"Now … you don't need my name … I am a friend. I don't care. I told you I am a friend … no, you're wrong. That's not my name. I don't care …"

A long pause followed, and I heard a few mio dios and curses. "Okay. You want to know who I am? Do you? Okay, I'll tell you. I am the mother of his child," she proclaimed loudly before slamming the receiver down. With a huff, she retreated into the kitchen.

I threw down the sheet and stared at the moon through the starlit skylight, dissecting what had just happened. Below, dishes rattled, and cupboards slammed. An object fell onto the floor, and I sat up, imagining an injured Electra crumpled beside the sink. Bleary-eyed, I got out of bed and hurried down to the kitchen, where Electra held her head at the small table, visibly upset. The smell of alcohol lingered in the air, and an uncorked wine bottle was on the counter next to an open bar of dark chocolate. I turned, ready to leave her in this private moment, until Electra thumped her hand onto the table. "It's not fair."

"Okay," I said cautiously as she peered through a tangled mess of hair. "I heard you on the phone. Everything all right?" She was an infrequent drinker, so the wine bottle was surprising. I pointed to the empty glass next to her. "Are you okay?"

She gestured to the hallway. "I think she's very uneducated," she said sarcastically. "Definitely not Italian. English was our only way to communicate. Perfect for you. I hope *you* liked it."

My mouth dropped. "Are you joking? Your personal life is your business. I've got enough on my plate, thank you very much. And being able to speak a million languages isn't a sign of intelligence."

She jerked back into her seat with a slight moan. "You're right. I'm sorry."

I turned away. "Don't worry about it. Good night."

"Jayne," she called as I climbed the stairs to my loft. Afraid Alessandro would wake up, I rushed back into the room.

"Shhh," I whispered. "You're going to wake Alessandro."

She winced, realizing her mistake. "Sorry. I just wanted to tell you we'll leave Milan in two days."

"Are you sure you're okay?" I asked, flipping a grilled cheese as Electra stumbled into the kitchen. When I'd gathered Alessandro hours before from his crib, I noticed her bare leg above messy covers and an empty wineglass on the floor when passing her room. Proof of a tough night. At least she didn't pick up the phone again.

"No, I'm not. Please make me one of those fast-food things," Electra ordered, getting a glass from the cupboard. She filled it with apple juice, drank it in one gulp, and followed with a burp. After putting her glass into the sink, she wiped her mouth with the back of her hand. "I feel sick. The wine I drank wasn't my usual Chateau Margaux. I did and said stupid things."

That was an understatement. I didn't respond and cut up the grilled cheese as Electra rooted for medicine in her handbag. "Ready?" I asked, placing the cut sandwich bits in front of Alessandro. He stuffed a tiny square into his mouth while I silently prepared one for Electra.

"Who was she?" I mouthed, placing her grilled cheese on the table. She shrugged, and I stepped out on a limb. "His wife?"

"No, he's not married. At least, that's what he told me. A girlfriend, maybe," she said aloud, picking up half of the sandwich. It hovered near her mouth. "She wouldn't stop asking who I was, so I told her—too many questions. Curiosity killed the cat. Meow."

"Eek. But getting a call about a child must have been a huge shock."

"Shock? To her?" She straightened in her chair, her face growing redder. "What about me? I'm the one with a baby. I'm the one raising our child. He lives far away and …" She stopped and pursed her crumb-flecked lips.

"And what?"

She stared at Alessandro, and her eyes welled up. "I don't know. I've been alone for so long, and now Alessandro is with me. I don't need him to come and tell me what to do with our lives. You're here and helping us."

The kettle whistled, saving me from having to make an awkward reply. Afraid to give my opinion, I grabbed a mug. "Do you want tea?"

"Yes. The green organic one." She took a deep breath, and her shoulders relaxed. "Maybe you're right. I'm sure she's upset now."

"I'd say so. Do you think they will break up?" I asked.

She tsked at my question. "Jayne, this is Europe. Everyone has affairs in these Catholic countries. It's a sex free-for-all, and things happen whether we like them or not. Luckily, I have my Alessandro. His father knows I don't love him. I only love Alessandro. Do you want to come to the Philippines?" she added, like asking me to pass the salt.

I let out a laugh. "Philippines? The country?"

"Yes. I'm not joking—Palawan in the Philippines. I've been there five times. It's another world. Beautiful beaches. Wonderful people. So many islands to explore."

It sounded like she wanted to escape her predicament. "When would we go?" I'd never been to the Philippines, but I knew it was exotic and gorgeous from travel magazines. Long sandy alcoves, vodka-clear waters, and delicious coconut drinks. I'd read that their jewelry was fantastic.

She shrugged. "Oh, I have to plan it. You were in fashion; we could make children's clothes with your knowledge. I've been thinking about it for a while."

"You have?" I said, shocked, realizing she meant to live there, not just visit. And I was pleased she thought I was worthy enough to be in business with her. "Do they make clothes there? I've shipped fabric to garment factories in Asia but never to the Philippines. I imagine the islands have only hotels and spas, right?"

"The locals make the clothes in little shops." She got up to make her tea as I sat down to eat. "I'll bring them Alessandro's clothes. They copy the pattern and sew new outfits with different fabrics we choose. You buy yardage from the mills since you know how to do it from your time in New York. But we'll talk later. I need to apologize for last night. I'll call him at his office this time."

She planned to steal and copy Alessandro's clothes in the Philippines to sell in Europe. When did she dream this up? The idea was as strange as the phone call to her child's absent father. The former went against the unwritten rule of fashion that knockoffs were pirated creations of stolen brands and designs. "I don't know. Knockoffs are usually inferior …"

Her hands fluttered in front of me. "Okay. It was just a thought."

"Wait, just to be clear, the man who came yesterday was not Alessandro's father?"

Her hand trembled with the tea, and she steadied it. "No, Jayne. *That* man was the devil."

$ 269.44

JUNE 1ST

Nail polish remover + polish (pink) — 6.15

Moisturizer – olive oil? virgin or extra virgin? — 5.00

Vogue and toothbrush — 3.25

Nine cappuccinos — 10.00

MAY SALARY – woohoo! + 400.00

$ 645.04

KA CHING!

EXPRESS YOURSELF – MADONNA

CHAPTER SEVEN

AFTER A NIGHT OF TOSSING AND TURNING, I got up early and had my second cup of morning espresso in peace, enjoying a moment of calm before another storm. I wrote a letter to Flynn, telling her of my daily activities with Alessandro, and asked if she did the same with Kate and Quinn. How long did she stay at the playground? How many books did she read to them? What were her kids' favorite toys?

As I cared for Alessandro, I realized that raising children was a full-time responsibility only for the brave. It wasn't pleasant to face my ignorance, and I'd never given Flynn the credit she deserved for endless hours of commitment and patience. Yet her success spoke for itself; both her kids were kind and sweet. They shared lollipops, loved everyone, and asked silly but great questions. They called me Jayney, and my parents Pop-pop and Nana. I couldn't wait to see them soon and signed my letter with a request for pictures. Why didn't I bring any with me?

I licked the envelope and took a stamp from Electra's stash. On top of her messy writing desk was a colorful circus of fancy invitations, a silver bowl with paper clips, and child-rearing articles in every language.

Curious, I stopped for a closer look. On the right side of the desk, letters and official documents from Milanese law firms or Swiss banks poked out from a metal letter holder. I sighed, noting the beautiful antiques and décor around me. She never said she worked, and her time before Alessandro seemed full of social engagements. Except she was always alone. Her phone never rang, and she spent nights reading in her bedroom.

It added to Electra's aura.

A stack of unlined notecards lay next to a black, gold-nibbed fountain pen, and I leaned in for a closer look. An engraved card had *Principessa Contessa Electra Lucia di Caneva* below a mini yellow crown. Principessa? Another royal title? After the bookstore incident, the whole royal hierarchy idea piqued my curiosity, and I pulled out an Italian dictionary for the word Contessa. It said a Contessa was an Italian countess with the same ranking as an earl or count. Also, a countess or Contessa should be addressed as a lady. Now, was I to understand she was a princess?

I wandered through the stunning apartment, examining gold-framed photos and formal portraits that no longer creeped me out. They were treasures in Electra's royal life of kings and queens, and I wondered if she enjoyed the prestige. But Italy abolished its monarchy after World War II, so maybe that's why the bookshop lady was angry.

"Morning," she said, yawning down the hallway, tying her robe.

"Morning."

She followed me into the kitchen, where I would prepare the bottle. "I've got a special day today," she smiled, leaning against the sink. "An activity I've been looking forward to for a long time. It's outside of Milan."

"Great," I said, scooping the formula into the bottle. "When will you be back?" A free day with Alessandro to explore, I thought. My first stop would be Benetton, the colorful Italian knitwear store, to browse their spring sale. Then I'd stroll around Rinascente, the luxury department store near the Duomo, and fawn over their beautiful clothes while preventing

Alessandro from touching them with his gooey fingers. Their makeup counters had my favorite brand, and I'd pick up a new moisturizer and lip gloss.

She took the Moka pot off the stove to prepare an espresso. "It's not only *me*. It's all of us."

"Oh." Apprehensive, I warmed the bottle as she dumped the old grounds into the garbage. "Where are *we* going?" I asked, dabbing the formula on my wrist.

She took the bottle and assessed it. "Too hot," she complained, handing it back. "You'll burn the skin off my baby's little mouth. You know, forget the espresso. We don't have time. We're going to the racetrack."

Before we left for the taxi, Electra debuted a new foldable plastic stroller, the trendy navy item for new mothers. I had pointed it out on the street, hoping to plant the subconscious seed to step into modern times. It worked because Electra had a penchant for being up-to-date on every new baby item, and she'd soon had one delivered. While I brought the old one to the basement, Pedro put the new one in the taxi's trunk and gave me a high five before I jumped in the cab to leave.

Electra mentioned that her lawyer, Roberto, would also spend the day with us. When our taxi rolled up to the crowded San Siro hippodrome, the scent of fresh earth and horse dung filled the air, and I thought of my father. Sometimes, we'd go to the Belmont racetrack in Long Island at sunrise to watch the horses exercise and pretend we owned one. Once, he told a chatty trainer with a stopwatch that I was as unpredictable as a racehorse. I took it as a compliment, but maybe it wasn't.

Far away, the horses raced toward the finish line as an excited announcer spewed details in a blaring crackle. I turned to get the stroller from the trunk and almost missed a tall, gorgeous man gliding from the crowd to offer Electra a helping hand. My legs became spaghetti strands when he turned my way. The chiseled Roman god grinned above his aqua-green tie, and his dreamy eyes sparkled diamond chips. "Ciao, Jayne," he said, coming to my side. "It's finally nice to meet you. I'm Roberto, and I hear you're a wonderful nanny."

"Hi. I mean, ciao," I said, blushing from his wink, not the compliment.

Electra wriggled between us and motioned to the trunk. "The stroller, please."

"Oh, yes. Sorry." I hurried as the driver popped the trunk. Electra held Alessandro in her arms and pointed to a horse and jockey behind the racetrack barrier. "You have no accent," I gushed to Roberto, who had kick-started my dormant flirt gene. I grasped the stroller from the back and put it on the ground. "Where did you learn to speak English so well?"

He reached for the handle as I tried to pull the seat from its plastic body with a grunt. "You need a little help?" he asked with a grin.

"Sure." Sweat prickled under my arms, and I hoped I hadn't forgotten antiperspirant in the morning rush. He jerked the plastic handle from the back, pushing the canopy forward, but still, it didn't budge. The latch didn't release, so he repeated the action, this time with force.

"There should be a strap somewhere," I said, hunting beneath the plaid fabric. "Electra just got it, so I'm not sure where it is."

Glancing at the ground, I hid my chipped pink polished toes from his line of vision as his caramel suede shoe moved closer to my foot. I moaned internally. That varnish had been on since my au revoir pedicure on Third Avenue with Hannah. Why did I wear my sandals? Hello? Use nail polish remover?

He wiped his sweatless brow. "Back to your question. My English improved in New York. I was on Wall Street for three years." He attempted to free the stroller again. "God, this thing is impossible. How can anyone use it?"

"It was obviously designed by someone who never had a baby. Or disliked mothers," I said as his strong fingers clicked a latch on the side of the stroller, unlocking it like an accordion.

"There. Success. This little piece of plastic is the secret button." He stepped back, dusting his hands with the pride of an alligator wrestler, and glanced at the grandstand. "So. Are you going to place any bets today?"

"I don't think so. I used to go with my dad to Belmont when I was little. But I never won anything. Thanks for helping me. This stroller is brand new, so it has kinks in it." He turned to go, but I didn't want him to leave. "I was in New York. In midtown for a textile importing company," I offered. "Near Madison Avenue."

He opened his mouth to respond, but a voice boomed from behind. "Bravo, Roberto. We could have been waiting days for Jayne to open it," Electra bleated, plopping Alessandro into the stroller. She buckled his seat belt, and her eyes flashed to my feet. "Mio dio. Sandals? Americans never know how to dress. Better keep away from the horses. You could get foot rot."

I gave Roberto an eye roll, and he hid his smile.

Electra clucked her tongue. "There, Alessandro, Mama's got you safe and sound." She flicked her hand to the paddock area. "He'd love to see the horses, Jayne … and don't forget to bring him to the parade ring." An admit one ticket appeared, and she stuck it into my hand with a get-lost look. "This will get you into the restaurant area, so don't lose it. We'll have lunch at one in the clubhouse." She turned to Roberto and batted her eyelashes. "Is that okay with you?"

She was in her "kiss the ring" mode, bugling her marching orders. Roberto bowed slightly, and I wanted to puke at his submissiveness. She was his client, so he had to play the part. We both were clowns in her roadshow. "Have fun," I said, fastening the diaper bag. "See you later."

After ten steps, I peeked over my shoulder as Electra linked arms with

Roberto, cuddling him in an I've-got-a-secret-to-tell-you way. I stopped. Was Roberto the missing link to Alessandro's paternity? No, he wouldn't be so friendly after that nail-biting phone call. Or was Roberto Electra's boy toy? She *did* have ooh la la lingerie in that laundry pile.

"That little minx," I said under my breath. Yet he seemed too bright and sophisticated to be an easy touch, and Alessandro was born when Electra was nearly fifty, and Roberto was at least twenty years younger. I pushed the stroller forward— the mystery of Alessandro's paternity deepened.

As the crowd cheered again, the ground trembled from the roll of thundering hooves. "Let's go see the winner's circle," I said, catching whiffs of hay and leather in the soft breeze. "So, Mama can ride *her* hunky Italian stallion around the track."

After an hour of pointing out horses and waving to jockeys, I returned from the paddock, parking the stroller in a VIP area. When I arrived, the dynamic duo was deep in conversation, seated at a round table covered with a white tablecloth. Their empty plates and dirty utensils awaited removal, and Electra sipped wine from her lipstick-stained goblet while her arm smoldered on the back of Roberto's chair. She turned to watch my arrival with indifference, whispering secrets into Roberto's ear that made him nod.

After I cleared my throat, she put down her drained glass. "We had the most delicious prosciutto, Jayne. Best in Italy. Put Alessandro over here, please," she ordered, motioning to a highchair. I deposited him into the clumsy chair, and she gushed over her little boy, glancing at Roberto as she overplayed the part of an attentive mother. She ripped off a piece of bread and held it out to him. "You missed your mama, sweetie?"

I took the menu from the waiter. The only familiar entrée was penne, and I returned it with a smile. "Pene, per favore."

Roberto looked at Electra, and they burst into laughter. My face burned, and I seethed as the waiter walked away. "Excuse me. Italian isn't my first language." At this point, Electra was giggling into Roberto's shoulder, and he waved a finger at me in stitches. My eyes narrowed. "Can you please explain what's so funny?"

"I'm sorry." He pointed behind him. "You just ordered a penis."

"A bowl of the penis, please. I'm an American, so make it a large," Electra laughed.

"Ha ha," I said, leaning back in annoyance. Thanks for the warning on that one, Matteo. Jerk. "Can we get our minds out of the gutter? And taking potshots at Americans is getting kind of boring."

My comeback stunned Electra, and Roberto held her back when she leaned forward to respond. "We were just teasing you. It's pen-nay," Roberto said. "That second n is not silent. P-E-N-N-E. It's a very common mispronunciation."

"It's a very common mispronunciation," I mimicked in a child's voice, turning away. The stand shook as racing horses with whipping jockeys pounded past to the finish line. As everyone rose to their feet, the waiter appeared with my plate of pasta, and I took it begrudgingly, hoping I wasn't the laughingstock of the kitchen, too.

Luckily, the next race started minutes later, and I wolfed down my lunch, ignoring the squealing linguists jumping and shouting as if they owned the winner themselves. Roberto gave a play-by-play as he watched through his binoculars, and the pack of horses thundered by the stand. I barely acknowledged the performance, drinking from my water glass between sighs and shakes of my head.

"Did you see that? My horse won by a nose," Roberto said as Electra hugged him seconds later. "I can't believe how much I made on that bet."

"Let's go get your earnings," she said, taking his hand. I took over watching Alessandro as they hurried to collect the winnings. Half an hour later, Roberto returned alone as I savored the last bite of the shared tiramisu. His tall frame blocked the midday sun, and I wiped off any trace of chocolate from my mouth before glancing up at him.

"Everything okay, Jayne?" he asked, sitting beside me. A loud announcement for the next race prevented my response, so I waited as he proudly surveyed the green track like a thoroughbred owner. He turned with satisfaction. "I've been coming to this track since I was a little boy, and now I'm lucky enough to bring my clients. Like Electra."

"It's beautiful. Belmont is wooden like this one. The same atmosphere and garbled speakers," I said with a laugh. "Only that's what makes it special."

"Yes. It's a great track. The Belmont Stakes was a New York experience. And they've got decent hot dogs, too. The yellow mustard over here isn't the same. Too grainy." He glanced over his shoulder and turned back, fixing his cuffs. His voice lowered. "She can be … difficult."

I crossed my arms, afraid she'd sent him as a spy. "Everyone can be."

"Yes. I know, however, don't get me wrong. Electra is a decent woman," he chuckled. "I needed a place, and she let me stay in her apartment. She said you're up in the loft. That's where I was for a month when they renovated my bathroom. In fact, I left a suitcase that I need to get."

"A suitcase?" I gulped, remembering mine in Como—a funny, strange coincidence. "I still have one at my ex-boyfriend's place. He's the reason I'm here. But it's over … Looking forward to getting *my* piece of luggage to cut all ties with him …"

The corners of his lips twitched. "We have more in common than I thought." His eyes softened to a buttery brown haze. "Breakups are hard. I had an American girlfriend, and it didn't work out as I had hoped. She was from Dallas. I had never known what beauty was until I met Grace.

Kind, warm, loving. Champagne was her drink—I still feel sick whenever I see a glass of the stuff." He grimaced. "Listen to me babbling about the one who got away."

"It's okay, and I'm sorry. I know how it feels." I imagined Matteo's lips flecked with a white ricotta filling from a half-eaten cannoli I'd kiss with a giggle. "Champagne is a little more romantic than cannolis. They're my downfall. I can't pass a bakery without choking up."

He snickered. "You're more doomed than I am." He pointed to Alessandro. "He's reaching for the knife."

I turned and grabbed the knife from his grasp. "Thanks," I said, placing all the utensils far from his reach. An urge to leave the table overcame me, and I picked the toddler out of the highchair. "He's bored, and I should bring him back to the horses before he starts throwing silverware." I scanned the spectators and then looked across the stands to the exit. "Is Electra coming back?"

"Yes. She had to powder her nose. Hey, do you want to meet in Milan? Get a drink? I promise we won't pass a bakery," he said as I stood up with Alessandro.

"Um …" I said, taken aback. "Sure. And I won't order champagne."

"Great. I know Milan isn't New York. No place is. Although it does have cool neighborhoods and great clubs." He thought for a moment. "What about tomorrow night? Are you free from baby duty?"

Electra's face popped above the crowd and my arms tightened around Alessandro. I froze, flustered, while Roberto waited for my answer. "Sure. I think I can meet. Call me tomorrow to make plans," I said quickly, watching Electra walk nimbly down the steps. "I've got to go. Please tell Electra I'll be downstairs."

"Jayne," he said with a funny smirk, pointing to my shirt.

I looked down, and Alessandro had undone five top buttons of my pink Oxford shirt, exposing my boobs to the world. Luckily, I had on my good bra. "Jesus," I cried, plopping him into Roberto's arms. I quickly buttoned my shirt as laughing Roberto jiggled Alessandro. "He's a typical male, that's for sure. And the whole time you watched him do it."

"Why would I stop him?"

"Funny." I finished the top closure with a grunt. "Electra will be over the moon to know of this new achievement—a major milestone in finger dexterity. The Italian version, of course," I said before dashing off to the bathroom.

At the entrance, Electra was waiting, and we caught a taxi home after a quick send-off with Roberto. Alessandro fell asleep between us, tired from the busy day, and Electra gazed out the bright window in her sunglasses, deep in thought. Was she fantasizing about Roberto? I couldn't blame her, remembering his confidence and slight swagger. Nice butt, too. Where was he taking me, and, more importantly, what would I wear?

I applied more lip gloss. My social life had been nonexistent since arriving in Milan. I'd slid from an ambitious professional with a hot Mr. Darcy boyfriend to an expendable au pair who rated poops. Clubbing until dawn was fun before I met Matteo, and I wanted my nightlife to return to carefree dancing and concerts instead of catching up on current events. Those were the days when impulsive plans sprung up in a nanosecond.

I had always loved going out. Since I was thirteen, taking the subway into Manhattan was my weekend. Roaming Third Avenue with Flynn, going to Serendipity for wild chocolate desserts, or eating hot pretzels in Central Park and people-watching were my teen years' entertainment. Now, as a single woman, the inability to spontaneously grab a cocktail with Roberto was unnerving. Or enjoy the sunset from a rooftop bar. It would be just what the doctor ordered to forget about jerk Matteo.

I glanced at Electra. It wasn't her fault. Having her place to stay and the ability to earn back everything I spent was a gift. And I was so grateful she gave me a chance to experience Italy. What would have happened if she hadn't? Would *I* have employed a jilted Italian to stay with me in Manhattan? She'd taken a risk, and I was thankful for that. Still, I had never asked for a day off, working nonstop from Alessandro's first to last bottle, and his happiness was my top priority. Roberto had awoken my desire to go out and experience life after Matteo, yet I hesitated to approach the subject, seeing Electra massage her temples as I gnawed my thumbnail.

"Roberto is nice," I offered.

"Yes. He's a fantastic lawyer, unlike the others who rob you."

"I'm glad." I shifted in my seat. "I wanted to ask you a favor. Is it okay if I have tomorrow night off?"

"Why?" she asked, turning suddenly and clasping her pearl choker with a pained look. But her face softened. "Yes, yes. Of course, you can. You're a free woman. Except you don't know anyone here. Besides that terrible man in Como."

"I know. And don't worry, Matteo's not the reason." I yearned to feel wanted and alluring. Put on makeup other than lip gloss. Roberto could help raise my self-esteem. I couldn't spend another night waking up with dry, salt-stained cheeks; Electra even asked if I had allergies because my lids were so swollen one morning.

She sniffed. "Well, I hope so."

Going for a playful cocktail, then dinner, and if it led to a hot fling, why not? Casual sex could be the best way to forget my shattered fantasy. An evening where my mind was not punching itself for my failed relationship would be perfect. I smiled at the passing traffic, wondering if he'd kiss me. Or I'd kiss him. Energized, I turned and touched Electra's arm. "I guess I *won* today, too, only not with money. That hunk Roberto asked me to go for a drink—"

"He did what?" Electra sputtered, whipping off her sunglasses. Startled, Alessandro bolted awake with extended arms, ready to roar.

"He asked me after lunch," I said, soothing Alessandro. "To go out for the night."

She gritted her teeth, seething. "I told Roberto not to ask you out."

"You did *what*?" The taxi driver and I exchanged concerned glances in the rearview mirror. I gave Alessandro a toy to stop fussing. "Why would you tell him that?"

She shushed me and shut down for the rest of the ride, crossing her arms with a don't-bother-me expression. I thought she'd fallen asleep when she nodded into her chest, but she voiced annoyance when I poked her arm gently on our arrival. "I know where we are, Jayne. Take Alessandro and remember the stroller. I'm going for a drive. Alone."

An hour later, as I entertained Alessandro with a truck, she barged into the apartment, stomped to the phone, and dialed. Alessandro crawled toward the hallway, but I pulled him back into the bedroom and hid behind the open door. "Sono Electra di Caneva," she said in a too-loud voice. Was she calling an au pair agency? "Ho bisogno parlare Roberto." *I need to talk to Roberto.*

I stiffened. The muffle of Roberto's cheery voice greeted her at the other end.

"Yes," she switched to English, knowing I'd be eavesdropping. "No … It's not about my papers. You're fired."

Alessandro crawled again in her direction, and I closed the door silently. With my ear at the door, their conversation spun into a half-Italian, half-English vortex, with my name woven throughout as he and Electra bickered back and forth. Nauseous, I stepped away and entertained Alessandro on the rug in a confused daze.

Moments later, a knock. "Jayne? Alessandro? What are you doing in there? It's time for dinner."

"We're playing." The door opened, and Electra's flushed face offered a faint smile. Holding Alessandro, I followed her back to the kitchen to prepare dinner while she sat in the corner blankly, chewing the inside of her cheek. As I put on Alessandro's bib to begin the dinner service, there was a knock on the door, and Electra jumped up with her chest puffed out in anticipation. I hadn't noticed it before, but she held a sheet of paper. "I'll get that. You stay here," she snapped, running for the entrance.

I tried not to look, but I peeked when the argument grew louder. Roberto stood in the doorway with a suitcase in one hand and a piece of paper in the other. He tried to look past her at me, but Electra blocked his line of vision and pushed him out, ending the quarrel with a wall-vibrating door slam.

I jumped back and pretended to be busy. Electra trotted in with a satisfied grin, humming. "You know, I told him to leave you alone. A simple request," she said with a side glance, opening a cupboard. "You're not ready to date men. Especially Roberto."

"What? Are you serious? You can't tell me who I can and can't go out with."

"Jayne, please understand." She shut the cupboard with a heavy sigh. "I know it's not your fault," she said, coming over to adjust Alessandro's bib. Our eyes met when she glanced up at me. "If Roberto can't follow my rules, he can't be my lawyer. I don't think it's asking too much. When he came back from New York, he was devastated about Grace. And you? You cry every night. It's not ideal for the two of you to meet. And don't give me that face. It's not very pretty."

I bolted out of the apartment, ignoring her pleas to stop. Roberto's frame was visible on the bottom floor through the landing railing, and I shouted his name. He looked up and waited as I scrambled down the steps.

"Oh, my god. I'm so sorry," I panted. "I didn't expect her to lose it like that. Talk about jealous."

He shook his head. "It's not your fault."

"But firing you?"

He laughed. "Don't worry. It's happened before."

I gulped. "What? It has?"

His eyes darted toward the staircase. He looked afraid Electra would appear with a hatchet. "Jayne, look, believe it or not, she's watching out for you. That's a good thing."

I let out an exasperated breath. "Are you serious? I don't need her ladyship to manage my social life. I'm a big girl. And I was looking forward to going out with you. My first night off."

He put his hand on my shoulder. "Don't worry. We can get together when you come back from your trip. She said you're leaving this week."

"The prison warden said that? But we don't even have a car. She said there were no trains to where we are going."

His trim body turned to the door, and his hand gripped its brass knob. He swung around with a chuckle. "Don't worry about those minor details. Life with Electra," he said, opening the door into the night. "It's always full of surprises."

Sleepless from gnawing guilt about the incident with Roberto, I crawled out of bed and prepared the morning bottle and coffee, preoccupied if the American Express travel office would be open and what bargain airfares to New York it offered. I sipped my espresso as effusive Electra complimented me on how Alessandro loved being with me and what an excellent job I was doing. A backdoor apology, I thought. The lauding morphed into an explanation on the philosophy of *festina lente,* which meant the importance of taking small steps in the right direction instead of giant leaps in the wrong one. Weirdly, I understood her overbearing concern a bit better.

After breakfast, I stepped outside with Electra and Alessandro, and my mood brightened significantly. The early morning's relentless rain had transformed Milan into a sugar-coated, jeweled metropolis. Even the diesel-damaged air sparkled energy.

The grand piazza was bustling, and wealthy jet-setters laden with Gucci and Prada shopping bags jammed into the chalk-white arcades surrounding the Duomo. Apart from the shopaholics, a church tour leader gathered a group of priests to line up outside the Santa Maria Delle Grazie monastery wall to see *The Last Supper*, DaVinci's masterpiece. In the jumble of racing Milanese and visitors deciphering accordion maps of the must-see sites, I kept pace behind a full-throttled Electra as she snaked through the crowds.

Roberto's *GQ* magnetism bubbled into my mind. Was jealousy the reason she had fired him? Did she have feelings for Roberto? Her reddish waves bounced in front of me. The woman could be more challenging to read than Sanskrit.

Electra slowed to gaze at a store's display as I eyed the American Express office three doors away. Her cozy loft gave me stability as my black and blue ego healed. But the woman had secrets and would not divulge any of them. Who was the "devil" who'd come to the apartment? She'd never mentioned being a Contessa, but anyone could see that she had issues with her holier-than-thou and snobby attitude, plus her treatment of the public. However, her tough exterior concealed the insecurities of an imperfect woman. The absence of Alessandro's father might be the reason. Where was that man now? I wouldn't put it past her if I learned he was an FBI-wanted spy or a famous actor. Nothing would surprise me. I wished I knew more. Underneath all the elitist baloney, she and I were trudging through the same crap of our shredded lives.

Off again, I hurried behind her across the vast piazza, dodging crumb-hunting pigeons as her blazing locomotive stare scattered fearful Milanese as they darted away from her. I paused when Alessandro dropped his dinosaur onto the ground and rubbed the toy against the leg of my jeans to knock off any dirt, rushing to catch up with race walking Electra. As I circumvented a stagnant tour group, an imposing figure blocked my path, and I squinted at the alien-like landing.

It was Matteo, and my stomach dropped. "Hello. I didn't know you were in Milan," he smiled. His broad chest rose, and he clutched a leather briefcase in his light gray suit with the shiny brown shoes *I* had picked out at Brooks Brothers for an interview.

I swallowed the gob of dry sand in my throat. "What are you doing here?"

"A meeting," he said, lifting his briefcase. "It's in our Milan office." His eyes flashed to Alessandro, pumping his legs in the stroller and then back to me. "Who's this little guy?"

"Him?" I said, noticing Electra slow down. She turned to find us, and my pulse jumped. "A friend's kid. I've got to go. See ya."

He stepped closer to prevent me. "Which friend?" he said, crouching down to Alessandro's level. "Is there someone new in your life?"

"Funny. I wish." I pulled the stroller into my stomach. "It's a friend you never met. She's waiting for me."

He wiggled his finger on Alessandro's knee, but the little boy swiped it away with his dinosaur. They say children sense evil, I thought. Maybe they're right. "Hey, what's your name? Come ti chiami?"

Electra neared, and I panicked. "I really have to go," I told him, swiveling its hi-tech wheels into his unsuspecting calf. He winced in pain, but it was too late to escape.

"What's going on, Jayne?" she asked, sizing up Matteo on arrival.

I shrugged. "Nothing."

She studied Matteo, then me. Her eyebrows hit her hairline. "Nothing?"

"Electra, this is my … my friend, Matteo."

Her face set like cement. She'd heard too many details of the Como annihilation for any other reaction.

"It's a pleasure to meet you, Electra," Matteo smiled, extending his hand.

Electra shot her nose in the air and dismissed him as a queen would flick off a peasant offering rotten fruit. "No," she said, turning away in disgust. The move was Shakespearean, and I couldn't have asked for a better reaction to lacerate his ego.

Matteo's face dripped skin at the rejection. Electra yanked the stroller's handlebars from me with such force that Alessandro's body snapped back. "Did you tell him you were here?" she said gruffly, staring at the ground.

My hand flew to my chest. "Me? No. No way. Never."

"I hope so." She blinked with suspicion, exhaling like a bull ready to charge. Before I could defend myself more, she abruptly marched away.

Matteo leered at her figure, crossing the piazza. "What a bitch."

"I ... She can be tough," I said, confused. Why would she ever think I would invite Matteo to Milan?

He spat in her direction, and the thick glob landed with a plop. "Who does she think she is?"

His rage was familiar, frothing into an angry, red, ugly mug I'd seen before when a guy in Washington Square Park played his boom box too loud or when he discovered a job he'd interviewed for went to somebody else. The caged demon I had once ignored. He now aimed it at someone who'd biblically taken me in. She wasn't perfect, but at least she didn't throw me out onto the streets. "Stop it. I don't want to hear anymore. And who are you to judge anyone, anyway?"

I looked over as Alessandro's dinosaur dropped again onto the pavement. Electra picked it up, glancing in our direction as she dusted it off and handed it back to him, forgetting her own rules about germs. Matteo kept on his verbal attack, except his words meant nothing. Electra heard my late-night sobs and fretted about why I didn't eat much. She knew he was the reason behind my faraway stare of disbelief, and even though her Roberto reaction had been over the top, at least I knew she cared.

I turned to Matteo, his thin red lips still spewing vulgarities. “Electra helped me when I had no place to go. After you *abandoned* me in Como.”

He pointed across the square. “She’s a rude and awful woman. A stronza. Bitch.” I remembered the word from the woman’s rant at the bookstore. “A new word for you to know. And for the record, you left me.”

“*After* you dumped me because I was cramping your Casanova style.” I spun to Electra, who was nearing Alessandro’s favorite gelato counter, and turned back to him. “Your selfish lies put me here,” I sneered. “I’m working my ass off to earn back my life savings I wasted on you. But thank you for teaching me the big secret for a great relationship. It’s not having one. Especially with you.”

“Wait, wait,” he said, stepping forward with a melancholy gaze. He took a deep breath and blew it out with force. “This is stupid. Let’s talk about this. I thought we could—”

“Are you serious, Matteo? *Now* you want to talk?” I said with a sarcastic laugh. “That bitch, as you say …” I scanned the gaping crowd around us. Their faces blurred, and I tried to catch my breath. “She has her flaws, but at least she was there for me.”

He reached for my hand. “I—”

“She’s not perfect, but it was a lifeline I needed,” I said, moving away from him. “From you and your harem. Remember that gesture you told me to use if a guy bothered me and I wanted him to disappear?” I swiped my fingers under the tip of my chin and flicked him off. "Vai a farti fottere. Ciao.” *Go screw yourself. Bye.*

$645.04

Stamps	- 4.00
Postcards - send one to Jim?	- 3.00
Film for Kodak Instamatic	- 5.25
Supplies - do you need soap for bidet?	- 13.49
Mood board scissors / colored pencils	- 34.00
Market finds - vintage lace	- 2.00
Gettoni's	- 5.50
Panino & Pizza - best ever - Via Durini	- 6.50
	$571.30

ST. MARCO

CHAPTER EIGHT

THE RUN-IN WITH MATTEO HAUNTED ME. The bitter resentment and my endless harping about crushed love weren't in my playbook. I had to forgive and forget. Move on. Time would heal me.

Like in all European countries, August was the month everyone in Italy fled to their country houses or beautiful seaside resorts and called Ferragosto. Besides the standard daily closing of stores at lunchtime, Electra warned that cities became ghost towns. As in all things, she wanted to be weeks ahead of the mass exodus of the commoners. However, we still had no car, so her plan was sketchy.

Upon returning from the park with Alessandro, a frantic Electra met us at the building's doorway, wildly flapping a piece of paper. Nearby, Pedro swept as Dante sniffed a big box with a picture of a car seat on its label. "There you are! Come on. We're going to buy a car now, and they're waiting for us. Hurry and park the stroller inside," she said, scooping up Alessandro and marching to the taxi stand. "The seller said many people are interested in it. Pedro, grab the box and follow me. I'm not going to lose this deal."

After pushing us all into the backseat, Electra explained in the taxi that she'd seen an advertisement in the morning newspaper and had contacted the number. Excited, she proclaimed the car was the Ambassador of Ghana's automobile. "Is that so?" I smirked. "How interesting."

Pedro and I exchanged glances as he placed the box on the passenger front seat. "Buono fortuna," he said as he closed the door.

Near the outskirts of Milan, the taxi dropped us off in an empty industrial parking lot where two figures wearing long, orange robes stood next to a shiny black Mercedes and another funky car I had seen in old French movies. The Mercedes' silver hubcaps glistened, and I imagined myself in sunglasses cruising the Italian Riviera, blasting music, and waving to gorgeous guys. Then I remembered my passengers, which zoomed me back to reality. "That Mercedes looks nice. And very safe."

She nodded. "It does. German cars are the best."

As we approached, the tall, thin men eyed us with concern—two women with a baby weren't the buyers they'd expected. But when Electra greeted them with crossed arms, her passive-aggressive behavior caused them to step back.

"You two keep quiet," she ordered over her shoulder. While the group talked, I kicked loose gravel, listening to snippets about cars and price negotiations. Of course, both men spoke perfect English and Italian and answered her every concern. After a while, she beckoned me closer.

"Here are the keys," she said, handing them over as the men leaned against the dark Mercedes. I gave her Alessandro, but she grabbed my arm when I approached the Mercedes. She pointed to the other car. "Take that one for a drive. Let me know what you think."

"Not the Mercedes?" The car was odd—a Citroen DS, a classic French automobile; I'd never seen one up close. The copper-colored vehicle was a massive, space-age ladybug on wheels, and I hoped Electra knew about cars because, to me, it didn't seem roadworthy.

She gawked at my hesitancy. "Go on. It's fine. They said all French presidents drive in this car. Even Prince Rainier in Monaco has one."

Electra waited until I creaked open the door. The first shocking sight was the futuristic steering wheel protruding from the dashboard. It was vastly different from the last car I had driven: my mom's Buick station wagon. The column held a one-spoke steering wheel; the rest was a hollow circle. The unconventional dashboard had gauges and dials surrounded by plastic switches and knobs that belonged on a jumbo jet, or the Starship Enterprise.

"Go on. It looks a bit different, but it's just a car with four wheels," she prodded. I sank into the seat of tobacco-colored leather, clutching the steering wheel to save myself from disappearing further into its depths. Barely able to see through the windshield, my fingers fumbled for any button to adjust my position. The ignition was hiding somewhere, though I dared not ask for help in finding it. I finally found it in the last place I imagined—the center of the long dashboard.

The key turned, and the panel of dials and switches lit up with monochromatic beeps, chiming my success. The vehicle rose off the ground, and I panicked at its unforeseen lift. "This car is rising for some reason," I shouted, grabbing the door handle, ready to jump out.

By this time, the men had joined Electra. "It's okay," one of the men chuckled, pumping his fists into the air as if lifting and lowering an invisible object. "It's got hydropneumatics."

I flashed a smile. Of course, it couldn't be a *regular* car; it probably ran on Cabernet Sauvignon. Or champagne. In the background, Electra mouthed mio dio with disapproval while Alessandro stared with a gaping mouth, concerned by my fear. At least somebody cared.

I put it into drive and circled the parking lot at various speeds, assessing its steering and handling. The car was surprisingly smooth, and although it was quirky and unusual, I found that I liked it. After parking,

Electra scurried over. "How was it? Did it drive well?" she asked, sticking her face into my window. Her voice lowered. "Should I buy it?"

"Yes. It's great. Extremely comfortable to drive. Plus, it's huge inside," I said, twisting my body to examine the rear seat. I threw back my hand to show Electra. "There's so much space between the backseat and the driver. You could literally sleep in this car."

We discussed it more and decided it was a satisfactory purchase with low mileage. After they agreed to file the paperwork, Electra wrote a check to the thankful men, and I stuffed the necessary papers into the glove box before leaving. Electra tethered Alessandro into his new car seat with the seat belt, equating it to the preparation of an astronaut's safety check before liftoff. Once done, I removed my bag from the passenger seat for Electra to sit, but she plunged beside Alessandro and closed the door.

"Why are you sitting back there?" I said with concern. "There's plenty of room up here."

She put on her seat belt. "No, I'm fine. What if Alessandro needs me? I'm right here."

"Oh. Yes. If Alessandro needs you. Of course." I pursed my lips, realizing the real reason. The men had mentioned that the Ghanaian ambassador never sat in the front. Also, while expounding on the safety features, they declared that French President Charles de Gaulle survived an assassination attempt by a terrorist group because he'd been sitting in the backseat of his presidential Citroen DS. That's all Electra had to hear to claim her new spot.

"You need to pack a bag for Alessandro," she declared as I drove onto the main boulevard after a litany of backseat outbursts of lefts and rights since leaving the parking lot. "As soon as we get back."

"Wait. So, we're leaving *today*?" I said in disbelief. "Why not tomorrow?"

"No, we can't. My friend is waiting for us."

My hand squeezed the steering wheel. "Okay. But I need time to pack *my* bag. And do a load of washing. A heads-up in the future would be nice, you know."

"I'm sorry. You're right. There's been a lot of things running through my mind." She wagged her finger at my reflection in the rearview mirror. "We can't fit those two large suitcases, you know. I'll put one of my bags in your room. And no wasting time daydreaming because we must get there by sunset."

I thought about Gino; I needed to call him before leaving. The clock in the car read two, and sunset was eight hours away. "Where are we going?"

She peered out, watching the world pass from her lady ambassador's perch. "Venice is our first stop. After that? Other places."

"Venezia? The floating city. Exciting," Gino said, handing me a tiny cup of espresso.

"I hope so. And then after that, who knows? I may be gone for the whole summer. My Italian is improving. Ask me to name any farm animal. And I can quote *Pinocchio*. When I come back, it's only *come stai* and *va bene*, okay? No English."

"Perfetto." He paused, stroking his chin stubble. "Why don't you prepare a project I can show the designers I meet? To let them know you better and your fashion aesthetics."

I sat up. "Like what? A list of fabrics I sold?"

"No, no one wants to know about last season. More of the daily grind you faced up there at Trendary. The tools you used, how you collaborated with designers, their feedback ..."

I was unsure of his request. "Usually, the designer gives me a mood board, and then—"

"That's it." He clapped and pointed his two index fingers at me. "Create an Italian mood board. I can see it now. An interpretation of your travels, and Venice is a perfect place to start. Jayne Boland all the way," he said, growing excited. "Let's see what triggers those American impulses fresh from the streets of cold, dismal Manhattan—your use of color and texture. *La vita e bella* feeling through a new lens. A tapestry of consciousness communicated by you."

La vita e bella was a phrase Matteo would say when we'd walk on a beach and sit with a bottle of wine on the dunes. The unwritten ability to appreciate the small things in life. "It sounds intense," I said, wondering if he was asking too much as I sipped my espresso. I didn't have a design degree and having just been on the selling side of fabrics, I was unsure of the entire process.

He read my mind and shrugged. "Well, if you want to play in the big leagues, it should be. Step out of your comfort zone."

"I hear you. And accept the challenge. Still, don't forget, I just got dumped by one of your fellow countrymen, so my mood board could be a nasty kaleidoscope of raw emotion," I scowled. "Blood and guts."

He deflected my comment with a sly smile. "Love and hate are the best inspirations, my dear. Ask any renowned artist."

When I left Gino's office with my new assignment, my stomach flip-flopped with trepidation. And I had even forgotten to tell him about my run-in with Luca Rosso. An art shop nearby had scissors, and I added a pack of colored pencils to my mood board purchases. The undertaking would be challenging but fun, and I was excited to prove my worth to Gino.

Since I had taken a detour to Gino's, buying organic potatoes and jars of Alessandro's favorite mixed berry puree was a mad dash, and I returned sweaty and ready to pack. The car was outside the building, and I grinned at the cleaning spray bottle and paper towels near the vehicle. Pedro bent over the engine, and I gave Dante the leftover cornetto from my pocket, listening to his owner's grunts.

"Grazie, Pedro," I said when he came up for air with a dipstick in his hand. "I mean, thank you, Pedro, for cleaning the car. And the oil. Olio."

He laughed. "Stai imparando. You leave for how long?" he said in his broken English. We had a friendly language exchange agreement of no judgment.

I shrugged. "I don't know." He seemed upset with my answer and scratched his arm. "Why? Perche?"

He eyed his surroundings and opened his mouth to answer, but Dante barked instead. He laughed and patted the dog. "Dante sad. See? He says don't go," he said before grabbing a wrench from his pocket. "But I teach you oil now."

"Oh. Okay." I wondered what he had really wanted to tell me. "We're going to Venice first. After that, I don't know." My eyes narrowed. "Is everything okay? Va tutto bene?"

He swung the wrench up at Electra's window. "Too long time away from apartment," Pedro said. Then, his attention diverted, and he signaled to someone behind me with a grin. "Ciao, Signore Rosso! Come sta?"

I swung around as Luca Rosso swooshed past me. "Tutto e meravi-glioso. Grazie mille," he said as he hurried into the building. I wanted to trail him, but since Pedro said I needed to learn to check the oil, I didn't leave and instead took the opportunity to quiz him about Luca Rosso. From what I could understand from our simple conversation, he was super friendly and used his place as a private design studio because it was more peaceful than his larger office. My desire to talk to Luca Rosso doubled with that new knowledge. I would love to see what design goodies brewed in his secret workplace.

When I arrived back at the apartment, I took the mini duffle bag on my bed and held it over the loft railing for Electra's attention. "You're joking. This little thing for me?" I said in disbelief. "Electra, it barely holds a toothbrush."

She glanced up. "We don't have enough space in the car for all your … dresses and things. You'll need comfortable clothes because of all the driving. That's all."

"Still, I need more than one outfit."

"Who are you going to see?" She left for the kitchen, disappearing from my view. "You Americans need to learn to work with what you have," she added.

"I know what this American would like to do. Have NASA freeze-dry you, put you in this minuscule bag, and rocket you to the moon," I griped quietly, ready to heave the bag back at her. Frustrated, I murmured expletives instead, placing the bare minimum of my unwashed clothes inside. A pair of shorts, shirts, a sundress, and jeans made it bulge, and I tied my Tretorn sneakers onto its strap. The bulky bag's seams stretched apart when I tossed in mascara, lip gloss, and my notepad. Then, I crammed a fistful of underwear and miscellaneous items into the limited space of my backpack. Luckily, Electra reevaluated her proposal when she saw I could not zip it close and gave me a larger sack, which I greatly appreciated.

Pedro had the car packed with the highchair, stroller, assorted toys, groceries, kitchen gadgets, luggage, Alessandro's three suitcases, Electra's two Louis Vuitton garment bags, her makeup case, and a year's supply of diapers. As Electra wedged herself into the back seat, Dante whined to get in the car while Pedro laughed, pulling him away. We waved as we departed, joining the other vehicles in broiling hot mid-afternoon traffic, ready for an adventure.

Venice was less than two hundred miles away, and an unexpected peach pit mushroomed in my throat when the car zoomed past the Como exit. I stewed silently, grinding my teeth while Electra and Alessandro slept in the back seat. But I had to release my angst if I was hoping to improve myself.

We reached our destination at the San Giuliano parking lot at sunset. Electra trotted off to buy a five-day parking ticket, and I wandered to the edge of the lot, admiring the postcard-perfect Venetian skyline. I had to pinch myself as the warm night breeze whipped off the lagoon: gondolas, water taxis, and vaporetto's danced a harmonious ballet of crisscrosses over the Grand Canal. Although Matteo wasn't by my side, I wasn't that upset that Alessandro was instead. Electra was upbeat when she returned, and her smile was infectious. Our threesome was strange and different, but we shared an appreciation for the beauty, reachable just across the canal.

The water taxi cut across the lagoon like a knife into an aquamarine cake as the golden sunset framed the grand palaces. Electra pointed out the famous landmarks: Rialto Bridge, Ponte dell'Academia, and Marco Polo's house as we cruised into the renowned city. Venetian gothic facades floated magically on the canal's boulevard while parked boats bucked in the whitecaps, ready for the next trip. Along the promenades, some walkers played with their dogs while others casually strolled hand in hand, transforming the travel poster into a living city.

My body slowly relaxed. Lapping waves tapped lightly against the thousand-year-old walls and arches in a rhythmic caress. The city was still tourist-free because the August season of travel hadn't begun. The sprinkle of sightseers were the usual Australians taking their lifetime trip, Japanese shoppers, exchange students, older American tourists, or other Europeans, mostly retired.

After disembarking, we found the apartment tucked away from the center of Venice on a cobblestone-lined canal, down a narrow lane called a *calle*. Electra's friend, Freja, greeted us, and she seemed wholesome and hospitable. Tall with long blonde hair, she was Electra's friend from university. The apartment's atypical wood-lined interior was like a boat's hull with a wide upstairs loft area for guests, and I was lucky to snag the high, serene nook since the others shared the oversized main bedroom downstairs.

"There is justice," I exhaled, fixing the edges of a patchwork quilt on the bed. The cozy attic space separated me from the friendly chaos downstairs, and the old Christmas tinsel dangling from the ceiling beams added to its charm. In the acoustic paradise, I relaxed as the rhythm of pedestrians mixed with telephone rings or clanking dishes echoed outside against the rock walls. The sounds of Venetian life sifted through the air, and I listened, amused.

After Alessandro went to bed, my voyeurism into the private world of Venetians was reignited as I strolled the alleys; lit interiors beamed dinner preparations as adults read newspapers while children watched television. A family cat asleep on a steamy window sill or a dog waiting for falling food added life. My look-see might have been creepy, yet I didn't care, and binged nightly on the compelling documentary.

I thought of my mood board, anxious to begin its creation. How, with fabric, do you represent hollow echoes of leather soles on ancient stone or the nature of water? Since Electra said we'd be stopping in different regions, I decided to have a theme for each destination. For Venice, when I passed an open window's fluttering white curtains, ethereal seemed to fit the city's essence. Delicate and light.

Luckily, Electra and Freja left daily for the Save Venice meetings they joined or took trips to explore the many Venetian islands. My assignment was to take Alessandro in his stroller for mini adventures, mixing with day trippers, locals, and the occasional priest or holy nun who always seemed to be sprinting to an ecumenical emergency.

The Venetian marketplaces became a treasure trove for my mood board. Besides drooling over incredible pecorinos and parmesans, fresh fish, and sausages, I picked up monogrammed linen napkins, old silver spoons, and textiles with tiny beading or embroidery designs, appreciating the intricate, delicate handiwork. Postcards, vintage clothes, silk scarves, and old tapestry pieces packed the open-air stalls, and I haggled to buy a nice trinket of inspiration for less than ten dollars.

To help my quest, I imagined being on Luca Rosso's design team as I rummaged through a bin of old velvet slippers, finding an azure one with a hole in the toe. I brushed the soft fibers with a smile, and the seller let me have it for free. Its mesmerizing color matched the crystal waters. "Perfetto."

During a side trip, I called my mom to tell her I was in Venice—the one place she had always wanted to visit. "Mom," I shouted as soon as the phone clicked the connection. "It's me. Jayne. I'm in Venice. Your favorite place."

"Jayne?" It was Flynn, not my mother. Her usual chipper voice was dull.

I clenched the phone, clinking more coins into the metal box. "Yes, it's me. Why are you home? What happened? Is it Mom?"

"What? No. Mom's fine."

I sensed her holding back through the static of a crinkling potato chip bag. It was a weekday; she'd have driven two hours from Millbrook. My voice rose. "Then why are you there? Is everything okay with you guys? The kids?"

She ignored my question. "How's Italy?"

"Fine. Fine. I wanted to tell Mom I was in Venice. What's going on, Flynn? My radar says there is something wrong."

She grunted. "Your ears must have been burning because we just finished talking about you. So, you're touring Venice now? Nice," she said with sarcasm. "You know Mom is scrounging to get your airfare back here, and the whole nanny thing is ridiculous. You had a career here. Get out of there."

I glanced down at Alessandro and saw that he had fallen asleep. I had five gettoni left, meaning a minute of talk time. "Please tell Mom to stop saving, I don't need a plane ticket. And it's called a job, and you know how hard childcare it is."

The static became louder. "I do. But they're my *own* kids and not someone else's. I don't understand the point."

"I'm trying to save and get my life together. And I called Mom to tell her I was in her favorite city, not to hear your insults. Is she there?"

"Please tell me you're not waiting for Matteo to crawl out of his brothel and take you back. 'Cause that's not happening. Ambrose and I are working like dogs, like most responsible people."

I refrained from blowing up, and the phone clicked. "Wait, one of the coins stuck. Don't go," I yelled into the receiver, hitting the machine. It was located outside a *bacaro*, a tiny bar, and a patron peeked out to see the commotion. "Hello?"

"It's not just me. Mom and Dad think you're wasting your life. Why don't you get on a plane and return to reality?"

The phone died before I could answer, and I stood seething at her last remark as I pried the stuck gettonis out with my fingertips. Twenty-four-seven of sweat wasn't reality? She had no idea how hard my days were, and I knew she had always thought I was flaky because my job was in fashion and didn't adhere to her "norm." Her words balled like a cold fist in my chest. Why was she so bitchy? This job was helping me out of my financial hole. And why didn't my parents trust me to succeed?

Alessandro blinked awake due to the noise of the argument. "Go back to sleep, little man," I said, tempted to enter the bar. Flynn's expectations for me had always been sky-high; I thought that was behind us. Our sisterly bond had changed when I joined her in high school. Friends said it was normal. She'd barely acknowledged me, the nerdy freshman, as she played the part of an uppity senior on the volleyball team. That was okay, except her hip friends let her borrow expensive clothes for parties, and she set the bar high. I was her awkward sister fighting an endless battle with acne. But she got homesick when she went to college, and I talked to her every night to help her cope with a demanding schedule, an unfriendly roommate, and insomnia. She was better after Thanksgiving and said our nightly chats saved her life. What was her problem now?

I felt isolated from our sisterly cohesiveness for the past year. After Matteo dumped me, I missed her so much and was dying to smoke a cigarette with a glass of wine on the beach, like old times when we had a problem. Then follow it with a good scream, cry, and bear hug.

I watched a gondola pass under a bridge, thinking. After Flynn first met Matteo, she asked a strange question. Would I have hooked up with Matteo if he had been from the Bronx? Was it the simple fact of Matteo being different, exotic, cultured—an Italian—that kept it exciting? Did I love him only because of that? Would we have made it to the second date if he were from the tri-state area? Staten Island?

Was wanderlust the reason I was with him in the first place?

Flynn's last words on the phone hung in the air like skunk spray, and I wrote to her and my parents, explaining my plan to earn enough moolah to get back on my feet while plugging away on my mood board. I didn't understand why they couldn't see my goal as feasible and avoided telling them that I could stay in Italy. Or go to the Philippines. Or even return to New York. My future had become Spin the Wheel, and I had no idea where the pointer was to land.

Electra took Alessandro to run errands the following day and left Freja and me alone at lunchtime. I liked that Freja's outgoing manner had a Bohemian edge, highlighted by an apartment full of hanging tapestries and smoky twirls of sandalwood incense. Of course, she also spoke perfect Italian and English along with her Norwegian, humming Boy George while preparing smoked salmon sandwiches in her country kitchen. She sized me up with a glint in her eye, and my body tensed under the scrutiny. "So, how do you like Electra?" she asked with a sly curl to her tone.

"That's the question everyone likes to ask. She's all right," I replied with a shrug.

"All right? That's American for bearable," she said, cutting a lemon in half. My hunger spiked, watching her squeeze lemon juice over the pink fillets. "You know, we met at university in a film class and kept in touch because we love Venice. She stays here because I have the space, and we gossip about old classmates. She's tough as nails, however. And stubborn. She'll break you down if possible. Can't imagine what it would be like to have her as my boss."

"You're not the first person to say that to me." She wanted me to confess my true feelings, except I hesitated to confide in her. "Electra is tough, yes. But she was the only one who opened her door when I was at my lowest. Looks great," I said, picking up a loose caper and popping it into my mouth. "Everyone has their baggage. God knows I do."

"Her last au pair only lasted a week, and the one before that, a day," she said, handing me a napkin as she sat down. "She said it was about the ironing."

"Oh, yes," I snorted. "I think crisp collars and perfect pleats are better than sex for Electra."

She laughed. "It's a European thing. In Norway, we're lucky because people are laidback, and it's all sweaters for us. Oops, I forgot the wine."

I waited while she poured us each a glass, and we both took a sip after toasting Electra. The wine was refreshing and cold, and we munched in silence until I cleared my throat. "Is Electra a real-life royal?"

Intrigued, she put down her glass. "Of course, she is. What do you want to know?"

"Is she … is she a real princess? Like Princess Diana princess?"

"Well, she's not as big as Princess Diana. I mean, she's untouchable." She lifted her sandwich off the plate. "Still," she said, "Electra is a princess. One hundred percent."

I took a moment to let that fact seep in. "And what about the Contessa part?"

"All of it." She took a sip of wine. "She's not the Queen of England level but her family is still part of the noble aristocracy. Counts and countesses own thousands of hectares of land. She is below a marquess and duchess in the pecking order but above a viscountess and baroness. That's the lowest member. I'm not an expert on her family, but I know that she's a princess, but doesn't use the title much."

"It's mind-boggling that she has two titles."

"Especially for someone from the States. Norway is still a constitutional monarchy, so we have our King and Queen. For centuries, nobility was the old source of wealth and power, and her family has been noble since the Middle Ages. And part of the Habsburg monarchy. She's more Austrian than Italian. You know she's fluent in German, right?"

I gulped. "She is?"

"Yes. I believe Electra went to boarding school in Austria. My friends always want to hear how my weekend with the princess was," she laughed. "As you can see, I'm as common as a potato. Have you visited her town?"

"No. But I think we're stopping there. And I'm below a potato in terms of being common. I could be corn. Or air," I laughed. "Before I met Electra, I thought England was the only place with a monarchy." History classes taught about medieval lords controlling fiefdoms, marrying their daughters off for more land, and beating serfs for rent. Henry VIII was the center of it all. I'm sure Electra would have loved to live in that world. Long gowns and pointy headdresses. Dungeons and hot tar. "Exploring her town will be very interesting. She wants to tour places in the north she visited as a child. I think this trip is an emotional one for her."

"Oh, yes. And you're lucky. For Electra to ask you to drive her and Alessandro is a big honor. You're seeing a personal side of her that no one else does. When you see Caneva, you'll understand. The family has a castle there and owns all the land." She sat back and emitted a breezy sigh. "She's an interesting woman with that sprezzatura you can't buy."

I had heard that word on the television yet didn't know what it meant. "What is sprezzatura?"

"It's the biggest compliment you can receive. The ability to look effortless but still have chic style and cool elegance. See how today Electra looped her red scarf as a belt? If I did that, I'd look like a clown. And it would take me hours to make that bow."

She was right. Electra made superb bows with her silk scarves. And her simple makeup was always flawless. I glanced at my jeans and smirked. With my limited wardrobe, claiming my career was in fashion was embarrassing. Electra could combine chic shirts, corduroy pants, and cashmere cardigans without fear of judgment and always look stylish. "I hear you, and it's depressing," I laughed.

"Her mother lives in the hills near Caneva, and the family has country houses throughout Italy. Electra has a sister, too: Anna Maria. When Electra told them she was pregnant with Alessandro, they said the baby was a bastard and could never be a di Caneva. She had to go to court, I think."

"What? That's awful. A bastard? Didn't that go out with jousting and minstrels? And how sad that she is fighting with her family. That's the last thing she needs. They should be in her life and especially her son's."

I clasped my hands, letting this latest information sink in as Freja refilled her wine glass. Why would her sister shun her? Flynn wouldn't do that to me. She'd be there if needed, especially with a new baby. Electra's absent relatives explained a lot. But there had to be more to the story. Who did she have in her life besides Freja, Alessandro, and me?

"I'm sure it has to do with her inheritance. However, we may never know because Electra is *very* private and would rather drink bleach than talk about her affairs. I could be wrong."

"What about her father?"

"Oh. Such an elegant man. He died five years ago. Electra never mentioned him to you?" she asked, puzzled. "I met him in Milan, and he seemed to be the only one who cared for her. She always wears his wedding ring. You know, the big solid gold band."

"Yes. It clinks whenever she picks up a glass." Electra always twisted the thick ring—a nervous habit. On her dresser was a photo of a man in a movie star pose, his hand under his chin. Distinguishably handsome with a mustache, debonair would be a perfect word to describe him. "Electra and I don't get into deep conversations, so this is all new to me. She is always reading a book or the newspaper. She never goes out except to get the paper or lunch at one of the charities she supports." A rush of sympathy shot through me, and I didn't want to gossip about her anymore.

"That's too bad."

I fingered the sandwich as Freja ate. Electra's public image was a façade to hide her distress. The toxic situation with her mother and sister must have eaten away her self-esteem and made her suspicious of people. And it explained her obsession with Alessandro; he was all she had in her lonely life.

Questions like how she could afford to live in an incredible apartment on Milan's most expensive street were unanswerable. The photos I found and the story I'd heard said family wealth, but how? Investments? Land? Or was her financier now Alessandro's father? And the big one that no one had addressed yet. I took a sip of wine. "I hate to be nosy, but who and where is Alessandro's dad?"

Freja grabbed my hand and leaned closer. "You mean mystery man?" she said in a barely audible whisper. "No one knows. And Electra won't give away any secrets. Not that I ever asked." She took a small orange from a fruit bowl, and her fingers pressed into the skin, spraying zest into the air. "Orange?"

I got her subtle change of subject. "No thanks." I cleared my throat. "One day, this blond guy knocked on the door and asked for her, and then he asked for Alessandro. I said they weren't there, and then he left. When she arrived later, she was upset he came by but didn't quiz me for his name, although she called him the devil. Could he be the father's brother? She was furious."

"Interesting. The plot thickens."

"I know. I feel bad. I mean, Electra should take Alessandro to see his grandmother. And Anna Maria, his aunt. They'd eat him up; he's such a cupcake."

Freja eyed her orange slices and nodded. "Thank God she had that little boy. Especially after losing her father. Funny how things happen, isn't it?"

"Yes," I agreed. Now I understood why there were so many tissue boxes around the Milan apartment. We were both basket cases, I thought.

But at least we had each other.

$ 571.30

JULY 1st

Bikini - find sunglasses — 28.00

Gelato x 3 — 6.50

Diet Coke x 4 — 6.00

★ JUNE SALARY + 400.00

SUNSCREEN — 5.05

$ 925.75

10 X BIGGER

CHAPTER NINE

AFTER FIVE DAYS IN VENICE, the next destination was Lignano Sabbiadoro, a beach town absent from popular guidebooks. Electra said the village was on the sea, so I imagined a fabulous setting of limestone cliffs overlooking a celestial bay. The map showed it was sixty-five miles away, on the Adriatic coast in the Friuli Venezia Giulia region. Nearby was an inland town named Caneva.

We sped past trellised vineyards along the hillsides and wildflower-rimmed farmland on the rural roads. Commercial town centers had ubiquitous pizza joints, bars, and Agip gas stations with yellow and black six-legged dog signs barking every ten miles. On the radio, I listened to the news commentaries and would translate what I understood to Electra. With encouragement, she'd point out common phrases the announcer used and quiz me on random words. It helped the time pass, but when I switched to a music station for a break, my eyes glistened when a sappy Sinead O'Connor or romantic Eros Ramazotti song came on. That's when she would demand classical music.

We finally reached Lignano, where towering pine trees lined streets of cookie-cutter, white-washed homes topped with rusty slate roofs. Behind the simple metal gates, tranquil palm trees and pink-budded bushes bordered the houses and enclosed a family Fiat or Vespa in the driveway. People of various ages and sizes enjoyed the outdoors or biked toward the ocean in swimsuits with bright towels draped over their bodies. In the distance, the iridescent galaxy of the Adriatic spilled forth, and I breathed in the marine air, licking my salty lips with pleasure.

"This place is heaven," I said, feeling the sun. The warmth soaked into my bones as Electra tried to find the realtor's street on the map.

"Okay. I see where we are. Turn left down there." After I'd turned left and right multiple times, the real estate office was easy to spot with its balloon-dangling sidewalk sign. "There it is. Park over here," she said, pointing to a space near a gelateria. "Look, Alessandro, they've got gelato for you. Oh, I'm glad I picked this place."

She got out and skipped into the office, leaving Alessandro with me to gape at the colossal rainbow-painted ice cream cone. My forehead rested on the window, allowing the sunshine to toast my pale face. Kids ran by with sand buckets, and nearby cafés buzzed with bronzed locals enjoying boisterous late lunches, adding to the town's party atmosphere. It had a laid-back, different beat than secretive Venice. Its mood board theme would be fun.

Minutes later, Electra bounded down the steps, jingling the rental key. "Okay," she said, popping into the car, "the house is close to here. She gave me a local map, so I'll show you."

Two blocks away, we found the house down a side street near the beach. The no-frills interior matched the outside with simple, indestructible furniture and a comfy couch. Midnight blue curtains framed the expansive sliding glass exit to the garden, where a metal table and chairs awaited on a concrete slab decorated with potted daisies and lavender. The fenced-in area, shaded by pine trees, was a perfect space for Alessandro to play and investigate. There was even a croquet set.

After bringing in the luggage, I got Alessandro ready for the beach. There, we strolled onto the endless soft sand, deserted by the post-lunch siesta Italians loved. One or two modern hotels dotted the curve of the five-mile-long beach, worthy of a spread in any travel magazine. There must be so many fantastic hidden bays and little nooks to visit in Italy that I had yet to discover—oases where the locals escape the loud, obnoxious invasion of tourists.

I straightened the corners of the big beach towel claiming our patch of sand, while Electra twisted in the umbrella post. Her big worries were sunburns and pesky food-stealing seagulls. Alessandro crawled underneath the shade, and it wasn't long before sand entered his mouth. Luckily, a juice box helped with the sand extraction procedure, though he impatiently pushed my hand away. Electra lay on her stomach to read her book about toddler development while Alessandro dug with a yellow toy shovel, filling and refilling a bucket under my eagle eye. By this time, I was used to tending to his every need like a valet.

After a big stretch, Electra arose and dusted the sand off her body. "Alessandro, my love," Electra purred, taking off her sunglasses. "Let's go for a swim."

I smiled. "Will this be his first time in the ocean?"

She scanned the beach. "No, it will be his first time in the *sea*. The Adriatic is not an ocean. Seas are partially closed by land, and oceans are bigger." She turned and noted my reaction. "There is nothing wrong in being corrected. It's how you learn. I can teach you more than Italian."

"My mind is open for any knowledge," I said, batting my eyelashes. She picked up Alessandro and walked to the tiny ripples of the surf. He clung to her bathing suit, eyeing the vast bathtub below him with trepidation. Not wanting to miss his first dip or a chance to offer help, I followed as she meandered further into the shallow water. Soon, she was thigh-deep with a wailing Alessandro. I lowered down to float close by, using my hands to propel myself along the sandy bottom as I blew bubbles into the water like a motorboat.

"You got this, Alessandro," I cheered as he quieted, watching my sputtering.

Electra softly bounced up and down with wide-eyed Alessandro in her arms, acclimating him with little splashes. Her disfiguring scar was more visible on her bare throat, and she covered the crimson mark with her hand when she caught my glance.

"It's not pretty, I know. The doctors said the scar will always be there. It happened when I was five years old," she said. "An accident." Her fingers smoothed over the scar tenderly. "My fault."

I flipped over to my back. "Can I ask what happened?"

"Of course. You should hear this story." She looked into the distance, deep in thought. "I was in the kitchen with my young nanny, Xinyi. She cooked my special pasta that day. She told me to wait in my chair while she went to get herbs from the garden. Because I was stupid and spoiled, I didn't wait and grabbed grapes from the fruit bowl and put the bunch in my mouth." She cringed at the memory.

I knew where she was going with the story. "Oh."

"Oh, is right. I don't know why I even drink wine," Electra lamented, fixing Alessandro on her hip before kissing him. "I heard Xinyi's footsteps and was afraid she'd be mad at me. I choked when I tried to swallow them all. She found me with blue lips and couldn't get the grapes out. Luckily, Xinyi picked me up and ran to our doctor's house, which was close by. It was so bad that he had to perform a tracheotomy. I was very lucky. Xinyi and the doctor saved my life. But my parents always blamed the accident on Xinyi."

"I'm sorry. That's awful."

"It was my fault; except they did not want to believe it. I stayed in the hospital for a month, wrapped in bandages. Xinyi was gone when I returned home, and I never saw her again. My parents had sent her away. She was more than a nanny to me. I miss her so much."

"You can't blame them. Any parent would have reacted the same way."

"I wouldn't have. I asked everyone where Xinyi went, but they played dumb. Back to China, I don't know. I wrote letters to her that my mother said she mailed. She lied though; I know that. I think of Xinyi often and the guilt she must have felt. I know she would love to see me, especially with Alessandro." The setting sun changed her eyes into sad green embers, and she kissed Alessandro again. Her face had a strange eeriness and seemed years younger through the filter of the clear water droplets. Alessandro's cherubic body glistened under a sheath of shine, and the pair became an idyllic sculpture of mother and child. She smirked. "You remind me of her."

"I do?"

"Yes. You'd do anything for my son. I know that in my soul." She came closer. "If anything happened, you'd have to contact Alessandro's father. I'll give you his number."

I thought of Anna Maria and the mother that Freja mentioned. "Are there any other family members I should contact in case of emergency?" I asked, the name Anna Maria on the tip of my tongue. "Just in case."

She shook her head, pursing her lips. "No. No one else matters." She held out Alessandro to me. "Can you take him? I want to get in a swim before dinner."

"Of course."

Her long arms carved the calm surface with perfect strokes, and the distance grew between us. The now-fearless Alessandro splashed his chubby fist into the warm sea and sputtered with a smile at his adorable reaction. I wiped his face, thinking of Electra's deep childhood pain,

Xinyi, and the teasing she must have gotten over the years. No wonder she seemed made of granite.

After changing our clothes in a cabana, we ate a late dinner at the café on the boardwalk. At sunset, visitors gathered under lamp-lit pagodas, sipping cocktails as kids played around, burning their ice cream-fueled adrenaline. Electra was her usual aloof self, fussing with Alessandro's hair or clothes as a distraction. Her invisible wall was back up, and now I understood why she was never interested in talking to people or offering a pleasant smile. She wasn't just shy—she was terrified to let her guard down.

We strolled back to the house after a quick stop for milk. Exhausted, Alessandro fell asleep without his usual nighttime bottle, and Electra and I watched *Charlie's Angels* dubbed in Italian. I tried to stay alert as the characters chattered, but the effects of the sun, salt, and sand took hold of my heavy eyelids. I fell asleep on the couch, content to have peeked into Electra's soul to answer a handful of my questions.

The following morning, while everyone slept, I slipped to the beach to photograph the sunrise. Also, I took pictures of forgotten sand buckets and a child's lone flip-flop for the mood board. Later, I hoped to get one of Alessandro eating a bowl of gelato. His dripping face would be the epitome of joy.

After my return, the morning hummed along its usual slow way. Alessandro played in the garden while Electra made breakfast. I was swinging in a hammock between tree trunks when Electra exited the sliding door with a platter of cut-up cantaloupe. A loud plunk hit the ground before her, and she almost dropped the tray. With a mio dio, Electra glared up at the sky and down at her feet. "What is this?" she said, kicking the object. "Ow. It's huge."

I squinted at the dark object, then went closer to examine it. I looked upward through the tree branches and noticed the large ornaments. "It fell from the pine tree. I think it's the world's biggest pinecone," I said, swiping it from the ground and weighing it in my hand. The mango-sized brown object was at least a pound.

"A pinecone?" She put the melon tray down, scanning the five-story pine trees with thick trunks and broad canopies. Jagged outlines of large pinecone clusters were visible, clinging to branches like grenades against the lazy Sunday morning sky. "That bomb fell from that tree!"

Another plummeted, landing next to Alessandro, who was depetalling a tulip in the garden. With a blood-curdling scream, Electra bolted to protect his body as she squinted upwards for another to drop with horror. "Help, Jayne. Call the police."

"The police?"

"Yes. Oh, for god's sake." She grabbed Alessandro and fled into the house, crouching as if under enemy fire. Alessandro protested while I scrambled inside with his bottle and the tray. Electra grabbed the phone and waved to me to be quiet. Minutes later, she ended her conversation. "Si. Ora. Grazie." *Yes. Now. Thanks.* She hung up, visibly shaking.

I doubted they'd dispatch squad cars for falling pinecones and hoped she wouldn't be disappointed. "What did they say?" I finally asked.

"They're on their way."

Minutes later, two police officers arrived and inspected the yard, sharing amused glances about the situation. Electra gesticulated about a pinecone falling on Alessandro, and the men frowned with skepticism, perhaps assessing her mental stability. I helped her case by pointing to the significant dent where the pinecone had landed. Unimpressed, they uneasily shifted their weight, taking notes on a tiny pad as we went inside.

They left after a quick indoor inspection, yet Electra wasn't satisfied. Her face became an abstract configuration of worry and concern as she paced the floor, talking to herself. She barely noticed I'd burned Alessandro's oatmeal and mistakenly used part of an overripe banana for his puree. Finally, she stopped and slammed the counter with her hands, declaring the agency would return her rent. We were in the car and outside the rental office ten minutes later.

"Don't say a word," she said, fixing her blouse. "Let me do the talking."

Electra, Alessandro, and I entered the agency's modern, slick office with shiny marble floors and glossy walls decorated with Lignano travel posters. A man at the front table said ciao to us but grew concerned when Electra rushed past with clenched fists. At a back table, an older couple in Hawaiian-print clothes talked to an overly made-up agent dressed in white jeans and a coral beachy top. Electra barreled into the conversation, and the male customer jumped back in fright, clutching his chest. Stunned, the agent gave a little yelp and stood up.

Electra pulled the giant pinecone from her bag and slammed it on the workspace. "This almost killed my son," she said in Italian.

The agent picked up the pinecone, glaring at Electra. "E pigno. Lignano e pigno tutti," she said, twirling a finger around her temple at the couple and commenting on Electra's inability to understand the pinecones were a part of Lignano's natural habitat. She went to a poster and pointed to the pine trees with an exaggerated eye roll. "Tutto Lignano."

Electra signaled for me to come forward. She then took Alessandro out of the stroller, using him as a prop as she balanced him on her hip. Petting his hair with a sad face, the retelling of the near-death story got personal and tragic. When she finished, the agent tossed the pinecone in the air with a smile, remarking to the other couple as she raised her arms, exasperated. They let out a peal of laughter that infuriated the nostril-flaring Electra.

"Uh oh," I said under my breath. I glanced at the door, ready to run.

"Mio dio." She pulled the contract from her bag and waved it in the agent's face. At this time, the agent from the front hurried to join the conversation. He took the contract from Electra and pointed to the signature line. "Non possible," he said, reading the clause that said the rent was nonrefundable.

The nodding agent joined in. "Non possible, Signora di Caneva."

She took the paper from him and handed it back to Electra. "Finito. Arrivederci," she said with disgust. *I'm finished. Goodbye.*

Fuming, Electra stuffed it into her bag and shouted words I didn't understand. She beelined to the exit with Alessandro, and I trailed behind as the group murmured and laughed.

When I opened my car door, I found her sitting silently in the front seat, twisting her ring. I held my keys, waiting for her to erupt. Was she going to go back to the police station? Or a lawyer? Staring ahead, she was too quiet. I didn't know what to do.

An older man closed the car door next to us, and she snapped out of her fog. Her door flew open, and she jumped out to knock on his window. He rolled it down, answering her rapid-fire questions with the word *municipio*, which means town hall. He pointed across the parking lot to the exit, spewing directions. She thanked him and got back in the car. "We're going to the town hall," she said as I turned the ignition.

"What are you going to do? Talk to the mayor? Sue the agency?"

"No." She gave me the stink eye. "That's so American. I will do this *my* way."

Five minutes later, we arrived in front of the stucco town hall, and Electra marched in after dropping Alessandro and me off at a bustling café. I drummed my fingers on the table while he gobbled a cornetto, curious about what she was doing. With her, anything was possible, and I was worried. I had never seen her so upset.

After an hour, she returned in better spirits, urging me to hurry and finish my Diet Coke. She proclaimed that someone was coming by the house in less than two hours. "Why?" I asked before taking the last sip. "Are they going to rent it from you?"

She smirked. "You'll see," she said coyly.

After Alessandro went down for his nap, her unknown plan began. First, she found her Rolleiflex camera, which she treated with the utmost care. The odd camera had been her father's, and she had used it to take hundreds of pictures.

But she didn't need the camera. In the case was a black plastic light meter. Electra often used the light meter when taking a picture of Alessandro with a dark background. However, this time it was different. She slinked around the house, pointing the instrument at corners and jotting down its readings near sunlight and furniture. After loosening a dark curtain from its hook, she brought it to the large glass doors and glanced at the meter with a satisfied smirk.

"What's the plan?" I asked, trying to decipher her actions. Was she going to photograph the house? Send pictures to the newspapers?

She ignored my question. "Get me all the dark towels from the bathroom," she ordered, glancing at her watch. "Hurry. They'll be here soon."

I gathered the navy towels and waited for further instructions while she rushed outside, scanning the sky. Returning, she snapped her fingers and pointed to the arm of the couch. "Put a towel there," she said, gliding her hand over the armrest. "Any spots with sunshine are a no-no. Bright places will make the readings too high." I did what she asked, and after she unscrewed the lightbulbs, she finally seemed satisfied with what she had accomplished.

"What now?" I said with a laugh. "Turn off the sun?"

"Funny. I wish I could." Overwhelmed, she scrutinized the room, biting her nails. "When they come, I want you to stand before the sliding door." The doorbell rang, and she jumped in a panic. "If he wakes up, put Alessandro's highchair closer to you and block the window." She pointed to a sunspot on a chair. “Put his bib there now. Pretend you don’t speak Italian,” she whispered, reaching for the door handle.

Two older men stood outside, and she ushered them in with a smile. Dressed in jeans and polo shirts, one had a briefcase and the other a notepad. Both entered with apprehension. Maybe they had been forewarned.

“Grazie,” Electra said before launching into the story as she brought the men into the garden. She reenacted the landing of the colossal pinecone and pointed to the crime scene. On cue, a pinecone fell with a kaboom, confirming her claim.

They returned inside, and one of the men explained with a sympathetic voice that people loved Lignano Sabbiadoro for the pine trees, which were part of the landscape and aura. Electra patiently listened with folded arms as he explained that a pinecone falling from a tree was as normal as a bird flying in the sky.

After he finished, she pulled the light meter out of her pocket like a gun from a holster. With confidence and a flick of her hair, she bounced around the room, reading aloud numbers as the men trailed behind her. One jotted each reading, sharing confused expressions with his colleague with each notation. When she completed ten, a document appeared from her bag, and she offered it with the authority of a Julius Caesar proclamation. “My defense,” she said in Italian, puffing out her chest and pointing to the paper.

The men gazed at the document before their attention darted to the light meter and around the house. They exchanged knowing glances and turned their backs to whisper. Electra winked at me with her hands behind her back and waited while they conversed in hushed tones, comparing numbers. Finally, the expressionless men spun around and handed back the paper. “Si. La casa non buona abitare.” *Yes. The house is uninhabitable.*

Electra released an elated yelp and gave me a thumbs up as one of the men completed an official certificate that the house was uninhabitable with a heavy sigh. He signed it with a flourish and ripped off one of the copies with a dejected look. "Grazie," she said, taking the copy from his hands.

Alessandro made a noise in the back bedroom, and I absconded to check on him. The front door shut, and Electra removed the towels from the couch as I returned to the room. "Very impressive. Touché. I'm sure that was a first for them," I remarked as Alessandro shuffled across the floor, holding my hand. "Were they mad?"

"Mad? Them? Jayne, you must stop being the victim. Why should *they* be angry at me? The law shows this house is not habitable." She took Alessandro and hugged him tightly. "The lady at the agency with her Bazooka outfit didn't care about my family's safety. She made your mama very upset. And that is one thing you do not want to do. How can I live in a place that will hurt you?"

"They came from the town hall?"

"Yes. Those men were officials. When I went into the town hall, I asked about the pinecones, and they said everyone has them and it was part of life in Lignano. They say tourists paint them. Do you believe it?"

"Wow. They could use them as doorstops. Or weapons."

She basked in her glory with a wide grin. "Yes. Wow, as you Americans say. Wow, wow, wow."

"But how did you know about the light needed for a house to be considered habitable?"

She tapped the side of her temple. "Oh. I don't think like other people, you know. I'm a fox and look for any hole to escape. My father always said I was smart." She seemed pleased at my interest and became animated. "First, the town hall person said to go to the public health department and complain. So, I did, and a woman with a duck face gave me a list of regulations. I read the long list in her office, and there was nothing about garden safety or those awful pinecones. So, I thought it was over."

Her face brightened. "*But* before I closed the book, a chapter on health codes stopped me. That's when I read the standard for natural light must be no less than thirty lux," she said, sweeping her hand across the room. "I know how much light there is because I always use my light meter to take photos; this place has less than thirty lux."

"That's wild," I said, scanning the dark room. "And I agree with your father. You're a sly one." It was darker when the massive pine trees blocked the late afternoon sunlight, so her timing was impeccable. It was her last-ditch attempt against all odds, and the countess had played a perfect hand. Nothing could stand in her way when fighting for what she believed was right. Admirable. "So, I guess we're outta here?"

"Yes, it's justice for us, and we are leaving this terrible house," she sang, picking up Alessandro. She danced around as he giggled at her silliness. "We'll have a beautiful dinner inside, so we don't get killed, and then go to the rental company tomorrow to get back what they owe me."

"Umm," I said, opening the empty refrigerator with only eggs, milk, and a head of lettuce. "There's not much here. Should I go to the store? Or are we going out?"

Electra stopped dancing. "No. I don't want to see anyone. That little pizza place near the supermarket smelled delicious. Take the car, and let's get a pie for tonight. It will be our adios dinner in Pinecone City Lignano. Then we'll pack and leave forever."

$ 925.75

Pizza	- 9.56
International Herald Tribune	- 1.50
Gettoni's	-10.00
Wooden train for Alessandro's birthday!	- 10.00
Tronky bar - amazing when dipped in espresso	-.86

$ 893.83

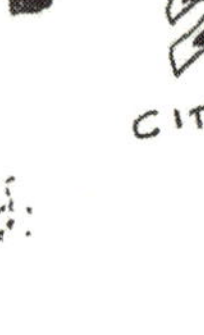

CHAPTER TEN

I PLACED THE WARM PIZZA on the front seat, still smiling from the town officials' double take when Electra pulled out her light meter. I don't know if her aristocratic upbringing or the centuries of wheeling and dealing with merchants had left a warrior imprint on her genes, but she could be a wrecking ball if someone got in her way. Poor victims like Roberto and the rental agent had no idea of her desire to win. Was it another explanation why there was no one in her life, perhaps? And what happened to Alessandro's father? How could he disappear from his son's life, I wondered? Perhaps he tried to stay but found it impossible. Her defiance strengthened my belief that her past must have been brutal. Xinyi. Her family. The loss of her father. The scar. Her desire for justice was more complex than I had imagined.

The garlic aroma engulfed the car, and I happily reversed, tasting a slice in my mouth. The night would be easy with little packing since half of Alessandro's clothes were still in the suitcase. An evening stroll to the beach would be pretty, and I'm sure Electra would get gelato since she'd succeeded in her goal and beat the rental agency. I giggled to myself, imagining the unsuspecting agency woman entering the gelateria and a cone landing on her head.

Suddenly, a *Titanic*-hitting-an-iceberg crunch sounded, and my body jerked forward. In my rear-view mirror was a block of dimpled grey—a large tree trunk.

"What the hell?" I pulled the car forward to a ripping metal sound and cringed with fear as I got out to investigate. The facts were black and white. I hit a tree, and there was now a giant horseshoe-shaped dent in the car's bumper.

"Oh. My. God. Electra will kill me," I cried, touching the U-shaped indentation. I checked the parking lot for witnesses, but it was before the dinner rush, and the only person there was me. But another tree stood in the distance. Trees planted in the middle of a parking lot? I had never seen it before and cursed my luck. How had I not seen it when I'd driven into the space? Hunger and derelict pinecones were on my mind, and I'd missed it. "Who puts trees in the middle of a frigging parking lot?" My hands fell to my side. "Italy, of course, where even parking lots must be beautiful."

I got back in the car, weighing my options. Electra would freak out with the shocking news that her precious presidential mobile now had a sledgehammer-sized dent. I prepared myself for whining about how she should have bought an army tank. And the cost of a fancy bumper replacement? Also, the plan was to leave for the rental agency early in the morning, and now, with this new disaster, a stop at a garage would delay us.

"Argh," I wailed, hitting my palm against the steering wheel. A pizza employee exited his establishment and lit a cigarette, oblivious to my accident. Gray poured from his smokestack nostrils, and I swallowed my nicotine urge earned during stressful college days, trying to think of a reasonable excuse for the dent. Of course, the Citroen DS bumper wasn't a cheap Fiat one that two taps of a teaspoon would fix.

"Damn those baguette eaters." Even *if* I could keep it a secret, it wouldn't be like I could swing into any garage and have it replaced in an hour. Body shops were closing, and I had only passed one Citroen DS on the road. The non-Italian bumper would have to be an expensive order from France. That price tag would be astronomical. Also, whenever the speedometer got close to the speed limit, Electra repeatedly warned me to slow down because she hadn't bought insurance. Of course, the offices had closed for the summer. Since this was my fault, I'd be at least three hundred—if not more—out of pocket. How could I fix this?

Frustrated, I quickly drove to the gas station we had passed on the edge of town, praying for a miracle. Luckily, when I screeched in, a mechanic on duty examined the mishap with his oily hands. From what I understood in his broken English and my elementary Italian, the bumper could take five days to arrive. And when he rubbed his fingertips together, I got the universal meaning of expensive.

Discouraged, I drove back, my stomach in turmoil. When I pulled up to the house, a pile of suitcases was by the front door, and I groaned. Not wanting Electra to see the dent, I rushed from the car to collect the bags and stuffed them into the trunk. Before I could close it, Electra hurried into the front yard with a handful of Alessandro's toys. "Oh, you're back. You were gone for an hour. I was getting worried," she said.

"Sorry. The guy took a long time. Hey, I got those," I said, wrangling the toys from her. "Go back in. I'll bring the pizza."

She ignored my request. "I'll get it. You finish the bags."

I blocked her, pointing to the house. "No. Go inside," I ordered as if I had pulled a sheriff's badge on her. Electra's breath sucked in at my audacity, yet I remained stoic. "You … you might get killed with a pinecone … and Alessandro will be without a mother. Then what?"

She paused, uncertain if I was joking or not. But it worked, and she hurried into the home with her hands over her head.

Wiping away perspiration, I packed the trunk quickly, leaving enough space for my little bag. When I returned to the kitchen, an impatient Alessandro pounded a fork on his highchair tray for dinner. Electra had set the table with a salad, and she was rifling through the drawers for more utensils, mumbling to herself.

"Here's the pizza," I trilled, putting it on the counter with the car keys. I wrinkled my nose when she neared the box. "You know what? Can I finish packing? I'm not too hungry now," I said as my stomach growled in disdain. "If you don't mind, just save me a slice for later."

"*You're* not hungry? It's pizza. Your favorite. Do you feel okay?" She slid a slice onto a plate and handed it to me. "Before you go, can you cut this up for Alessandro? I need to get the plastic bib," she said, taking the car keys. "It's in the beach bag."

"No," I shouted a little too loudly. I had thrown the bag to the back and knew exactly where it was. The dish landed back in Electra's hands. "*I'll* get the bib. You cut and sit. It's been an incredibly stressful day, and you need to rest. Have a glass of wine."

"We don't have any." She placed the plate slowly on the counter with an unbroken stare. "And I got rid of the stress, remember? I'm fine … I'll be right back."

"No. Eat your pizza," I demanded as I took the keys from her. "*I'll* be two seconds."

I flew out before she could stop me and raced to the back of the car. When I opened the trunk, its contents fell onto the driveway, and I tossed them back haphazardly. The beach hemp bag was on the bottom, and I yanked it free.

"I found the bib," Electra yelled over my shoulder. I swung around, and she cradled Alessandro, now wearing his plastic elephant bib and sucking a pizza crust in his mouth. Her hat was a spaghetti strainer, and she balanced a metal pot above Alessandro with her free hand. "It was on the rail on the oven door. You must have put it there after breakfast."

"Oh. Good." The trunk was still open, and I twisted my body to block her view. I sat on the bumper and pointed up to the clouds. "Look. A bird has a pinecone!" Their attention turned, and I put my hands on Electra's back to twist her body from the car. "Oops. Too bad. It flew away. But let's have pizza. I'm starving," I said with an after-you gesture as she gave me a curious stare. "What? My appetite is back. Time to celebrate our victory. Let's par-tay."

The following day, I snuck out to the Citroen and reversed it to within centimeters of the house so Electra wouldn't spot the bumper damage. After breakfast, there was enough chaos that she didn't notice the dent, and we arrived at the agency mid-morning. Alessandro and I waited in the car while Electra barged in, waving the official certificate, and demanding a refund. She bounded out of the office five minutes later with a big smile.

"That dragon lady was so mad. She called the police to say I was wrong, but they said no. Ha. Do you believe I got my refund?" she panted, jumping into the back seat of our getaway car. She dangled the paper at the agency, sticking her tongue out as I peeled out of the parking spot. The agent gesticulated wildly in the doorway while her colleagues threw up their arms in protest.

Electra blew out her cheeks and sat back. "The police told her it's not their business, and they said if the town signed the document, they could do nothing. The law is the law, and there is nothing she can do about it."

"Well, she will never forget you,' I said. "You definitely made an impression."

She smiled at my comment, twirling the ring around her finger. "I thought of my father, and he'd do the same thing." She included more details, and I listened, glad to have the whole incident behind us. She finally went back to reading her book, and Alessandro fell asleep. I thought of my fun mood board, pressing my lips together. At least I'd gotten five beach photos.

A red light dinged on the dashboard, and I squinted to view it better. The car needed gas. Miles later, I pulled into a gas station, worried about the dent. Electra closed her book and took off her cat-eye readers to scan the pump activity. I didn't move while an unshaven attendant in cobalt overalls pumped our gas after I quickly instructed him to fill it up. He took the credit card and put it into the manual machine while the tank filled loudly underneath us.

But when he crouched to study the bumper, my pulse skyrocketed. I watched him straighten up to write the license plate on the slip with a concerned look. He came to my side and pointed to the back of the car, ready to talk, until I cut him off.

"Si, lo so. *Yes, I know*," I said, smiling to take the slip to be signed. I handed it to Electra, clenching my teeth.

"Oh boy," Electra said, handing me back the signed slip. She unbuckled her seat belt. "Don't leave yet. You know what again."

The man took the receipt, and I sniffed the air. "What? He's fine. It's only baby gas. Too many onions." I turned the ignition and grimaced. The man didn't leave, peering at Electra and Alessandro in the back and then me.

His mouth opened again to speak. "Grazie mille," I said, closing the window before he said anything. I pulled away from the pump a bit too fast.

Electra tapped me on the shoulder. "Jayne. Your nose isn't smelling. This car stinks," she said, waving to a free parking space. "Go there. He needs a new diaper. I can't let him sit in poop."

Reluctantly, I parked the car and unbuckled. A glance over my shoulder told me the man had gone on to his next customer. "I'll take him. You don't need to come," I said, reaching for the diaper bag. "Just stay where you are, and you know, read."

But she already had him out of the seat when my door closed. She studied the small convenience store across the lot and put on her sunglasses. "I'm going to see if they've got fresh fruit."

"Fresh fruit from that place? Are you serious? If they do, it's *definitely* not organic," I said, growing impatient. "It's glow-in-the-dark junk from Chernobyl. Let's find a healthy supermarket and a clean bathroom, so I can change Alessandro there."

"Signora, signora," the attendant called to Electra.

Electra turned to look at him and then at me. "What does he want? Didn't we pay him?"

"Of course, we did. Let's go. He looks weird," I said, wheeling around to the store as the man approached us. I tried to shepherd Electra and Alessandro faster into the mini mart; however, the man caught up.

"Signora? Signora?" he said, stopping right in front of Electra. "Hai visto la tua ammaccatura?" *Did you see your dent?*

Her face fell. "Ammaccatura?" *Dent?*

The attendant nodded with "Si," and beckoned her to join him at the car's rear. I gave her an I-don't-know shrug, and she reluctantly followed him. At the car, he slid his hand over the bumper, shaking his head with disapproval while a bewildered Electra fingered her pearl choker with tuts, listening. My insides tightened when she looked at me aghast. "Did you see this damage? I can't believe those agents did this."

I hesitated before responding, stepping closer to touch the smooth rubber and metal. My mouth dropped with feigned disbelief. "This is outrageous. I can't believe they did this to the car. What monsters."

She looked back towards Lignano. "They must have smashed it this morning. The officials must have told them about the refund and that rental mafioso came and hammered the car when we were sleeping."

I gulped at her imagination. "That's … unreal."

She felt the dent again. "Did you see or hear anything last night when packing the car? Anything suspicious?"

I put my hand on my chin and thought for a moment. "I don't know. There was someone who passed me when I was packing."

Her finger wagged in the air. "See? See?"

"But I was busy, so that could have been a neighbor or someone going to the beach." I put my finger on my lips and looked skyward. "There was a slight push. I mean, it was a little windy, so maybe it was—"

"Scusi." The man broke into my story. "I speak little, little English. Poco. I hear you say. No one smash," he said, pretending to strike the car at the dent sight. "Not possible."

Electra folded her arms. "Why?"

"No possible. Il palo." *A pole.* My stomach sank as he guessed the exact scenario from the parking lot but said a pole-like structure, not a tree. He described his theory, and we all got the gist. Every detail was correct except for the pizza in the front seat. "Perfetto," he said, outlining the dent. His eyes met mine for the final blow. "Only drivers do this."

Electra frowned at his hard-to-believe explanation. "No. Non possible," she protested. The man shrugged, and she spun in my direction. "Did *you* back into a pole?"

"Me?" Technically, it was a tree, not a pole, I thought, playing it cool. "A pole? No. Absolutely not."

The man didn't help my case by reenacting the scene, and his theatrical whiplash of a driver backing into an object was Oscar-worthy. I shrugged and tried to look blameless, but my conscience couldn't take it. I snapped my fingers. "Wait. Now I remember. I thought it was just another pinecone. When I picked up the pizza, I did feel this itsy-bitsy tap in the back of the car," I confessed, putting my thumb and forefinger together as close as possible without touching.

The man beamed, and Electra gave me an are-you-serious expression. She turned to him. "I miel piu sinceri ringraziamenti per la vostra attenzione. Il mistero e risolto." *Thank you very much for your attention to this matter. The mystery is solved.*

Alessandro pulled at Electra's shirt as the man proposed to fix it for a million lire, which meant a thousand dollars. She waved him away, and the man shrugged, retreating to the pumps. Left alone, I watched her carry Alessandro and the diaper bag through the automatic doors, knowing I was going to need a solution to pay for this goddamn stupid dent.

The drive was going to be tense. Should I admit defeat and go home?

A subtle scenic transformation happened when we left Lignano, and the fascinating view quelled my anxiety about the cost of the dent, which could send me back to square one. Vineyards, towering forests, and endless meadows with grazing cows and sheep entertained me. I had never heard of the Friuli Venezia Giulia region or its significant towns, Pordenone, Udine, or Gorizia, but I had heard of its harbor capital, Trieste. Tucked into Italy's eastern corner, its territory extended from the Julian Alps to the Adriatic Sea and was not a must-see destination like Tuscany or Sardinia. Its shared borders with Austria and Yugoslavia had been the gateway for German and Slavic invaders centuries ago, and the dark forests gave the area a chilly edge. The marauder element still lurked in its hills, at least that's how it seemed to me.

Heading north, the biting cold veins of cascading streams enlivened the rocky uplands below ominous skies. Although it was a gorgeous area that caused gasps around every curve, from snow-capped peaks to overflowing lush pine forests, the warm soul of southern Italy was missing. Even the menu was different in the rustic trattoria where we stopped for lunch—sausages, mustard, cabbage, and a million white wines. Because it was Alessandro's birthday, Electra put a candle in an apple tart for Alessandro to blow out, and he was happy to open my present.

But every five miles, Electra brought up the subject of the dent. That, followed by deep sighs and casual murmurs highlighted with signs of the cross over her chest, added to my well-deserved guilt. Nevertheless, the root of her stress could also have been visiting her hometown of Caneva. Her name was di Caneva, the *di* meaning *of* Caneva. She was vague on any specific details or plans. I didn't know if we would visit her mother or sister and was afraid to ask as we passed a road sign for Caneva.

My mind drifted, imagining driving up a manicured driveway past cawing black ravens as high-spired towers and well-built fortresses dotted distant peaks. A stodgy tuxedoed butler would answer a gold-knobbed door with a sniveling expression as Electra's mother refused us admittance from the top of a staircase in a blood-red velvet dress, and her evil sister watched with glee behind heavy brocade curtains.

"I can't wait to visit the town named after your family," I said gingerly, glancing at her fingering her choker in the rear-view mirror. "Not many people have that opportunity." She shivered like my words stung her ears, so I tried to lighten the mood. "Near Milan, there was a sign for a town called Gorgonzola, and I couldn't believe it. It was so funny. Is there a Gorgonzola family in Italy?"

"I've never heard anyone with that last name. They must have immigrated to America," she huffed. "To follow dollar roads, diamond lakes, or whatever they say."

I held back from conveying my parents' inspiring immigration story. They came over with two-hundred-fifty bucks and a dream. It wasn't easy, yet they had succeeded. Seeing the rewards of hard work and perseverance was a lesson I learned to appreciate.

"Yes, America, those awful immigrants that made it into today's powerhouse. If it weren't for their risk-taking voyage for a better life, we'd be …" I'd let her finish it, I thought with an eye roll.

"Oh, please." She pulled out lipstick, which signaled a step onto her soapbox. Alessandro pawed to swipe it away, although he missed while she carefully applied it. "Have you heard of the Brenner Pass?" she said, smacking her lips.

High school history class of WWI soldiers running through the snow shooting at one another jumped into my brain. "The valleys between Austria and Italy? What about them? Does your family own one?" I scoffed.

"Yes … and no. It's a small mountain valley between Italy and Austria and has been important for centuries, millennia even, ever since the Romans came to the area. Our valley was on a major trading route between Europe and Asia. My ancestors were toll collectors for centuries. And back then, they were paid with *gold*," she said with a smile. "Gold never loses its value, you know. This area was part of the Austro-Hungarian empire before Italy stole it. So, we're not like other Italian families. We're more Austrian than Italian."

La-di-da. But I remember Freja's information, and I needed to know more. "How so?"

"Before the First World War, Tyrol and other parts of Italy were part of Austria. Venice owned half of Yugoslavia until it fell because of weak men, and the Hapsburgs took over. I'm fluent in German and consider it my language."

She droned on about the history of Italy and its northern neighbors, and I listened, passing signs for roadways to Innsbruck, Lienz, and other cities. She was her own favorite subject, and I wished I had a pinecone to toss in the back seat to stop her continuous history lesson. It was too much information to absorb, spewed from someone who assumed Italy and history had wronged her family.

The Alps in the foreground grew larger with each mile, squeezing fields and valleys tighter into their slice of land, and my mind drifted to Matteo. The stadium-sized green and yellow farming hills graced the side of the road as gusts blew acres of grass back and forth. Last year, we had a picnic in Central Park. I sighed. My body didn't ache for him anymore, although the disappointment still sloshed in our love's once-occupied sinkhole. But I had to look on the bright side. I was learning Italian from a real-life countess and experiencing the country off the beaten track added to the incredible gift of discovery.

"Jayne? Did you hear me?" Electra asked, tapping her ring against her armrest.

"No, I'm sorry. What did you say?"

"I said, let's pull over in one of the fields so that Alessandro can have his yogurt," she said slowly. "I'm stiff and need to stretch my legs."

"Will do, boss." The high meadows exploded with bee-hopping summer wildflowers, and I needed to pick and press pretty ones for my mood board, as blossoms were always inspirational. Electra gave me an old shopping bag to hold my discoveries and didn't blink when I said I was doing a mood board. I explained that it was a fashion travel journal and didn't mention it was for Gino.

"We can use it in Palawan," she said as I quietly groaned. A mowed hayfield looked like a promising spot for a picnic, and I slowed down at a shoulder pull-off underneath a tree's wide canopy. "This looks like a perfect place to stop," Electra directed from the back seat.

After gathering Alessandro's bag and a blanket from the back, we trudged to the top of a low hill as Alessandro's little hand delicately picked buttercups and pale blue forget-me-nots. He held them tightly, enjoying the gusts of fresh air and hillside exercise. When we reached the top, spruce forests garnished the grey rim of the mountains, and a cardinal-red cable car descended slowly as another passed it on its way up.

Electra read my awe. "It's the tramway at the Piancavallo ski resort. You can go to the top for the gorgeous view. I skied there as a child and may bring Alessandro next year. He'll love it."

She threw down the old blanket, and we sat on the warm grass surrounded by the craggy glacial summits of the snow-salted Dolomites. "If I break out into 'The Hills Are Alive,' you can't blame me," I said, laughing. "This is just like the opening scene of *The Sound of Music*."

"It is. Please don't ruin the moment," Electra said, hiding a smile.

We ate a simple picnic of yogurt and fruit, three specks in a painter's dream. From our vantage point, golden rapeseed fields pooled in the valley below, and slow-moving cows and sheep animated the far-reaching view. The sugary air of cut grass and pine brought back summer memories of barefoot hikes at a Catskills Girl Scout camp, and I lay back for a peaceful moment, watching birds soar across the sky and wondering how to put the spectacle on my mood board. "Nature is so kind," I said softly, closing my eyes.

"It is special here. My roots are deep in these valleys." Electra stood up and stretched. "The light is different—clearest in the world. The dry sweet air meets the breeze from the Adriatic, and the sun cuts through it so well. Do you feel the energy coming from the mountains?" she asked, glancing upward.

I squinted into the sunlight, taking a deep breath. "In the air, you mean?"

In a dream-like state, she made graceful Tai Chi-like motions around her. "Yes, it's magical. When I was little, Xinyi taught me to appreciate it. The shiny beams. Strong. Clear. The way it sharpens the trees and flowers. Me. You. Alessandro. Don't you see it? There is no humidity, and the particles weave a dance between the rays so well that it's pure harmony of nature. I can't explain it. This is Friuli."

I watched her move slowly like a long-legged crane, her arms extending out into the air like silk ribbons. "I let the tension leave my body," she said, bowing and wiggling her fingertips. "My breathing is centered, and my body balanced."

I rose and copied her gentle movements. Alessandro joined, and we all did twirls and yoga-like poses with gales of laughter. It felt good to release the anxiety of the past days through the moving meditation, and I felt better. After more twists and turns, she returned to the blanket, scooped up the resting Alessandro, and kissed him as he giggled. She turned to me. "Don't you feel divine? It's not healthy to sit all day and not move. But it's getting late. We should go."

I shook out the blanket as she hiked to the car with Alessandro. Xinyi had had an impact on Electra, that's for sure. Like a guru. Where was the woman now? Was she alive?

Suddenly, Electra screamed. "My ring," she exclaimed, swinging her arm around the grass. "My ring. It fell off." She held up her empty right hand at me.

"You're kidding," I shouted. "Where?"

"I don't know. My beautiful ring," she wailed. She put Alessandro on the ground and patted her clothes like they were on fire. She delved into Alessandro's tiny pockets and pulled out his petal pieces. Not finding the ring, Electra spun in circles, overwhelmed by the loss, moaning in despair.

"We'll find it, don't worry," I said, scanning the huge surrounding pasture. "When did you last remember twirling it?"

Her gaze ricocheted around the mown meadow. "When I got out of the car. The food. You got Alessandro," she listed on her fingers. "I think I had it then, and I twirled it, remembering when my father and I went hunting for a bear nearby."

"A bear?" I asked, distracted, and glanced at the vast lands and gulped. I held back from asking about bears in the area, and my desire to find the ring and leave increased. The green grass stained my sneakers, but I tried to stay positive, kicking the blades around me. “Okay … so when was the next time you remember having it? Did you have it when Alessandro had his yogurt?”

“Yes. No.” She paused, ready to cry. “I don’t know. Let’s go to the car and check if it’s there.”

We rushed to the car, and after a quick search, she poked out of the side. “It’s not here. It’s out there somewhere,” she cried, desperately throwing her hand to the field. “I know it is.” She clutched the fabric of her shirt. “I feel it.”

Frustrated, I scanned the acres of green. “I’m so sorry it’s gone,” I said, turning to her. “We should inform the farmer who owns the field about it. He may find it one day and can send it back to you.”

“One day?” she screamed. “No. It’s here. We are finding it now.”

“Look, I know this is important, and I’m really sorry it fell off your finger, but how can we find it in all this grass? It’s impossible. That field is huge, and we walked everywhere,” I said, putting sleepy Alessandro in his car seat.

“No, it’s possible. For you, no. For me, yes.” She stomped onto the field, tossing her hair over her shoulder before raising her stretched arms to the sky with artistic execution. Her face tilted upward, and her eyes shut tightly. “Papa, please come down and help me find your ring. All my departed ancestors, relatives, and friends, please help me. I need your guidance, *please*.” She paused and whispered, thinking I couldn’t hear. “Papa, I know you are there. Help us.” Then she prayed and made a sign of the cross when she finished.

Before I could react, she had already found a stick and swatted the hay from her path with gusto. I found another and reluctantly began the same procedure, hoping she’d give up soon. Luckily, Alessandro was asleep and didn’t have to witness the futility.

The endless green grass made me dizzy under the blazing sun. I cursed, using every expletive to relieve the stress of inspecting each inch of the field. The knees and hem of my jeans turned dark green, and my throat burned from dehydration. "This is ridiculous," I said aloud. "Are you okay?"

Electra looked up, full of hope. "What? You found it?"

My shoulders dropped. "No. I was asking if you're okay."

"I am. Continue." Electra was now army crawling on hands and knees, examining each tuft of grass in her woolen blazer and heavy pants. Sweat poured off her face; she was on a mission and determined. The plea to her ancestors from wherever was weird and a homage I'd never experienced—yet still, I respected it.

"We need to drink water before we pass out." Perspiration trickled down my back, and I glanced at the scribble of trees, dying to lie down under their canopy and rest. My temples twinged with an oncoming migraine, and my legs ached. Wanting to stop this nutty charade before we died of heatstroke, I was ready to open my mouth to complain when a band of gold flashed on the green path.

I bent down and picked it up. Warm and round. The ring.

"I found it!" I shouted, holding it up in victory. Electra whooped joyfully and raised her fists, cheering in Italian as she ran to me.

She put the ring on and then threw her arms around me. Seconds later, she stepped back and held my shoulders, staring deep into my soul. I expected a ton of gratitude, and my cheek muscles hurt.

"*You* said it was impossible," she said, "and that's when *I* knew it was possible."

$ 893.83

AUGUST 1ST

-20.00

Gettoni's -24.69

Supplies - Candy, Vogue, map - 7.60

Gelato x 4 - TORRONE AND TIRAMISU - BEST!

-12.43

MOOD BOARD PURCHASES - NEED MORE PICS!

JULY SALARY - HIT ONE THOUSAND! + 400.00

$ 1,229.11

CHAPTER ELEVEN

"YOU'RE NOT TALKING," she said from the back seat.

I harrumphed, still stewing over her cutthroat comment. Her passive-aggressive quips were beyond annoying. You think she'd be grateful I had found her family heirloom. If I had more money, and if it weren't for my suitcase full of expensive clothes at Matteo's or being in the middle of nowhere with her and Alessandro, I'd be on the side of the road hitchhiking to the airport.

She sighed. "It's not healthy. Doctors say—"

"I didn't appreciate your comment *after* I found your precious ring," I exploded.

"I don't know why you're taking it so out of context," she started. "You Americans—"

"Stop," I said, raising my hand. "*You Americans this, you Americans that*. I'm sick of you running down my country. What about you Italians? The Italian men? Hello? *Bella this, Bella that,* they say it every time they pass anything with cleavage. In New York, men never do that. Here, men ogle women so blatantly, like slobbering wolves. And let's not talk about governments. At least we have decades of stability instead of three days. What about the recession here? Your economy? How many years has your damn government been in chaos?"

"Watch your language, please." She shifted in her seat. "I didn't mean to hurt you. I'm sorry."

"You did. I mean, look at me. I left my life in New York, came to Italy with everything I owned, was dumped like used furniture on the side of the street by my would-be fiancé, and then moved to a city I'd never even been to. Here I am with you, and I'm a surprisingly capable au pair. And chauffeur. Talk about making the impossible possible."

"You're right. You were left with nothing. Now you have us, and I appreciate you driving us to each destination."

I groaned quietly. It wasn't what I meant, but I knew any argument was already a dead-end. While Hannah and friends were busy with active and fulfilling lives in Manhattan, I was playing the part of Julie Andrews in this wannabe tour of whatever-the-hell-history. "I just needed to vent. Let's drop it."

Electra sighed. "I didn't mean to hurt you. You're on a journey as much as I am. When I asked my relatives to help me, maybe they said up there, *Electra, we did that already. She's standing right next to you.*"

I was speechless at her sentimental outpouring. Did she just imply I was a godsend? We passed a sign for Caneva, and I snatched the opportunity to change the subject because my thoughts were all over the place. "I think we're in your town," I said, driving over a bridge above a turquoise river.

We entered the village of three-story white stucco houses with a beautiful church on a hill with a grey campanile. The next sign had a knife and fork pizzeria logo next to a small castello sign and an arrow. Castello meant castle, and I canvassed the hills for a magical chateau, waiting for a magnificent fortress to appear on a rock promontory as a chorus of Hallelujah echoed in the valley. Alessandro threw his toy to the front seat, tired of the drive, and I slowed down, searching the landscape for a castle. "Am I going the right way?"

"There," she said, pointing to a large stone wall punctured with small gaps and a sign saying PROPRIETA PRIVATA. Behind it was a large iron gate. "I'll open the gate."

It was heavy, but she pushed it open through the overgrown grass. Soon, we were slowly bobbing up the steep lane as I avoided potholes on the dusty driveway, passing small structures that Electra would randomly call out. "That's the slaughterhouse. Over there is the dovecote. See that tree. My father said it had the best apples."

The driveway widened and around the last corner, an abandoned, three-story grey stone structure with massive arches had nefarious ivy dressing it into a swamp monster. I drove through the broken down gates, confused. A large watchtower was in its center, and the missing massive doors sent a chill down my back. "Is this it?" I asked, wondering if the real one was behind it.

"Of course, it is. It has been here for almost a thousand years. What did you expect? Disneyland?"

I pursed my lips and parked the car fifty feet away. While I gathered Alessandro, she enthusiastically hurried to the abandoned building like she was home for Christmas. I trotted behind, stepping over thick tree roots and trying not to slip on the moss-coated rocks surrounding the stone structure, dodging curious lizards who had come out to greet us. When I entered, Electra had already climbed the dark windy stairs to the top of the watch tower. Following her voice, I found her patting the twenty-foot rudimentary wall like a well-behaved horse.

"This is our history, my beautiful boy," she said, taking Alessandro from me. She brought him closer to the wet wall and put his hand on a stone next to a large opening. "This is where our ancestors began it all.

We made this valley. Our blood is in its earth. Once upon a time, long ago, we ruled as far as you can see." She then pointed to the bell tower I'd missed behind the castle. "See that over there? It's been here for hundreds of years. The bell still tolls when they have harvest festivals in the village. It's a tradition. We have to come in the autumn for the next one."

I nodded, sensing importance as the stronghold's history emanated from the stones under my feet. Not everyone could wander around the ruins of an ancient fortress and trace where relatives built their legacy before the Middle Ages. An eerie feeling that ghosts of courtiers and fair pretty maidens were all around us swirled in the wind, surrounded by pots of gold and exotic spices. Torch flames of sunlight framed the stone archway and flickered from past battles and death. Taking a step back to appreciate the ruins and the grandeur after Electra left, I absorbed the centuries of history with its wide-arched opening and medieval damp rawness, wishing to know more.

"Come see here," Electra shouted to me. I scrambled up the opening as she tried to control her hair from the high vista's gusts. "Look at my view."

"It's wonderful." A timeless jumble of red-tiled roofs and pointy spires of her ancestral village bordered a large azure lake, and northward, the Alps rose like a gray, heavy dough. "And it is so cool that all your ancestors stood here as well," I said into the sharp breeze as I took a picture for my mood board. "I'm sure this view hasn't changed at all."

"Yes, the view is the same. Except so much of the castle is gone from wars and weather. The archaeologists have taken truckloads of the artifacts away, and I should demand to see them." She pulled a stray hair from her mouth. "They're in a museum now, I'm sure."

She seemed to be on the verge of tears. "That's a great contribution to this region's Italian history. It should make you feel like you're giving back."

She didn't look enthused. "I guess. But I let my father down. He used to come here as a child and kept it like a park. He told me they would have fires in the fireplaces and roast a pig. Now the farmers use the land for grazing, so at least the castle grounds were better preserved. That's important."

We stepped back and trekked to the center of the citadel, its high walls protecting us from the sharp channeled winds. A lone sparrow nibbled on the ground, and I glanced at pensive Electra. "Are you ... *sad* when you come here? Is that why you haven't been here in years?"

Her lips formed a thin line. "Yes. Very. More disappointment than anything. Every time I visit, it looks worse than before. My father would be depressed to see it this way. Empty and abandoned. No love. The wear and tear of time steals our history from my family daily. The fruit trees need pruning and the soil tilling. I've let him down." She threw her arms in all different directions. "Rocks are missing. Trespassers walk all over the walls and ruin them. There is no respect for my family's history. Even the trees are taller and allow no sunlight, so the vines strangle the past like snakes," she said, wringing her hands. "My only hope is that Alessandro visits it with his family one day, and one wall will still stand here. A piece of glory from the di Caneva family."

"Can you work with the locals to help your castle? Do you want to stay in the area and try to fix it up?"

She groaned. "I would love to, but there is a trust, and the family controls it. It's out of my hands."

I left her alone to grapple with her family's fight against time. A mood board theme with a nostalgic lean toward bygone eras seemed appropriate. Speculating on the castle's future, I took pictures of arches and porticos while Alessandro threw pebbles over the earthen walls. Around the castle perimeter, beer cans and broken boxes hid in the tall grasses, and cigarette butts dotted the green grass. Passing a fire pit full of wine bottles, I was relieved that at least no graffiti vandalized the castle's rocks. Abstract art and lettering would be the beginning of the end.

We left the dispiriting area and returned to the town for dinner. "I need local food to brighten my day. You must try the cjalsons," she said, showing them to me on the special menu of the local trattoria we had found. She caught my questioning gaze. "I used to eat them all the time, and they have them tonight. They are a specialty in Friuli. Little ravioli."

"Sounds like just what the doctor ordered." Although cjalson didn't seem Italian, they tasted it. Like ravioli or dumplings, the spinach-stuffed dish had Parmesan and cinnamon flavors, which was different from the usual. The desserts had the same name, and we split a plate with assorted jam fillings.

After my stomach was Thanksgiving-level full, I secretly unsnapped my jeans button for relief. "Do you ever visit *any* of your family? Do they live nearby?" I asked as she took her last sip of wine.

"My mother and sister, never." She turned to admire Alessandro. "We don't need them anyway, now that I've got my little boy. They hate me. It's a long story," she fake yawned, looking for the server. "They said awful things to hurt me. But my real problem is my cousin."

I sat up. Someone new. "Your cousin?"

She tapped her lips with her napkin, debating whether she would tell me her story. She folded the napkin and met my curious gaze with a traumatized intensity. "My cousin is the meanest man I know. He lives in his Tuscany villa, and all he does is feed his stupid pigeons." She flicked her hand into the air. "He's mad because I struck him with a candela … thing."

"A candle?"

"I'll think of the word in English. It's the massive thing that holds candles," she said. "It's in the middle of the table."

I knew what she meant. "A candelabra," I said. "Big and silver?"

"Yes." She repeated the word candelabra slowly before continuing. "He invited me to dinner, and we drank two bottles of wine because he poured nonstop. He said the Milan apartment was not mine, even though my father told our family on his deathbed that he wanted *me* to live there. Then he said Alessandro is a bastard and not an heir to my family's fortune. My mother and sister told him to do this."

"Are you *sure?*"

"Yes. Of course, I am. My sister wanted my apartment for herself since she works in Milan. That was her lawyer who came to the door and asked for me. And my cousin? I shouldn't have struck him on the head," she said, her eyes narrowing. "I should have gone between his legs."

I pictured the encounter—not a pretty sight—and pressed my knees together. "Yikes. Geez."

"Geez," Alessandro said, pointing to the cheese on the table.

"Yes, it's cheese," I laughed, grabbing the cheese to show. "I think that's his first English word."

She laughed at my comment. "Alessandro will know English better than Italian. However, I have to say you are improving. You speak very well. I hope I have helped you."

"You have. Thank you. I mean, grazie mille."

"Prego." Her face softened. "You talk to my son, and it doesn't matter what language it is. Engagement. It's vital for his development and an unexpected gift that I appreciate very much. He loves you, you know."

I didn't know what to say and took an uncomfortable sip. At least one man in Italy loved me.

Later that night, we arrived in the bigger, neighboring town, Udine. We strolled through its beautiful Renaissance squares and grand buildings the following morning. After breakfast, we crossed small bridges over the Torre's frothy waters, which added to its surreal allure. The high Roman-Gothic bell tower of the cathedral resembled the campanile of St. Marco in Venice and set the stage for the pretty town.

"See those numerals," Electra said, pointing to MCDXC chiseled into a building. "That building is from the fifteenth century."

"Wow. There are zero tourists here. These beautiful towns we visit are never in my guidebooks. Why?"

"Of course. That's the way we want it. You Americans sip wine in Tuscany or make pizza in Rome. That's what you see in the movies and want to experience. You're so limited in your knowledge of the world."

I gave her a good-natured smirk. "Excuse me. Remember, we are going to stay away from stereotypes. And more people travel to Rome to see the Vatican and the Pope than to make pizza."

"They see him because of *guilt*. That's the south of Italy. You don't see fat people in the north because *this* area of Italy works hard compared to the rest of the country. Did you notice the factories on the side of the highway? It's a very industrial area."

I wasn't in the mood to argue or to call out her prejudices.

Tour guide Electra played the part of a returning family member, reliving childhood memories as we passed stores and restaurants. Quaint colonnaded porticos and antique houses decorated with coats of arms and geometric patterns once held her family friends, but they had left for the countryside, she told me. Cheerful locals greeted one another with shopping baskets in one hand and the leash of a well-behaved dachshund in the other, which was part of the subtle tinges of town life. The bakery trays stuffed with Linzer tortes and fruit cobbler added the best diversion, and we finally stopped to order three warm apple strudels, admiring the strange city.

The Italian, German, and Slavic influences reflected the Friulian culture and architecture, echoing its yo-yo history between bordering countries. It must have been strange to live in a chunk of territory that had switched nationalities so many times; awakening to the announcement that New England was now part of Canada would be a go-back-to-bed moment.

We entered a big palazzo with frescoed chubby cherubs reaching out to each other between palatial doorways. The large building with grandiose arches had a sign, *Palazzo di Caneva*. My gut twinged, remembering the notecard from her desk, and then it dawned on me. "Is this your house, also?" I asked, staring at the impressive façade and a noble family coat of arms with a lion in the center.

"Yes and no," she said, grasping the entrance handle. "My father was the last in his family to live here before the government took it after the war. Did I mention Napoleon Bonaparte slept here?"

"No. That's so cool. It's like when we say George Washington slept somewhere." The plaque outside the portal said the Caneva family was a noble twelfth-century family from Venice who had transferred to Udine. The Austrian Army used their house during World War I, and it had gone under restoration recently. Compared to the castle relic, the prestigious home was more noble and regal with its location in the town center. "My parents are Irish, but I'm not even sure of the name of their hometown. Bally dee whatever. I'm going to ask them more questions about their past."

She nodded. "Before they're gone."

Somber, we entered the large building, which was twenty degrees cooler than outside. Oblivious tradesmen whitewashed a long wall with antlers and rifles, unaware that the woman passing beside them was a descendant of the family who had owned the house for centuries. A crystal chandelier hung from the plaster-inlaid, vaulted ceiling in the massive room, and I imagined Napoleon arriving underneath it with his horse-drawn carriages and military entourage. Scrolled details and encircling artisan decorative touches with debonair portrait paintings on the wall added immense regality. This building reflected Electra's bespoke heritage. And her faint smile said it all.

On the second floor, an embroidered tapestry depicting a battle scene hung the length of the thirty-foot hallway, and Electra strolled past it, absorbing the majesty of her family dynasty while her father's ring spun around her finger. She was in her element, although I sensed an inner struggle hidden in her smirk.

I needed mental clarity, too, stewing over what she'd said about Alessandro loving me. The words were sweet, but why did it feel like quicksand? It seemed like Electra was enticing me, first with exotic places and now the emotional tug of Alessandro's love. A pang gripped me, and I let her walk away, pointing out gnarling dogs and rearing horses on the tapestry to her son. Gino was a possibility, I thought, and I had to keep my options open. I'd also call Hannah to check if my old position was still available at Trendary. My goal from "normal life" was to earn an income and visit more of Italy. But now, was it time to return home?

After excusing myself, I rushed down the stairs and out the door to find a faithful phone booth. When Hannah answered, her cheery voice said Gino had just called and asked for my new number.

"That's tricky as we are being very nomadic. I'll call him today to explain. But the real reason I'm calling is to see if Jim has filled my spot yet?"

She let out a groan. "I didn't want to tell you. I mean, it was totally unexpected. Something I never saw coming. I swear," she whined.

"Shit. Are you serious? Did he hire someone else? Tell me," I demanded. "I can take it. I want to hear *every* detail."

"Oh god." Hannah hemmed and hawed. "Really? I mean, this is so hard … It was me, Jayne. He gave me *your* job … Jayne, are you there? I said I couldn't do that to you."

"And what did he say? Don't sugarcoat it."

"He said, well, we can't wait for Jayne to get her head out of the clouds. If it's not you, then I'll hire someone else."

"That idiot said that? My head was in the clouds? What the hell is that supposed to mean?"

"He's pissed. I think he thought you would be back after Matteo ended things. Like, be back at your desk the following week. He's doing the typical woe-is-me bullshit. You were his perfect employee. I don't think I can meet his high standards."

"Stop. Of course, you can. I should have called from Lignano, except we had this pinecone thing … which sounds crazy, but I can't talk about it now."

"I feel so awful. I'm sorry. If I told Jim you're coming back, I swear, he'd give me a raise from happiness. But what about Gino? Maybe he's got a job for you. Are you staying in Italy?"

"Yes. No. I don't know. It's getting complicated now. Electra's talking about the Philippines and all this stuff."

"The Philippines? With her? Are you nuts?"

"Yes, that's where I am. Nuts, bananas, lost my marbles, etcetera. But Gino has me doing a mood board. I may be in over my head but at least I have a chance to make it here. I've got to go."

"Wait, Jayne. Are you mad at me? I can totally understand if you are."

"No. I'm not. I'm literally smiling right now for you. You always said you wanted to get out of shipping, so this is perfect. And I'm here if you need me," I said, mustering optimism. "But you'll be fine."

"Well … okay … like I said, I was shocked when he asked me …"

I thought of Hannah sitting at my desk. She deserved a promotion. "I would have done the same thing. Relax. You're going to be great." I spotted Electra coming toward me, pushing the stroller. "She's coming," I said. "But I've got a ton of stories to tell you later. We're now in this town where Electra's family lived for a thousand years. And thanks for the info on Gino. But wait, Hannah, can I ask you one thing?"

"Sure."

"Am I an airhead?"

"You? No. You're the best."

Back on the street, I stopped underneath the Gioielli sign and glanced through the glass. Gioelli meant jewelry; if I sold Matteo's ring, I could get my struggling finances back on track.

Excited at the prospect, I whipped around to Electra and thumbed to the store. "Can I get a piece of jewelry appraised here? I want to sell this ring," I said, rifling through my backpack for the little box. The bauble lay on my palm seconds later, and I held it out. "Matteo gave me this in New York. It's not an engagement ring, he said. Kind of a pre-engagement ring. Still, it was enough to clinch the deal for me to come here. Obviously, I don't want it anymore."

"Strange. A pre-engagement ring? I never heard of that. *We* don't do *those* in Italy." She snorted. "Where did he buy it? Bulgari? Tiffany? Or was it Manfredi?"

"I wish. Except Matteo never had that kind of dough," I peered down at it. "But it has a diamond. He said it was platinum and gold, so it must be worth *something*."

She took it from my hand and squinted at the band. "A diamond? That speck?" She glanced at the jewelry store. "Gold is valuable, so we'll see what they say."

Entering with high expectations, the glass cases with diamonds, sapphires, and precious jewels twinkled in the perfumed sanctuary of welcoming dazzle. Black velvet boards lay silent with eye-popping presentations, and I hesitated, replacing my puffed out chest optimism with dread.

"Buongiorno." A bespectacled man in a charcoal suit strolled across the thick beige carpet and greeted Electra with a slight bow. Her voice rose three octaves to explain why we were there. He nodded, noting her chunky gold ring and pearl choker with interest.

She switched her explanation to me. The man's face recalibrated, looking me over for my bauble credibility: zero. In my bedroom at my parents' house, my ballerina jewelry box had three silver bracelets and gold hoop earrings from my sixteenth birthday. Flynn was the one who could compete with her two-carat rock engagement ring and a sleeve of 24-karat bracelets. She'd also inherited Ambrose's grandmother's bling. I wished she were here with me to raise my status.

Without a word, he took the ring and pulled a jeweler's loupe from his pocket. After a quick examination, he retreated into his office. Minutes later, he returned with a tiny cream silk bag and dropped it into Electra's hand, explaining the results with a pinched face. It didn't take Leonardo da Vinci to realize I didn't have crown jewels.

Electra thanked him, and we were back on the street before she spoke. "It's made from cheap metal. I think you call it tin."

"Tin? That cheapskate gave me a ring made of a Coke can. Or better yet, tuna. He told me it was platinum. What about the diamond?"

Electra wrinkled her nose with a wry grin. "Zirconia cubica."

"That jerk. Is it worth *anything*?"

She scrunched her face. "Two thousand lire. About two dollars."

"Two effing dollars? He probably got it in a gumball machine."

"The man said it is a type of ring they sell in toy stores."

Was there a toy store at JFK? "Insert knife and twist," I mumbled, throwing it into a gutter. It clattered into oblivion as I thought of Jim's words. "My head wasn't in the clouds. It was stuck in the worst fairy tale ever written."

Our visit was brief in Udine, and soon, we were back on the road to Trieste, a city nestled on a thin, narrow strip of land separating the Adriatic and

Italy's five-mile border with Yugoslavia. However, I couldn't appreciate the beauty of the landscape, driving the car on autopilot. My naivety was annoyingly visible. I should have known better at my age with a pretty decent dating history. But that is every teary swan song. Love was a drug, and I had overdosed big time. Why had he begged me to come to Italy?

"I'm sorry about Roberto. I should have let him take you out."

My brain slammed the brakes. I frowned over my shoulder at Electra. "Yes. It would have been nice. Why didn't you?"

"Jayne, I was worried about you. I didn't want Roberto to hurt you more than you already were. You were so fragile."

"It was only a drink," I said. "But thanks for your concern. Are you going to rehire Roberto?"

She snorted. "I did that the next day."

On the outskirts of Trieste, children played along the narrow coast-hugging lanes as dogs wandered the streets and laundry billowed in the wind. High above the city, neat concrete houses overlooked the wave-crashing Adriatic Sea, and I observed that Trieste had Dublin's rawness with its coastal and city landscape. Its horseshoe harbor glazed in a misty thicket of flagged masts added excitement to the gray facades and dark pier. Electra tapped my shoulder with a wink. "You'll love Trieste. It's very international. The gateway of the East."

The grand Piazza dell' Unita's central square was surrounded by eighteenth and nineteenth-century buildings and each had a matte black tarnish from a century of exhaust fumes and sooty coal burning smoke. The ornate details were barely visible under the grime, yet a sense of power from generations of importance were obvious.

And it was diverse. Greek Orthodox churches sat next to the eclectic city's synagogues, mosques, and cathedrals. Animated conversations of foreign languages matched the men in long beards sipping espressos with white-collared priests. I noticed the black and flame-red Illy coffee signs at every street corner as Electra babbled that Trieste had the most cafes in Italy. That triggered a memory of the first time Matteo had shown me how to make espresso. It was when pulled it out of his suitcase when he moved into my apartment. A snowy day of love. The urge to call him surfaced unexpectedly, like an awakened dragon.

I extinguished that flickering flame quickly. Gino was the person I needed to contact, not Matteo. "I'm going to show Alessandro the boats," I said after we parked in front of the hotel. While Electra checked in, I wheeled Alessandro down the pier, hunting for a vacant phone booth.

I spotted one and beelined for it. Kids played along the promenade, passing a soccer ball back and forth, causing a ginger cat to scatter for cover. While Alessandro watched the game, I leaned into the pier's solitary metal and plexiglass box, second-guessing my decision for the Saturday morning phone call. The harbor gale was strong, and I put my back to its force, jabbing my finger into the crud-covered slot for any forgotten coins. Finding none, I rattled in my gettonis and dialed.

"Jayne," Gino said in a long drawl. "Are you still in Venice?"

"No. I'm in Trieste."

"Trieste? So, you're going up the coast."

I glanced back to Alessandro in the stroller, kicking his legs in an imaginary soccer match while watching the others play. "Yes. Sort of. We're crossing over into Yugoslavia tomorrow."

"What? There's a possible war starting there."

I knew of the troubles and had been following the headlines in the *International Herald Tribune*. "I know. But we're far from the center, she said. We'll be in and out in a week."

"Okay," he said with uncertainty. "I hope you make it back because I may have a spot for you."

I smiled at the wads of bubble gum stuck to the booth's glass. "Really? I can't believe it. With who?"

"Me." He lowered his voice. "I may be jumping the gun on this, but I think Tatiana may leave. I won't go into details, but I've seen the signs, and I'm sure she'll tell me soon."

"She got another job?"

"Kind of. Her uncle has a small mill in Prato, and he's getting older. It's a solid business. She told me she'd inherit it from him one day because he never married."

"Wow. Well, that's great. The timing is perfect because I don't think we'll be back this month."

"That's better for my schedule. It's the summer, so business is nonexistent 'til everyone returns in September. How's the mood board coming along? I'm very interested to see it."

The soccer ball rolled towards me, and I kicked it back to the waiting group. "It's alive," I said. "A work in progress."

"Wonderful. An American perspective is always interesting. Clear and strong. No sentimental bullshit. Be safe and call me when you're back."

My next phone call was to Flynn.

"Hey, how's it going?" she asked. "Where are you now?"

"In Trieste. James Joyce's city."

"Cool. Dad will want all those details when you get back. Hey, sorry about the last time we talked. I was having a bad day. You know, throw up and all that fun stuff. Mom said she got your postcard and you mentioned the *Philippines*. You are coming back, aren't you?"

"Um, I don't know. Things have changed, and I'm trying to figure it out. My job at Trendary is gonzo, but there may be another one in Milan. Electra wants to start an overseas kids clothing company, but she's all over the place with her family problems, and I don't see that happening. But who am I to see the future? As we've all seen, my track record hasn't been that great. But I miss you all."

"Miss you, too. It sounds like you have a lot of choices. But, what do you want to do, Jayne? You have to think about what will make *you* happy. Not us. Please don't listen to me or mom and dad. Do what is best for you. Weigh your options. Tick your boxes. Call me if you want any advice. I'm here."

"Thanks. But it's so hard to decide."

"I know it is. Except when you've weighed all your options, you know you have made the right decision. For you only. That's what is most important."

$1,229.11

- 5.25

Film - cheaper - develop? - 12.50

Café lunch - 4.00

Postcards - need more stamps - 7.50

Dinner tip - amazing meal

*sardines, lemon, salt

$ 1,199.86

CHAPTER TWELVE

OUR NEXT DESTINATION WAS PULA, a Yugoslavian town on the Istrian peninsula. We had a boat reservation to Losinj, a small island in the northern Adriatic Sea where Electra had rented a house in the town, Mali Losinij. On the Italian-Yugoslavian border, twenty minutes from Trieste, my jaw dropped as soon as we hit the checkpoint with armed guards and military-camouflaged tanks. Alessandro had discovered Toasty and now the stuffed animal sat in the passenger seat, giving me comfort while we idled in the queue of cars waiting to pass the border control gate.

"Those guns are scary," I said. "I thought you said the war was far away. Are you sure it is okay to enter a war zone?"

"Use your Irish passport. Not your American," Electra hissed as we inched forward. "No sudden moves."

"Great. So, I could be shot dead for sneezing," I said under my breath, rummaging through my bag while my panicking fear thumped volumes of blood. "Next time, please give me a little notice so I can prepare my stuff. And my will," I added, glancing at the menacing firearms. Luckily, I found the right passport before a gun-toting guard moseyed toward us.

Staring ahead, Electra remained stoic, and I followed her lead. The officers took our passports and ordered us out of the car for border inspection. Europe had been in flux since the Berlin Wall had fallen the previous year, and the inter-ethnic relations of Yugoslavia were a tinderbox of uncertainty. I wanted to go back to Italy.

As I watched the soldiers, Electra told me their teetering government was coming off its high of hosting the 1984 Winter Olympics. The unrest between its Serb, Croat, and Slovene factions was brewing as each wanted their independence. Her information didn't make me feel better and I wished I knew more.

"Why is it taking so long?" I said, eyeing the rifle-bearing soldiers leaning against a building. "What if they take us prisoner? And *why* are we the only ones still here? Those cars that were in front of us are long gone."

Electra put her finger to her lips.

Two men led us to a bench, motioning to sit outside the stone hut that had been transformed into a damp border control office. The soldiers examined our passports as their guns swung with tiny tik-tocks. Most were young, strong, and baby-faced. They seemed inexperienced with their averted gazes and constant repositioning of their weapons. Wide-eyed Alessandro was beaming, kicking his legs as the tough guys cruised around him, eyeing us with mistrust.

After a half-hour, an older bearded guard with a cigarette dangling from his mouth returned with our passports. His eyes were barely visible under his patrol cap. "Your car is French, you are Irish, she's German, and the baby has a diplomat's passport. He's your baby?" the man said with skepticism to Electra. His body angled away from her for a better look, and he squinted at me. "Not yours?"

Electra blinked as if awoken from a deep sleep. "No, no, this little boy is mine."

He quipped to his comrades, and they snickered. He then held out our passports. "Keep these with you all the time. If you don't, you go to jail," he warned as he returned them.

We hurried into the car, and their curious double take at why Electra jumped in the back seat was priceless. "That was interesting. I hope we can get back into Italy," I said, driving underneath the arm of the border gate.

"I wanted to kick that imbecile for asking if Alessandro is mine. Who does that scum think he is?" she sulked.

"I know. Super obnoxious. Why does Alessandro have a diplomat's passport? And why don't you have an Italian one?"

She fixed her hair and looked out the window with a shrug. "I know someone in the embassy. They helped me."

Who? I was dying to ask. "Oh. I guess it's nice to have friends in high places."

She winked. "It is."

The tension dissipated as the car sped past rolling vineyards and pretty hills of Istria, reminding me of Tuscan photos I had drooled over too many times. I mentally put the yellow and green on my mood board and already understood that Yugoslavia would be an exciting destination after our hair-raising welcome. Along the road, frequent hand-painted signs for miele poked from the wildflower-filled shoulders, and I realized miele meant honey after driving by a painted bee on the signpost. "Maybe we can try the honey here," I suggested. "It seems to be everywhere."

Electra busied herself by pointing out the countryside and cows to Alessandro. Weathered farmers with sunburnt arms drove rusted tractors bringing life to the area, while sunbathing sheep communed with fly-swatting cows in a romantic folk-tale setting.

On the road, Yugo cars—Yugoslavia's contribution to the auto market and the cheapest automobile ever produced—were the number one car. The mighty Citroen DS passed dozens of Yugos, which was not difficult.

Yet unsafe practices, such as babies on mothers' laps or live sheep and goats in the backseat, made me shudder as we drove by.

I was still nervous. Military trucks also thundered past us, full of grim faces dressed in camouflage gear. I worried we were heading toward the unrest and was relieved to see signs for Pula. Electra had booked the two o'clock ferry, and I coasted down the hills into the glittery seafront town with a half-hour to spare. Electra said the city was part of the Roman Empire, and a massive coliseum was next to the harbor, proving her point. I hadn't known Roman ruins would be in that part of the world and voiced my ignorance.

"Are you sure you studied history?" Electra asked. She added that, because of the area's turbulent history over the past hundred years, one could have been born in Austria, married in Italy, and raised kids in Yugoslavia—without moving an inch from Pula.

"You should give tours. You know so much."

"Thank you for your confidence. If I am helping you understand Europe better, that's all that matters."

"You are. I really appreciate it."

When we got closer, an indigo and white passenger boat bobbed in the silver-dimpled bay. A worker directed us to the ferry parking area, where we unloaded our suitcases. I followed Electra as she held Alessandro, pointing out the boat while we headed to the ticket counter where a handful of people queued for tickets. Once onboard, we sat on the open deck in the velvety breeze, and I finally unwound with a big exhale. "We made it. Woohoo."

"Yes. We did." Seagulls floated above while men threw cigarette butts into the harbor, hauling up the thick ropes for cast-off as each yelled orders back-and-forth. Locals held their tickets as they inched forward towing dogs and children up the gangway. No one else had suitcases, so I guessed that we were the only tourists.

The boat's engines sputtered and chugged into action. Soon, we were in the middle of the small harbor, but the incessant honking of a car horn echoed across the bay, and I turned to locate the noisy vehicle. Down a narrow street, I could see a cream van careening to the dock with its passengers waving their arms wildly outside each window. I looked up to the boat's wheelhouse as the captain grabbed his binoculars. Another man pointed at the group, and the engine slowed as the vessel banked to the right within seconds.

"He's turning the boat around," I said to Electra. Her mouth opened in astonishment.

The car had kept beeping, but the grateful group jumped out as soon as the ferry changed its course, waving with glee. I grinned, knowing the Staten Island Ferry would never have been so gracious. My admiration grew for Yugoslavian culture, and I felt safer.

After we'd picked up our final passengers and got back on course, eventually the ferry docked on the island of Losinj in the Adriatic. Electra chose the island because she had visited it as a child. Long ago, it was once a climatic health resort for asthmatic patients because of its vast forest of filtering pine trees that purified the air. Off the ferry, rocky paths and stone steps led us to the sheltered cove on the other side of the lush, stunning island. A church bell rang out into the quiet pathways, and besides chirping birds and sleepy cats, we were alone. Signs wound us through narrow alleys with high clotheslines zigzagging across balconies to the village on Kvarner Bay.

"See over there," Electra said, pointing to a hill across the bay with grand houses. "There are villas up there that my relatives owned before the war. They came here for the air and beauty." She scanned the horizon as she waved more air into her lungs. "So clean. Don't you smell it?"

The sweet scent threaded the sea air. "Yes. Those green needles combed the air for everyone," I commented. "I think this is the best air I've ever breathed."

Descending the last stone stairs, I looped onto the small harbor where chipped façades of three-story pastel townhouses knit together to form a colorful setting. Simple fishing boats rocked in the translucent bay, and men pulled their heavy nets onto the pier surrounded with bright, pearly flashes. However, I did a double take at the statue of a yelling man raising his fist in the middle of a cobblestone square. It was a stark reminder that Yugoslavia was still a Communist country.

Nearby, an outdoor café seemed inviting with its chalked sign featuring a smiling sun. I glanced into the shadowy bar full of men with dark caps and unshaven faces. Their chapped hands held shot glasses full of a transparent liquid, and each stared at us with unwelcome suspicion.

"Looks a little sketchy." I turned to Electra. "That crowd doesn't seem very friendly."

"Oh yes, they hate tourists. And they drink bottles of this vile drink, Loza, here, so watch out. It's very potent." Electra nudged me to move forward. "This is where I'm supposed to pick up the rental key." Entering the establishment, the men murmured to one another to look at the strangers, but Electra plowed her way to the white-aproned manager and started to speak a mix of Italian and German. A shiver went up my spine when I spotted three soldiers nursing pints of beer in a corner. Was it safe to be here while a civil war smoldered? I glanced at a portrait of Josip Tito near the back, wondering if there were any payphones on the island. But when I looked back at the bar, the thin bartender drying glasses gazed my way, and our eyes locked. His warm smile melted any worries.

After obtaining the key, we entered the sea captain's townhouse on the pier, three doors down from the bar. Its weather-beaten door opened into the kitchen, and I unloaded Alessandro's bag onto the table with chairs, noting the thick layer of dust. The adjoining dark room had an overstuffed lime green couch with ominous stains of unknown origins, plus a large window opened onto the harbor. Once I unlatched the window, a grey-haired woman shuffled by with a shopping basket and nodded to me. Curtainless, I questioned our fishbowl existence as another person passed with a curious glance into our rental. Worried again, I hoped our week's stay would end quickly.

Our daily side trips were long meandering strolls around the village or hikes in the nearby aromatic hills. Although it was heavenly, I couldn't understand why we had come to such a remote island, and the villagers' suspicious glances relayed the same question. Besides the drifting boats in the sleepy harbor, locals at the café also entertained us with their centuries' old routine: unloading fresh catches while seagulls screeched for any leftovers. In the hot afternoons at the café, they sipped cold beers or lemonade and smoked cigarettes while laughing and chatting.

We always took the farthest table from the door, and Electra hid behind her sunglasses, reading newspapers in various languages. Alessandro and I watched the fishermen or entertained the local tabby cat who followed us everywhere. The little harbor was unnaturally clear, with twenty-foot visibility to the bottom. Colorful fish and crabs crawled and swam in a pristine environment, and we'd observe their activity. In the distance, long sandy beaches and simple fisherman houses spiced up the barren dunes, creating a peaceful fit on my mood board.

"Jayne, can you please get me another espresso?" That was music to my ears because I loved to order from the handsome bartender and barista. Tan with large copper-salted brown eyes and thick black hair, we had quick, shy exchanges at the café counter while I waited. From our simple conversations, I learned he was from Sarajevo and was thrilled to practice his English with me. After the third day, when all eyes were on me, he asked me to come to the restaurant after Electra went to sleep. Blushing, I mumbled no and gave a weak excuse. Not that I didn't want to, but after the debacle when I had gotten Roberto fired, I couldn't risk hurting someone else with Electra's nonsensical actions, especially in a country with such harsh sentences for any crime.

Our last day on the island was sweltering hot, and Electra caught me off-guard with a suggestion. "You can have the afternoon off if you'd like," she said mid-morning as she mixed the ice in her lemonade. She then fanned Alessandro with her raffia hat. "The heat is awful, and Alessandro got too much sun yesterday. I'm staying in the house where it's cool to read with him."

Her gift of time was unexpected. "Um … great. I'll go for a swim and get some sun."

"Yes, that sounds *very* fun," she said in a curious voice. "But don't burn your Irish skin."

After lunch, I threw my cover-up over my bikini and wandered from the pier, unsure of where to go. Older sunbathers lay along a rocky outcropping further down the road, and I did a double take. Everyone was naked—full birthday suit mode. Was I the only one with a tan line?

Awkward because of their immodesty, I sat on the nearest rock and tried to blend in, laying my towel out and watching the horizon to avoid gawking at jiggling body parts as nudists tossed beach balls around. However, the noon sun seared my skin to a crisp pink within minutes, and I applied sunblock, trying to be inconspicuous. A group of stout women came to my area and threw off their tops, exposing their ample bare breasts with buxom pride as they surveyed the water.

"When in Rome …" I said, untying my top. Average in the chest department, I lay down, shy yet content, as my delicate skin grew warmer. Luckily, I turned on my stomach as a group of men slowly walked by, perhaps interested to investigate the uncommon sight of small breasts. Unsettled by my immodesty, I tried to close my eyes, but a shadow loomed over me, and a finger tapped me on my shoulder.

I squinted into the sun, and the outline of his messy hair gave him away. It was my bar friend. "Hi."

"Me sit here?" he said, motioning to a nearby rock. I sat up and grabbed my bikini top, causing him to wave his hands. "No. Don't. You stay same. Nice."

Before I could respond, he dropped his towel and perfectly dived into the shallow water. When he came up for air, he flapped his arms in distress and submerged again. My lifeguard intuition from a summer stint at a Boy's Club community pool kicked in, and I ran to the rock and dove. As I neared his thrashing arms, he went under again. Ready to do a surface dive, someone yanked my leg from below, and I kicked my foot, thinking of the shark movie that had scarred me for life. A force pulled me under, and I swallowed a mouthful of salt water. The sides of my body tightened under his grip, and I broke through the surface. Coughing, I looked down, and my crush lifted me higher with a big smile.

"Not funny," I yelled, kicking and wriggling from his grasp. People onshore laughed at his antics, and I splashed at his face until he freed me. "Go away."

Then he dove under, and his head went between my legs. His strength hoisted me onto his shoulders. "Stop," I cried, hitting him for freedom.

He let me go, and I took ten strong strokes to reach the rock on the beach. Scrambling out, I grabbed my towel and wound it around my body, gulping deep breaths as my pulse slowed. But it rose again when his lean, muscular, glistening body walked out of the sea toward me.

"Don't come near me," I glared, holding up my palms to him.

With a droop-lipped stare, he came closer slowly. "I'm sorry. I thought you like."

I began to towel off. "Pretending to drown is not funny."

He ran his hand through his thick hair. "You're right."

At this point, I could have sold tickets from the open-mouthed interest of the attentive cluster of naked people surrounding us. I took a deep breath and put on my cover-up, muttering, "You should be."

"Lunch?" he asked when I began to walk away. I shook my head no. He ran in front of me and placed his hand over his chest with a frown. "Please?"

I was tired and angry. If he weren't so damn manly and handsome....

In the distance, laughing kids played on the rocks, and I sighed, kicking the fine, golden sand while trying to suppress a smile. His bright eyes waited for my answer. *Life is short. I'm here and alive. A nanosecond decision.* He had just been teasing and stupid—a flirt. Don't be such a diva, I chided myself. I did have a sense of humor and offered a shy smile. "Okay."

He nodded his boyish grin approval and wiped clinging droplets from his tight, six-pack abdomen. I enjoyed watching his drying demonstration, limb by limb. And he knew it.

As we walked, he told me his name was Bojan. His parents, worried about the war, had sent him to work at his cousin's bar, far away from Sarajevo. He had friends already enlisted, and I told him about the border patrol when we entered. He asked questions about my family and told me he had always wanted to visit America. It was one of his dreams.

"You should. America has its pluses and minuses, as does every country. I can't say it's better. Simply different. Especially here. Capitalism is fundamental, except being overseas, I realize we don't appreciate the little things. For one, here I notice nature much more. There's not the urgency of New York to "make it" any way you can," I said, gazing at the surreal coastal oasis around me.

We entered the café, and the friendly owner gave Bojan a knowing smirk. He sat us down with a welcoming gesture and, minutes later, laid an oversized plate of grilled silver and black sardines on the table. "For you," he said, looking at me. "Mali Losinj's best dish."

"Thank you," I swooned. Drizzled with lemony olive oil and covered in crispy salted skin, I ate two inches of delicious fish in one bite—bones and all. Bojan and I popped dozens into our mouths and then sopped up the perfectly infused oil with a basket full of warm, crusty bread. It was one of the best dishes I'd ever tasted, and the house white wine combined with the sun and drowning psychodrama made me beyond sleepy.

When we left the bar, my brown-eyed friend wasn't ready for a nap. When I yawned, he put his arm around my shoulder. "You come with me?" he flirted, waggling his perfect bushy eyebrows. "Walk?"

I didn't need prodding. "Sure."

As we hurried to the far end of the harbor, two fishermen shouted to him, but he ignored their calls with a swipe of his hand. Though I laughed, I was afraid Electra would appear and demand that I return to work, so we hurried down the promenade like runaway teenagers.

"Boat?" he panted, pointing to a small sailboat docked at the end of the harbor. He winked when I nodded, and we scrambled onto the rig with its peeling paint hull and interior. In the back was a bottle of wine and two paper cups, adding to the fun. With ease, he sailed into the middle of the bay, and we drank warm wine and shared crackers and salami slices between our piecemeal conversation.

As he maneuvered past a buoy, his expression changed. "Jayne, there will be war. My father sent me here because he didn't want me to fight. But they find me, I know. I fight for Serbian land."

I grabbed his hand, already feeling a pang of his absence. "I'm so sorry. It must be terrible to know there may be a war."

He squeezed it. "I will come to America. One day," he said. "I hope then I see you. Maybe? You show the Big Apple to me. And we see Mick Jagger."

"It's not that easy," I laughed, which segued into a conversation about the concerts I had attended, including coincidentally, his favorite group's. Returning to the harbor, we chatted about our favorite bands, the distant hills clustered with boarded-up ornate villas and a derelict clock tower adding to the romantic setting. It was so spontaneous and beautiful that I wondered what would happen next, watching his tanned arms pull in the billowing sail as the lights in the captain's house twinkled as our beacon.

Before docking, he leaned over with a silly grin and kissed me. His soft, wine-tainted lips caused my body to dissolve as his arms wrapped around me. "Bojan, we leave tomorrow. I don't know you that well, but I like you a lot," I breathed between kisses.

"Mali Losinj now, New York later," he said. The thought of him firing a gun or being wounded by a bullet was unnerving. I didn't explain I may stay in Milan and confuse him because I didn't need to pull him into my nervous breakdown.

"'Till the Next Goodbye,'" I said.

"Ha. Yes." He was impressed. "Great song. And album."

Once out of the boat, crickets serenaded from the tall trees, and we held hands at the rental door. We giggled when our fingers finally pulled apart as Bojan reluctantly let go. "Laku noc, draga" he said with a final kiss.

I learned the following day the words meant, *Good night, darling.*

Rough seas confined us to the main deck on the trip back to Pula. The lukewarm coffee in thin plastic white cups was a better choice in the cafe than the suffocating clouds of cigarette smoke in the enclosed lounge polluting my pine-sanitized airways. Only I didn't care.

My mind was on Bojan. I didn't have that "can't eat, can't sleep" feeling, but sipping wine on his sailboat as the sun set had left my insides squiggly. It was a memory I replayed as a cocktail of hormones conducted an uplifting symphony after months of hibernation. However, his ties to Yugoslavia and the possibility of war tethered me to reality and halted any imaginations of a future with him. Been there and done that with Matteo.

Everything had to be well planned before I committed to anything.

I sighed. The quick visit to Mali Losinj had been an odd destination, especially since the communist country was on the brink of a civil war. I knew Electra had brought us here for a reason, and I couldn't figure out why.

"You never talk about your family," Electra said unexpectedly.

I shrugged. "It's just my sister Flynn, and my parents. Yugoslavia would have blown them away. The beaches, scenery, wharf. I wished they could see it. They're always busy, you know, with their jobs and all that. Flynn has her husband, Ambrose, Quinn, and Kate. They've got a nice house and work very hard to pay bills and the mortgage." I looked at Electra's inquisitive expression. "Don't get me wrong. I love working in fashion. And you can't survive on a smile in New York. But this experience with you has shown me there is more to life."

"Yes. Americans try too hard." She looked out into the bay with a raised chin. "Mali Losinj was the last place I traveled with my father. We went for the summer because he needed to breathe healthy air. He died of throat cancer—a terrible ending for such a beautiful man. We cried and told each other all we had to say on that trip. He was a wonderful human being. I loved him so much."

"I knew it was more than an island for you." She nodded, and I grabbed her hand, rubbing her forearm. "He was lucky to have you as a daughter."

Her lips trembled. "Thank you."

We sailed on, and as my stomach dipped and rolled with the boat, I listened as Electra explained our next destination, Cortina D'Ampezzo. We were heading back to Italy. Famous as a winter destination, my apparent curiosity made her rattle off a litany of information about James Bond and other movies filmed in Cortina. I read in chic magazines that wealthy Italians skied there, but she said it was also the place to be in the summer.

As we gathered our things to disembark, Electra gave me a side-eye.

"You were out most of last night. Did you have a fun time?"

"Yes. It was spectacular. I met up with Bojan, the bartender. Totally spontaneous. He brought me on his boat." Her eyebrows rose, and I wondered if she had somehow known that yesterday was Bojan's day off. I opened my mouth to ask but realized I didn't want the answer. "So, tell me more about Cortina. I'll send Bojan a postcard from there."

"Oh, it will be quite different than Mali Losinj. We will be with a *very* old aristocratic family," she said as she straightened her neck scarf. "I showed you their palazzo in Venice, if you remember. The three-story one with two terraces? On the Grand Canal?"

I held back from laughing aloud. I wasn't an architecture enthusiast, so all the regal palaces had looked identical to me. I drummed my fingers on my chin, holding back a giggle. "Oh, yes, I remember. The one with two terraces. Beautiful."

"Yes. The Bellagos have wonderful taste."

Back on the road, things seemed safer as we passed silver-spiked olive groves separated by knee-high stone walls. The crossing into Italy was more manageable, and a police officer shepherded us with ten other cars under the border gate. I was pensive, wondering about Bojan and cursing that I hadn't taken a picture of the plate of sardines for my mood board.

My only tokens from our visit to Yugoslavia were the café's embroidered sailboat napkin and a snippet of pink cotton from an apron in the captain's kitchen. The tiny island touched me with its simplicity and squeezed negativity out of my being with its soft breezes to rebalance my life. Nothing could translate how the blanket of despair was no longer a burden on my shoulders. It might have been Bojan's kiss or the moonlit night when I felt in sync with the world. Whatever elixir of emotion had occurred, I was finally content with myself again.

$ 1,199.86
Gettonis - 20.00
Cappuccino x5 - 7.30
Jar of Nutella - limit one tablespoon a day - 2.00
Dinner and drinks with Valentina - 22.00
Postcards and stamps - 5.00
$ 1,143.56
GRAPPA
DOLOMITI
RIFUGIO

CHAPTER THIRTEEN

WE EXITED THE HIGHWAY towards Monfalcone and crossed into a mountainous region. Traditional wooden houses in the charming towns had flower boxes overflowing with rosy geraniums. Besides the alpine homes, village lots were crammed with campers from every European country and family-packed VW vans overloaded with bicycles. Soon, I was greeted by massive tourist buses veering around hairpin turns. Their too-wide sweeps turned my white knuckles arthritic. Besides worrying that the car could careen over the mountain precipice, Electra's catastrophic-like gasps added undeserved pressure as we climbed upward on roads with no shoulders or guard rails for protection.

"You may get sick from the altitude," Electra stated from the back. "The higher we go, the thinner the air. It's not going to affect Alessandro, but it will you."

The shrouded figures of the elephantine Dolomites grew more prominent, and the silvered granite transformed into its tell-tale pink from the sun's westward rays, adding to their overwhelming presence. Turnoffs for picture-taking, parking areas for summer gondola rides, and open-mouthed ski stations thousands of feet above the road added to the panorama. "How high are we going?"

"Cortina is at five thousand feet. The summits are, I think, two thousand feet higher. I've never skied here. Do you ski?" she asked.

"I did. Once. In Vermont with you-know-who. It was my first time," I said.

"Hmm, well, at least you had a little fun with him ..." she said with a smirk.

I imagined Bojan flying down the slopes. He was probably an excellent skier. I blew air from my lips. "My former life."

On cue, the clock tower pealed its welcoming toll as we arrived at Cortina's bustling center. Range Rovers were apparently the car of choice, with Porsches and Mercedes also dotting the roads, sprinkled with an occasional Ferrari's throaty rumble. My first thought was that reflective sunglasses and long-haired toy dogs were must-have accessories. High-end brand names flashed across sweatshirts while locals wore outfits that reminded me of the Octoberfest at the Yorkville German festival I used to enjoy with friends on the Upper East Side.

As we drove by a café, professional-looking climbers with carabiners and ropes sat outside and shared beers with hikers, adding to the athletic alpine aura. We passed a woman in a ski jacket, and I doubted my clothes would be warm enough—the mountain weather was thirty degrees cooler than Mali Losinj. "Where is this house you're renting?" I asked, circling another roundabout.

"Follow those parking signs," she said, directing from her map. I drove down the main road until she shouted, "Stop!"

I slammed the brakes, and my face nearly hit the dashboard. "What?" I gasped. "Did I hit a person?" She put on her sunglasses and straightened Alessandro's hair, ignoring my concern. "Hello?"

"Mio dio." She skimmed her finger over her choker, her lips forming a thin line. “Of course, you didn’t hit anything. We’re here, that’s all,” she announced, fixing the lapel of her loden-green blazer. Her outfit, with its horn buttons and olive pants with brown boots, fit perfectly in this new Alpine scene, and I glanced down at my formula-stained denim shirt.

“I hope there’s a washing machine and dryer at this place,” I said self-consciously.

“Oh. Oh. I see a parking space. I’ll get out with Alessandro with his stuff, and you can bring the rest of the bags. Move up further.”

The car behind me beeped for me to move and I tried to find the parking space she mentioned. “Where to? I don’t see a space …”

“Go on. Move. I told you to park closer.”

Cars honked. “Where? I don’t see a space. This is as close as I can get.” Another car blasted its horn and roared past us.

“Okay. Let us out here.” She mumbled in Italian as she unbuckled Alessandro. Glaring pedestrians shook their fists at my audacity as I raised my hands at her impossible request that I move. “Oh, you are always right. Jayne is always right, isn’t she, Alessandro?” she gnarled. She ripped Alessandro from his car seat before slamming the door. She passed the passenger side and said, “Fuck you, Jayne.”

I wouldn’t have believed it if I didn’t see the f-bomb coming out of her mouth. A pedestrian then stopped her and fawned over her propped-on-one-hip Alessandro, a usual occurrence because he was a showstopper. I held back from blasting the horn in anger.

“Fuck you, princess of parking.” My nails dug into the leather steering wheel as I pulled away. I didn’t do anything wrong—there were no free spaces. “Stupid bitch,” I added, snapping up the visor. A man jaywalked as I slowed down for the parking sign, and I beeped, causing him to run like a scared rabbit to the other side. Feeling horrible for my actions, I took it down a few notches before I hurt someone.

After finding parking on an upper street, I retraced my route to Corso

Italia, the main shopping boulevard of Cortina, and found number ten, a pretty chalet. Two entrances—one street level and the other through a flower-full porch on the first floor—were eye-catching, with decorative planters bursting with geraniums and daisies. I climbed the stairs and pressed the bell, trying to remain calm.

"Buongiorno," I said to the pink-cheeked young woman who answered the door. She was my age, in sweatpants and an oversized hooded sweatshirt. Her licorice-black hair was in a sleek ponytail. "Sono Jayne. E Electra qui?" *Is Electra here?*

"Hi," she said in English, ushering me into the house. "You don't have to speak Italian with us. I'm Valentina, and Electra is with my mother."

"Oh, great." I gave her a once-over. "Did you go for a run?" I asked with envy. I felt like I hadn't exercised in so long. "I'm jealous."

She seemed embarrassed. "Yes. I only ran three miles today. I'm training for a half-marathon."

"Three miles is great. Especially at this altitude."

"Do you run?" she asked as we walked down the hall. The scent of cookies baking was a pleasant surprise.

"Yes, but not much lately. It's hard in Tretorns. But I did in New York."

She stopped short. "Did you run the marathon? That's my dream," she said, swooning. "The pre-race pasta dinner. Race through Queens. Crowds cheering all the way. The Brooklyn Bridge. The finish line in Central Park, where everyone claps for you. That's the best."

"Yes, it's exciting like that. I'm from Queens, so I've watched it for years. I never ran, but I handed out water in my teens. A friend of mine ran it last year and loved it. He said the bridges bounced up and down with all the runners. Pretty cool."

We reached a room with a beamed ceiling and two large windows opening onto a breathtaking view of the alabaster Dolomites. Electra chatted on a teal velvet couch with Alessandro on her lap to an elegant older lady sitting opposite her in an armchair. Her grey hair was short, and diamond earrings hung from her earlobes.

She rose when I entered, her pale eyes friendly with a welcoming smile. "Hello, Jayne," she said, stretching out her hand.

"Hi," I said, shaking her hand.

"Americans. Their manners are nonexistent. It's never 'how do you do' or 'nice to meet you,'" Electra piped up, eyeing me contemptuously. She made a funny face as her voice rose, parroting me, "Hi, guys. What's up?"

My face warmed, and I glanced at Valentina, but she stared at the floor. Electra had her claws out even longer than usual today, and I responded with a perfect smile. "Excuse my unintentional homegrown rudeness." I turned to the woman with a half-curtsy. "I hail from the Excelsior state of New York. It is of the greatest pleasure to make your acquaintance …"

"Signora Bellago," Electra offered with disdain. She rose and handed Alessandro over to me like a bag of groceries, not appreciating my humor. "He needs a change," she said, checking her watch. "And it's almost dinnertime. Take him to La Cooperativa and buy a piece of salmon for you both," she said, her tone dripping with superiority.

Signora Bellago clutched her jade bead necklace and exchanged a glance with Valentina. I looked around for the diaper bag, but only deer antlers and a set of old books were on the table, and the bag was nowhere. "Don't you have the diaper bag?" I asked Electra.

Stunned at my question, she flicked her hair over her shoulder. "No, I don't have it. Didn't you bring it from the car?" she complained. "I told you to. You never listen. Never."

"No. I … I parked the car. The cars were beeping to move. When you jumped out, I thought you …"

She sat back down, reached into her handbag, and pulled out a diaper and wipes. "You're saying it's my fault? At least one of us is prepared to take care of a baby," she said, handing them over with an exaggeratedly pained expression.

Without a response, I hurried out with Alessandro, swearing under my breath. What had happened to Electra? The altitude? I got lost in the big chalet and did not know if I should use the Bellago's bathroom or another room to change Alessandro. Can't be the *rude* American again, I thought. Flustered, I opened a random door, and a man chatting on the telephone looked up at me with surprise. I closed it and finally found an exit to escape the house like it was on fire.

"Jayne." I looked back and saw Valentina waving from the top of the stairs and waited for her to catch up. "Electra," she panted, glancing around. "What was that? Is she always that mean?"

"Mean? Electra?" I said, feigning shock. "Yes and no. But today, this is off the charts. I'll blame the altitude. Or she must have double-dosed on her witch pills. And she loves to put America down in any way she can. It's part of her act."

"God," she laughed. "She's awful. Why don't you leave her and work somewhere else?"

"Everyone asks me that question. Easier said than done. Believe it or not, Medusa can be really nice sometimes. She was my shelter in a storm when I was down to zero. But I don't want to bore you with my sob story. I've become a duck, and her insults roll off my back. I'm trying to save enough to return to a sane life. There *may* be a job over here. I don't know. It's all up in the air."

She nodded. "At least you have options. Better than nothing."

"Yes. I'm halfway there." Alessandro watched with interest, and I bent down to his sweet face. "Your mommy can be a full-blown bitch sometimes," I told him.

"A bith," he said, kicking his legs.

I laughed. "Uh oh. Electra will grill me on how Alessandro knows the word 'bitch.' Luckily, I haven't used the c-word… Tempting, though… Oh my god, I've got to get my life together," I said, feeling overwhelmed. "But it's my fault. When I left Manhattan, I never thought I'd end up an au pair in Italy for a contessa. My boyfriend broke up with me the day I landed in Milan. Everything's a mess."

"Sounds like it. Relationships can be tough, especially long distance ones. Hopefully, Electra is just having a bad day. Hey, do you want to go out one night?'

My jaw dropped. "Me?" I said with disbelief. She was wide-eyed at my strange reaction, and I tried to act normal. "Yes, let's go out. I haven't been out in *so* long. Except for this great guy I met in Yugoslavia. We had a nice time."

"Sounds *interesting*."

"It was one night on a boat and pretty harmless. But I swear, his body was like Michelangelo's David. We'll see what happens between us, if anything. But yes, let's make plans to meet."

"Okay. What about... tonight," Valentina suggested, pulling at Alessandro's shoe and clucking her tongue for his attention.

"Tonight?" Her last-minute invitation took me off-guard, and I hesitated to answer. Electra would go to bed early after the long drive, hopefully. She hadn't gone out since Venice and would probably unpack or read. "Sure. Sounds like fun."

"Okay. I'll come down and get you at eight?"

"How about eight-thirty so I know he's asleep," I replied.

Her brow furrowed at my request, but she shrugged. "Okay. Eight-thirty."

Because of its lower location on a sloping street, the Corso Italia rental apartment's basement window looked up to the main church's Gothic bell tower in the square's center. The pine interior had forest green and white linoleum floors and sparse, simple furniture. An oversized robin egg blue couch in the living room became my pullout bed, and a burgundy-and-white gingham-covered table with two benches served for dining. Electra and Alessandro slept in the main bedroom, and we'd share a large bathroom in the hallway.

Crammed in the rear closet of the apartment was a bike with flat tires, dry, lifeless plants, and a mishmash of downhill and cross-country skis and boots. Next to this heap was a thin door to the staircase into the Bellago's kitchen. Electra's voice swirled above in animated conversation while I unpacked the suitcases, and I hoped she would stay there for a long time.

After unloading the car, I bought salmon and other necessities. Electra didn't come down for dinner; I'm sure she knew I wasn't tickled pink about how she had acted. After finishing my bedtime rituals for Alessandro, I heard her arrive. I tiptoed out of the bedroom to get ready but stopped. Electra was applying blush in the mirror in the bathroom, humming.

I hesitated. "Are you going out tonight?

She put her brush down and checked her teeth for lipstick. "Yes. I'm going back upstairs. Why?"

"Um," I put my hand on my chest. "I was going to go for drinks with Valentina."

She guffawed. "You're *what*? Does she know this?"

"Of course, she does. She's the one who asked me." I straightened my shoulders and took a deep breath. It was one hundred percent my right to have a night free. She wasn't going to stop me. "We're going into town," I said slowly. "To have fun."

Her face reacted like she'd tasted acid. "To have fun. Okay. I… I didn't know."

"I think it's okay since I've worked *every* night since I have been with you, except for the one time with Bojan. It's not a big deal, right?

Alessandro is fast asleep. The kitchen is clean, and there is no ironing to do."

She turned to the mirror and fixed her hair before flashing a saccharine smile. "No, it's not a big deal, Jayne, as you say. Okay… then go." She swatted at me like a fly. "I'll stay here and read the paper. Have a nice night."

"Great. Thank you." Electra disappeared into her room and locked her door—a passive-aggressive message—but that didn't stop me from throwing on mascara and brushing my hair before running out of the rental. Valentina waited outside in the traditional Alpine dirndl folk costume, and I covered my mouth when I saw her. "What are you wearing?" The tight white bodice and long cerulean full skirt with a blueberry embroidered apron could have come from the costume department of *Heidi*.

She strutted like a runway model and spun. "I know it looks funny, but it's a tradition in Cortina. Everyone wears them at night. It's our custom."

I was amazed to find that she was right. As we strolled through the town to the bar, I soon became the odd one out because everyone except me wore Tyrolean clothes. Men in grey leather suspenders smiled with regal feathers poking from their olive-green wool hats and strolled with partners in outfits matching Valentina's. Children wore mini versions of their parents' clothes, following behind like a herd of unruly goats.

Valentina said in Cortina that the *passeggiata*—the before dinner stroll Italians love—was the time for families to parade alpine heritage and say hello to one another. It was sweet and very Old World. Although I felt underdressed in my jeans, I was glad to be part of the tradition.

When we arrived, we joined her friends who were also dressed in traditional clothes, although two were dressed like me. Valentina and I exchanged names of New York and Italy's best clubs and restaurants, laughing as we told stories of our past partying adventures. I danced with handsome guys and ate sausage rolls with borscht soup, loving every moment. Yet I still wished Bojan were there when a Rolling Stones song blasted over the speakers. I bet he was a fun dancer.

"I miss this so much," I shouted as I sat down after dancing to "Tainted Love" by Soft Cell. "The music, the dancing, everything. I used to go out *all* the time in New York. Who knew this club would exist in this tiny town."

"We love our nightclubs. In the winter, there are ten times more people. The Ski Hut is another club nearby, up in the mountains. It's an old chalet they've converted into a bar. Hey, have you tried grappa?"

"No. What's that?"

"Wait." Valentina went to the bar and whispered in the ear of the Tyrolean-dressed bartender. He grinned and rang a bell, causing the crowd to grow quiet. The guy pointed at me and announced that the American would drink grappa for the first time. The place went wild as he poured a shot. Valentina brought over the small tulip-shaped glass and placed it in front of me. "Here you go. Take a deep breath and have a sip."

I picked up the glass while everyone watched. I put it to my nose, smelling the grape lollipop scent with a tinge of allspice. I placed the glass to my lips, expecting a sweeter liquid than the harsh one I soon swallowed. My face distorted like drinking orange juice after brushing my teeth. "Oh my god," I said, trying to control my reaction and not offend anyone. "Reminds me of whiskey."

"It's a digestive. Great for the stomach," Valentina said. She spun to the patrons with a thumbs up, and they applauded my bravery.

We celebrated the night and howled at each other's dance moves. It was a wake-up call that in my cloistered life, I had been missing the simple joy of being able to giggle and enjoy people. Being with friends was what I missed. I had to get back to normalcy. I just needed to figure out where and how.

The next morning's mild hangover was the price to pay for a good time. My sour mouth and donkey-kicked temples reminded me of past overdone soirees, and after hydrating with a drink of water, I pressed my ear to Electra's door and heard Alessandro's morning rumblings. I cracked open the door, and a foot moved under the scattered, colorful pile of baby books on the bed. Alessandro's sweet gaze met mine as he lay beside his sleeping mother. My finger went to my lips as I smiled, imagining them curled together as they fell asleep. Then I remembered her f-bomb and sighed.

Alessandro's arms shot up, and Electra moaned in pain. "You kept me up all night when you came in."

"Sorry," I said, rubbing where I'd hit my leg during my clumsy stumble into a pitch-black foyer. I had fallen against the hallway chair, chuckling with Valentina. She took the stairs to the upper floor.

"Let me stay here for a while," her creased face croaked. "I need to sleep."

"Sure. No problem. Come here, little guy." I whizzed in to pluck the cub from his mama bear so Electra could catch up on her beauty sleep. His compact body smelled like marshmallows, and I squeezed him tightly.

"Valentina and I had fun," I whispered into his ear when he grabbed his bottle. I went back into the kitchen and twirled around the room. "I had grappa for the first time," I sang in a funny voice, making him giggle with my reactions. Milk pooled in the corners of his mouth, and I made funny faces as he sucked down the bottle's contents. "We got back a little past midnight. I'm sorry if I woke you up. We're going out again, and she invited me to another town for a party. In a chalet."

Suddenly, dogs barked wildly outside, and I went out to investigate the commotion. Two men untangled their snarling, wired-haired dachshunds, and the cool mountain air pressed against my bare calves and arms as I watched. Across the street, a bed-headed couple kissed outside on a hotel balcony. They looked so romantic, and my lips pouted, kissing the air and thinking of my lovely kisses with Bojan. Not Matteo.

Above, chalet shutters opened, and Valentina's Pavarotti-looking father, whom I had met on the street the day before, leaned out into the bright morning sky. "Buongiorno," I called, waving for his attention.

"Ciao, Jayne. Ciao, Alessandro," he said with a grin. He punched his chest, inhaling the fresh air. "A beautiful day. Dov'è Electra?" *Where's Electra?*

I made a sleeping gesture, and he smiled before ducking back into his house. Electra mentioned he owned a media company. She also emphasized with a locked jaw that the family was like hers. Curious about what she meant, I asked how. "We run in the same circles. The House of Bellago. They're an old, noble aristocratic family," was her response. "Venetian, of course."

I returned, ready to start breakfast and enjoy the hour away from Electra's eagle eyes. Usually, she would roll out of bed around ten and have a boiled egg and toast. While she ate, I'd shower and prepare for the day. On a kitchen chair was a Tyrolean outfit and a red Robin Hood hat with a big pheasant feather protruding from its band. Electra had bought it for Alessandro, and I couldn't wait to dress him after his morning bath.

Her bedroom door suddenly opened, and she lumbered like a coal miner into the sunlight. "I forgot. We're going to the mountains this morning," she announced, squinting at me. "I need an espresso. Pronto."

I hurried to take the espresso out of the cabinet. "When are we leaving?" I asked, scooping coffee into the machine as fast as I could.

She glanced at the clock. "Uh-oh. It's so late. Forget about the coffee. We must leave now. They're waiting."

"Who?" I asked, taking his cereal down from the shelf. "Do I have time for a shower?"

She scrambled to the bathroom. "No. It's the Bellago's."

"Great," I responded with a grin—more fun with Valentina and her family.

$ 1,143.56
− 4.25

Lunch after brush with death!

RIP

$ 1,139.31

edelweiss

CHAPTER FOURTEEN

"WHERE ARE MY HIKING BOOTS? They're missing," Electra cried, running around the house in her pajamas.

I joined the hunt, listening to the usual chorus of mio dios. She hadn't used the f-bomb again; had I imagined it the first time? But my instinct said no. Of course, it came out of her mouth. "Did you forget to put them in the car? Where did you hide my boots?" she asked, throwing up her hands.

I frowned at her accusatory tone. "Nowhere. I didn't touch them." My blood pressure rose, and I rechecked every corner in the tiny rental. I pointed to the ceiling. "Did you leave them upstairs?"

Her face brightened. "Yes. Yes, I did."

"What meals should I pack for Alessandro? Or is it just snacks?" I asked as she bounded up the steps. She didn't hear me, and I wrangled him into the cute outfit and red hat. Minutes later, Electra plodded in, holding her boots, fully dressed.

"I'm going to ride with them," she said, pulling the boot on her foot.

I stopped yanking up his pants. "So, we're not going?" I said, hoping for a free day to explore Cortina.

She pushed the hair from her face. "No, we're all going. But you and Alessandro are in the car alone. I'm going in the Range Rover," she said, letting the Rs roll over her tongue like a true Italian.

I stopped. "Wait. How do I find you? I don't know this area at all."

"You can read a map, can't you?" she asked, tying the laces of the other boot. "And you can follow us in the car." She stood up and stomped on the floor. "But they can't wait forever. We have a noon reservation at the rifugio, so we're leaving now."

Matteo had told me about rifugios, rugged mountain huts or simple chalets set high in the mountains that served hearty, ethnic dishes to starving hikers. I jogged back and grabbed the keys, imagining a warm, home-cooked meal. My backpack was in the corner, and I emptied the contents onto the couch before throwing in my emergency essentials and Alessandro's necessities: a bottle, diapers, wipes, and a bag of Cheerios.

Back in the hall, I reevaluated my worn Tretorn sneakers next to her professional lace-up hiking boots. "Am I okay with sneakers?"

She grimaced. "Well, we are in the mountains and hiking."

"Ugh. My bag only fits so much, remember? The one you gave me. In case you haven't noticed, I've worn the same jeans since we left Milan. So, I couldn't bring my Imelda Marcos collection of hiking boots," I said with sarcasm, running to the backroom, "But I saw an old pair back here somewhere."

The weather-beaten leather boots were cardboard stiff, and if I weren't so desperate, the small mound of petrified animal droppings near them would have been a major turnoff. Still, beggars can't be choosers, and I took the spiderweb-veiled shoes from the floor. My only hope was that every creature, insect, and fecal deposit had vacated or dissolved as I crammed my feet in with a nauseous wince.

"I'm ready," I said, running to where two food jars sat near my backpack. A horn beeped outside as I zipped them shut into my bag. "Hold your horses, people."

"Basta. I put the map in your bag," she barked. "If you don't come now, you've got to wind up the mountain yourself." Someone yelled her name, and she opened the door to greet them before spinning to me. "I'll meet you there," she trilled like a lovestruck girl. "Got to go."

"Wait," I yelled, taking Alessandro and the backpack as I hurried outside. The Range Rover's door was open, and Electra's body was halfway into the back of the car. From what I could see, there must have been at least three others inside.

I shut the door and threw the backpack over my shoulder. My legs burned as I ran to the parking lot to the Citroen while their SUV followed me. Out of breath, I placed Alessandro in his car seat as they watched me fumble with the seatbelt.

"Follow us," shouted Electra as I jumped into the driver's seat.

The army-green Range Rover roared up the mountain road, passing shimmering alpine lakes as the snaggled, serrated mountainous ridges loomed closer. Screeching around hairpin turns, I corkscrewed up the sides of the Dolomites, swerving away from backpackers and bicyclists. The Citroen DS's power was equal to the high-performance SUV, and I was determined not to lose them as Alessandro gurgled in the back seat, unaware of the hairy situation.

We got off the main road and sped onto a dirt lane. The local road was wide enough for only one car, and I followed their beige cloud of dirt, climbing upward and feeling a bit carsick. My ears became blocked by the rising altitude, and I pinched my nose to relieve the pressure. Finally, a painted *rifugio* with a large cherry-red arrow appeared on a timber post, pointing down the road. I followed the Range Rover into a dead-end parking area, relieved. A single space was free, and their car zipped into it.

"Sure, take the last spot," I grumbled, leaning forward to peer at the peaks of the majestic Dolomites. At the base was a brown chalet with a flapping Italian flag. My appetite increased as I checked where to park, eyeing hikers at picnic tables spooning mouth-watering food into their mouths. I drummed my fingers on the steering wheel, wondering where to go.

Electra piled out of the SUV, followed by Valentina and her parents. She stepped away from the car and gawked in my direction, visibly annoyed. Valentina glanced back but ignored my predicament to join the others on the worn path to the chalet. Electra hurried over with a red grimace, huffing with impatience. "What are you doing? Park over there," she barked, throwing her hand to the viridian edge.

The sidewalk-sized sliver of land looked dubious. "Over there?" All I could see was an ocean of pine trees behind it. "It's tiny. And it doesn't look very safe."

She opened the back door and scooped Alessandro out. "Yes. It's fine. We're in the mountains, not Bloomingdale's garage. People park anywhere," she said before grabbing his diaper bag. "Mio dio. It's not *that* hard. Hurry up, though. The reservation for lunch will be gone; we're already late."

She rushed away, and I evaluated the situation, fuming. The hood of the Citroen DS had a quirk that was discombobulating when driving and parking: the air vent for the engine was on top of the hood—but it wasn't centered in the middle as one may think would be practical for the driver. It was in the middle of the passenger side and tricked the driver, or at least me, into incorrectly relying on it as a marker for the car's center.

I checked my mirror and put it into reverse to park on the small tuft of land. As I slowed into the spot, I glimpsed Alessandro's red hat disappear up the path. "No use to help and guide me," I fretted. The Citroen inched closer to the side with a slight angle in the terrain, and I succeeded in parking it. The motor stopped, and the hydraulic system groaned as it lowered the chassis to its resting position with an alarming tilt to the left side.

I gasped when I opened the door. It swung out over the chasm below, and the car's running board was inches from the edge of a thousand-foot drop. The chassis creaked again, and I braced for the worst. "Holy shit." I leaned to the right, searching for Electra and Alessandro, but they were nowhere in my view. I couldn't even honk for help as it only operated when the car was on, and I couldn't risk it moving again.

A gust spurted from the valley's pine canopy, and the car's metal grated in the wind. The door handle was reachable, and I leaned forward slowly and put my fingers around its cool steel handle. Any creak was hair-raising, but the car was my friend and wouldn't disappoint me. "We got this, girl. We'll get through this." The door eased forward under my grasp, and I shut it soundly while my heart thudded in my chest. "You're getting an oil change for that," I exhaled.

Now what? In the rear-view mirror, a couple in long khaki shorts wandered up one of the hiking trails, deep in conversation. They approached the parking lot with hi-tech walking sticks, oblivious to my dilemma. Luckily, the thin man spotted the car and scratched his bald head at what moron had parked there, not knowing I was sitting there. He called out to the woman, and she came over to gasp at my situation.

My sudden movement startled them, and I pointed to the drop below me. The man understood and went into action, motioning to start the engine.

The car spurted alive and rose. His face dropped, and the car tilted toward the cliffside. I shifted my weight as his frightened partner clenched her teeth and tried to stay calm as he came to the passenger side window and spoke in German.

"Non sprachen Deutsch," I said, my lips quivering.

He nodded. "Okay. Don't worry," he said with a heavy accent. "I will help you. Be slow. Elephant slow."

His partner remained frozen; her hands locked in prayer. Slowly, the car tilted as the man watched my back and front wheels. Inch by inch, I did as he commanded. Soon, the car was back in the flat parking area. Relieved, I blew a kiss to them as tears welled and my hands trembled. "Thank you. Thank you so much."

He walked over. "I had a Citroen like this. Worst car ever," he said, rejecting my adulations with amusement. "We all need a beer after that."

The couple gave me the thumbs-up and left me to gather my wits. I had almost just become a mountain statistic. The slap with death was a wake-up call to new dangers, and the image of an upside-down crumpled car in a ravine haunted me as I scouted for any parking oasis. There was one, albeit cramped and tight, and I slunk into it, cursing Electra. How could she have missed it?

The friendly owner, dressed in jeans and a green flannel shirt, welcomed me into the room's heavenly smell of a beef stew. Her busy husband stirred a big pot in the open kitchen while their teenage kids scrambled with plates full of mouth-watering meaty chunks, onions, potatoes, and carrots. Electra, Valentina, and her parents convened in the corner, and I sat alone, too overwhelmed for chitchat. The lukewarm feast helped me unwind, and the gigantic chantarelle mushrooms were a surprising help in taking my mind off what just happened. Around me, people drank pints of beer, and I just sipped a glass, absorbing the incredible view through red gingham curtains as a need-to-be-brushed sheepdog sniffed the ground for crumbs.

I caught Valentina's eye and raised my hand to tell her my horrific story, but she ignored me. She must have the same post-party hangover with a throbbing head, I thought, chewing. Each mouthful of food eradicated the achiness of last night's drinking, and my parking debacle faded in the enjoyment. The lunch ended with a slab of homemade cheesecake smothered with mountain berries, and I devoured it in record time since everyone else had packed up and left to hike. When I hurried outside, Electra stood before a rusted chrome and flimsy nylon baby carrier with her hand on her chin. She perked up when she spotted me. "Jayne. Look at what we got. This carrier was in the back of their car."

Aluminum poles poked out from the cloth side, and a corner had a tear. "Is that for Alessandro?" I said, my eyes widening as I got closer.

She gave it a wobbly shake. "Of course, it is. It's fine, and it held all the Bellagos for years through these mountains. I'd be honored to put Alessandro in it."

I didn't have the energy to argue and counted to ten with a sigh. "You're the mother. Help me put it on," I said, turning my back to her. She held the carrier up, and I looped my arms through the straps. Electra secured its delicate buckles, and the thin straps cut into my flesh. "Ow. It's not a straitjacket, you know. Can you loosen it? Please?" I gasped in pain.

"Then it won't be tight."

I raised my eyes to heaven with the hypocrisy. I shimmied my shoulders a bit and found that moving the strap closer to my shoulder became more comfortable. "Can this thing hold him? What if he falls out?"

"Stop. You Americans and safety." She put in Alessandro, and his heaviness twinged my back muscles. "Lawyers ruined your country."

I was ready to respond, but my neck jerked back from Alessandro's brutal hair pull. I stared at the sky, wincing. "Ow."

"Look at you two. Ready to hike, my little boy?" she asked, stepping back. "He looks so regal. Like an Austrian prince."

On his steed, I thought, fixing my hair as he let go.

On the crushed stone path, Electra skipped off to join the others, and I studied the trail map with its red capillary lines of trails. When I gazed at the high peaks, suspicious vultures soared kite-like below the ridges, and I adjusted the straps, trying to ignore the blisters forming in my new boots.

"Keep your eyes peeled for bears, bubs." As we started to walk, the Dolomites stood guard on the rim of the lush grasslands with razor-sharp ridgelines. Trudging behind the group, I reached the first metallic marker. A simple wooden cross with a coffee can for donations at its base. Valentina dumped a coin into the slit of its plastic cover, and the group trekked to the next marker.

A mile later, the thunderous roar of a rushing river greeted us, and the posse stopped for a break. I stepped close to the aquamarine runoff that seemed pure in its beautiful, chaotic way, thinking of my mood board. Valentina sat cross-legged on a rock nearby, rifling through her backpack pocket, and I walked toward her with a smile. However, she arose quickly as soon as she noticed me. Then Alessandro pulled my hair to the right, and I marched to his new command, albeit curious of her strange reaction. "Be gentle up there, Lone Ranger," I grimaced. "I'm still the sheriff in this town."

Steps later, a pale, woolly flower with a fuzzy yellow center peeked out from a boulder's fracture like a snowflake that had forgotten to thaw. "Ooh, look. A pretty flower," I said, touching its tiny cotton ball's soft petals. I plucked it to show Alessandro, and he held the blossom gently in his chubby fingers to smell.

"Jayne. Do you want water?" Electra called.

"Sure," I yelled back. I grabbed his soft foot near my armpit. "Let's show Momma your little flower."

Valentina's mom stepped back when I approached the group, staring at Alessandro dumbstruck. She hit Electra's arm for attention and pointed at me. Electra's mouth dropped, and she snatched the tiny flower out of Alessandro's hand without warning. "No," she scolded with over-the-top gruffness, causing him to wail. "Mio dio. No, no, no."

"Why? Is it poisonous?" I gasped, bouncing the carrier to calm his sudden crying.

"Worse." She threw up her arms, ranting in Italian with the word *American* mixed with great emphasis. Valentina's mother crowded around her, and before I could ask Valentina to explain the problem, she joined the group, scowling in my direction.

How could a small flower cause such chaos and anger? The only person amused was Valentina's father. I sidled up to him with my tail between my legs, and his lips twitched. He enjoyed the stage-worthy spectacle, which bordered on comedic hysteria. "What is that little flower?" I asked under my breath.

"It's edelweiss. A mountain flower that belongs in the daisy family."

"Daisy family? Then why are they all freaking out?" I said, watching them gawk at the flower's corpse on Electra's palm.

"Well, it's illegal to pick. I'd say in this crowd, it's equal to burning your flag," he said, shaking his head at the group. "It's silly. You didn't know."

I slapped the side of my thighs. "Of course, I didn't."

Electra stomped over to us. "You destroyed this … centuries of nature," she claimed, sticking the wilted flower in my face. "Do you know Edelweiss is almost extinct? This prehistoric gem of nature could be one of the last ones in the world. You have no respect."

"I'm sorry. I didn't know."

"Well, you know all the songs from *Sound of Music*, so you should have."

"Electra," Mr. Bellago rubbed his stubbly chin. "To me, what Jayne has done is beyond admirable. It would be best if you forgave her. She is trying to cultivate in your son an appreciation of the beauty of the universe. There are pictures of flowers in books, whereas to touch, feel, and share the experience with the ones he loves makes it memorable and special." He swung around to me. "They don't have edelweiss in the United States, do they?"

"Not that I know of. And just so you know, this is my first time in the Italian Alps, and there are no signs to warn people not to pick flowers. I just thought it was pretty for Alessandro," I said, glaring at Electra. "Excuse me for expanding his horizons. And for your information, the edelweiss song doesn't say do not pick."

Mr. Bellago followed me as I left the noisy group. "Oh, let them rant about the injustice. Aren't you tired from carrying Alessandro for so long? He's too heavy for that old carrier. What does she feed him? Spinach porridge? Rocks?" he asked, scowling. "Let me take him."

"No. I'm okay," I said, dejected. "He's just a big eater. Thanks for coming to my defense. What you said was almost poetic and really hit me as the truth. Before I came to Italy, I never really noticed the natural world around me; it's like that part of my brain was turned off. But since I've been here, I hear birds, wonder what a butterfly thinks as it flutters, and watch a leaf fall from a tree. And brooks do babble. Nature is now my secret inspiration." I knew it would be my theme for Cortina. "I'm embracing the wonder."

"So, you're saying you can see now."

I laughed. "Yes. Exactly. Better late than never."

I slipped away while Electra restarted her edelweiss rant as Mr. Bellago returned to defend my actions yet again. Alessandro yanked on my sweater to steer right; I was relieved to escape, hoping the argument wouldn't grow too heated. Electra hated to lose, and from what I could see, Mr. Bellago didn't enjoy defeat either.

Valentina's family had a certain sophistication that Electra didn't. And they were genuine and kind, even though the reaction was a bit over the top with the edelweiss. Even on the hike, they put on no airs in their ripped sweaters and tattered jeans and contrasted the expensive wool tweed jacket and jodhpur-like pants of Electra's high-priced outfit. In it, she belonged in a Tyrolean catalog, not on a treacherous hike. Electra talked the talk, but the Bellago's walked the walk. They whispered wealth, they didn't shout about it.

But Valentina acted like the previous night had never happened. Why?

I slowed down to enjoy the mile-wide views and took more photos, delighted to be alone in the highland without distractions or ridiculous squabbles. Between ancient mountain ranges, hammocked valleys hung, and I picked up a piece of dry wood and a pretty stone as I walked. Cowbells tinkled nearby, and a pair of brown and cream heifers munched on grasslands below the cottony clouds, watching with interest. "I wish I could tack this peacefulness on my mood board. Isn't this beautiful, Alessandro?"

Hiking up a steep hill, I spotted a bucolic hay barn with cut-out hearts on its weathered boards, adding to the serenity. At the top, an endless carpet of violets, lupines, forget-me-nots, and daisies blended with purple-and-white clover stretched to the horizon. Next stop, heaven.

"I'll come back here one day with my family, Alessandro. We'll stand right here and tell them my story. And I'll say one person was my true friend in Italy. You know who? You, little man."

I blinked back tears, squeezing his tiny foot. The fact that my little sidekick would never remember was kind of upsetting. I already missed him.

"Jayne, Jayne." I turned to see a panting Electra trudging up the hill. Her flushed face was damp from sweat. "You need to go back with Alessandro. Do you think you have enough water?"

"Where? Back to the restaurant?"

She scowled. "No. To the house. You have the car. Alessandro needs his nap. There's enough food for dinner there." She thumbed back down the trail. "I'll eat with them tonight. Okay?"

I scanned the multiple narrow paths in the distance, and the mountains seemed to have huddled around us. My mind spun like a needle in a broken compass, and I surveyed every direction. "Okay. Umm . . . which way to the car? This way, right? Do I hike straight back?"

She flung out her hand. "Follow the signs for either they say *rifugio* or *hutte*," she said, glancing at her watch. "Ask anyone along the way if you need to. But you'll be fine. It's easy . . . and, Jayne, the flower you picked?"

My jaw clenched. "Yes."

"Just a misunderstanding. I appreciate your showing Alessandro flowers and all the wonderful things around us," she said. "I'm sorry for overreacting."

"It's okay." I hobbled away, aiming for a signpost in the distance and mumbling about whether my return could be her punishment for picking the flower. The path was familiar, and I relaxed, glancing over my shoulder 'til the group was out of sight. I spotted a dandelion puffball and picked its stem with a grin. "This isn't on an endangered list, that's for sure. Let's blow on this together, and if we do it in one breath, all our wishes will come true," I said, holding the white, fluffy ball of seeds between us.

He put his little hand on my shoulder, and I squeezed his warm fingers. "Ready? One. Two. Three."

Together, we blew, and the seeds dispersed into the rollercoaster wind. Giggling, I watched them all float away, hoping my wish would come true.

Whatever decision I made would be the right one.

$1,139.31

Magnesium pills for anxiety - pharmacist said 2x a day	- 5.50
Red Robin Hood hat - Quinn	- 12.00
Wildflower dress for Kate - machine washable?	- 30.00
Alpine flower book	- 8.50
Pint of beer - grande really means a gallon!!	- 4.00
More mood board stuff - ribbon - grouse feathers are $$	- 9.65
Candy, Toblerone	- 6.56
Rest Stop pizza/soda	- 6.50

$ 1,056.60

12
DOWN UP
6

CHAPTER FIFTEEN

AT THE RIFUGIO PARKING LOT, more hiking groups had arrived on foot. I slipped a half-asleep Alessandro into his car seat and hoped the drive down would be more leisurely as I snapped my seat belt buckle with a big yawn. If all went as planned, I could revisit the tourist shop in Cortina, where painted cowbells and ceramic beer steins crowded the shelves. The red Robin Hood hats were there also, and I wondered if I should buy one for Flynn's son, Quinn. It would be perfect for him. And a cowbell for musical Kate would be fun. She'd drive Flynn and Ambrose crazy, clanging it in the house.

At first, the one-lane road was pleasant, although my foot hovered above the brake pedal, fearing the cliff's edge, never more than a few inches away. Could the group stay overnight on the mountain? I read in the guidebooks that rifugios had simple bunkrooms and trails that connected mountain huts for those interested in weeklong treks. Would Electra have informed me of their plan, or would I have a sleepless night of not knowing? Electra would love alone time in a rustic shed with the family to pick their brain or gossip about the world of aristocracy. Or throw me under the bus with exaggerated stories.

I took a deep breath. Why had Valentina acted like I was a stranger all day? She stuck to her mother like a baby fawn. I hoped I hadn't been an idiot the previous night.

Preoccupied, I gasped when another large car came into view and slowed. "Crap." There was no shoulder on the narrow road to pull over, and neither vehicle could pass. However, the driver thought otherwise and sped in my direction.

"Jesus, slow down." After I stopped, I checked Alessandro; he was asleep with a river of drool leaking out of his rosebud mouth. I turned back, and the obnoxious car with Magnum 4x4 on its hood stopped, our bumpers almost kissing. After my last fright, reversing the Citroen DS up a dangerous road with no guardrails would be as easy as docking a cruise ship in a bathtub, and I raised my arms in frustration.

The woman driver gesticulated for me to reverse, and I gestured for *her* to move back. After we formed Italian finger purses at each other, she leaped out in her fur-trimmed fancy hiking boots with silver bells and marched over with fury. I lowered my window, ready to defend myself, and she began a spit-firing tirade in Italian. Too tired to reply, I listened. The last place to pull over was half a mile back, and I held my ground, puffing at the enraged lady while ignoring her insults.

Her passenger in a down vest got out to join our conversation. Something snapped in my brain, and I heaved the door open, hitting her belted canteen. "Scusi. Stop. Basta. You're speaking too fast for me," I said in half Italian, half English, ready to have a nervous breakdown. I grabbed my hair, circling the cars with a deep moan. "I can't back up this … this boat. I almost fell off a cliff already. I don't want to die."

They both gawked at my strange outburst. "We speak English, you know," the driver said calmly.

"Of course, you do." My body relaxed a tad, and I rubbed my eyelids. "Then please help me. I … I can't drive here in these ridiculously high mountains," I said, exasperated. "These scary roads are too narrow, and I'm not used to driving where one wrong move means farewell world."

"All roads are like this in the Alps. There is a rule—you drive up from the hour to the half-hour and drive down from the half-hour to the hour." She glanced at her friend and then at her big gold watch. She held up her wrist and pointed to it. "My watch says *I* have the right of way."

"If it makes you feel better, okay, that's fine. Congratulations. And I'm sorry. It's my mistake. Like everything else that's happened since I got to this country." I kicked the dirt, swearing under my breath at the unfairness. "No one told me there were road rules. But why would they? I'm just the hired help. But what am I supposed to do now? Chitty Chitty Bang Bang over your car?"

"I don't know what the shitty chitty thing is." The driver stepped forward, puzzled. She held out her hand. "Give me your keys, and I'll help you."

I examined the road, and it still seemed hopeless. "How? Your car is huge, and so is mine. Let's leave our cars here," I wailed, throwing my hands up in defeat. "We can walk off this mountain, have a beer …"

"I want to hike, not drink beer. It's easy," the woman said, approaching slowly with a coaxing smile. "Trust me. The keys?"

I hesitated, then went to the car and pulled them from the ignition. I dropped the keys into her palm. "It's my boss's car. So, please be careful."

"I will." She jumped in the car and rolled it back a centimeter but stopped with a jerk. She popped out of the driver's side. "Hey. There's a baby in here," she shouted.

"I know." I ran to the car. "Did you wake him up?"

She looked back. "No. But I'm shocked your hysterics didn't."

The other woman was now in their SUV and followed my car as it reversed slowly. I followed, watching as they signaled to each other. A slight shoulder was a quarter of a mile up the road, and she quickly maneuvered into the space. The other squeaked by, and I clapped at the victory. "Yay," I shouted. "Thank you."

I hurried to the Citroen as the driver got out. Except my joy was short-lived. "Wait. What if another car comes up like you did?"

"Hmm. That could be a problem because we're right at the half-hour." She thought for a moment, then shouted to her waiting friend in German. The red brake lights flashed, and the car drove off. She pivoted back to me. "I'll drive you both down."

I refrained from hugging her but was overjoyed and overwhelmed by her generosity. I jumped in the passenger seat and had the pleasure of someone else driving as the car zigzagged down the road, loving the big-ticket views I had missed on the ascent. At the bottom, she pulled over, and I gushed my appreciation. Her friend arrived soon after, and both waved as they drove back up the mountain road.

I needed that beer. Pronto.

For the next week, I busied myself with small hikes and wandered around Cortina, imagining my exit as I scouted for inspiration. Nature opened my mind and influenced my depiction of Italy, and the Dolomites' rawness and the setting sun's melancholy added tragic touches. The poetry of nature created a sensuous homage I was eager to portray.

A book about wood nymphs was on a small bookcase, and I felt like one as I flitted around, examining flowers and trees. There were not only nature references; my mood board became a collage of old postcards and snippets from various sources, and I even found a piece of cotton with the texture and color of edelweiss. At the *il mercato delle pulci* flea market in Cortina, I bought a silky ribbon the color of the glacial rivers and a piece of brocade that reminded me of the curtains at the Bellagos' chalet. My scissors snipped velvet trim, silver buttons, and earthy-colored yarn skeins as my mind wandered. I wrote lines from a book of poems I found for inspiration and gathered every memento, even buying a grouse feather from a clothing store's replacement stock.

I checked in with Gino, but he had no updates about Tatiana's decision. I also called the café in Yugoslavia and spoke to Bojan. Hearing his smoky voice tell me he wished he were with me in Cortina was nice. Exploring the area with hikes and picnics would have been so romantic, especially since Valentina had given me the cold shoulder. I guess I must have said ridiculous things when I was drunk. I racked my brain to remember what.

On Friday, Electra rushed down the stairs earlier than usual from her nightly rendezvous. She broke down at the end of my pullout bed with a big wail. "They just informed me the apartment is booked next week with another family. It's too late to find another rental, and we must return to Milan."

It was a week earlier than planned, yet positive news. I could meet with Gino sooner and discuss my possibilities. I held back my excitement and feigned disappointment. "Aw. That sucks. When are we going to leave?"

"You can drive back tomorrow, and I will take the train with Alessandro the next day," she said, taking a piece of fluff off her sweater and depositing it on the floor. "You can unpack and prepare the apartment for our arrival."

Classic move. I gritted my teeth with a sudden sympathy for Cinderella. That meant a day of washing dirty clothes and ironing. "That's not much time to pack or even take my last look at Cortina. How long is the drive?"

"Long enough. You'll be fine, though. Go to the store and buy that special honey Alessandro loves on his cereal. Oh, and remember the mountain apples for his applesauce. Organic, of course."

I squinted a smile. "Of course."

After breakfast the next morning, the first customer through the doors of La Cooperativa was me as the bleary-eyed staff prepared for a busy day. The honey aisle had various brands, and I scanned labels for Alessandro's local favorite. Shoppers trickled in, and my casual glance caught Valentina in jeans and a red sweater walking down an aisle. I ducked behind the bakery goods to spy. She always looked so chic. Maybe her reason for snubbing me was that I was too unsophisticated with my limited jeans and tee shirt wardrobe. I hoped she'd traipse off to the women's department upstairs so I could finish. Luckily, an elderly couple stopped her to say hello, and I crept to the back area for the special apples.

Hugging the wall to escape any notice, I made my way to the cashier with a bag of apples, honey, and a Toblerone bar for the long car ride to Milan. While I debated whether I should buy a touristy Cortina key chain of a timbered chalet, a shadow loomed over my shoulder, and I turned.

Valentina.

I swung back, avoiding her gaze.

"Hi, Jayne," she said, tapping my back.

I took a step away, staring at the counter, confused. "Oh. Hi."

"I heard you're leaving today."

I flashed a grin. "Yup."

She touched my arm, scanning nearby shoppers, and then leaned forward. "I … I came to tell you," she whispered. "It's …"

"What?" I gulped, feeling nauseous. "Tell me what?"

She stepped closer. "It's about Electra."

My body stiffened. "Electra? I just left her. Is she okay?"

"No, it's nothing like that. *I* wanted to tell you what she said after the night we went out. She went up to my mother and said it was improper for her nanny to be seen with me in Cortina. She said people would talk, and it didn't look right."

"What?" I asked a little too loud. "*Are you serious?*"

"I wish I wasn't. My mother didn't know what to say." Valentina glanced at the waiting cashier, who seemed enthralled by the story, and she motioned to me. "She needs lire."

"Mi dispiace." The cashier took the wad while I seethed with anger. The saboteur. First Roberto, then Valentina. No wonder my social life was nonexistent. I thought it was me, but it was my gatekeeper. What was wrong with Electra? Jealousy? "This is so unreal. She's really stepped over the line this time. Too bad closed-minded people come with an open mouth."

"I know, I'm so sorry. I feel awful. My mother told me not to go out with you because Electra rents the apartment, and it would be too awkward to have her mad at us. She didn't trust her because she heard she could be mean. I told her it was wrong, but she said Electra could be a nightmare when she doesn't get her way. She knew her in Milan and Venice, and she has a reputation."

"I'm sure she does," I sneered. "Ugh, she needs to be dethroned. What a piece of work that woman is." I flapped my arms to the side. "But do you know what? I should have known."

"I'm sorry about the edelweiss too. I guess we went overboard. My dad screamed at us when we got home. He and my mother are still not talking. We had fun at the bar that night, and I wanted to go out again. I'm so sorry. My friends loved you."

I felt vindicated. But what was I going to say to Electra? "I know, it was so fun. You were my Cortina drinking buddy." I reached out and touched her arm. "Thanks for letting me know. I'm sure it was hard to do, and you didn't have to, although I appreciate it. I mean," I said, my face warming, "I thought *I* had done something wrong."

"No. Not at all. You're so funny. My family doesn't really like Electra. Especially my father. My parents argue about her all the time." She leaned closer again. "We couldn't stand it when she came up every night. We even locked the basement door one night, but she came to the front door and knocked till we opened it."

"Is that so?" I said, faking astonishment. "Wasn't Electra the life of the party? She said you were waiting for her *every* night."

"Waiting for her to leave," she said, rolling her eyes. "That's the only thing we wanted. We don't have another family coming, you know. My father said enough. Basta. He wanted to enjoy the rest of his summer."

When I returned to the apartment, I barely acknowledged Electra as she flitted around packing. She'd gone too far, and this trip to Milan was a perfect way to tell her I wanted to quit. After putting the honey in the suitcase, I stuffed the luggage, toys, and knick-knacks in the car. Of course, Electra bought a bespoke, child-size wooden table and chairs from a local craftsman, and I had to jam them in the back seat as well. Along with the mass of children's Tyrolean clothing she'd bought, probably to knock off in the Phillipines, wine, and assorted glass purchases from Venice, the only breathing room left was two inches around me.

"I hope I don't get pulled over," I said, checking the rearview mirror. "Not that I'd be able to see a police car behind me." A shopping bag blocked my vision, and I pushed it down, causing a box to fall into the backseat with a muffled crash. I pulled out the map from the door pocket, examining the route I'd be taking. It was rural mountain roads till a toll highway started.

"You'll be fine," Electra said, holding Alessandro. "Follow the signs to Milano. It's easy."

"Easy?" I heard that word from Electra before and knew it could mean disaster.

"Call me when you get to Milan," she said, glancing at her watch. "You should be there by eight."

I turned the ignition and thought of the mood board items I had stowed by my pull-out bed. I didn't remember placing the bag in the hurried chaos. "I forgot my stuff. Did you see that bag with the paper in it?" I asked as I got out of the car. "It was near the door."

"That bag of paper and junk? I threw it out for you." I felt ill and held my stomach as I turned back to her. My shocked face caused her to flick her hand with a hint of regret. "It's still in the trash if you want it. In the kitchen. I can get it."

"No, I'll get it. Next time, if you don't know, ask me, please." I bolted into the kitchen and found it under gooey eggshells and leaky coffee grounds. Luckily, there wasn't any damage to the contents, although the fabric was now stained brown. I picked it up, and the now-aged patina wasn't as bad as I thought. "Not the usual tea-dyeing, but I'll make it work."

I hurried back and was caught off guard to see Valentina and her parents standing beside the car. As soon as Valentina spotted me, she ran up and gave me a big hug. Over her shoulder, I saw Electra's jaw drop while Valentina's father winked at me behind the stunned Electra.

"We're here to say farewell," Valentina said, stepping away. "And good luck with your future."

Her father cleared his throat. "Jayne, I hope you visit us and stay in the main house for as long as you like. We can enjoy the passeggiata together," he bellowed with a loud voice in Electra's direction.

I nodded with a big smile. "I will certainly do that."

Back on schedule, I left via gentle switchbacks that took me through pastoral villages and fluffy meadows dotted with weathered barns and rolls of hay. Tunnels cut through the mountain's stone, and vast bridges reached over roaring rivers, enlivening the gorgeous drive. Delighted being passenger-less, I blared pop music and sang along, eating my

Toblerone in the party mobile. I wondered what Bojan was doing; I hoped he was safe. I had sent another postcard to the café before I left. A Rolling Stone song on the radio reminded me of his warm kiss. Was he thinking of me?

An hour later, the weather changed, and torrential downpours kept me swearing like a sailor while tractor-trailers barreled past with their wheels at eye level. As the wipers swished back and forth, I squinted for road signs while praying the car wouldn't hydroplane into a ditch. But Gino's offer kept my spirits high, and I imagined a different life from the chauffeur slash babysitter one I was currently leading. Although I had chickened out and decided to reveal my news to Electra when she returned to Milan, the shackles were off metaphorically. Roberto and I could now get a drink. I'd make new friends. My parents could visit with Flynn and her family, and I'd show them my success. I sighed. My days with Electra would be over, though I'd miss sweet Alessandro.

The splashing traffic slowed when a toll loomed from the fog. Milan was nearby. I grabbed my wallet as the arm of the toll collector popped out. "Milano?" I handed him the cash. It was already nine o'clock, and my ETA to Milan would be after eleven p.m. with this awful weather without more traffic or accidents.

"Si," he said, handing back the change.

Off again, encapsulated in a metal box, I had time to reflect. It was bizarre how Electra and I had ended up together. Me, the dumped American, abandoning the dream of what was supposed to be Matteo's true love, and her, the snooty single mother with relationship problems. Two lost women with broken lives. Hiring me to drive on the greatest hit tour of her royal di Caneva family was exciting but odd. Was it because I was an American and she wanted to impress me? And why did she tell Valentina's mom my friendship with her daughter was improper? I guess she did think I was inferior to her. But I knew deep down she didn't feel that way. Her underlying insecurities were from dark wounds, and I found them sad. But it doesn't matter how rich you are; you can't buy people or their respect. It costs nothing to be decent.

One thing was sure—Gino's offer gave me an out. There would be no Philippines. And he'd be a fantastic mentor because he had incredible connections throughout the industry. I'd collaborate with designers from Gucci, Prada, and other big names. I wondered if he worked with the great Luca Rosso and turned up the music, whooping with the prospect. This exciting chapter in Milan would be mine to write.

Heavy fog slowed late-night Saturday traffic funneling from the suburban outskirts, and thankfully, Electra's apartment was close to the Duomo in the city center. The rotten weather had added hours to the trip, and I pulled onto her street around midnight to unload. Bleary-eyed and exhausted, I parked at the building's front door for easy unloading.

The foyer was eerily quiet, and the elevator's cables echoed against the plastered walls as it faithfully descended. Pedro's lights were off, and I quickly squeezed myself and the first bags onto the lift. Outside Electra's door, Pedro had left a stack of mail. I persevered, unloading piles of stuff, including the table and chairs. After multiple trips, the car was empty, my body ready for a Swedish massage, and I climbed over the heap to Electra's door, anxious for sleep.

But when the door opened, I gagged from the unexpected nose-burning musty smell. Coughing, I stumbled to the side table's lamp and screamed as soon as the room brightened—a hundred giant black bugs on the floor charged in every direction, fleeing for their lives.

As a New Yorker, I knew the antennae trespassers too well. Cockroaches.

"Oh my god," I cried, frozen in fear. Electra's landline began to ring. Over and over, each *bring-bring* scraped my fried nerves. I stepped forward, but a renegade cockroach kamikazed full throttle towards me, and I shrieked, jumping onto a nearby chair. Afraid to move, I watched the bug's two, thin appendages seek my scent while the phone rang mercilessly.

The stack of new mail was still in my hands, and I slowly pulled out an envelope, fixated on the bloodthirsty cockroach. Another joined the demon, and I screamed when two came out of nowhere to coordinate a stampede. Holding the envelope over the creatures, I dropped the paper grenade on the bullseye and stomped on it.

I became hyper-focused on any moving speck. With an armful of letters, I strategically deposited each aerial bombing and blazed a trail to the phone that wouldn't shut up. It took six cockroach bombardments before I shouted into the receiver. "Hello?"

"There you are. I've been phoning for hours. Where were you?"

"Cockroaches are *everywhere* in this apartment," I yelled, feeling phantom creepy-crawly sensations over my body as I searched the floor for recruits. "It's an effing infestation."

"Oh, the summer roaches? They're harmless and only come out in the humidity. Is it raining there?"

"Yes. It rained buckets the whole way. It was like driving five hours in a car wash," I said, watching a scout investigate an envelope with its antennae. A book was close by, and I pitched it with a big thud. Another man down. "There were so many huge trucks too. I did a few Hail Mary's, praying to live another day. That's how scary it was."

She didn't care. "Did Pedro leave the mail outside the door?" she asked. "I have to go over it when I return. Was the car okay?"

"Your precious automobile is fine," I said sarcastically. "And my back aches, but the luggage is safe and sound. Table and chairs, too. What about these cockroaches? Where do they come from? Do they bite?"

"What am I? A bug expert? You're the New Yorker; don't you know how to deal with them? The spray is under the sink. Make sure you open everything because the fumes will kill us all."

Great, I thought, death by roach or cancer-causing toxins. "Okay, let me go."

I hung up and, after opening the windows, found the spray with an alarming skull and crossbones label. Its chemical fumes caused dizziness, and after a few random squirts, I stopped. Afraid of trespassers in my loft, I checked under the bed skirt ten times and opened the skylight an inch for fresh air. Worn out, I went back down and dragged the suitcases and other bags into Electra's room, where, after another quick scan, I was satisfied there were no more creatures.

It was three in the morning, and my body was shutting down from fatigue. After scooping out a few tablespoons of Nutella into my mouth, I took a swig of disgusting peach brandy from Electra's dusty bamboo bar stand and stumbled upstairs. Rain pounded on the skylight as I fell into bed, content to be back in my familiar loft. The soft pillow was beyond wonderful, and not even a wayward cockroach could have moved me from my safe, warm bed.

Or even a sexy Bojan.

September 1st $1,056.60

August salary	+ 400.00
Gettonis	− 20.00
Espressos - need to drink with no sugar - ugh	− 8.00
Supplies and new lip gloss	−12.10
White foam for mood board	− 4.00
Tronky	− 0.86
	$1,411.64

Luca Rosso

BOJAN

XO

CHAPTER SIXTEEN

THE JANGLE OF THE FRONT DOOR'S LOCK jolted me awake, and I sat up as Electra's auburn profile burst through the doorway. I scrambled out of bed, realizing the debris field from last night's guerilla warfare would send her off the rails. Letters and upside-down carcasses littered the floor, and the scent of nose-twitching toxins made me gag. I threw on my Colby sweatshirt as Electra gasped in an endless thread of mio dios below me.

"What ... what happened?" she asked as I ran down the steps. Alessandro's face lit up when he saw me, and a cute smile spread across his face. He wriggled to get down, yet Electra cradled him tightly, stepping into the room like hardwood planks were suddenly missing. "Why are my letters on the floor?"

She pushed one with her shoe, and I yelped. "I ... Wait, don't do that. Those cockroaches are under them," I warned. "Crushed and unbelievably gross."

"This place is a disgrace," she said indignantly. Her eyes bulged in horror as she took in the combat zone. "Look at this mess. A little bug is harmless. I thought you said you were a New Yorker. They've got cockroaches all over apartments and restaurants there. You act as if you've never seen one before."

"Yes, they do, but I've only ever seen two in my apartment. There was an army of them here. Hideous and big. They ran to every corner to hide, and one tried to crawl on me. You'll see what's left. Only a tapioca of guts," I said, hopping toward her. "They're bigger than the ones in New York. It must be the pasta. Ha-ha."

My joke did not alleviate the situation. Expressionless, Electra pointed to a book under my feet. "That's a *very* expensive book. A first edition. It's extremely rare and signed by the author on the day he died," she said, putting her hand on her forehead. "All of the damage ... My priceless treasure ruined."

I forgot I had used it as a weapon. "I'm sorry, I didn't know. But these cockroaches are faster and spread like wildfire, and I didn't know what else to do," I said, bending to retrieve it. I turned it over, and the flat brown cockroach lay in a splat of grainy yellow. "Ugh."

"Don't tell me any details," she moaned.

I grabbed a tissue to wipe. "If I do this—"

"No. Don't use that. It will tear the fibers and remove the gold lettering ... Only a book specialist in Florence can fix it. Years of special training is the only thing that can repair the damage you've done."

I tried to smile, surveying the unappealing war zone. It was now a wasteland in a fog of chemicals. "I'm so sorry. The phone was ringing ... Did I mention I have this fear of cockroaches because the last time I saw one, it was right here," I said, pointing to the tip of my right shoulder, "I looked in the mirror and almost died when it crawled closer to my hair. I can still feel the hard shell when my finger flicked it and—"

She pointed to the ground. "Those letters are for you."

My mouth went dry when I saw children's crayon scrawls. The letters were from Quinn and Kate. I grabbed them off the floor and turned over the colorful envelopes decorated with simple flowers, Italian flags, and big hearts. Bug cadavers had ruined their artistry, and I choked up. "Quinn and Kate wrote me letters." I felt the stiff photos in one of them and ripped it open to pull out their pictures. Their smiles were contagious. And they looked older. Quinn was hamming it up in front of the camera with an Incredible Hulk pose, and Kate held a bunch of daisies in my parents' backyard.

I showed the photo to Electra. "Aren't they adorable?"

She pulled her readers from her pocket and smiled. "Yes. Very. Oh. The smell of the bug spray," she said, swaying. Beads of sweat popped onto her pale face, and I rushed to take her son from her arms while she fanned her face. "It's hard to breathe. How much of the spray did you use?"

"Not much at all." I panicked and pulled a chair towards her, glancing at the opened windows. "Here, sit. Let me get you water. Want a coffee? Stay calm," I said, running to the kitchen. Thoughts of blaring ambulances and her leaving on a stretcher made me scramble faster. "Try to relax."

"My brain hurts." She followed, lamenting how she'd have to get the apartment sanitized because of all the poisonous chemicals. "I need more fresh air. A coffee is an excellent idea," she shouted, opening the kitchen back door to let in the breeze. The noises and heat of Milan filtered in, and I plunked Alessandro onto the counter to prepare the coffee as she gulped fresh air from the small terrace.

"Feeling better?" I called, getting a cup as Alessandro watched from the counter.

"I think so. Is the coffee ready?" Electra asked, bumbling back into the kitchen.

"One more minute." I fiddled with tea towels, my stomach churning with the cost of repairing the book. Electra pulled a pastry from her bag and threw it on the counter. "I forgot. I got this at the station for you."

"Thanks." The shattered, flaky, crushed pieces of a cornetto looked unappealing. "I'll eat it later."

I poured the coffee, and she sipped it loudly. Color returned to her face, and I breathed a sigh of relief. "Oh, I feel better with this. Thank you. By the way, the car. Why didn't you park it in the lot last night?" she asked, putting the cup onto the counter. "You know, you parked it in the red zone, and it's still there."

I gasped. I forgot about the car! "Oh my god," I said, running to look at the car on the street. Why didn't she mention it before? "I got back so late … and the bugs were all over the place … I fell asleep at three in the morning … I'll move it now."

"Yes, do that." Her eyebrows rose. "There's a ticket on it, also."

What? It was Sunday in late August. The Italian police were supposed to be on beaches in Sardinia, not giving out parking violations. "There is? I can't see it. A real one? I mean, it's only been there for, like …" I said, glancing at the clock with a wince. "Ten hours?"

"The police don't give out fake tickets, Jayne. As I *told* you before, they are everywhere in Milan. Ten minutes in a tow-away zone, forget it. It is the way they finance the city police department. Everyone knows about this. I don't understand why you think you are so special."

Before I could chime in, she gave me another once-over. "You know the fine will cost hundreds of dollars, and you are paying for that mistake because I'm not. Too many problems have happened with that poor car already," she added. "And now my book. It needs a restoration expert. The gold-leaf lettering is from the eighteenth century and will be expensive."

Seriously? Gold-leaf lettering? The cost would be astronomical. After the parking ticket fee, my bank balance would be on life support. "I … I guess …"

She pulled off a corner of the pastry. "No guesses, Jayne," she said with a you-better-believe-it tone. "You're a big girl. These are your problems now, not mine."

I soared down the apartment building stairs, flew past Pedro sorting keys, and almost did a face-plant after tripping over a dozing Dante. The Citroen DS was where I'd parked, though with a piece of paper flapping against the windshield. "Argh," I said, ripping it off the glass. A plastic bag protected it from the rain, and I dried it on the side of my sweatpants.

Pedro came to my side with a pained look. "No good, Jayne. I sleep at my sister's house. I don't hear the police. They do not like cars in this district," he sympathized. "Only taxis. Historic. Molto lire." *A lot of lire.*

"Lo so." *I know.* The ticket had five hundred thousand in a small box. Almost five hundred dollars. Aghast, I showed it to the porter and played with Dante's silky ears as he studied it.

His mouth twisted to the side when he handed it back to me. "Mi dispiace." *I'm sorry.*

"Grazie," I mumbled, opening the driver-side door. A deluge of the previous night's rain fell onto the seat to add to my misery, and I wiped away the puddle, calculating numbers.

Pedro greeted someone, and I looked up as Luca Rosso entered the building with his confident stroll. Dante lopped behind as Pedro ran in after him, and I left the car, hoping to meet the designer. Again, he was too quick, so I only glimpsed the bottom of the ascending elevator's cabin.

Pedro turned with a smile, surprised to see me. He glanced at the elevator shaft and back to me, noticing my disappointment. "Next time, you talk."

After parking the car, I hurried back, distressed about ruining my budget because of an auto body shop and now a book restorer and an astronomical parking violation. My anxiety tingled like tinfoil in my veins, and I had to call Gino to find out the details of my employment. I rounded the corner, ready to lament to sympathetic Pedro, but he was talking with a pretty woman in a trench coat and long wavy hair. As I got closer, the woman's monosyllabic verbal jabs reminded me of high school Flynn yelling insults at me for stealing her clothes, and I slowed. The argument climaxed when the woman pointed to the building and rushed to enter, but Pedro yelled, gesturing upwards with finger purses and blocking her with his body. The enraged woman hesitated and then huffed away in anger.

I approached a furious Pedro, who was wiping his neck with a red bandanna. "Who was that?"

Rattled, he told me it was Electra's sister, Anna Maria. Before he said another word, I shot after her and touched her arm. "Wait," I said in Italian.

She spun around with the same intense green eyes as Electra, glaring daggers. "Who are you?" she asked in Italian.

I told her, and she glanced at the building. "How is my terrible sister?" she then asked in English.

"She's fine. She's with Alessandro, who is the most beautiful little boy. She'd love to see you."

Her eyebrows arched higher. "She said *that*?"

I didn't have time to think but had nothing to lose. "Yes. Electra misses you very much. And your mother."

Her face relaxed, and she threaded her fingers through her chestnut locks. "Well. She never calls me. Or my mother. The apartment is for everyone, not just her. She doesn't understand that little fact."

"I don't know the whole story. It would be best if you discussed it with Electra. She'll be home later."

She jutted her chin into the air, a family trait. "We'll see," she said, walking away.

Pedro had disappeared from the entry, and when I entered the smelly apartment, a bucket and mop sat in the middle of the yellow blob-stained parquet floor with a pair of latex gloves nearby. The book was on the ledge. I coughed, opening the windows wider for fresh air.

"Hello? Anyone home?" I yelled, checking rooms. Alessandro's bedroom was quiet, and his little suitcase sat in the corner, ready for unpacking. The purr of the washing machine signaled its use, and Electra's rouge lipstick was capless on her bureau. I read it as a hasty departure and wondered if she had spotted her sister with me or Pedro.

The deep cleaning allowed me time to rehearse my departure speech while scrubbing on bruised knees. The dried bug residue came off the floor quickly with the bristled brush and forgotten dust bunnies vanished in the process. The humid, damp smell dissipated slowly, and the apartment returned to its earlier state of lemon-tinged cleanliness.

In my post-cleaning free time, I concentrated on the mood board. The stiff stock bought from a local art store came alive with my selection of beautiful clippings and colors, sandblasting the last despondent grit out of my soul. The experience of Italy and its first-class sights spoke in each fragile item, though some held a sadness that mystified me. But for the first time in a long time, I was hopeful of my future, gazing at the foam board of diverse interpretations and inspirations. The serenity of nature was my focal message. The peace bestowed on me from my travels with Electra had been therapeutic. Of course, we'd had issues, yet how could I repay her for giving me back my self-esteem? And dignity?

The door clicked, and I hurried into the living room as a brochure fell from Electra's bag onto her writing desk. The front cover picture was of a beach umbrella stuck into golden sand, and then Electra placed another pamphlet on top of it —the Japan Airlines timetable booklet.

I moseyed behind the couch, fixing the pillows as she organized the pile of information. Palawan would never happen, and I couldn't dodge the issue. She gave me a side glance with a sniff. "I received a quote to repair the Citroen's CX Prestige bumper—the cost is about a thousand dollars. And I called a book dealer in Florence. He's sending me a quote for the damage. He couldn't believe what you did." She inhaled deeply. "The place smells much better. Thank you. We must keep the windows open to get out the last bit of the poison. Lunchtime?" she said, pulling out her wallet.

"Sure," I said, eyeing the credit card between her fingers. Sweat prickled everywhere from my fear that she might have already bought tickets. Gino's job offer dangled at the tip of my tongue, but I gulped and picked up Alessandro to bring him to the kitchen. "I'll make it now."

I whipped up the bowl of pastina and parmesan, regretting my chicken's inability to speak up on my behalf, or pump Electra for details. Half an hour later, she swooped into the room, blowing shiny ink on an envelope.

"Do you have a stamp?" she asked, waving it. "I forgot to buy them."

"No. Sorry." Electra changed the subject to spew about a luxury villa she wanted to rent, its proximity to the beach, and gibberish about a natural preserve with a Hindu temple. Her rant pushed me to my breaking point, and I blurted, "I'm not going with you. And I can't work for you anymore. It's been an amazing experience, but I've got a new opportunity, and I'm leaving."

She stared at me for what seemed like a football field of time and finally snapped out of her trance. "Oh, you are, are you? How expensive was that parking ticket?"

I froze. "Five hundred thousand lire. I'm going to try to get it reduced."

Her theatrical gasp made me feel worse. "Reduced? That will never happen. No one in Milan gets away without paying." She went to her wallet, pulled out a wad of cash, and handed it to me. "Take this to pay for your ticket. You can't leave with all your debts on my shoulders. We'll have to discuss how much you will pay since now *my* car will have this big fine against it and the insurance will be astronomical. No one will be able to drive it. And you haven't mentioned once how you plan to pay for the dent. Or my valuable book."

Unable to listen anymore, I quickly wiped stray pasta stars from Alessandro's face. "I don't need your money," I protested, throwing the lire on the table and marching out with her at my heels. "You can't keep me here if I don't want to stay. It's called kidnapping. I'll go to the police station now and resolve the whole thing. And then deal with the other stuff."

She snorted. "You're wasting your time, Jayne. The police won't let you, a foreigner, get away with not paying a ticket. They never let anyone off. It's impossible."

I crossed my arms with a sneer. "I thought nothing was impossible."

She closed her wallet. "We'll travel to the Philippines, and then you can pay me back. Of course, I'll pay you more as my assistant. You won't be an au pair anymore. You'll be too busy with our new company," she said with conviction as I opened the door. "And you don't even have time to talk to the police today."

I whipped around. "And why not?"

"You know the event I tried so hard for?" she said, fanning herself with a notecard she had taken from her desk.

I hated it when she assumed my interest in her activities. "No."

She gave a little shriek. "Miss Boland, wait 'til you hear where we are going." She became animated, and her attitude switched into euphoria. "I just opened the envelope before I came into the kitchen. It's for the Venice Film Festival. Someone likes me upstairs because I got an invitation! *Everyone* will be there for the Golden Lion. It's very exclusive, you know. It will be great to be with all the celebrities, filmmakers, directors, and actors ..."

"When is it?" I asked, afraid of the answer.

"Tomorrow. I got the last room at the Hotel des Bains for us. The Lido is the *only* place to stay at the festival. We'll be there for three days. You must pack quickly because the train is in four hours."

"Four hours? Well, I must see a friend first. I'll be back to catch the train. And, by the way, your sister may stop by," I said before slamming the door.

Gino's office was a mess when I arrived. Bolts of fabric lay on the floor like corpses on a colorful achoo of swatches. Ginghams, plaids, and geometric patterns clashed against raspberry-pink silk mohair, leopard prints, and Scottish tartans. I tiptoed by the explosion of material, knowing the debilitating jumble of textiles must have driven the perfectionist, Gino, mad.

"Jayne, thank god you're here," Gino said, giving me a one-armed hug as he put out his cigarette. "It's a disaster. I've got late deliveries, vomit-looking lab dips, and I'm going bonkers with this new grunge look. Flannel shirts are the rage; my mills are trying to meet the demand. I'm blaming MTV. It's the death of tailoring as we know it." He clapped his hands together. "So, when can you start? I can't wait for Tatiana; I need you now."

I gulped. "I can't leave my job yet. This thing came up."

"Hmm. That's a bummer, as you Americans say. But that's okay. I've still got time. Tatiana asked for another week at her uncle's, so it will be any day that she tells me she's leaving. And what are you doing now exactly? Hannah said you're with this champagne-sipping duchess royal tyrant who wants you to be her slave in India? Is that true?"

"It's the Philippines. And yes, she's a countess. Or a princess. Whatever. But I'm not leaving Italy."

“Who is this tea sipping Marie Antoinette, anyway? Hannah said she’s a hardcore member of royalty, and you went to her castle. Does she know Princess Diana?”

“Princess Diana wouldn’t hang with her. She’s no fun. Her name is Electra di Caneva.”

He gasped. “I know her. I’m friends with her sister, Maria.”

Another sister? “Who?”

“Maria La Motta? You know her. The big fashion writer? Hell hath no fury like a negative review from Maria La Motta.”

My eyes narrowed. “Wait. Is her real name Anna Maria?”

“Yes, only she goes by Maria.”

“*That’s* her sister? You’re kidding.” Stunned that Anna Maria was Maria La Motta, my shriveled heart bloomed. Maria loved Damian and had written a wonderful tear-jerking tribute in *Women’s Wear Daily* as his faithful, loving friend. But I stopped mid-swoon. She was still dangerous. Every reputable designer sought the omnipotent La Motta’s approval after their shows, knowing the power of her influence. With one negative word, a disparaging review could collapse a fashion house into oblivion. Supremacy ran in the blood of the di Caneva family, it seemed. No wonder they had been successful for centuries.

He nodded slowly. “I can pick up the phone and call Maria right now if you don’t believe me.”

“Don’t,” I cried. “Maria La Motta was outside Electra’s building a few hours ago, and I told her to visit her. She’s never met her nephew, Alessandro.”

“What?”

“Electra said the family is calling him illegitimate for the purposes of their inheritance. The ‘ole medieval bastard argument.”

“Money,” he said, shaking his head with disgust. “Root of all evil and everything in between.”

"What is Maria like? Is she nice? Does she have kids?"

"No. She's divorced. Word on the street is that she's living with a billionaire and might have tied the knot with him. She's a workaholic and the face of Italian fashion. The whole body of Italian fashion, when you think of it. You want to be on her good side. Let me rephrase that. You *must* be on her good side, or else you go home. And I don't see *any* kids in her future," he said as I unzipped my backpack.

"Before I forget." I pulled out the mood board and held it out. "Here's what you asked for. I hope you like it."

He took the board and sat at his desk, poring over my creation. "Love these eclectic swatches." He sniffed one. "This smells like a clove cigarette mixed with Earl Gray. And I like how you used the map of northern Italy as your background. I've never seen that before." He looked up like a satisfied teacher. "This speaks to me. A lot of its elements are very original. And organic. I'm getting sublime elegance with a touch of sporty magic in a wispy forest. I can see a runway with natural rawness in each garment. What is this?" he asked, touching a piece of gray fabric.

"It's wool I picked out of barbed wire while hiking in Cortina. I boiled it and then ironed it over a piece of slate. You can feel the wrinkles in its texture."

He fingered the piece. "I can see them too. You were a busy girl up in the north. I see your direction. We tend to overlook nature, and the mix of trees, flowers, and appealing serenity is an untouched inspiration. You show it here. Unusual. Not the typical mishmash of trending color, but it works."

"Italy was my muse," I said. "This only shows ten percent of how the landscape inspired me. My concept isn't what people expect when they think of this country. You know—art, culture, architecture. Hot red Ferraris or the Amalfi Coast. My board represents the chaotic elements that give Italy energy and the hidden overall connection to nature."

He tapped a small photo. "This couple on the balcony?" he asked, raising his eyebrows with a smirk. "You and who?"

I laughed. "I only took the picture. But you can't have Italy without romance."

He broke out into a smile. "Intriguing. Tell me more."

"Well," I blushed. "I did meet a nice guy. And for the record, I tried to find a beautiful piece of nature that would match the warmth of his angelic, coppery pools of innocence but couldn't," I sighed.

"I'm sure," he smiled.

"My focus was different before I came to Italy, and this opportunity to channel my slow awakening onto a mood board was monumental. Thank you. Fabric is key in every design and learning more about it is beyond thrilling. And for me, nature paints the flowers, leaves, sky, and sunsets with unbelievable beauty. I realized my peace isn't in a church or a bible."

He seemed pleased. "I don't think you're alone."

On cue, church bells clanged, and I stepped back from his desk, my muscles tightening. "Gino, I've got to go."

His face dropped. "Wait, where are you going now? We're just getting philosophical. Stay and have a coffee. You only just got here."

"I wish I could. I'm off to a place I never thought I'd go to in Milan. The police station."

"You're not serious. You didn't steal a sheep, did you?"

I twirled my finger in the air. "A girl's gotta do what a girl's gotta do."

Two police cars parked outside the limestone police station with fluttering flags snapping in the breeze above the entry. *Polizia*, the police, mingled by their squad cars as I repeated conjugations, dashing up the steps two at a time. Practicing how to reduce the traffic ticket, I researched the pocket dictionary for unfamiliar words, like *scarafaggi*, which meant cockroaches, as I scrambled through the entrance. Every detail was important.

The uniformed officer at the front desk helped a middle-aged couple, visibly upset. "Me no lire," the beer-bellied man wailed with a British accent. "Traino. Stolen." I felt terrible for their troubles, remembering when Italy had been that foreign to me.

The police officer sat poker-faced. "I speak little English. Complete this," he said with a heavy accent, handing the man a piece of paper and a pen. The couple studied the form while the officer went to the filing cabinet. He took a brochure from a file and handed it to them with authority. "This is the embassy address. You go there after this."

The couple shuffled to a red leather bench below a line of pay phones, and I asked them if they needed help. Excited to have a translator, the couple let me complete the form as they dictated information. With a cheerio, they were off to the embassy within minutes, and I continued my plan. With my clammy clasped hands, I stepped forward to the desk and cleared my throat. "Scusi," I said when he glanced up.

He took a deep breath. "Si."

I pulled the ticket out of my pocket and presented it without a word. After a quick scan, the officer pointed to the left and directed me to the parking department. "Grazie," I said.

The waiting area was humid with warm bodies, and the impatient Milanese complained to each other. Everyone turned to see my law-breaking newcomer entrance, and I yanked a number off the paper-spitting machine and slunk into a seat. One by one, citizens reluctantly paid or argued fines with the two exasperated female agents who spat no-nonsense abrupt dismissals of "Basta" with a raised hand. The big-haired blonde seemed faster than the other lady with thick penciled-in eyebrows over her peacock eyeshadow. Both women's nails matched the vase of artificial geraniums between them, and I smiled sinlessly whenever either looked my way.

Finally, my glowing number flashed on the wall monitor, and the peacock woman checked her polish as I hurried over to her. I tried to appear not guilty while she examined my ticket with disinterest. "Cinquecentomila," she said, opening her cash drawer.

"No," I said, showing empty hands. "Non ho." *I don't have any.*

She glared at my insubordination. "Perche?" *Why?*

"Non ho," I repeated. I didn't have money to pay an overnight parking fine, and I pulled out my wallet, showing the vacant slots. "Mi dispiace."

Unsure of what to do, she focused on the other agent, busy flirting with a tattooed guy holding a motorcycle helmet. Sensing a waste of time, she dialed an old rotary phone, staring at the violation while waiting for an answer. Her face brightened in a flurry of Italian, and she explained my situation to the listening party, sizing me up and down. Nods later, she clicked the receiver down and handed the ticket back. "Il capo," she cackled, pointing out the door.

Capo. Cap. *Il capo* means the chief of the police. I swallowed my courage. "Il capo," I repeated slowly. I hoped my refusal to pay wouldn't double the fee. What if they locked me up?

"Si. Si. Il capo," she broadcast loudly, gesturing for me to go away. The other agent and the guy stopped talking, their attention shifting to me with sudden interest. Not wanting to cause a scene, I rushed out of the waiting room, petrified about what would happen next. A passing police officer noticed my nail-chomping demeanor and stopped. "Va bene?" he said. *Is everything okay?*

"Si. Yes. Um … il capo?" I squeaked.

"The captain?" he said, noting the bewilderment on my face. He refrained from asking another question and pointed down the hall. "He second floor. Stairs to go up. Elevator broken."

"Parla Inglese?" *Does he speak English?*

He snorted at the question. "No. He don't."

"Grazie mille. Thanks," I said, hesitating. I thought of the ruined book and the bumper. All my earnings were paying for stupid mistakes. Trudging up the stone steps, my anxiety took over. I pulled an Electra call-to-anyone and prayed for all my deceased relatives to send powerful karma and mega luck with this monumental undertaking. I stopped mid-step. What if I had to pay for it today? Or they threw me in jail for insubordination? Ready to cry, I climbed onward.

The only sound on the second floor was clicking typewriter keys. Waxy fumes from the bright linoleum varnish hung in the air, and offices lined the long hallway. The block letter directory guided me to the captain's office at the end, and my fingers skimmed the paneled wall while I rehearsed my speech on poverty. I wouldn't tell the woe-is-me Matteo story. It was a weak argument. And it would show my naivety.

Behind the captain's frosted glass door, a shadowy figure answered a ringing telephone, and I cautiously turned the brass knob. A receiver-holding brunette woman held her finger up for silence, and I stopped. Behind her small desk was another enclosed glass office where the captain laughed on the phone as he leaned back into his leather chair. His jet-black eyebrows, mustache, and lean body in a crisp uniform drained my confidence. A grey curl of smoke twirled above his smoldering cigarette, and when he spotted my gawking, he motioned for me to enter.

"Ciao, Hugo. A domani," his husky voice said as he smushed his cigarette into the ashtray. After hanging up, he eyed me with curiosity and a smirk. "Si, signorina?" he said, smoothing his mustache.

I placed the offense in front of him before I sat. "Mi dispiace," I said, "Non ho i soldi per pagare. Ho tante multe. Uno e per un incidente con una macchina ..." *I'm sorry. I have no money to pay. I've many bills. One is for an accident with a car ...*

"No." His face clouded, and he put up his hand. I wasn't the first to cry poor in his office, and his handsome face held firm. "Cinquecentoamila lire," he said, tapping his forefinger on the wood desk.

"Ho lasciato New York per Milano," I said as his chin lifted. "Per lavorare per una donna ed il suo bambino." *I left New York for Milan to work with a woman and a baby.*

"New York?" His face lit up with a smile, and he set off with a barrage of questions. Have you been to the Statue of Liberty? Times Square? He said his wife loved Broadway shows, and then he sang a snippet from *Phantom of the Opera.*

I was losing control of the situation. When I tried to answer the captain's question if I ever met famous people, he shouted, "Agua," to his assistant. She rushed in with a plastic cup of water and stuck it into my hands. As I took little sips, he again examined the ticket, and I smiled whenever he looked up, hoping my wide-eyed demeanor would win a pardon.

But he pointed to the bold lettering in the first line. "É una zona limitata. Mi spiace ma è cinquecentomila lire." *It's a limited traffic zone. I'm sorry, but it's five hundred thousand lire.*

I clasped my hands together on my lap. "Capo, mi scusi …"

He was done with me and straightened his crooked blotter. "Cinquecentomila lire."

I took back the ticket and stared at the amount. "Cinquecentomila lire," I said under my breath, glancing around the office. A picture of his young family smiled from his bookcase, and I calculated how my bare-bones budget would take this financial hit. Hostel living, here I come.

He nodded. "È una zona limitata dove le macchine non sono autorizzate oltre i taxi ed autobus." *It is a limited traffic zone where the only cars allowed are taxis and buses.*

The familiar taxi sign outside Electra's building flashed before me, and I caught my breath. "Sono un autista come un taxi," I almost shouted. *I am a taxi driver*. His eyes narrowed, yet I didn't stop, thumping my chest. "La mia signora non sa guidare e dunque devo fare l'autista." *The woman doesn't drive so I am the chauffeur.* I mimed turning the steering wheel. "Ho guidato a traverso tutto l'Italia da Venezia a Cortina. A viaggiata anche la Yugoslavia. Lei rimane dietro! Ho il mestiere del taxi!" *I drove the car all over Italy from Venice to Cortina. I traveled to Yugoslavia. She sat in the back seat the whole time. It was my job.*

He gazed at me until his long arms reached for a cinder block-sized book on his shelf, and it landed on his desk with a big boom. For what seemed like a decade, he leafed through its pages 'til he found the one he wanted. I watched his finger find a passage, and he studied it before closing the volume with a loud thump. I was prepared for the worst when he suddenly rose and came around his desk to face me. I opened my mouth to defend myself, but he ripped the fine in half with exaggerated animation before I could speak.

"Basta," he said, tearing it again. "La multa non c'é piú. Un taxi puo parcheggiare nel centro storico." *The ticket is no more. A taxi can park in the historic district.* His hand landed on my shoulder in a fatherly way. "E mi spiace per i vostri problemi." *And I'm sorry for all your problems.*

My adrenaline pumped elation as he dropped the scraps of paper into the garbage. When I jumped up and stuck out my hand to shake his, he grabbed it with pleasure. Our happiness was mutual.

Leaving his office with a silent whoop, I gave the assistant a thumbs-up. She smiled and escorted me to the doorway, slipping a card into my hand. I glanced at an image of an automobile and a wrench with a telephone number.

"My cousin," she smirked. "Luigi. He fixes car for you. Say Teresa sent you."

Before she could react, I hugged her. "Teresa, grazie, grazie."

$ 1,411.64

Espressos	− 12.50
International Herald Tribune	− 1.50
Lunch with Gino (xoxo)	− 52.00
Gelato x 4	− 6.40
Car dent payment to Luigi	− 100.00
Bookshop ladies - bouquet	− 10.00

$ 1,229.24

BLOWN AWAY

~ VENEZIA ~

CHAPTER SEVENTEEN

ALTHOUGH I WAS DYING TO BROADCAST my get-out-of-jail-free ticket news to Electra, I held back in case another roadblock appeared. This spontaneous trip to Venice would be my last one with Electra and Alessandro and I wanted it to go smoothly. Everything was falling into place, and behind the scenes, I arranged that Luigi would pick up the Citroen with the help of Pedro to repair the dent.

We arrived at the stunning Santa Lucia station in Venice and pushed through the film crowd. As we moved through the throng with the cumbersome stroller, the international cast of characters eyed us, interlopers at their creative weekend. Luckily, Electra's aura of movie star glamour and nose-in-the-air attitude gave us status as a mysterious trio.

A La Biennale di Venezia banner draped over the glass exits that burst onto the breathtaking vista over the emerald waves of the Grand Canal. The energy was electric, and around us, film crews, actors, and executives milled about with clunky camera cases, tripods, and atypically shaped suitcases, waiting for the vaporetto, or water taxi. The chic elite dressed in monochrome colors gave a New York downtown feel, peppering the glamourous Hollywood atmosphere.

I thought of my quick phone call to Bojan at his uncle's restaurant before leaving Cortina. "Bojan loves movies and told me he wanted to be in the industry. He said seeing *Star Wars* as a kid changed his life," I remarked, plowing through people. A pang of sadness enveloped me, and I hoped he was okay. The news of the war hadn't been what I had hoped for.

She smirked. "He's still on your mind. That's good to hear. He's better than that other beast."

"Will the Bellagos be here? I asked Electra. "Or Freja?"

Her lips pursed. She was still stewing about the Bellago's bon voyage. It made me smile whenever I thought of it. "Maybe," she answered.

"I hope so," I said, scanning the crowd for Valentina. We filed onto the launch, and Electra maneuvered to the boat's port side. Scooting beside an English-speaking couple, I eavesdropped and learned every toilet flush in Venice sent sewage spewing into the lagoon till the ocean tide took it away. It's a tidbit of trivia I regretted hearing.

After disembarking on the island of Lido, we battled the line into the grand foyer of the opulent Belle Epoque hotel. On our arrival, giant green palm trees grouped with rattan furniture and massive gilded mirrors graced spacious hallways framed with palatial, Murano glass windows lit by multi-armed crystal chandeliers. "This hotel could be a movie set. Where's Tom Cruise? Harrison Ford?" I said in awe. "Those windows over the bar are huge."

"It is beautiful. Reservations are impossible to get. It's the only place to stay. Wait here." Electra marched up to the marble concierge desk and I remained with the stance of a faithful servant. Close to her stood a handsome man with glossy hair; from his dark profile, he looked familiar. Waiting for his key, the man smiled at our group, and my emotions fluttered. He was the handsome Omar Sharif, famous for his role as Yuri Zhivago in the film *Dr. Zhivago.*

I was stunned at my first celebrity sighting, and Electra urged me forward as he left. "Did you see who that was?" I asked, starstruck.

"Him? He's one of the judges," Electra said, glancing over her shoulder. She pulled a paper from her purse and held it out to read. "Here's this year's list if you're interested."

I wasn't a movie buff, and the only judge who popped out beside Omar Sharif was Gore Vidal, the writer. On the other side of the pamphlet were the competing films—including *Mr. and Mrs. Bridge*, with Paul Newman and Joanne Woodward, *Goodfellas*, directed by Martin Scorsese, and the soon-to-be winner of the Golden Lion, *Rosencrantz & Guildenstern Are Dead*, by Tom Stoppard.

However, there was another film, *The Elegant Man*—a documentary on Luca Rosso. "There's a movie about Luca Rosso. Do you think he's here?" I asked, scanning the crowds.

"If a famous director produced a film about me, I'd be here," she said, bustling to the elevator.

I didn't take issue with her obnoxious answer and sought out my hero. The hotel lobby buzzed with Hollywood types: agents, journalists, and fashion writers with *Corriere della Sera*, *Paris Match*, or other international publication press names on their lanyards. I tried to act calmly as I scoured the room for industry powerhouses and famous faces. I thought of Damian. It was his world, and my throat tightened. *Don't cry that it's over; smile because it happened.*

Was Maria La Motta here, I thought with a start?

"I'm going to get the paper. You go to the room," Electra said, handing me the key as we stopped outside the elevator.

"Okay." Tired from the trip, I leaned back onto the elevator's wall for support and was mid-yawn when none other than Luca Rosso jumped in as the doors closed. My body stiffened, knowing my resume was in my backpack. He nodded hello, and I took a deep breath, ready to spurt out my rehearsed "I love your fabulous clothes" speech as the elevator lifted. But Alessandro's dirty diaper odor engulfed the stale air, and his horrific reaction stopped me in my tracks.

"Mi dispiace," I chuckled.

He acknowledged my apology with curled lips of disgust. Sulphury fumes caused the designer to pinch his nose, and I cringed, remembering the broccoli mixed with pastina Alessandro had eaten for lunch. Thankfully, the doors opened, and the poor man gasped for relief as soon as he hurried off, leaving me with one less possibility of success.

"*The Elegant Man* number two," I frowned at Alessandro. "Really?"

The next day, Alessandro and I went to the pool area where loud, lounging drinkers and smokers chatted in lively conversation. Lido Beach was steps away, and we meandered through the crowd, listening to an orchestra play old show tunes on the balcony terrace. Another roped-off section had frolickers partying with pastel cocktails as they flitted in and out of large snow-white tents. Each structure had a ruffling banner, highlighting the film and its actors, and the venues required hard-to-get entry tickets. Since Electra had only one, I tried to melt in with the paparazzi, pushing the uncool stroller over thick cable wire and taking side trips through food buffets in pursuit of a dessert tray. Omar Sharif crossed my path and did a double take, trying to remember where he'd seen me. Life's a screenplay, I thought, and every role is up for grabs.

After lunch, the weather brightened, and Electra planned to meet Freja to watch another film. I had hours to kill, so I took a vaporetto to St. Mark's Square and looped through the shopping district known as Le

Mercerie. The who's who crowd stood elbow-to-elbow, and I took my time maneuvering through the slim lanes as artisans created beautiful products behind open doors or smudged glass. Hand-painted Venetian masks for Carnival entertained Alessandro with scary faces, and cobblers with velvet embroidered slippers competed against those made of shiny leather or featuring metal buckles. The rich, earthy smell of cowhide mixed with the sound of Turkish rug merchants yelling prices as pedestrian traffic stomped over their treasures.

Unsure where to go, I hopped on an empty vaporetto instead of the jam-packed one back to Lido. Seated with the best view of the Grand Canal, the clock tower of St. Mark's Square grew smaller while the wild wind ruffled my hair under a flock of squawking seagulls eyeing a cookie in Alessandro's hand. The boat sputtered across the lagoon, whooshing by net-laden boats mixed with camera crews, day-trippers, gondolas, and various expensive crafts, zigzagging in the unwritten but organized ballet. A brick building had FORTUNY in ten-foot letters across its façade; I loved the luxurious and costly Fortuny piece goods requested by designers. It was a perfect place to disembark.

The boat docked near a church with a wide staircase to its two-story tall, vibrant green entry. Its egg-shaped dome curved into the blank cloudless sky, and I trailed visitors streaming into the church from the pier, anxious to investigate.

Upon entry, a faint odor of campfire incense hit me as the stroller's squeaky wheel echoed life into its tranquility across the scarlet-and-white checkerboard floor. Sunlight streamed in from the barrel ceiling and highlighted simple nave paintings and statues. Bulb-popping cameras flashed in the church's alcoves against the peaceful setting of whispers and soft steps. The information desk had free pamphlets, and I selected the one in English from the slot.

The church was called Chiesa del Santissimo Redentore, built in the sixteenth century as a votive church to thank God for stopping the plague that had killed one-third of the Venetian population. It is one of the most famous of the Venetian churches. Every July, a festival held at the church celebrates its beginning with fireworks on its home, the island of Giudecca.

I closed my eyes and clasped my hands. "Please, bless my parents. And thank you for helping me make the right decision with my life." I glanced at the stroller. "And please bless Alessandro. He's a gem of a little guy. I guess you can throw in one for Electra, too. May she control her ego and repair her relationship with her family, and you know who. And Flynn and Ambrose and the kids."

I rose to continue my exploration of Giudecca, pausing to dip my forefingers into the holy water font to make the sign of the cross before facing the retina-crackling sunshine.

High hedges of cypress and ilex buffered the side of the water-lapping promenade, and children's giggles softened the air. At the end of the passage, a dockside restaurant with billowing black and silver flaps was busy, and I wondered if I could make a pit stop for a coffee.

The music grew louder as I drew closer, and inside, waifish patrons in short sequin skirts and feathery tank tops clinked fancy cocktails with older partyers. Screams of laughter and lively conversation lured my curiosity because the more fashion-oriented hosts were much more interesting than the Hollywood, yellow legal pad-holding snobs at Lido. Outside the venue, sleek, mahogany taxi boats crewed by uniformed captains chattered into radio headsets, and I remembered the stretch limousines that idled for famous clientele on Seventh Avenue during New York Fashion Week.

Glancing at a couple sharing a cigarette outside the entrance, I almost missed the black-and-white poster with Luca Rosso's handsome face. *The Elegant Man*. "Interesting." I slowed to gawk at the stepped-off-the-runway crowd in sequins, leather, cashmere, and every other expensive fabric. Of course, heavy hitters from New York and Milan were undoubtedly inside, partying with the fashion elite. I got giddy, expecting to see the show's star, chatting with Anna Wintour and her sidekick Andre Talley. Or off to the side with Linda Evangelista or Naomi Campbell. There had to be supermodels in there somewhere.

Starting to look suspicious to the black T-shirt bouncers, I shuffled down the canal, dreaming of when I'd be at a party like that. I missed the exciting fashion world and thought of Trendary Fabrics and how my career had just been starting to bloom. Self-doubt vanished, and I straightened my droopy posture, remembering my worth. I was great at sales and promoted in my first year. Now almost fluent in Italian, I would be an asset to Gino and learn so much.

An iron bridge loomed in the distance, and my weary legs needed a rest. Hunger also grumbled annoyance, and so I pressed onward, unsure of my location. In the distance, a lone phone booth beckoned me, and I walked towards it. I still had to tell my parents about my decision to stay and so I decided to take advantage of the opportunity.

"Mom," I gushed as the coin clattered into the coin box. "How are you? I've got great news to tell you."

"Jayne, sweetie. It's not a good time."

My body stiffened. "Is it Dad?"

"No. It's not. It's Flynn."

"What happened?"

There was a pause and a gush of breath. "She had a miscarriage."

My body swayed. "What? When? I didn't even know she was pregnant."

"She was a few months along. And it happened last night. She's still at the hospital. They tried everything to save the baby," she said, her voice cracking.

"Mom. I … I'm so sorry."

"I know, honey. Look, your father is outside waiting in the car. We're driving up there now to take care of Kate and Quinn. I'll call you. I mean, you call me. If you can."

"I will, Mom. I will. Tell Flynn I love her."

I hung up the phone, my body trembling with the news. Flynn was pregnant and lost the baby? Why hadn't anyone told me?

I clenched my fist, wishing to hold my sister's hand like she had when I got pneumonia after a too-long ice-skating party as a kid. Mom and Dad worked, so she'd tried to make macaroni and cheese for the first time and played nurse with constant temperature-taking. Also, I'd spilled ginger ale on her favorite *Tiger Beat* magazine, and she hadn't yelled at me. Should I call the hospital? But I'd forgotten to ask which one.

A clock tower tolled, pushing me to get back to the hotel, though I didn't want to move, wiping away tears. Flynn is in a cold hospital bed, alone. My heart ached for her family and the baby. She was such a great mother. Ambrose was a doting father and husband. And what about the little ones? Had they known they were going to have a new sibling?

In the distance, a lone figure stood on the black bridge over a canal. Perhaps the person could point me in the right direction to the nearest stop. I broke into a jog with the stroller. As I got closer, the tourist in a navy-striped sailor's sweater leaned against the metal rails, deep in thought, soaking in the beauty of Venice's golden silhouette. A lucky man, without any of my despair. I hated to disturb his special moment, but I needed to leave ASAP.

Behind me, a big cheer erupted from the crowd at the designer's party, and I looked back, suddenly sickened by their unmitigated shallow joy. When I turned around, the stranger gazed at the noise, also. I caught my breath. It was Luca Rosso.

I nipped into a doorway, and when the rowdy celebration resounded with another big cheer, he grimaced but not in the good way. Why wasn't the star of the show with his adoring crowd?

Then it hit me. Exposed on the bridge, Luca Rosso was his authentic self. A Renaissance artist in a contemporary setting. He absorbed the world with his vitality. True to himself, he'd stepped away from a party even though it celebrated his fashion accomplishments. His solitary moment of inspiration designed his next season stroke by stroke in front of the incredible Venetian spine of skyline under a wispy scarf of clouds—his mental mood board.

I collapsed against the heavy oak door, thinking about Flynn, New York, Matteo, everything. Across the canal, Manhattan rose in my mind's eye like a phoenix from the water. The Art Deco Chrysler and Empire State Building leaped like joyous dolphins, and my spirit, weathered with ache and pain, restored itself with the power of the almighty Statue of Liberty. Vaporetto's turned into yellow taxis, and the gondola traffic was as heavy as Fifth Avenue's five o'clock rush hour. A massive Times Square billboard appeared over the canal, and its banner read: *Come home, Jayne. Matteo didn't make it in the Big Apple. But you succeeded in Italy and can triumph anywhere. Especially in New York. Close to your family.*

I turned away and doubled back to the vaporetto stop, almost panicking that my mirage of Manhattan would disappear. People like Matteo burrow into a corner inside your mind, and the memories of them will never die. But there are spaces owned only by you that no one can intrude upon. New York occupied a prime area of my mind, and my family claimed their importance in another. One thing for sure was that Flynn needed me, and I needed her. I didn't want to lead my life like a lonely Electra. In my heart, Italy would be a unique footnote in my turbulent time, though my gut said I needed to be back in America. Immediately.

When I returned to the dark hotel room at last, out of breath, I presumed Electra had gone out with Freja. A note with cash for dinner was on the coffee table, but I needed Alessandro's blanket in her room. Without knocking, I barged in and saw the outline of Electra asleep in a fetal position.

I tiptoed to her chest of drawers, but she loudly sobbed, and I went closer to her. A light went on; her raccoon eyes were bloodshot, and her cheeks had black mascara streaks. "Are you okay? Why are you crying? What happened?" I asked, hurrying to the bedside and trying not to bawl myself. A bouquet of pink roses was on the nightstand, and her hand clutched a tiny card.

"It's nothing." She waved me away. "Go. I'm fine. I am."

"You don't look it. Who sent the roses?"

She tried to sit up but slumped back into her sheets with a whimper. "I don't want to talk about it. Go eat with Alessandro at the hotel restaurant. I'll be fine."

I fixed her blanket, and she turned away, swatting me to leave. Unsure, I took the bag and walked to the doorway. "Wait. Tell me. Did Alessandro have a fun day? Did he like the beach?" she sniffed under the covers.

I nodded, grabbing a box of tissues from the bathroom. "Yes, he had a wonderful day. He loved the tents and the costume shops. We wandered around St. Marco's and went to one of the islands." I handed her a tissue. "Are you sure you're alright? I can stay."

"I'm fine." She glanced at the flowers with disgust. "Don't ask me about these. They were very unexpected—the biggest surprise of my life. A harbinger, I think. But no more questions, please."

"Okay." Having my past problems with unexpected roses, I pursed my lips. "Hey, guess what? I saw Luca Rosso twice today."

She snorted and got ready to blow her nose. "You're obsessed with that man."

"Well, I can't say it's mutual. However, Mr. Rosso influenced me more than he'll ever know," I said, remembering my New York moment at the canal. "I'll tell you later."

“Okay. Close my door,” Electra said, burrowing in the bedding with a wad of tissues. “You won’t see me until the morning.”

Electra blamed the harsh weather for leaving Venice the following day, though I knew the flowers had triggered her retreat to Milan. The card and roses had disappeared, and the subject was another topic added to her taboo file. But that was the least of my worries. Flynn was my focus as I made a list of what to do, obsessing about my decision to return to New York and regretting I’d have to tell Gino of my change of plans.

“By the way, the police chief ripped up the offense,” I said to Electra as we waited for the water taxi. “He let me go for free.”

“I … I can’t believe it. I’ve never heard anyone getting off from paying for a ticket,” Electra said, searching my face for any crack of deception. “Are you sure? Maybe you didn’t understand him.”

I grinned at her incredulity. “No, I understood the captain one hundred percent. He stood right in front of me and ripped it in half. The impossible became possible.”

She lifted her chin with a slight grunt. “What did you do to make him let you off?” *Hello paranoia*, I thought. “I should have gone with you. You must have told a crazy story.”

“Nope. Actually, it was pretty boring. And you would have been very proud of me. There was a loophole in my favor. The zone is for taxis. And what did I do for the past months besides being a nanny?” I asked with a grin.

“You drove a taxi for a mean woman and her not-so-mean son,” she said with a laugh.

“You? Mean? I wouldn’t go that far. Difficult, yes. And my get-out-of-jail speech was done in tutto Italiano.”

She smiled and patted my back with a wink. "I'm proud of you. What you did is bigger than the pinecone in Lignano. I knew you were very smart."

On the way to the restaurant to meet Gino, I stopped at an international florist to send a bouquet to Flynn's house. I couldn't stop tearing up when writing my emotional message on the slip. Flynn and I were sisters, and I'd do anything for her. I hope she believed that.

"Ciao, bella," Gino said, planting a big kiss on both cheeks and putting me at ease. I was nervous about his reaction when I asked him to meet me at the trendy bistro. I hadn't talked to Hannah in days, so no leaked info would have alerted him. He would be shocked to learn I had decided to go back home.

He sat in the restaurant's turquoise chair, glancing at the sophisticated crowd. "Snazzy place you picked for a newbie. It's been on my radar, but I was waiting for a mill to take me here. You know, pick up the tab," he laughed. "The many fringe benefits of my fabric world."

"Electra recommended it," I said, dreading the bombshell I had to drop as I took a breadstick. "She said it's the *only* place to eat in Milan. I hope you like it."

"Like it? It's much better than my usual cornetto and espresso lunch," he said, studying the menu. "I hear the tasting menu has the best parmigiana di melanzane. One of us must order it." He leaned forward. "Are you sure you can afford this?"

"Yes. One hundred percent." A server took our martini order before I continued. "Gino, I wanted it to be special because I ... something happened, I ..." I sputtered, wiping stray crumbs from the tablecloth.

He grabbed my hand. "You're getting married?"

I laughed at his wild imagination. "No way. Are you kidding? First,

I haven't even had sex in almost a year. I mean, I kissed someone, but that's it. Hopefully, I'll see him in … soon. But enough about my love life. You've been such an incredible person since I arrived on your doorstep like a pathetic, broken-hearted fool. I mean, I didn't know anyone except Matteo, and you answered my first phone call and gave me hope. Thank you. If it weren't for you and Electra, I don't know what would have happened … You took care of this New Yorker you barely knew, which was beyond nice. It was so kind and incredible. I'll never forget it. And that's why this is so hard. I wanted to say that even though it's what I had hoped for, I can't accept your offer. It was a super hard decision, and I am so grateful for all your sweet help, but I'm returning to New York. I'm sorry."

He folded his hands. "Can I ask why? Is it your old job? Did Jim—that rat—snag you from under me?"

"No, he didn't. I don't think I'd even work at Trendary if Jim offered me a better job. This experience has changed me." I looked around for the waiter, hoping to have a drink in my hand within seconds. Gino had been a special friend, and I hated disappointing him. "You know that whole 'you bloom where you're planted' thing," I said, thinking about Flynn. "I feel so bad leaving you high and dry. Last time in your office, you looked so overwhelmed."

"Yes, that's true. I was drowning in problems." He waved his hand to shoo away the memory. "But don't worry about that. Grunge just took me by the you-know-what. I'll survive. It would have been great to have you with me as my schedule has heavy hitters coming in for the next few weeks, and your Seventh Avenue training and expertise could have been an asset. But I've got a friend who works at Missoni. Maybe she can fill your place."

"Really?" I said, placing my hand on my chest. "That makes me feel so much better."

"Her name is Allegra, and she knows the business. But I'm curious. What changed your mind? I thought you loved it here. I mean, your mood board on Italy. *Hello*? The aesthetics. Textures. Colors. A masterclass of creativity. You brought me on your adventure. I saw your wonder."

"It was a trip, all right. And I guess I have to thank Matteo in some bizarre way. I can only describe my odyssey as finding awareness. And growth. Driving all over Italy gave me the time to examine my life. And being with Electra, I discovered what matters. Or what's important. I'll feel the effects of this experience forever."

His eyebrows lifted. "A little spark in you awoke. Your insight is undeniable." He tapped my hand and raised his finger at me. "Your board made me feel like I was lying in a field of daisies, gazing up at this wonderful world. You've got talent, Jayne Boland. Use it."

"Grazie. I did the proverbial 'I found myself,'" I said, making air quotes.

"I don't think you found yourself. I think you *created* yourself."

I won't lie—his words put my ego into the stratosphere. Our drinks appeared, and I raised my glass to him with a lopsided grin. "May grunge last one season, and our friendship be endless on the runway of life."

"Hear, hear. And to perfect lab dips and on-time deliveries," Gino said as our glasses clinked. "And may we never see another massive shoulder pad on a woman's jacket."

"Or neon lace gloves."

My days in Milan were going fast, and I circled the park a bit longer on my walks with Alessandro, getting sentimental about my departure.

"Jayne?" Alessandro twirled a leaf to see. "Weaf."

"Yes. Leaf. Isn't it beautiful? And you said my name, Alessandro. Good for you."

His marble eyes were full of amazement, and I thought of Flynn's loss. Overcome with emotion, I knelt at his level and hugged him. The little guy was my rock, the perfect pal who gave me a purpose without judgment. We bonded, and I'd become part of the family. He'd never remember our time together, but his tiny handprint had left its mark on my soul.

"No," he protested with a pouty face when I released him.

"Okay. I won't hug you; you're a big boy now," I laughed. His chubby fingers offered the leaf by the stem, and I carefully took the thin filament. "Can I have this?"

"Sì." I placed it in my bag with his first crayon drawing and the napkin of the café where we shared his first meal in Venice. "Thank you, sweetie. I will treasure this always."

Our last excursion was to a new gelateria where I ordered all the flavors for us to try. Behind the counter, the server sensed a special moment and scooped mini mounds of pastel-colored gelato into his bowl. Alessandro's eyes bulged at the rainbow blob, and the cute attention and kindness triggered another gulp of emotion for Italy and its people.

After a few bites, pink ice cream dropped off Alessandro's spoon onto his ironed shirt. I had forgotten his bib and would have normally freaked out. Today though, I figured a misguided dollop was an excellent way to leave my mark. "That's okay, Alessandro. You've been my best buddy, but I want to tell you I will be leaving soon," I said with a frown, wiping the stain. "I'm going home."

He looked around the gelateria. "Home. Mama?"

"Yes. Mama is there, but my home is in New York. Far away." I smiled, aiming my spoon for another scoop. He pulled his bowl closer to his chest, making me smile. Would we ever meet again so I could tell him how the cutest little boy was the best part of my Italian adventure?

"I'll miss you," I said, fixing his blond bangs. "We've had fun, right? Your first time down the slide was with me. We fed ducks in the park, walked with Dante, and played at the playground. And had all that yummy gelato, of course."

Since he was too busy enjoying the sugar fiasco, I let him finish without my walk down memory lane. There would be someone to take my place. I wonder who it would be. Electra hadn't put any notices on the community board or called an agency. She'll place a flyer at the Irish Embassy, I thought with an eye roll.

With my spoon, I swooped in for a last taste. The caramel sweetness melted in my mouth, and I planned my following tasks. Luigi ordered the fender part and charged me only a hundred dollars when I picked up the car. The plan for the damaged book was next. After that, picking up my suitcase from Matteo would be the last hurdle. The end of my Italian detour.

The bookshop was empty when I rolled in with a sleeping Alessandro. A new salesperson hurried from the back, excited to see an incoming baby. Since she was unfamiliar, I was thankful she didn't associate me with the crass Electra. After the woman cooed every synonym for *beautiful* at Alessandro, I showed her the damaged book and explained the cockroach massacre in Italian, pointing to the smear. She flipped the book back and forth and surprised me by asking if it was Electra's.

"Si," I gulped, ready to leave. Her mouth puckered, and she told me she'd bought it at the store last year, refuting what Electra told me. "So che il libro è molto vecchio e costoso. Puoi aggiustare la copertina del libro?" *I know the book is antique and expensive. Can you repair the book cover?*

She took a deep breath, and the manager strolled out from the backroom to join her. Both women gave me a side-eye while examining the book in conspiratorial whispers. After a quick discussion, they hurried to the back of the store, leaving me in limbo.

As I waited, I glanced out their storefront and spotted Electra on the street with the "devil" man who had come looking for her in the apartment. They argued with explosive gesticulations, and she finally stomped away. He shouted after her, and she turned around and gave him the middle finger.

"Ouch," I said aloud.

"We are done with the book," the team said as I turned, presenting the book. The stain was gone, yet I flipped it over in disbelief. I looked up with surprise. "Co'me?" *How?*

"Veni." The women brought me into the back room, where their magical tools lay on a table: a blow dryer and a gum eraser. They explained that the book was a reprint with a polyester cover, and the lettering was not gold but yellow paint. They also added that Electra knew this, and the book was not valuable.

Why would she be so dishonest? Furious at Electra's lies, I offered to pay, and they refused my offer, saying it was their pleasure with winks and giggles.

Upon returning to the apartment, I lay Alessandro down for his nap and slipped out to find Electra at her writing desk. "Do you have a second to talk?" I asked, holding the repaired book.

She removed her reading glasses and placed them on her papers, eyeing the book with a scowl. "Yes. What's the matter now?"

I gave her my last eye roll. "Nothing. Your book has been repaired."

"No. That's impossible," she huffed, taking it from my hands to examine. "Hm, it seems up to my standard. I'm afraid to ask who did this, but I consider it satisfactory."

I snorted. "*That* book isn't as valuable as you proclaimed, so you owe me an apology for lying."

"What?" Her face reddened, though her hand flew to her chest. "I must have confused it with another book. I'm sorry."

"Also, the bumper is fixed and brand new. Better than before."

"How did you get the car fixed so fast?"

"This wonderful friend of mine, Teresa, gave me a name. Only a hundred dollars." She smirked at my response, and I cut her off before she bombarded me with questions. "Electra, I don't want to leave on a bad note. Thank you for the opportunity and a place to live after that nightmare with Matteo. I learned about Italy through you and traveled to incredible places and even Yugoslavia. Alessandro is a beautiful little boy, and every day was so fun with him. It's a hard decision, but I'm returning to New York."

Her mouth fell open. "I thought you were staying in Milan."

"I did have an offer, but I … I should have told you on the train back from Venice—New York is my city. My family is there. And a lot of friends, too. It's where I belong. Like you belong in Milan. Your sister is here and your life."

"My sister?" she said with a funny face, placing a pen between her lips. "When do you want to leave?"

"Um … when can I? I mean, when is it okay for you?"

She put up her hand. "Don't worry about me, Jayne. Or Alessandro." Her voice rose. "Go tomorrow if it's better for you."

Her answer was unexpected. "Tomorrow? But don't you need a few days to find someone for Alessandro?"

She sighed. "No. And I was going to let you go, anyway."

"You were?"

"Yes. What does it matter? You were leaving anyway. There are many things."

"Many things, meaning me?"

She smiled. "No. Not you. Me. This big apartment is worth at least a million dollars and is a big problem for my family. That lawyer representing my cousin told me I had to leave. Three country houses and five villas throughout Italy aren't enough for them. It's called greed. Roberto will discuss the best solution to move forward."

"What are you going to do?" I asked, concerned. The thought of Electra and Alessandro being homeless was scary.

"First, I'm going to meet with Alessandro's father. John Hanover is his name, and he's American and wants to be in his son's life."

I grabbed the corner of her desk. "What? Did you say he's American?" She smiled and shrugged. "Wait, so let me get this straight. Your principe azzuro is American? But you *hate* Americans," I said, trying not to get too hysterical at this latest info about his nationality. My brain wasn't wired for such earth-shattering information. "That's all you talked about—America this, America that."

"I know. What else could I say? Obviously, I don't hate Americans *that* much."

"Oh my god. Alessandro is American!"

She put up her hands. "Calm down. He's *half*-American, and that's all."

"That's half too much for you." I joked.

"I'm glad you're going back to New York and fashion. You're almost thirty, so you must make serious decisions about your life. Is there anyone special that I should know about?"

"Yes. My sister, Flynn. And for the record, I'm not close to thirty. So, I've got over five decent years left in me. Men aren't a high priority right now, and poor Bojan is stuck in Mali Losinj. Hey, did John Hanover send you the roses?"

Her eyebrows furrowed. "No, those were from Anna Maria. She and my mother want to meet Alessandro. That's what was on the note. She wants to solve the apartment problem the best way possible, so I feel better about the whole thing. She was always jealous of the special attention my father gave me after I got my scar. She's remarkably successful, you know. It's a long story, and I understand her frustration. We'll find a solution. It will take time, but hopefully, we can be sisters again one day."

The understanding and honesty in her words were moving, and she seemed ecstatic with her sister's attempt at reconciliation. "And now I know whom to thank for telling her to contact me," she said softly. "If it weren't for you, I don't think it would have *ever* happened. You're not only a great au pair, but also a good friend, Jayne. Alessandro and I need Anna Maria in our lives. My mother, too. This can be a new beginning."

"Yes, a new, wonderful beginning. How about your sister helping you start your business overseas?"

"No," she sputtered, batting her eyelashes. "We'll take baby steps first."

I laughed. "And talking about brand new starts, I will get my suitcase from Matteo tomorrow. Then I'll buy my ticket home."

"That's great. It will give me time to prepare my son's emotions for your departure." She smiled with a wink. "And mine, too."

$1,229.24

SEPTEMBER 15TH

English dictionary for Pedro	-15.00
Cappuccino w/Matteo - bittersweet	-2.50
Guilt payment - GRAZIE MILLE!	+1,000.00
Last gettoni purchase - hallelujah!	-20.00
Children's book about America for Alessandro	-5.30
Ticket to JFK!	-572.84
Preboarding drink	-4.50
Pink roses for Flynn	-50.00
Last pay from Electra - TUTTO FINITO!	+400.00

$1,959.10

TO-DO

- phone book for addresses
- White out
- Walkman??
- need nylons
- call Ava and Maeve?

I ♡ NY

LOVE

CHAPTER EIGHTEEN

"THANKS FOR THE FLOWERS," Flynn said when Ambrose handed her the phone. "They're beautiful."

"You're beautiful," I said, choking back tears. "I'm so sorry."

Flynn sniffed. "I know. We're not telling the kids yet. It's too much for them. You know what I mean?"

"Of course, I do."

"Jayne, I feel bad. Are you coming back here for me?"

"What?"

"Aren't you going to miss Italy? It's what you always wanted."

"Once I did. It was incredible and I learned a lot and have too many unbelievable stories to tell you now. But family is family, and it took eight thousand miles and six months to figure that out. I can't wait for us to get together. Can I drive up and see you all over the weekend? I can also care for the kids if you and Ambrose want a breather. I am a highly qualified nanny, you know. Contessa approved, and that's the third rank from a queen. And I cook, too."

"You cook? No more using the smoke alarm as your timer?" she joked. "That is hard to believe. Remember when you made those brownies for my fifth grade class? I still had to bring those hockey pucks to school, and Fiona Dumont chipped her tooth on one."

I smiled. Our parents had to pay for Fiona's dental work. "Don't remind me. Who knew vegetable oil played such a vital role in baking?"

"Mom said Electra was tougher than Stalin."

"She was. Everyone has issues. But maybe a bit of a revolution is what I needed on this wild journey. You'll see."

"I can't wait."

Elegant train stations were on my list of what I'd miss about Italy, along with hourly tolling of church bells and women in cotton house dresses riding bicycles to the market. Of course, I had to add the innate ability to make magic with simple ingredients and the little cobblestone streets that meandered into mind-blowing piazzas that no artist could do justice. Wandering cats, gelato, and espresso, too.

I agreed to meet Matteo at the Milan train station and collect the suitcase. Our encounter would be a simple transaction—but to me, the stress level was equal to dropping off a ransom. I hoped it would be unemotional and brief.

The long mosaic corridor led me into a massive glass-domed area in the station. Space-like chimes and blasting train horns were the perfect backdrop to prevent a sloppy sentimental parting. A tall blonde man who looked like Damian passed, and I put my hand on my chest. It was over a year since he had died. He would have loved to hear my wild Italian story over gin and tonics. Yet, even though he was gone, I had constantly felt his presence in my adventure. He was my co-pilot in that empty passenger seat. I sniffed, remembering Matteo's tight hugs at the funeral. The saddest day of my life.

"Jayne!"

I sucked in a deep breath as Matteo approached with the suitcase. His bloated belly hung over his tight belt, and his ruddy face shone under drops of sweat. Was he drinking and partying too much? I was relieved to sense the familiar horse prance of my pulse had long gone to pasture. It was hard to believe that Matteo had been the center of my world only months ago; now, all I cared about was that a girlfriend hadn't stolen anything from my luggage.

In keeping with the usual greeting, we exchanged uneasy cheek kisses. I wiped away the linger of his lips and my thoughts jumbled into a pasty mess as I tried to stay in control, pulling out a chair.

"Looks like Italy agreed with you. Did you get your old job back in New York?" he said, swiping back the bangs of his hair.

I fidgeted in the seat. "No, I think this time, I'd like to be on the *buying* side of fabrics instead of selling. Work one-on-one with a design team and then source their inspiration. Be a part of the process, you know. I'll start networking when I return and send the 'ole resume around. My parents will be ecstatic to have me in Queens until I figure out my future," I said as a waiter approached to take our order. "Espresso per me, per favore."

Matteo's eyebrows rose with a smile, and he put up two fingers for a second coffee. "What about Gore-Tex? And can Jim help you in any way? Hannah?"

His interest irked me. I shrugged and faked a smile. "Who knows? I'll weigh all my options when I'm home safe and sound."

His voice softened. "How are your parents?"

"What's with the twenty questions? *Now* you're asking about my parents? They're fine. Overjoyed to have me away from you. You know, it was hard, Matteo." I didn't want to leave on a sour note and took a deep, cleansing breath. "This is what is best for me. Jayne Boland. But, please, tell me, just for future reference. Was it my cooking? The sex?"

"Sex? Are you kidding? It was great. And your cooking?" Matteo protested. "I miss your meatloaf. I can't believe you're leaving. To see you here. Your dimple, hair … I …"

His words were just elements of speech at this point. The bitterness was gone, but annoyance had replaced it. The waiter left our espressos, and I scalded my mouth with a massive gulp to finish it quickly. Matteo looked confused, and I felt sorry for him. "Matteo, it's over," I said gently. "What happened, happened. Time to move on."

He nodded. "My parents didn't talk to me for months after I told them what I'd done," he said meekly. "I'm sorry for the mess in Como and the pain I put you through. In New York, my life was too overwhelming with all my problems. You were doing so well, paying the rent, and then got promoted while your useless boyfriend couldn't even buy a bagel. I had to prove myself."

"I always had faith in you." I turned away, remembering my cheering sessions before his interviews. It wasn't time to be sentimental. Or resentful. Bojan and Roberto had rebuilt my threadbare confidence, and I would always hold a special place for them in my heart.

Matteo touched my arm. "I know that. You never let me down and look at what I did. Jerk 101. I'm sorry," he said, pulling an envelope from his pocket. "This is for you."

I took the envelope and opened the flap. Inside were American dollars.

Our eyes locked, and he smiled at my shocked expression. "It's a thousand dollars, Jayne. To pay for your plane ticket into and out of this disaster. You were right with what you said in the apartment. Instead of making you come here, I should have gotten on a plane and told you like a man. My father calls me *vigliacco* now. But that's my problem, not yours. I'm sorry. I hope it makes you feel a little better."

"It does." His gift was so unexpected. But a welcome apology. And I liked his father because *vigliacco* means a coward.

After Matteo's infusion of cash, everything fell into place. On the way to the airport two days later, Electra told me more about Alessandro's father, smoothing over any awkwardness on our last day. John was an entrepreneur working in Paris, and they'd met in Venice at the film festival two years prior. His cousin, not a Russian girlfriend, was the one who had answered the phone, and she'd gotten the ball rolling for their reconciliation. Also, he told Electra he had always loved her, but she refused to believe him, so following her insecurity, she cut him out of her life. But when he heard about the eviction, the Blue Prince came to the rescue in a big way. That rekindled their romance, and I was glad to see her face gleaming with hope.

I closed my spiral notepad. "Wait. How did John hear about your eviction if you had no contact with him?"

She smirked. "Pedro, of course. He met John when we used to date. That man can't keep a secret. He's worse than an old lady. And his dog is just as guilty."

"I'm going to miss him and Dante," I said, appreciating the funny duo. After I presented him with the English dictionary, Pedro gave a parting hug, whispering to visit the next time I was in Milan. I'd laughed at his sly offer and given Dante my last cornetto before I waved arrivederci.

Electra pointed to my lap. "That little notebook. What do you write in it?" she asked defensively. "Are you writing a book about how terrible I was?"

"No. But don't tempt me. It's just a journal of pluses and minuses to keep track of my finances," I quipped, skimming the pages. One penciled jot was on July 5th, when we celebrated Alessandro's birthday. Such a strange diary of my adventure, I thought. "My dad gave it to me before I left to record all the exciting restaurants and romantic hotels I was supposed to visit. You know, a travel journal. That went out the window fast. But it shows a better story of a young woman whose life broke apart but, in a way, fell back together when she found herself."

"Are you stronger?"

I sighed and thought for a moment. "This is the best way I can describe it. Say you go into a gourmet restaurant known for their osso bucco. The interior is first-rate, the people, wow, and the atmosphere is alive. But you're upset when the waiter tells you the kitchen is out of osso bucco. So, what do you do? Leave? No, you order another entree and savor it. Each bite is more delicious than you ever imagined. You realize it was a better choice than what you originally wanted. Life has to be a positive experience. Difficulties make you stronger. Does that make sense?"

"Always search for the truth. Matteo was osso bucco, I am guessing?"

I laughed. "Yes, the veal shank that fell on the floor that the dog licked after the chef stepped on it. But since he gave me enough funds for my plane tickets, I'll put him back on the counter minus the saliva."

At the airport, I happily wheeled the luggage-laden cart into the departure hall, excited to finally see my parents and hug Flynn. And the kids and Ambrose. The flight was on time, and after the conveyor belt had swallowed my suitcases, I stepped from the check-in area, ready for the big send-off. What could I say to this fluky pair who helped me see the importance of love, family, and home? "You guys don't have to stay," I said on the verge of tears, glancing at the gates. "It's too long for Alessandro to wait, and it's lunchtime, and he could start screaming soon."

Electra held Alessandro and smiled at my suggestion, upbeat to have a reason for a quick exit. She blinked her dewy eyes and was also trying to keep it together. "Yes. We should go. Alessandro," she said, putting him down, "you give Jayne a big hug and kiss bye bye, okay."

Alessandro seemed confused, and I stooped to his level. He opened his little baby-lotioned arms and threw them around my neck. My chest ached with emotion, and I squeezed him tightly. "Bye, little man," I said, kissing his cheek. "I'll never forget you."

"Bye, Jayne."

I clapped his tiny hands together. "Alessandro, think of this goofy American when you eat gelato, okay?" He smiled, and I stood up, wiping my eyes. "When are you leaving to see John?"

"John may come here for a month, and Roberto is preparing papers before we go. Oh, he told me to tell you he'd call you the next time he was in New York. I hope that is okay."

I crossed my arms with a wry grin and tapped my foot. She pretended not to understand but threw up her arms in defeat seconds later. "Okay. Yes, I was a bit jealous that he asked you out. You're so young and pretty. I'm very sorry. John said horrible things to me when I told him the story. He says I should see a therapist about my past. He's right … Please forgive me."

I like this John a lot, I thought. It was a perfect segue to leave. "I do. Look, I better get going," I said, repositioning my backpack on my shoulder. "Thank you, Electra. Our incredible road trips and your history lessons opened my world to not only knowledge but also nature, northern Italy, and Yugoslavia. Being with you and your son was a life lesson I never expected. And I'm sure I also drove you over the edge with my problems and mistakes. I admire that you're a powerful woman who knows how to fight. And I'm so happy for you and John. And I forgive you and your hormones."

She kissed me on both cheeks. "Thank you. I admire you for smiling each morning in all your chaos. Never be ashamed of what you've been through. I wanted to show you a better Italy after Matteo, and I hope I did."

"You did. And much more. Life is pretty challenging, and you taught me to stand up for myself. I am not the same hopeless person who landed on your doorstep with a shattered life. Thank you for taking a chance on this Irish American. I'm truly grateful. And Alessandro? I'll miss him so much," I said, fanning my face from crying. She tousled his hair as I kissed him again. "I'll never forget my time in Italy. Ciao."

She handed me a box with a promise not to open it until the flight passed into North American air space. Confused, I agreed and left as Electra held Alessandro in her arms, waving and shouting ciao. *Ciao* meant *hello* and *goodbye* in Italy—which always made me wonder if any other country had that strange dichotomy. I turned away with a big wave and another ciao, ready to start my newest project: Me.

Stupid me, I should have followed her instructions because as soon as the plane took off, I opened her package and sobbed. Even the guy next to me got an unprovoked explanation for my river of emotions.

Inside were photos of Alessandro and me. And the weird thing, I never knew she had taken them. That sneak. She must have hidden in the park when I pushed him on the swing or had mini picnics of Nutella and crackers. One was even taken from behind when I had Alessandro in the toddler backpack in Cortina, and we admired the Alpine view. I realized my journey was hers as well. A rollercoaster ride for us both.

When I finally arrived home, my parents were low-key and didn't drill me with too many questions about what had happened overseas. My jaw-dropping photos told the tale I wanted to convey, and the delicious seafood risotto created from scratch was a thank you for their support during my time of need. When my dad handed me a letter from Yugoslavia, I told them about Bojan but not how much I prayed for his safety. They understood.

Flynn and I had a wonderful reunion, and I baked a killer lasagna with homemade sauce she swore was the best she'd ever tasted. Kate loved the embroidered wildflower dress I'd bought in Cortina, and Quinn was excited to wear his red hat that hadn't gotten too squished in my suitcase. Flynn and Ambrose laughed at my stories and were extremely impressed with my Italian. I told Flynn about Bojan; she said she knew someone at the United Nations who may be helpful in the future.

A week later, while the heat clanked autumn into my bedroom's radiator, I searched the classifieds in the *New York Times* and *Women's Wear Daily*, my go-to fashion authority, for any job opportunity. My mood wasn't the best, and a Nutella and espresso withdrawal could have triggered it since my too-weak how-do-people-drink-this-stuff instant coffee and grainy chocolate bars weren't giving me the same sugar kick to override the sick feeling of failure ambushing my confidence. If I was going to get anything done, one thing was for sure: I needed to go to a grocery store and get my supplies.

"Jayne? You up there?" my mother shouted from downstairs.

"Yes," I yelled back, crumpling another letter with an obvious typo. "I need a word processor, but since I'm flat broke, this will have to do," I commented to Toasty, reloading paper into the typewriter for another tapping frenzy.

My mother came into my room, scanning my scattered newspaper sections, coffee cups, and stained sweatshirt with concern. "Oh, honey, you've got to straighten this place up. I don't know how you can concentrate in this mess. Why don't you take a break and go to the city to see your friends? Have fun and go to a party. You're working too hard up here."

I groaned at her suggestion. “Not until I have some news to talk about other than Matteo.”

“You have Italy and your travels,” she frowned. “And they'll understand. You're not the first person with a broken heart. What about Hannah?”

“She's busy with my old job. She's trying to help but has been busy clubbing with all these new friends. After six months away from New York, I feel like I arrived on a different planet.” I fell onto my bed and grabbed my pillow to scream. Afterward, I turned to my worried mother. “I'd have almost ten thousand in the bank if Matteo didn't get me on that plane,” I sulked.

“You can't think that way. It changed you for the better. I can see it. Think of all the magical things you did. You traveled with a real Venetian countess who showed you a secret side of Italy hidden from everyone else. You visited her castle and even saw where Napoleon slept. Not many people get that opportunity.” She picked up my empty coffee mugs and sighed. “No wonder you don't sleep. You are drinking way too much caffeine.”

“Because American coffee can't compete with a perfect hair-on-your-chest espresso.”

She laughed and walked to my messy desk. “Oh, did you see that letter from Italy you got today? I put it on a stack of papers,” she said, shuffling through the classified pages of the job section. She grabbed an envelope and walked it over to me. “Here it is.”

I opened the white envelope and pulled out a formal letter from Luca Rosso Milan. My mouth dropped when I read the following sentences. *Luca was impressed by your mood board and its ability to portray Italy's grace and lush beauty with thoughtful and creative pieces. Your organic color choices brought an overlooked natural palette to the forefront. He'd like you to interview for the assistant fabric buyer position at our New York office for his exciting new sports division, Rosso Red.*

I put the letter to my pounding chest, unable to breathe. "Mom, this is … is incredible. Luca Rosso, the epitome of fashion, is giving me a chance to work in their New York office. The king of fashion wants yours truly to interview for his new division. I can't believe it."

"Jayne, that's incredible. Did you meet him over there?"

"That's what's so weird. I didn't. Luca Rosso has his studio in Electra's building, but whenever I had the chance to talk to him, it's like there was a supernatural force that stopped us from speaking." I sat down on the side of my bed with a huge smile. "Gino," I whispered. "I love you."

"Who is Gino?"

"My dear, dear friend. He had me do a travel mood board, which is why I got this …" I trailed off and paced the room, flapping the letter. "Mom, Luca Rosso is the hottest designer around. I'm surprised the poor man didn't have me arrested as a stalker. I mean, he, me, and elevators … Oh my god. I can't believe he liked my mood board."

"Liked? Sounds like he loved it. Call his office and set up the interview before he forgets. Clearly, he knows a good thing when he sees it," she said with a hug. "Your time in Italy pushed you to unfamiliar places. I knew it was hard but look at the doors it opened."

I stepped back. "Mom, this isn't a door. This is the frigging gateway to another galaxy."

"I can see that by the way you're acting. What's this?" She picked up the notebook I used to record my bank balance off the bed. "The mood board?"

"No. That's my survival bible." I took it from her and flipped it open to the last page. My pencil circled the ending balance of $1,959.10 several times. "One thousand nine hundred and fifty-nine dollars and ten cents. *If* I get this unbelievable chance to be on the elegant man's design team in New York, that's enough for the first month's rent and an IKEA futon. Also, an espresso maker. And sporty clothes for the interview. I can't go in looking like I'm not a team player. It's going to be tight, but I'm much better off than I was with just four hundred dollars in my pocket when I landed in Milan." A thought struck me. Did Electra or Anna Maria have anything to do with this? I let out a chuckle.

She smiled. "See? Everything works out in the end."

I grabbed her hands, and our eyes met. "Mom, this isn't the end. It's the beginning."

LA FINE

ACKNOWLEDGMENTS

FROM MEMOIR TO FICTION, *Lost in Lombardy* has had several U-turns and detours in its creation. I am truly thankful to everyone who cared about my endless pursuit of writing this book and other endeavors. Heartfelt gratitude to my amazing late parents, Veronica and Patrick Neligan, who may have gritted their teeth a few times with my antics but had always let me be me; to the unnamed countess who left a lasting impression in my life; to Peter Dowling for his sincere interest in this journey plus the keys to Bayside; to Mia McDonald and her unwavering faith with my writing and fantastic author photo; to Eve Matheson who got the ball rolling in Newport; to Esmond Harmsworth for the good ole college try; to Laurie Hepburn whose creativity and support was always a phone call away; to my Colby besties, Jane Smyth Sutton and Lynn Fuller Scarfo, (Jayne and Flynn?) can't wait to celebrate on the Cape; to my first reader, Nicole Kynast, your positive energy was monumental; a toast of appreciation to my book club support gang, the amazing Kristin Liapunov, Siw Potter, Ayesha Siddiqi, Hilary Flanagan, Berit Hessen, Anette Bonswetch, Anita Husebaek-Shaw, Terry Cigno, Mary Viggiano,

Jenny McCann, Donna Schole, Michelle Cautley, and a special shout out to Diane Guzy for reading updated versions in her busy life; to Mairead Gallagher and O'Donohoe family for the cozy Dublin warmth; to Bonnie Mann for unlimited words of encouragement; to Peter Mann, grazie per tutto; to the Marshall and Kazmierczak contingents for their confidence; to Donald Savitz for sincere enthusiasm and much appreciated agent help; to Taylor Swift, whose lyrics transported me to the days of letters never read and lying traitors; to my team of astute editors – developmental editor Danielle Barthel, copy editor Claire Strombeck, and proofreader Cassidy Sachs; to Bailey McGinn for a beautiful cover; to Victoria Wolf for interior design; to Nancy Treacy and her support; to Catherine Neligan for going above sister-in-law duty; to all my Curtis Brown Creative buddies whom I've passed in the literary trenches.

And to my fun-loving Neligan siblings, David, Brian, Deirdre, Patrick, and Aideen Neligan Vergara, plus their fantastic spouses and my wonderful nieces and nephews, our shared memories at Innisfree cement the theme of this story – family.

Lastly, to my incredible family and their unwavering encouragement. To Frank, thank you for letting me vent without interruption, being my best reader, and supplying a shot of Jameson's when needed. To sweet Ava, your upbeat words were helium to my deflated self and always lovingly appreciated at the needed moment. And to fearless Maeve, I would never have written Lost in Lombardy if you hadn't urged me to write "my Italian story." I am deeply indebted to your optimism and foresight.

Xoxo

ABOUT THE AUTHOR

LORNA NELIGAN has had an eventful life – falling off the Great Wall of China and being pursued by Marlon Brando are just two of her many stories. As an East Asian Studies graduate of Colby College, she headed to New York City and entered the exciting world of international high fashion as a fabric buyer for luxury design teams. Her last job was based in Paris with Ralph Lauren.

Lorna now divides her time between New York and her parents' hometown of Dublin, Ireland. If not writing, reading, or editing, she is debating with her husband and two daughters if they should rescue another English bulldog. She is also the President of the Friends of American Section of the Lycée International de Saint-Germain-en-Laye in France.

I hope you have enjoyed reading *Lost in Lombardy* and its wild travels through Italy.

Please leave a review on Amazon.com and Goodreads.com.
Your feedback is truly appreciated. Thank you.

MY NEXT BOOK WILL BE RELEASED
LATE 2024

THE BUTTERFLY AND THE WEB

All hell breaks loose at elite Branson University when a young female geologist from South Dakota unwittingly joins an exclusive secret society.

For a sneak peek and more visit
www.lornaneligan.com or scan this QR code:

Made in the USA
Middletown, DE
10 June 2024